He was Vampire, a threat to  **her very existence, but that didn't stop her from wanting him . . .**

M000316988

He was still laughing when he happened to glance over and caught sight of Emma. He lifted a hand, palm out, to stop Miguel, then tilted his head slightly as he took in the unlikely sight of Emma standing in his gym wearing her somber gray suit and high heels. He grinned at her, his muscled chest heaving, gleaming with sweat, drawstring gi pants hanging low on narrow hips to reveal a hard, flat abdomen and just a glimpse of that sweet narrowing of muscle into a man's groin.

Emma stared, her mouth dry and her heart twisting oddly in her chest. She *wanted*. And if the hunger on Duncan's face was anything to go by, he wanted her right back.

Or maybe he was just hungry. As in blood. She watched warily as Duncan prowled over to her, his hips rolling bonelessly like a big cat's, his gaze raking up and down her form before settling on her face with a lazy, slow blink of his eyes.

"Emma." His voice was a seductive purr that turned her name into a caress.

Dedicated with love to my sister Bridget,
who fights the good fight every damn day

Other Books by D. B. Reynolds

Raphael
Jabril
Rajmund
Sophia

Coming Soon
Lucas

Duncan

***

D. B. Reynolds

ImaJinn Books

The sale of this book without its cover is unauthorized. If you purchased this book without a cover, you should be aware that it was reported to the publisher as "unsold and destroyed." Neither the author nor the publisher has received payment for the sale of this "stripped book."

Duncan
Published by ImaJinn Books, Inc.

Copyright ©2011 by Donna Beltz
All rights reserved. No part of this book may be reproduced in any form or by any means (electronic, mechanical, photocopying, recording, or otherwise) without prior written permission of both the copyright holder and the above publisher of this book, except by a reviewer, who may quote brief passages in a review. For information, address: ImaJinn Books, Inc., P.O. Box 74274, Phoenix, AZ 85087, or call toll free 1-877-625-3592.

ISBN: 978-1-61026-083-1

10 9 8 7 6 5 4 3 2 1

PUBLISHER'S NOTE:
This book is a work of fiction. Names, characters, places and incidents are products of the author's imagination or are used fictitiously. Any resemblance to actual events or locales or persons, living or dead, is entirely coincidental.

Books are available at quantity discounts when used to promote products or services. For information please write to: Marketing Division, ImaJinn Books, Inc., P.O. Box 74274, Phoenix, AZ 85087, or call toll free 1-877-625-3592.

Cover design by Patricia Lazarus
Cover credits:
stryjek@dreamstime - male model
matthew_carroll@dreamstime -washington
konradbak@dreamstime -female model
geotrac@dreamstime -suit

ImaJinn Books, Inc.
P.O. Box 74274, Phoenix, AZ 85087
Toll Free: 1-877-625-3592
http://www.imajinnbooks.com

Chapter One

Cyn shivered slightly and moved closer to the wave of heat coming from the Learjet's engines. It made the frigid hangar marginally bearable. She hunched deeper into her coat and peered through the dim light. Raphael was down near the nose of the aircraft, deep in conversation with Juro. She could only make them out because of the multicolored glow of the jet's cockpit coming through the windshield. Raphael looked up briefly, and his eyes flashed silver. Her heart twisted at the sight. He was so gorgeous. It still took her breath away sometimes.

"He worries about you."

Cyn controlled an involuntary jerk of surprise at the sound of Duncan's voice over her left shoulder. "Duh," she said, rolling her eyes in his direction.

Duncan laughed as she turned towards him. "I will miss you, Cyn, you and Raphael more than anyone else."

"It's all happening so fast," she complained softly.

Duncan leaned forward. "Not really. We've planned this for some time, but it's been only days that we knew the time was right. And you haven't been yourself lately—"

"What? You thought I'd have a relapse or something if you told me? It's my body that was injured, Duncan, not my mind. I'm not *that* fragile."

He was silent for a long time, standing perfectly still, the way he did sometimes, until she could almost forget he was there.

"You didn't see him, Cynthia," he said at last. "When we thought you would die, you didn't see what it did to him. You weren't the only person damaged that night, and you need to take care of him now, because I won't be here to do so."

Cyn grabbed his hand when he would have turned away. "I love him, Duncan. More than anything in the world."

"I know that. But you need to *care* for him as well. I couldn't leave otherwise." He tightened his hold on her hand and raised it to his lips, kissing it softly.

"Duncan," Raphael's deep voice interrupted, his hand leaving a line of welcome heat as he trailed his fingers down Cyn's back before resting a hand on her hip.

"My lord," Duncan responded with a respectful nod.

Raphael grinned. "Not for much longer."

Duncan lifted one shoulder. "You may no longer be my lord officially, Sire. But in truth, it will always be so."

Cyn stepped back to give the two of them their moment, their voices a bare rumble of sound over the whine of the jet's engines. It was pathetic the way they stood there pretending to be all manly about their feelings. Far better if they'd just hug, maybe shed a tear or two, and get it over with. But no, that wasn't going to happen. Raphael shot her a glance over his shoulder, looking as close to desperate as she'd ever seen him. She snickered. Apparently, the hugs and tears were going to be left entirely to her.

"All right, my turn," she said, taking pity at last. She stepped up to Duncan and threw her arms around him in a big, honest-to-goodness hug. No back patting to nullify the emotion of the moment, no quick kiss-kiss sort of fakery. She hugged him long and hard. He hugged her back, too, although she was certain he was being careful of his vampire strength and her still-healing body. But despite all of that, he hugged her, and she felt his head turn away from Raphael, as if to conceal the emotion on his face.

"I'll miss you, Duncan," she whispered. "He'll miss you, too."

"I know," he murmured at her ear.

"And I'll take care of him for you."

"For both of us."

"That, too."

He laughed then, and she stepped back, slipping her arm around Raphael's waist while still holding Duncan's hand.

"We'll visit," she promised. "And you can visit us. None of that vampire territorial bullshit, okay?"

Duncan exchanged a look over her head with Raphael, and Cyn pursed her lips in thought. Those two were up to something. They wouldn't tell her what it was, of course, but she'd figure it out. She frowned, glancing at the big, industrial clock on the wall of the hangar. Nearly ten p.m. here in California. By the time they got clearance and were off the ground . . .

"Aren't you cutting it kind of close?" she asked worriedly. Duncan was taking the smaller of Raphael's two jets. Small was a relative term when it came to private jets, but she couldn't remember how fast this particular aircraft could go, assuming she'd ever known. She was pretty sure it couldn't make D.C. before sunrise, though, and both of the pilots were Vampire, too.

Duncan squeezed her fingers in reassurance. "We'll be stopping in Atlanta tonight, going on to D.C. tomorrow night."

"There are things Duncan must do immediately upon arriving," Raphael explained. "He needs to land in Washington as soon as possible after sunset so he has the entire night to work with."

Raphael dropped his arm over Cyn's shoulder and tightened his hold, effectively pulling her hand away from Duncan. She smiled privately. His move seemed casual enough, but she knew he'd planned it. His vampire possessiveness couldn't permit even Duncan to hold her hand for long. Which brought her back to her biggest complaint about this whole affair.

"I still don't see why he has to go there all alone. Why can't some of your people—"

"It's taken care of, *lubimaya*," Raphael said patiently. "You must trust us."

Cyn tightened her lips against the automatic comeback that came to mind. She did trust them, but it was always possible they hadn't thought of some detail or other. Sometimes these guys couldn't see the forest for all those testosterone-laden trees.

Juro appeared at Raphael's elbow. "Everything is set, my lord." He gave Duncan a brief nod. "Good fortune, Duncan," he said, then walked back to stand near the waiting limo.

"Sire," Duncan said, straightening into something like attention and bowing slightly from the waist. "It is has been an honor to serve at your side for so long."

"The honor has been mine, Duncan. But Cyn was right. We'll see you often."

Cyn put a gloved hand over her mouth, trying not to cry. Now that the time was here—

Raphael tugged her back against his chest, wrapping both arms around her. "Go while you can, Duncan. I believe my Cyn feels another hug coming on."

Duncan laughed and gave her a wink, then spun on one heel and, with vampire speed, disappeared into the Learjet in the blink of an eye. The pilot made a brief appearance in the hatchway as the stairs retracted and the hatch was sealed, and before she knew it, the jet was taxiing out of the hangar and Duncan was gone.

She turned in Raphael's arms, burying her face against his neck. "I feel like a mother sending her baby off to college or something," she muttered, rubbing the tears from her eyes on the soft wool of his coat.

Raphael chuckled and gave her a tight hug, before leading her over to the limo. Cyn paused long enough to look up at him and say, "Duncan tells me I'm supposed to take care of you now that he's gone." As she slid into the cushy interior of the limo, she saw Raphael stiffen in reaction to her comment and grinned in satisfaction.

"What was he thinking?" Raphael muttered before he ducked inside and pulled the door closed.

"I heard that," she said as he settled her in the curve of his arm.

"Of course, you did."

She huffed a laugh, then pulled back to see his face. "I love you, you know," she said seriously. "Even when I'm a bitch, I still love you."

Raphael touched his lips to hers in a lingering kiss. "And I love you, my Cyn. Always and forever."

The big vehicle rolled away from the airport, winding its way down the hill to Marina del Rey and through Santa Monica before they finally hit Pacific Coast Highway. Raphael held her against his side the entire ride, one hand stroking absently up and down her arm, as he stared at the dark city rushing past. Cyn was quiet, too, content to be with him, and to know that, like her, his thoughts were with Duncan far overhead as he winged his way into the most dangerous challenge of his long life.

Chapter Two

A few miles outside Washington, D.C.

The Learjet rolled up to the darkened hangar, a pale ghost of a plane appearing out of the shadows of a moonless night. Miguel Martinez scanned the private airfield, his vampire sight piercing the near darkness easily. The place was nearly abandoned. No one around but the lone tower controller who'd been paid well to look the other way and ask no questions.

He returned his gaze to the arriving jet. It was running nearly as dark as the night, with nothing but the gleam of the cockpit's instrument panel through the windshield to light the pilot's way into the black interior of the hangar. It should have been impossible. It would have been if the pilots had been human. But, like Miguel, they were vampires and starlight was enough to see by.

The aircraft eased to a gentle stop, its engines a loud burr of sound that hurt the ears and echoed off the flat spaces and high walls of the empty hangar. The pilot shut down the engines and the sudden silence was nearly as shocking as the noise had been.

Miguel crossed the bare concrete of the hangar, nerves singing with excitement, with the awareness that his Sire was here at last. He fisted his hands at his sides and straightened his back, determined to make a good impression, to prove himself worthy of the honor he'd been given.

The hatch opened. Miguel took one step and then another, until he was only a few feet from the open door. The stairs deployed with a hydraulic hiss.

A figure appeared in the hatchway, a tall and broad-shouldered male, little more than a darker shadow against the unlit interior. He paused briefly before ducking his head to clear the low overhead, then took the stairs downward quickly and with purpose.

Miguel went to one knee. "Sire," he said reverently, pleased that his voice revealed none of the jittery nerves making his muscles twitch beneath his finely tailored suit.

"Miguel." A hand touched the back of his head. "Now, get up and give me a proper greeting."

There was laughter in his Sire's voice, and Miguel jumped to his feet with a grin, reaching out to take the proffered hand, feeling himself pulled into a quick embrace.

"Duncan," Miguel said. "It's so very good to see you."

* * * *

"Victor?" Duncan asked, as they strode directly to the BMW Miguel had left idling on the far side of the hangar.

"He's at the house, hosting a small dinner party."

"With humans?"

"Always. The only vamps he keeps around are his four guards."

"The humans will have to be dealt with, then."

"Not a problem, my lord," Miguel said as he dropped into the driver's seat of the sumptuous vehicle. "Louis and I can handle it."

"Where is Louis?" Duncan asked, closing the passenger side door with a muted thump.

"Waiting outside the house, keeping an eye on things."

"You anticipate trouble?"

"No, but tonight's too important to leave to chance."

Miguel drove out of the hangar and made a sharp right turn toward the access road. Duncan saw the doors of the hangar begin to close behind them almost immediately.

"How was your journey, my lord?" Miguel asked.

"Uneventful. Raphael sends his regards."

"I'm honored."

"So," Duncan said, settling in for the drive back to the city. "What do I need to know about Victor's setup tonight?"

"Same as always. He has his four vampire guards, two in his presence, two on guard elsewhere inside the house. They're complacent in the routine, and the two not with Victor personally usually sit in a room near the front door, watching TV or playing video games. I've never seen them leave the house unless Victor's with them. Exterior security, including the gate, is handled by humans around the clock, and they're *never* permitted inside the residence. There's a guest house that's set up as a barracks if the human guards want it, but most of them have homes of their own and go there at the end of their shift. The estate is walled, with the only gate locked down during the day. At night, the human guards pretty much limit their duties to guarding the gate, with only the occasional perimeter patrol."

An accident had snarled traffic on the Beltway, and Miguel zipped across several lanes, utilizing the lightning fast reflexes granted by his vampire blood. Duncan grinned. "Still a terrible driver, I see."

"Not true, my lord. The accident was already there."

Duncan laughed, but sobered immediately. "What about Victor's guests?"

"It's a small dinner party, just Victor and three humans—a couple of legislators and a K Street scumbag with lots of money to hand out. All males, which is par for the course with Victor. As far as I know, he has no plans to bring in any women tonight, but even if he did, it wouldn't be until much later."

"Prostitutes?"

"I don't think so. Not most of them, anyway. There's no shortage of women in this city who will party with a man if he's got enough power. And power is what matters here. Money goes hand in hand, but power means access, and that's everyone's number one prize."

"Very well. You and Louis handle the human gate guards. I'll take care of Victor's two vampires at the front door. That needs to be done quickly and carefully so he doesn't sense anything amiss too soon. Once we reach the dining room, I'll deal with the human dinner guests. I want them out of the way. After that, Victor has to be mine, but we can play it by ear when it comes to taking down his remaining two vampires. You need to be ready to deal with them."

"My lord, we can wash the human gate guards' memories after Victor is taken care of. Let Louis and me deal with the vamp guards at the door, while you—"

Duncan turned to look at Miguel, keeping his voice even, but frosting it with the slightest touch of his power. "I want the humans secured first, Miguel. I can handle Victor *and* his guards, if necessary."

"Yes, my lord."

They turned off the Beltway, zipping down streets one after the other, all of them nearly empty late on a Tuesday night. Duncan had studied maps of the neighborhood, but it wasn't the same as being here. He'd also memorized floor plans of the vampires' official residence in the city. Some humans referred to the house as the vampire embassy, which was a good enough, if inaccurate, description.

The residence itself was a big 19th century colonial that in pictures reminded Duncan of the great mansions of his youth in the Deep South. He could only hope this particular house had enjoyed significant renovation since its construction a hundred years ago. If not, it would soon. He had no intention of living with cranky plumbing or nonexistent air conditioning.

Fortunately, the residence sat on an unusually large parcel of land adjacent to the embassy district. With two full acres backed by Rock Creek, a wall surrounding the entire property and only a single gate, the estate should have been nearly impregnable. But it wasn't. There were holes in the house's security that one could literally drive a truck through. And that, too, would change once Duncan took over.

Because the vampire embassy was about to get a new ambassador. They just didn't know it yet.

Chapter Three

Miguel called Louis on his cell to let him know they were coming in. When they made the final turn, Louis was waiting in the middle of the street, his pale eyes gleaming nearly white in the headlights. He grinned when he saw them and stepped to the side so that Miguel could pull up next to him.

"Sire," Louis said as he climbed into the back seat. "Thank you for letting me be a part of this."

Duncan turned around enough to hold out his hand. Louis took it carefully at first, then gripped it tightly when Duncan did the same. Duncan could feel the calluses on Louis's palm and fingers from the weights he'd lifted most of his life, even before Duncan had turned him.

"It's good to see you, Louis. As I told Miguel, the two of you will take care of the humans at the gate, while I deal with the vampire guards just inside the residence. And once we get into dining room, I want the humans out of there. I can hold off Victor."

"My lord, all *four* of Victor's guards will be inside the house with him."

"I'm aware of that," Duncan said. He held back a smile as he remembered all the times he'd been overly protective of Raphael—and how much it had irritated the Western Vampire Lord.

"It's the house in the cul-de-sac, my lord," Miguel said, his voice tight with anticipation as they drew closer to the estate.

Duncan turned to get his first in-person view of the residence. It didn't *look* like a fortified embassy. With cherry trees peeking over the top of a too-short perimeter wall and two chimneys puffing white smoke into the cold air, it looked more like a place where Mom and Dad were raising their 2.5 children and letting the dogs run in the yard. Assuming Mom and Dad had a whole lot of money and enough paranoia to build a wall around their home, even a short one.

"Time to rock and roll," Louis whispered, and Duncan smiled grimly.

They rolled up to the wrought-iron gate, and Miguel dropped his side window with a faint buzz of sound. Frosty air rushed in, and Duncan smelled the creek which ran behind the house, along with a faint hint of snow. All of that disappeared beneath the overwhelming scent of human as the guard bent into the window to check them out.

Miguel had been on the premises once before, ostensibly to offer his services when he'd first moved here from California and set up a security business in Virginia. "Miguel Martinez," he told the guard. "Lord Victor is expecting us."

The human opened his mouth to say something, probably to protest that he wasn't aware of Lord Victor expecting *anyone*, but then his eyes glazed over and he blinked slowly. He smiled and nodded, waving them in.

"These aren't the droids you're looking for," Louis murmured from the back seat.

Miguel nearly choked on a laugh as the guard stepped back into the shed and triggered the gate mechanism.

"Enough, gentlemen," Duncan said quietly. He understood their excitement. His own blood was thundering with anticipation. But this was a dangerous thing they were about to do, and he didn't want them to fool themselves into thinking otherwise.

"Forgive me, my lord," Louis breathed.

Duncan nodded, but his attention was already on the big, white house, his power reaching out to lightly touch the vampires inside. All but Victor. The others wouldn't notice his touch, but Victor might.

"Very lax security," he commented mostly to himself. "Two vampires together inside, near the front door." He frowned. There was a buzz of something, some underlying power that confused him. He wanted to explore it further, but there was no time, and it was too weak and unfocused to represent a danger to his plans for the evening. It would have to wait.

"Miguel," he said, "you and Louis take out the remaining human guards gently. Check the barracks, as well. I don't want anyone raising an alarm, but there's no reason to hurt them either. Then join me inside. We'll take the dining room together."

"Yes, my lord."

Duncan opened the car door while Miguel was still braking. He sped up the brick steps two at a time, sending a tight needle of power ahead of him to burn out the electronic lock on the front door. The security bolts released with a solid thunk and the door swung open. Duncan stepped inside, his eyes doing a fast sweep of the area while the two vampires on guard were still dragging their attention from the big screen TV to stare at him in surprise. He didn't wait for them to recover their wits. He reached out with his power and seized their hearts, squeezing until they dropped to the floor. They weren't dead. Victor was corrupt, but he wasn't weak. As the Sire of these two vampires, and especially at such close proximity, he would certainly feel it if they died, and he'd know something was wrong. So Duncan let them live for now. But when Victor died, these two vampires would die right along with him, most likely drained dry by Victor himself in a bid to survive Duncan's challenge.

Duncan had met Victor on more than one occasion when he'd accompanied Raphael to Vampire Council meetings, but he'd never matched strength with the vampire lord directly. The annual gatherings were carefully orchestrated affairs, bringing together the most powerful vampires in North America, vampires who were natural rivals at best and enemies at worst. Everyone was on their best behavior at those affairs, which meant there were no outright challenges and no blatant weighings of each other's power.

But Raphael had known Victor a long time, and there were other ways to measure the depth of a vampire's power. The upshot was that Duncan knew he could defeat Victor because Raphael wouldn't have risked him otherwise. And, more importantly, because he knew the depths of his own power. Victor would be ousted from his rule over the territory tonight in the usual vampire way . . . by assassination.

Miguel and Louis rushed through the front door behind him, their power brimming and ready to defend him if necessary. Again, it felt odd to be the recipient of that sort of devotion rather than the other way around. Something he'd have to get used to.

"Any problems?" he asked as his vampires hid the limp bodies of Victor's two guards behind the same couch they'd been sitting on when Duncan arrived.

Miguel let his burden drop, the comatose vampire's head cracking loudly against the wooden floor. "None, my lord. The gate is secured, the barracks empty. And all of the human guards on the estate are sound asleep."

"Excellent. This is it, then. Remember, once we're in the dining room, I'll put the humans under immediately. After that, we play it by ear. I don't care which of us takes down the two remaining vamp guards, but Victor himself is mine alone."

"Yes, my lord." Miguel was fairly bouncing on his toes. Louis stood as still as a statue, his muscles coiled for action. He nodded sharply, his eyes fixed on Duncan like a dog on point, awaiting the go-ahead.

"Let's go," Duncan said.

Miguel walked ahead of him, Louis behind. They went past the staircase and turned left down a long hallway, their footsteps nearly silent despite the old, wood plank floor. Doors stood open left and right, revealing rooms filled with furniture—a formal dining room with a table that could have seated thirty people easily, and a den or game room with another huge flat screen TV, several different video game consoles, and a foosball table in the corner. There was a spacious kitchen with open containers littering the counter tops and still smelling of the food Victor had brought in for his human guests. Duncan's research told him Victor typically had his parties catered, with his vampires serving as waiters where necessary. It wasn't particularly elegant, but then Duncan doubted it was a zeal for good food that brought the humans here in the first place.

The dining room they wanted—the one Victor was using tonight— was at the very end of the hallway, behind a pair of white pocket doors. Miguel reached for the doors and paused, hands resting lightly on the bronze handles.

Duncan tilted his head, listening with both his ears and his power. The conversation from inside was loud and boisterous, the human voices evidencing clear signs of intoxication or drugs. It could be either. Victor was here, too, his mind lazy and at ease, not expecting any trouble. His remaining two vampire guards were far more alert than their Sire, but at the same time they took their cue from him, and their minds were wandering, not at all concerned about what was going on in the room or out of it. What little attention they were paying was focused on the human guests, seeing them more as prey than anything else, while trusting that their now comatose fellow guards at the front of the house would alert them to any outside threat.

Duncan pulled back his probe, drew a breath and gave Miguel a quick nod of assent.

Miguel slid the door back and Duncan stepped through.

Conversation stopped dead as everyone turned to stare at him. Duncan gestured, and the three humans went glassy-eyed, their heads slumping to their chests in unconsciousness, one sliding to the floor beneath the table, while the others merely fell forward into the remnants of their dinner.

Victor's guards recovered before the first human's head hit the table, one of them vaulting the table, crystal flying and dishes breaking as he raced to protect his Sire. Miguel caught him in midair, his fingers digging into the other vampire's throat as he threw him to the floor and punched his chest hard enough to stop his heart in an instant. Victor's vampire gasped, eyes bulging, as he struggled to gather his power back into himself, to force his heart to pump once more. Given only a moment longer, it might have worked, but Miguel didn't grant him that moment. He grabbed an empty chair and smashed it against the floor until it produced what he needed. The piece of wood was jagged and raw, half varnished and half bare wood, but it was the perfect weapon. Miguel lifted the stake with a fang-baring grin of anticipation, and Victor's guard keened a wordless plea, the only noise he could still manage. Miguel brought the stake down in a single clean stroke, granting the only mercy he would—a quick death.

Louis and the other vampire guard were still battling one another, blood flowing as they exchanged brutal blows that would have killed a human with the first strike. Louis slammed his opponent into the wall, cracking the wainscoting and leaving a vampire-sized dent in the upper wall as plaster dust filled the air. Victor's vampire bellowed in anger. He tightened his grip, his fingers digging into Louis's arms as he tried to reverse their positions, but Louis used the vampire's momentum against him, spinning around completely and throwing him across the room. He crashed into one of the unconscious humans as he hit the table, eliciting an unwilling grunt of reaction.

Duncan felt more than saw Victor move, felt the vampire lord begin to gather his power. He glanced up, meeting Victor's reptilian gaze. The two powerful vampires studied each other for a long breath, but a sharp cry of denial drew their eyes to Louis and the remaining guard in time to see Louis impale his opponent with a jagged spear of wood.

Victor sucked in a breath as his vampire died, and Duncan turned in time to see the vampire lord slump forward, his fist clenched to his chest. As if he felt Duncan's gaze upon him, Victor relaxed his hand and raised his head with a defiant glare, showing no weakness to his enemy.

"This was unnecessary," Duncan observed after a moment, stepping back from the two piles of vampire dust with exaggerated distaste. He looked up and met Victor's angry gaze once more. "You should have taught them better, Victor."

At the head of the table, Victor remained perfectly still, his stare burning with hatred as a haze of crimson power began to seep over his brown eyes.

"Miguel," Duncan said, removing his overcoat and throwing it onto a nearby chair. "Get these humans out of here."

"My lord," Miguel murmured.

Louis reached under the table and yanked the fallen human out from under it, pulling him into a fireman's carry and heading down the hallway. Miguel dragged another of the guests—a large, florid man whom Duncan recognized as a U.S. Senator—through the doors, then came back and hefted the last human over his shoulder, before following Louis.

Duncan pulled the pocket doors shut, selected a chair that wasn't covered in broken dishes or food, and sat, crossing his legs at the knee. He scanned the room idly as he sat there, intentionally ignoring Victor's growing outrage. It was a small room, too narrow and, like all the others, crowded with too much furniture. The air reeked of cigar smoke and spilled food.

"So, Victor," Duncan said, finally turning his attention to the other vampire. "How are things in Washington?"

"Fuck you, Duncan," Victor growled. "You can't come in here and start killing my people."

"Apparently, I can," Duncan pointed out.

Victor snorted a dismissive laugh. "You? You'd never have dared this without Raphael." He spat to one side. "Where is the great man anyway?" He lifted his head as if sniffing the air. "He's not nearby; I'd sense him if he'd crossed into my territory."

"You should have sensed *me*, Victor. You've grown complacent."

"You're nothing but Raphael's lap dog. I don't waste my time on mutts."

Duncan merely smiled. "It's like this, Victor. We can do it the easy way or the hard way. The choice is yours."

A vicious grin split Victor's broad face as he stood and kicked his chair against the wall. He leaned forward, fangs bared and hands resting on the table as his power began to build, his eyes now gleaming like two burning coals of fury.

"Give it your best shot, puppy."

Duncan dipped his head in agreement. "The hard way it is then." He stood, and for the first time since he'd left California, the first time in the presence of anyone but Raphael and the California lord's most trusted vampires, Duncan loosed the full measure of his power. He let it build until it was a firestorm in his chest, the pressure both excruciating and exhilarating. Lights flickered as energy danced around the room.

Duncan blinked lazily and met Victor's surprised stare with a quiet question. "You were saying?"

With a roar of defiance, Victor launched a preemptive volley, a tight ball of incredible energy that must have drawn heavily on his power. It was a bid to weaken Duncan before he was ready, before he could muster his own power into a shield around himself. But Duncan had trained with the best the vampire world had to offer. His shields snapped closed with a concussion of sound. Victor's attack slammed into them with tremendous force. They flexed, but held, and Duncan flicked both hands forward, as if brushing away Victor's assault, a move calculated to enrage the other vampire lord.

Victor growled, his teeth grinding together as he smashed one thick fist into the table, amplifying the blow with his power and shattering the whole thing into kindling. He looked up and grinned at Duncan, then raised both hands flat in the air, palms up, lifting the bits of splintered table as if it were still whole. With another power-filled gesture, he flung all of the shards at Duncan, a flying wave of deadly sharp wooden stakes.

It was a clever move. Duncan admired it even as he defended against it, twisting the power of his shields into a whirlwind of energy that sent most of the table shards whipping out in all directions while others exploded upon impact into harmless matchsticks.

Victor was sweating blood and shaking with fury, his shields weakening perceptibly. Duncan suspected the other vampire had concentrated too much of his reserve power into that first preemptive strike, but Victor wasn't done yet. His shields might be weaker, but they held against Duncan's discreet probes. Duncan frowned as Victor's power suddenly surged, as if he was drawing energy from somewhere outside the room. But the most likely source of that sort of power would be Victor's vampire children, and two of them were already piles of dust, with the other two near death. Even if Victor had drained them dry, they couldn't have given him this much of a power boost. Did Victor have minions they hadn't uncovered? Someone beyond the four that had been with him for centuries? Impossible, unless . . .

Duncan concentrated, remembering that odd buzz of power he'd felt as they approached the house. He spared a bit of power, a fraction of his awareness, and searched the house, looking for the source of that buzz. It had to be here somewhere, and it had to be what Victor was feeding from. *There!* In the basement, there were . . . Duncan's eyes widened first in shock, then in revulsion as he looked up and met the old vampire lord's confident glare.

"Abomination!" Duncan hissed.

Victor laughed. "What a self-righteous little prick you are. I created them, and they live to serve me like any other."

Duncan's stomach turned. Victor had made vampires for the sole purpose of feeding his own power. There were at least twenty of them down there, trapped in the basement, half-starved, mindless, little better than feral animals, existing only to provide Victor with enough strength to hold onto his territory. It was a practice forbidden by the very Council Victor was a member of, and it was precisely what Duncan had called it—abomination.

Victor grinned maliciously. "Still think you can take me, puppy?"

Duncan felt his purpose harden into granite, his anger turn to cold intent. With a quick warning, he drew power from his own children, from Miguel and Louis. They sensed his need and gave it willingly, the two of them together far stronger than all of Victor's half-mad slaves, no matter how many there were.

Victor's victorious grin wilted, and Duncan saw awareness of his impending doom in the other vampire lord's eyes.

"Yield," Duncan offered, "and I'll make the end painless. For you and for those poor wretches downstairs."

"Go to hell," Victor snarled. He drew himself up, sucking up every last ounce of power remaining in the slaves in the basement, finally draining the two guards Duncan had left alive. Combining that with what was left of his own power, he fed it all into a wall before him as he advanced physically on Duncan. He held a long, jagged piece of wood in one hand, his fingers gripping it so tightly that it sliced his skin, blood dripping between his fingers and running down his arm.

With a howl of rage, he rushed the last few feet, the rudimentary pike up and ready, his power a battering ram before him.

Duncan waited until the other vampire was nearly upon him, and then he clenched his right fist and punched it straight out before him as though slamming it into Victor's chest. A thunderbolt of power hit the other vampire's shields. Duncan felt them crack under the impact of his strike, heard the shattering of crystal as Victor's shields broke under the strain.

And he heard the mindless shrieking of those poor souls in the basement as their world collapsed.

Victor staggered, his face gray with shock, the red haze of power in his eyes already beginning to drain away, leaving them a dull brown. The stake he'd been gripping fell from limp fingers as he crumpled to the floor, first to his knees and then lower as he fell back to sit on his heels, hands hanging limply by his sides.

He looked up as Duncan crouched next to him, barely able to meet Duncan's gaze as his head lolled weakly backward.

"You should have taken the easy way, Victor," Duncan said, breathing hard from his own exertion.

Victor grinned one last time, blood staining his teeth and dripping down his chin. "Fuck you, Duncan," he rasped harshly.

Duncan laughed. "As you wish."

He slammed his fist into Victor's torso, ripping through skin and bone, to wrap his fingers around the vampire's beating heart and yank it out of his chest. As Victor sucked in a final groaning breath, Duncan held the still-beating heart before his eyes and sent a concentrated blast of power directly into the pulsing organ.

Victor shrieked as his heart burst into flames, as his body began to disintegrate, as he became nothing more than a pile of ash to mix with the broken china and crushed food of the too small room. In a far away faint echo of their Sire's passing, Victor's two remaining vampire guards—the two he'd left lying in a room near the front door—died along with their Sire, as did the pathetic creatures in the basement, falling into dust with barely a whisper.

Duncan started to stand, but he fell back to his knees as frantic cries filled his head, the vampires of Victor's territory screaming out for their Master, pleading for reassurance and understanding, begging to know what was happening. Duncan closed his eyes, groaning at the overwhelming flood of impressions, details, identities, hopes, wants. Raphael had told him what to expect when Victor died, when the burden of lordship fell upon Duncan, but nothing could have prepared him for the physical weight of it, for this sucking whirlpool of need that would bleed him dry if he didn't do *something*.

Throwing his head back, eyes still closed, he roared out a command for silence. As if cut by a blade, the flood of demands stopped dead. Duncan drew a deep breath and, despite his exhaustion, let his power flow out to every vampire in the territory, offering surety, offering support, letting them know that they had a new Master, but he was strong enough to take care of them. And that he would tolerate no rebellion, that challengers would die if they faced him.

Slowly he withdrew. The bond was established and it was strong. The territory's vampires were still there, a whisper of presence in his mind, like the nearly silent voices of an empty church. It was a weight on his heart that oddly reminded him of the first time he'd known he loved someone, that constant pressure in one's chest that is both a welcome presence and a frightening reminder of the persistent vulnerability that comes with love.

There were those among his new territory's vampires—*his* vampires, now—who remained uneasy, but that was expected. There were others who were curious enough that he knew they'd show up in the coming days, perhaps even to test his power, to see if he was as strong as he seemed. And that was expected, as well. But in the final analysis, no one had died—beyond Victor and his four bodyguards, and those pathetic creatures in the basement, who never should have been created at all—and that was a victory. The Capital Territory was small, only encompassing the District of Columbia, Delaware, Maryland, and Virginia. Several hundred vampires lived in those states, many of whom had been there longer than Duncan had been alive. He had taken the territory with relatively few meaningful deaths, but it remained to be seen if he could hold onto it without the need to kill a few more.

Footsteps thundered down the hallway behind him with unnatural speed. There was no need to turn around to know that it was Miguel and Louis, responding to his distress and ready to defend him. The two of them were his only children for now, although there would soon be more. But they would always be the first. He'd turned them both fifty years ago, when he and Raphael had decided to take the first real steps toward this day.

Victor had been right about one thing. Raphael supported this move. Victor's corruption had long chafed at Raphael, especially in the last few years, when it had become more and more difficult to maintain the secrecy of vampire existence. Victor's excesses had become an embarrassment and worse to the vampire community he was supposed to represent in the U. S. capital. But it wasn't until the recent alliances with both Rajmund and Sophia had been cemented that Raphael and Duncan had decided the time was finally right to make a move against the powerful Washington, D.C. Vampire Lord. It was time to install someone Raphael trusted, someone who shared his larger vision of the future of vampires on this continent, someone powerful enough to take on Victor and win.

If Duncan had asked for it, Raphael would have gladly lent him an army of vampires to take with him to D.C. But it had been important to Duncan to seize the territory on his own, with his own people. Miguel and Louis were his, and they would always be the ones who'd stood with him when this all began.

"My lord!" Miguel skidded into the room first, going to his knees next to where Duncan still knelt on the filthy floor. "Sire, are you all right?"

Duncan smiled. "The territory is ours." He stood, letting Miguel give him a hand up, and then turned to include Louis. "And now the real work begins."

Chapter Four

Emma Duquet parked her small Honda beneath a winter-bare cherry tree and stared at the elegant white mansion down the block. It was all lit up, sitting there like a queen lording it over the rest of the houses—the biggest lot and the biggest house on a block of big houses. Even the tiniest home on this street probably cost more than she'd earn in a lifetime. She frowned. Well, maybe not an entire lifetime. She planned to live long and well, if only to spite the Fates which seemed to have been against her so far.

A dump truck lumbered past, its headlights picking out the incongruous pile of debris sitting inside the house's fancy iron gate. In her neighborhood, that trash would have been dumped right on the street for pickup, but they probably had codes about that sort of thing around here.

The driver of the truck leaned out to speak into a receiver on the side of the mansion's small guard house, obviously announcing his arrival since the guard house itself was empty. The gate rolled open, but instead of driving forward, the truck reversed into a quick three point turn before backing through the gate and stopping with the rear of the truck bed right next to the pile of junk. Not seeming to care that their truck kept the gate from closing, two men jumped out and began tossing junk from the debris pile into the open bed of their vehicle.

Emma watched curiously, wishing she'd thought to bring some binoculars with her. On second thought, sitting in this district and staring through binoculars might get her arrested. For that matter, she'd better do something besides sit here, or someone would call the police on her. Washington was a very paranoid place these days.

Decision time. The gate was open, a golden opportunity if ever there was one. She could waltz right up to the front door of the vampire embassy and request an audience with the ambassador or whatever the hell they called him. She'd probably never get a better shot than this. Of course, it was also possible she'd waltz through the gate and into the arms of some angry guards. Maybe even a dog or two. Although, she didn't see any dogs and besides, the stories all said dogs didn't like vampires. Plus, with the gate open like that, if there *were* dogs, they'd surely be—

"Snap out of it, Em," she scolded herself. She had a tendency to overthink things as a way of postponing the inevitable. And this visit was definitely inevitable. Her roommate Lacey was missing, and Emma had run into a brick wall in her own attempts to find her. But someone in that house knew exactly where Lacey was, and Emma intended to find out.

She got out of her car and looked around. No one was watching.

She hurried down the street, slowing as she neared the battered truck. Changing her quick dash into a brisk, confident walk, she strode past the two busy men with a nod and a smile, as if she came this way every night.

The driveway was one of those long curving things, and between her nerves and the three inch heels she'd worn to work, she was a bit winded by the time she reached the pretty brick stairs. She paused at their foot and drew a calming breath.

"You can do this, Em," she whispered and took the stairs at a quick trot.

She reached the front door and stared in surprise. The lock had been destroyed. It looked like someone had fried it. Weird. But convenient. Between that and the open gate, the gods were clearly smiling on her mission tonight. She touched the knob delicately to be sure it was safe, then pushed the door open and stepped inside.

It was dark, although not spooky dark. There were a few lights down a hall that disappeared behind the big staircase right opposite the door. And a crystal chandelier overhead that looked as if it was on its dimmest setting. The crystals gleamed a yellowish gray, as though the light was not strong enough to punch through the glass.

Emma took another step inside, shivered, and closed the door behind her. It was surprisingly warm, despite the shadowy lighting. A part of her had expected it to be as cold as a tomb, like with the vampires from the movies. But there was a pleasant fire burning in the room to her right, the sight of which had been blocked by the open front door. The room had the look of a small library and was softly lit by pretty Tiffany-style lamps which were perched on a desk and on two small, round side tables. She heard the distinctive sound of someone sliding a book back onto a shelf and took a tentative step toward the doorway.

"Hello?" she called softly, somehow reluctant to announce her presence in this big empty-feeling house. She tiptoed closer to the room and shrieked, jumping back and nearly tripping on her own heels as a big, blond man suddenly stepped into view.

He eyed her curiously, his full lips curving into a faint smile. "May I help you?" His voice was smooth and easy, and it brought to mind the cool water running in gentle mountain streams back home.

Emma stared at him. He could definitely help her, but probably not in the way he meant. Emma liked tall guys, not giant tall, but tall enough that at five-six she could still wear high heels without being taller than her date. Not that she had that many dates with her work schedule, but one could always hope.

This guy was more than just tall, though. He was lovely. Late twenties, maybe a bit over six foot, with long blond hair falling loosely over broad shoulders. He had strong arms and a taut, muscled chest that filled out a dark blue, long-sleeved t-shirt and tapered down to a tight, flat abdomen. Faded denims clung to narrow hips and muscular thighs, and . . .

"Excuse me," he repeated in that same soothing voice, but with an undercurrent of amusement. "Did you want something in particular?"

Emma flushed, embarrassed at being caught ogling. What was she thinking? She wasn't here to pick up some guy, no matter how delicious he was.

"Yes," she started, then, discovering her throat was too dry to talk, swallowed. She coughed and started again. "Yes, I'd like to see the ambassador, please."

Warm brown eyes crinkled at the corners. "You may have noticed," he said, his gaze sweeping over what she could see of the obviously not-open-for-business embassy, "that we're in transition here. The old *ambassador* has been called home. However, his replacement will be in place soon, and when he is, I'm quite certain he'll be happy to meet with you."

"Oh," Emma said, suddenly worried. "You mean Victor's gone? Like for good?" When he nodded, she asked, "How long will it be before I can meet with whoever's in charge then?"

The blond tipped his head to one side appraisingly. Was he trying to decide if she was worth disturbing the new guy? Emma straightened self-consciously, wanting him to know she was a serious person, here on business, which might seem questionable after her earlier bout of hormonal gawking.

"Can you wait a few moments?" the hunk asked.

Emma jerked in surprise. "Sure," she said immediately. "I mean, yes, of course. Uh, where do you want me to wait?" She glanced around, then leaned to one side, looking past him into the library, which appeared to be full of intriguing books.

Oddly, the blond didn't seem to know where to put her while he went to check on the new ambassador's whereabouts. Maybe he'd arrived with the new guy. An unwelcome thought popped up its horny head. Considering the way he was dressed and his total fitness and general hunkiness, maybe he was the new guy's boyfriend. *Damn.* Why were all the gorgeous guys gay?

The blond suddenly grinned, as if he knew what she was thinking. "You can wait in—"

Fast, heavy footsteps thudded from somewhere deep in the house moments before a dark-haired man barreled in from the hallway behind the stairs. Moving incredibly fast, he did a standing slide and stopped in front of the blond like a runner into home plate.

"Forgive me, my—"

"It's all right, Miguel," the blond interrupted. "This young lady . . ." He turned to look at her. "I'm sorry. I didn't get your name."

"Oh. No, I'm sorry," she said quickly. "I should have introduced myself. Emma Duquet." She stepped forward and held out her hand.

The blond carefully took her hand into his, as if afraid he'd crush it. And maybe he could have, because his hands were just like the rest of him—beautiful and big, with broad palms and square fingers. Hard, too, not soft and pillowy like so many of the men here in Washington. Those strong fingers curled around hers and he squeezed gently, his grip lingering a touch longer than would have been perfectly polite. But who cared about polite? Emma was in love, or at least lust. Maybe he wasn't gay after all.

"I'm Duncan," he said. "And this is Miguel."

No last names for either of them. Huh. Weird. Maybe it was a vampire thing, although she was pretty sure neither one of these guys was a vampire. Not that she knew what a vampire looked like—that was more Lacey's thing. But these two looked more like frat boys getting ready for a party than all-powerful masters of the universe.

She offered her hand to Miguel in turn, but he only stared at it suspiciously and stepped between her and Duncan as if she had a disease or something.

"She can wait in the library, Miguel."

The dark-haired man gave Duncan a surprised look.

"The ambassador will definitely want to see her," Duncan added, glancing her way with a quick there-and-gone smile.

Miguel's eyebrows shot up, taking his whole hairline along for the ride.

"If you'll make Ms. Duquet comfortable," Duncan was saying, "I'll see to the ambassador."

Emma watched as Duncan disappeared back the way Miguel had come. He moved like a big, graceful cat, the way professional athletes moved, as if every muscle was in tune with all the others. And such a pleasure to watch, too.

"This way," Miguel said, interrupting her admiration of Duncan's departing studliness. He was frowning when she looked back at him. Miguel didn't seem to like her for some reason. No, it was more like he didn't approve of her. Well, tough. Emma didn't look for anyone's approval but her own. And she sure as hell hadn't clawed her way through college and law school in order to worry about what some diplomatic flunky thought about her. Besides, she wasn't here to make friends.

"Thanks," she said, and strolled confidently into the library as if she owned the place.

"Have a seat," Miguel said, making it sound more like an order than an invitation.

"I'll stand," Emma said. She actually would rather have sat, but she wouldn't give him the satisfaction. "Okay if I look around?"

Miguel's frown deepened. He scanned the room carefully, as if looking for things she might sneak into her pockets on the way out. Emma just gave him a droll look. For God's sake, this was obviously intended to be a waiting room for visitors. Look how close it was to the front door! If they were going to hide the embassy treasures, it wasn't going to be in this room, was it? Get a clue!

"Sure," he said finally. "I'll be nearby."

Emma smiled. "Fine."

* * * *

Duncan stripped off the comfortable denims and t-shirt he'd been wearing, albeit not without a regretful sigh. The confrontation with Victor had been less than twenty-four hours ago, and he'd hoped for at least a few days of privacy before the outside world intruded. They were still working on security, still searching every inch of this huge house for eavesdropping devices, hidden cameras, concealed doors and escape routes. It would be easier once the rest of Duncan's team arrived from California later tonight. If nothing else, it would be more eyes searching and ears listening. Several of Raphael's vampires had volunteered to accompany Duncan to this new posting, but he'd taken only a few and only the ones with a deep security background. Everything else could be taken care of later, but the first order of business had to be making this place secure.

Which brought up the fact of the lovely Ms. Duquet's unexpected appearance in his front parlor and how she'd managed to get there. As if summoned by the thought, Louis knocked lightly on the door of the bedroom suite that Duncan had taken for himself.

"Come in, Louis."

The stocky vampire cracked the door open just enough to slip through and assumed a parade rest position. Louis now belonged to Duncan body and soul, but before he'd become Vampire, he'd been a soldier, forged in the heat of battle, and he still had fond memories of his days as a military man.

Duncan buckled the belt on his suit trousers and sat down to put on a pair of black dress socks. "How'd she get in?"

"The dump truck, Sire. They blocked the gate open with their vehicle while they loaded the trash, and she slipped past. I take responsibility for—"

Duncan sighed. "It's not your fault. The three of us simply aren't enough to secure an estate of this size. It will be easier after the others get here—and after Miguel brings in the daylight team. In the meantime, I suggest we close the gate and ignore any callers."

"Yes, my lord."

Duncan pulled on his boots, stomped his feet as he stood, and slipped his suit jacket off the hanger. "Have you checked out the basement yet?"

"I was on my way when Miguel called me, my lord."

"Good. Thank you, Louis. I'm sorry to burden you with this. I expect it's pretty grim down there."

"No apology necessary, my lord. I'll take care of it." Louis dipped his head in a bow and slipped out of the room, leaving Duncan to his own thoughts, which immediately filled with images of Emma Duquet. He smiled as he finger-combed his hair back and tied it with a worn leather thong from the many scattered over the dresser top.

Emma, he thought. A lovely, old-fashioned name, although there was nothing old-fashioned about his visitor. Her long, chestnut colored hair had hung down her back in a wild tangle, and those unusual dark violet eyes had been sharp and intelligent, despite the almost manic energy she seemed to radiate. She wore her severely tailored suit like a knight wore his armor, but it didn't conceal nearly as much. No knight had ever flashed such shapely legs, nor donned a pair of high heels to make them look even longer than they were. Her legs had been covered in silk stockings, too. This weather was too cold for bare legs, but she hadn't given in to temptation and worn something less flattering than silk. He understood the need for modern women to wear pants, and thick tights were certainly practical in this climate. But the southern-raised man in him still preferred to see women in skirts and dresses, with the sweet curve of slender calves accented by the sheen of silk. Although, to be sure, no self-respecting woman of his time would have worn anything remotely resembling Emma's tight-fitting skirt and jacket, nor would they have worn silk stockings where a man other than her husband would ever see them, either. He grinned. Come to think of it, contemporary women's clothing had much to recommend it, after all.

And why was he spending so much time worrying about Ms. Duquet's clothes? He should be wondering instead what she was doing here. And what could be so urgent that her eyes had darkened with fear when he told her Victor was gone?

Chapter Five

Emma paged in awe through the last volume of what appeared to be a complete 1776 first edition of Edward Gibbon's *The History of the Decline and Fall of the Roman Empire*. And in remarkable condition, too. She was no rare book expert, but she'd have bet this particular set had never seen the inside of a bookshop. A well-preserved family heirloom was more like it.

She shook her head, suddenly impatient with herself. *Duh, Emma. Vampire.* They'd probably bought the whole set fresh off the press and shoved it on a shelf. Probably didn't even know they had it, much less what it was worth. She slid the book carefully next to the five other volumes and lifted her head, scanning the surrounding titles. She wondered if there were other treasures like that one, just sitting here with no one the wiser.

"Victor had a remarkable collection," said a cool voice.

Emma jumped guiltily and spun around. She stared at Duncan, her mouth hanging open in shock, until she realized it and snapped her jaw shut hard enough that it hurt. The man standing there was Duncan, but it wasn't him either. The t-shirt and jeans were gone, and didn't he fill out a suit nicely? Maybe the ambassador required him to dress for visitors, even the uninvited ones.

She blinked, tilting her head curiously as his words caught up with her thoughts. "You said *had* a collection. Past tense. Did something happen to Ambassador Victor? Is that why your boss is here now?" Her heart began to race at the idea that something had happened to Victor. The party Lacey had gone to was one hosted by the vampire ambassador himself, or so Lacey had told Emma. It wasn't the first time she'd gone to one of Victor's parties, but this one was supposed to be something special, a long weekend at a house outside the city. Lacey had been so excited. She'd blown her share of the rent money on a new dress and shoes, knowing Emma would forgive her and cover the whole rent—as always.

And right now, Emma would happily pay the rent for the next five years if Lacey would just show up safe and sound.

"Emma?"

She blinked. "I'm sorry," she told Duncan and shook her head to clear it. "Um, right. Past tense. *Did* something happen to the ambassador?" *Or to Lacey?*

"Nothing unexpected, no," Duncan assured her calmly. "But the book collection goes with the residence, so it's not really his anyway."

"Oh, of course. I guess that makes it your boss's now, right?"

Duncan smiled, seeming genuinely happy with her conclusion, or maybe it was more like he was amused. She scowled as he turned gracefully and strolled over to the heavy, ornate desk. Miguel slipped into the room like a dark ghost, making no more noise than Duncan had. He'd changed clothes, too, and now took up a position behind Duncan's left shoulder as Duncan sat behind the desk.

"Have a seat, Ms. Duquet," Duncan said, "and tell me what brings you here."

Emma looked up in surprise as she settled into the chair. "Wait, I thought I was meeting . . ." *Shit.* Emma barely managed to keep from swearing out loud as she realized what was going on.

Duncan, meanwhile, turned sideways to the desk, leaning back in the big leather chair and crossing his legs at the knee, one arm on the desk in front of him. He didn't fidget like some people would have, didn't tap so much as a single finger on the desk. He just watched her intently, as if curious to see how she would react.

"You're the ambassador?" Emma croaked.

"We don't actually refer to it as an ambassador, but, yes."

"That means . . . You're a vampire? But that's impossible. I mean, how old *are* you?"

Miguel stiffened and gave her an outraged glare, but Duncan tsked softly and said, "That's a very rude question in vampire culture, Ms. Duquet. You work in this city. At least I assume you do. Surely they've taught you to be more delicate than that when dealing with other cultures."

Emma narrowed her eyes in irritation. He was right, of course. She did know better than to ask a question like that, but he'd shocked her right out of her cultural awareness classes. And he knew it. He was toying with her, and she didn't like to be toyed with.

"Look, Duncan, or whatever your name really is—"

Miguel actually growled at that, but Duncan raised a hand to stop him. "It's all right, Miguel. She meant no insult, did you, Ms. Duquet?"

Emma didn't answer for a moment. She was too busy staring at Miguel. She'd never heard a man actually growl before. A real, teeth-bared, saliva-dripping, I'm-going-to-rip-your-throat-out growl. Wow.

"Ms. Duquet?"

"Yes! I mean, no, I didn't mean to insult you. I'm . . . I'm usually better than this."

"But you're worried about something. Something that brought you to see us, even though you've never been here before. Something important enough that you snuck through the gate and into our house without invitation."

"The gate was open," she protested.

"The gate was blocked by a truck actively engaged in loading trash," Duncan corrected gently. "Obviously, it was not *supposed* to be open."

Okay, so he had her there. "You're right," she conceded. "I'm sorry. *Again.*"

Duncan laughed softly, his warm brown eyes dancing. He sure didn't look like a vampire. Miguel she could buy. He'd *growled* for God's sake. Duncan looked like a blue blood Harvard business graduate with an expensive tailor and enough rebellion in his soul to let his hair grow long. But maybe that was the point. What better face to put on the vampire culture than someone who looked like the corporate executive next door?

"Your problem?" Duncan prompted her.

Emma drew in a deep breath and let it out slowly. "My roommate, Lacey," she started, then stopped. Lacey was way more than just a roommate, but he didn't need to know that. "She went to one of Victor's parties. It was a weekend thing, but she should have been home by at least Sunday night, because she had to work Monday morning. That was three days ago, and I still haven't heard from her. Lacey wouldn't do that."

She looked at Duncan, waiting for him to respond somehow. To tell her everything was okay, that the party was still going on, or they'd decided to take a plane to the Bahamas and there was no cell coverage. Something, anything, to explain Lacey's silence. He didn't say anything right away. He sat almost perfectly still, clearly thinking about everything she'd said, but not rushing to respond. It was frustrating for someone like Emma, who tended to live life at full throttle, but at the same time, there was something mesmerizing about his stillness. She didn't think she'd ever met anyone who could remain so still. She would have attributed it to him being a vampire, except that Miguel, standing right next to him, was fairly bristling with energy, his muscles bunching beneath the lines of his elegant suit.

Duncan, on the other hand, was like a big cat—a tiger, maybe—so beautiful and sleek on the outside. But even as you admire his beauty, your heart's racing with fear, because some part of you knows that this is danger, this is death. There was a coiled power to Duncan, as if it was barely contained within his skin. It demanded all her attention, and yet, outwardly, he was just sitting there, still and quiet, waiting. Just like that tiger.

Emma wasn't a tiger. She was always fiddling with *something*. Her teachers used to scold her constantly for her twitching, as they called it. But the truth was she had too much energy to be still. It would burn her up from the inside if she didn't use it somehow.

"Was this the first time your friend joined Victor at one of his events?" Duncan asked.

Emma stifled her jerk of surprise at his sudden question. "No," she admitted. "Lacey likes to party. Working and living in D.C. was my idea, but she agreed to come with me for the social scene. There's a party of some sort almost every night in this town. More than one most nights, and on weekends—" Emma shrugged, then hesitated. She didn't want to tell Duncan the rest of it, didn't want him to think badly of Lacey, but . . .

"Lacey's sort of obsessed with you all," she added reluctantly.

"You 'all' what?" Duncan prompted.

"Vampires," Emma said, wincing. "She must read ten books a week, absolutely gobbles them up. Paranormal romance mostly, and most of that vampires. She met Victor at a VIP function hosted by the company she works for. They're a K Street lobbying firm—big, big money. Anyway, she came home that night happier than I've ever seen her, because she'd finally met a real live vampire. Two days later, there was an invite in her work e-mail, a party here at the embassy."

"Here."

"The first party, yeah. That was maybe two months ago. I'd have to look it up to be sure. I don't keep track of Lacey's social calendar, but I'm sure she's partied with your vampire guys at least once a week since then."

"Were they feeding from her?"

Emma blanched at the straightforward question. She'd asked herself the same thing a thousand times, but she'd never asked Lacey. She didn't really want to know.

"I don't know," she admitted to Duncan. "I never saw—" She drew a shaky breath. "I never saw any marks on her neck or anything."

"You wouldn't necessarily. It is likely, however, that your friend was permitting—"

"Lacey," Emma interrupted. "Her name is Lacey."

Duncan acknowledged the correction with a dip of his head. "As charming as I'm sure Lacey is, I doubt Victor would have continued to invite her unless she was providing blood. It's not uncommon, you understand."

Emma looked at him blankly. "What's not uncommon?"

Duncan gave her a pitying look. "There are many humans, Ms. Duquet, who are eager to serve as a blood source for vampires. It can be quite enjoyable for them."

She frowned. "You mean for the humans? How can that be enjoyable?"

"Sexually," he drawled, and the word seemed to whisper seductively from his kissable mouth directly to her ear. It was so real she could feel the warmth of his breath teasing her cheek as his voice curled around her senses.

Emma's heart beat faster. Sweat popped delicately between her breasts, and moisture of an entirely different sort pooled deep between her thighs. She felt her nipples tightening and was glad for the heavy fabric of her jacket which would keep anyone from noticing. Except the heated look on Duncan's face said that he knew she was aroused, knew that her nipples were scraping exquisitely against the lace of her bra. She wanted to clench her legs together against the ache, but refused to give him the satisfaction. She clenched her fingers around the chair arms instead.

This was ridiculous.

She gritted her teeth, forcing her brain back on track. "Look," she said. "I don't know anything about human and vampire interactions. I don't even like the movies. All I know is that Lacey partied with you guys, and now she's missing. She hasn't come home or even called me in three days. Something's happened, and I want to know what you're going to do about it."

"Is it not possible, Ms. Duquet," Duncan said patiently, "that Lacey has met someone she enjoys and is spending an extra few days alone with him?"

"She'd have called me. She knows I'd worry."

"Did you call her office?"

"Yes, of course."

He gave her an inquiring look. "And?"

Emma pinched her mouth angrily. Damn him. "And she supposedly took the week off."

"Ah."

"No. No *ah*. She didn't tell *me* she was taking the week off, and she would have. Something is wrong here, and if I wait too long, I'll never—" Her voice broke as she fought back tears. Why couldn't she make anyone understand? Lacey was so much more than a roommate. They were best friends, sisters in every way that counted. They were all each other had in the world, and Lacey would *never have done this to her!*

Duncan didn't move except to frown thoughtfully. "I believe you," he said unexpectedly.

"Thank you," Emma whispered, nearly choking on the sob that was trying to force its way up her throat.

"Mind you," he cautioned, "I'm not convinced anything dire has occurred, but I do believe you know Lacey quite well, certainly better than I do. And if you say something is off about this situation, then it's worth looking into."

She nodded, biting her lip to keep from blubbering like an idiot.

Duncan's gaze sharpened on her mouth, and he stiffened from his relaxed sideways pose, turning smoothly until he once again faced her across the desk. "As I said earlier, Ms. Duquet, we've only just arrived in this city. Last night, as a matter of fact. Victor departed rather unexpectedly, which leaves us to dig through his records on our own."

"Can't you call him or something?"

"I'm afraid he's not reachable, but I'll do what I can."

Emma sighed. He was humoring her. He had no intention of trying to find Lacey. He wasn't even willing to call Victor, much less anything else.

"I'm not only saying this to appease you," he insisted, and she frowned. That was the second time he'd seemed to read her thoughts. Was it possible?

"And I'm not reading your thoughts either," he added, smiling. "What I have is many years experience reading human expressions, and your face is very expressive."

Emma blushed. "Um, thank you. I guess. So, how long—"

"I know you're anxious, but give me a couple of days. I *will* get back to you, I promise."

Emma wanted to protest. *Two more days!* But it was better than she'd honestly expected before she got here, and it was probably the best she was going to get. She drew a deep, calming breath, in and out.

"All right. Thank you," she said, and reached into her pocket to pull out her cell phone. "I left my purse in the car, so I don't have any business cards with me, but I can text my numbers to you, or—" She raised her head to meet his very human brown eyes. "Do vampires use cell phones?"

Duncan grinned. "We do indeed. All the modern conveniences." He slipped a hand into his jacket pocket, retrieved his own phone, and rapidly tapped a few keys. Then he slid it across the desk to her. "You can enter your number there."

Emma took the phone and glanced down at the screen. Her name had been typed in and was just waiting for a number. Feeling as if she were crossing some invisible line, she entered in her cell and work numbers, then put the phone back on the desk.

"I have a land line at home, but I never use it. Just the cell," she said. "And my office number. I gave you that, too."

"Very good, I'll—"

"Shouldn't I take your number?"

Duncan had already pushed away from the desk and stood, as if the interview was over. He stopped and gave her a bemused look. "Of course. Miguel."

Emma frowned. He couldn't tell her his number? He needed Miguel to do it for him? But Miguel was leaning across the desk, holding out a thick, white business card. Emma looked down as she took it. There were two lines on the card. Duncan's name, which apparently included a last name of Milford, even though he hadn't introduced himself that way, and a phone number. No title, no identifying affiliation of any kind.

"Okay," she said. "Thanks."

"Miguel, walk Ms. Duquet out to her car, would you? It's dark and slippery out there."

"Oh, no, really, I'm okay," she protested. The last thing she wanted was a stroll in the dark with the growler, Miguel.

"Of course, you are," Duncan said implacably. "Miguel."

* * * *

Duncan stood at an upstairs window and watched as Miguel escorted Emma Duquet out through the gate and down the street to her car, which was an older model Honda, he noted. A reliable car, but not an expensive one.

She said something to Miguel as she opened the car door. Probably thanking him, but nothing more than that. She wasn't comfortable with Miguel, or maybe she sensed his distrust of her. Whichever it was, Duncan didn't mind. If anyone was going to get closer to Ms. Duquet it would be him. He was attracted to her in a way he hadn't been to any woman in a very long time. He supposed it had something to do with the gentle hint of a drawl in her voice, one she'd clearly worked hard to lose. But it was still there to anyone who'd grown up in the South and knew what to listen for. It was said that a man's taste in women, and vice versa, was set when he was still a child, long before that taste was ever acted upon. If so, it was entirely possible that, even now, Duncan's taste in women was a throwback to his youth in Tennessee nearly two hundred years ago. But he suspected it was more than that, too.

"Sire?" Louis said behind him. "You called for me?"

"We need to break the security on Victor's computers," Duncan said without turning. "Forget the rest for now."

"Yes, my lord. I'll begin at once." There was an undercurrent of eagerness in Louis's voice. For all his skill at fighting, Louis was a geek at heart, a technical genius who'd never met a security system he couldn't break into. He'd been dying to get into Victor's computers.

"And Louis?"

"Sire?"

"I want everything you can find on Emma Duquet."

"How far back—"

"Everything, Louis."

"Yes, my lord."

Duncan continued to watch as Emma drove her car along the curve of the cul-de-sac, circling around before heading back the way she'd come. He thought of her lovely eyes, such an unusual color, the exact shade of pansies in the spring. He still remembered the flowers from his mother's garden in that other lifetime. Things had changed so much since then. It was more than a different time; it was a whole different world. He frowned at the thought. He rarely remembered those days anymore, and now Emma's pretty eyes had brought them to mind twice in one evening.

She'd been telling the truth about her friend. What she knew of it, anyway. Part of what made Duncan so successful with humans was his vampire-enhanced empathy. It was an unusual talent among his kind. Vampires were far more likely to lose any connection they'd once had to human emotion, rather than to gain it. But even as a human, Duncan had possessed an intuitive feel for other people's emotions. And somehow, when he'd become a vampire, that intuition had only grown. It had been too much at first, feeling every emotion of the people—human or vampire—around him. Even worse, emotions sometimes lingered in buildings or rooms, especially if the feelings were particularly strong or traumatic, like fear, hate, or even love. His abilities bordered on the psychic, but then many of the abilities bestowed by the Vampire transition did.

Over time he'd learned to block out the general noise, learned how to tap into feelings selectively. And he'd definitely selected to tap into Ms. Duquet this evening. Her feelings had been very straightforward, and, as frequently was the case, knowledge of her emotions had led to knowledge of her thoughts. The two went hand in hand, after all. People often lied with their mouths, but their thoughts were always truthful. Combined with all of the other clues humans gave off, he could generally judge a human as well as he could one of his own vampire children. And since a vampire Sire knew his children as well as he knew himself, that was saying something.

But if Emma Duquet was telling the truth, then Victor's activities went far beyond corruption, beyond even the abominations he'd kept imprisoned in his basement. Which meant Duncan had to find out exactly what Victor's crimes were before they came crashing down on Duncan's head.

Chapter Six

The next night, Duncan opened the door from his private suite and stepped into the hallway, wincing as something big plummeted through the open stairwell and hit the first floor with a resounding boom. This was his people's straightforward method of expeditious junk disposal. Unfortunately, it was creating a rapidly growing pile of debris in the foyer. Eventually, all that junk would have to be hauled out into the yard where it would sit until they had better security in place. There'd be no more uninvited visitors slipping past a heedlessly open gate.

The rest of the team from California had arrived right on schedule late last night, and the house was much busier than it had been. The newly arrived vampires had all knelt and sworn a blood oath to him, transferring their allegiance from Raphael to Duncan. It was all done with Raphael's blessing, which made the whole process much simpler. Duncan was their master now; their hearts beat at his command.

And his current command had much to do with cleaning up the remnants of Victor's corruption. All three levels of the old house were being searched thoroughly, which in many cases meant being literally torn apart. No one trusted Victor, but they weren't entirely certain what they were looking for, either. Listening or recording devices, certainly. When those were found, they were removed and traced back to their control base, which thus far had proven to be a windowless room secreted away next to Victor's daytime resting chamber on the third floor. That in itself was appalling, that he'd chosen to fashion a daytime resting place for himself on the highest floor. But then the basement would have been out of the question, since it had been filled with his half-sentient vampire slaves.

In any event, many of the recording devices they had found were located in bedrooms, and the video collection in Victor's hideaway gave proof that those bedrooms had been used frequently, if only for an hour or two at a time. More significantly, most of the men featured in those videos were faces Duncan and everyone else recognized from the evening news.

He didn't know yet if Victor had been actively blackmailing anyone—although he'd know even that before they were finished—but, if not, he'd certainly been stockpiling blackmail material against future needs.

Duncan walked down the hall to where Louis had set up his equipment in an ongoing effort to unravel the various files from Victor's computers. What he'd found so far was just more evidence of Victor's rampant paranoia. In the human world, he'd have been living in a small apartment with tin foil over the windows and newspapers piled up to the ceiling. Instead, he'd been a powerful vampire lord, hundreds of years old and nesting in the D.C. area before the city had even had a name. Duncan didn't know what Victor had done before they'd established the U.S. Capital here. Maybe haunted the battlefields of the revolution, preying on dying soldiers.

Or maybe, Duncan thought to himself, *I'm a tad bit prejudiced against the old vampire.* He smiled ruefully, then sighed. They didn't need him here. He supposed he could start ripping out walls with the rest of them, but—

"My lord!"

Louis's excited shout had Duncan crossing quickly to the desk where his security chief was bent over the keyboard of Victor's main computer. Two other vampire geeks crowded close and began making suggestions as Louis keyed through the data. Duncan stepped out of their way.

"I've broken the main encryption, my lord," Louis explained tersely as he continued to type. "But there are additional codes within some of these files."

"That one's a simple alpha designation," one of the others commented quietly. "Try opening—"

"Fuck, there it is. Pictures and everything."

"What?" Duncan demanded. The others slid out of his way as he moved to stand behind Louis once again.

"Women, my lord," Louis explained, paging through a file.

"Young, beautiful, *human* women," another added appreciatively.

"No names," Louis put in. "Initials only, but with the pictures, it shouldn't be too difficult . . . Did the woman the other night—"

"Emma Duquet," Duncan provided.

"Right. Did she leave a picture of her missing friend?"

"No."

"Okay, one minute." Louis swiveled his chair around to the desk behind him and pulled his laptop closer. "I started digging into Duquet's background like you asked," he said as he typed. "Her full name's Emmaline Marie Duquet, by the way, though she rarely uses it. She has a Facebook page she hasn't updated regularly in years, but let me check . . . Yep. There it is. Her friend's first name was Lacey, right?"

"Yes," Duncan said. He was watching over Louis's shoulder, seeing pictures of a younger, less sophisticated Emma Duquet flash by, pictures clearly taken either before or right after she arrived in Washington. Or maybe it was worry for her friend that had taken away the sparkle in her eyes, the grin that said she was going to take on the world and win.

"Lacey Cray," Louis muttered, settling on a single picture of Emma with her arm around a lovely blonde about her own age. "Pretty name. Pretty girl, too. Too bad."

Duncan wanted to dispute the finality of Louis's last words with their assumption that Lacey was already dead, but he couldn't. Despite his reassurances to Emma last night, and as much as he'd like to produce Lacey safe and sound for her, he knew that wasn't the most likely outcome.

Louis turned back to Victor's computer. "There are dates next to each woman's picture, my lord. And different initials after each date. I'm thinking . . ." He stopped typing and looked up at Duncan, as if to judge his reaction. "Given what we've already seen of Victor's personal porno collection, this is most likely a record of sexual encounters, my lord. The second set of initials are the men these women were paired off with, complete with dates."

"He was a fucking pimp," one of the vampires whispered in disgust. "Hell, maybe that's where his money came from. So far we've got him living like a Rockefeller, but no income."

Duncan glanced up. "Nothing?"

"He owned a lot of property, my lord," the vamp said. "But too much of it is in rundown neighborhoods, stuff he bought decades ago and forgot to sell before the market tanked. As far as I can find, he didn't even bother to collect rent on some of them."

"What about better properties, places he might be using himself?"

"A few of those, sure. I can get you a list—"

"Do that now, and e-mail the information to Louis and Miguel. And keep looking. If he didn't make money legitimately, where did it come from? It has to be there somewhere. Either that, or he didn't keep those records on any of the computers we've found so far, in which case—"

He grimaced as someone upstairs began laying into a plaster wall with what sounded like a sledge hammer. He let out a long, noisy breath and said, "If the records are in this house, I'm sure we'll find them very soon. But in the meantime, Louis . . ." He met his security chief's pale gaze. ". . . did Victor maintain any blood houses?"

Louis shook his head. "Not in the city of D.C., my lord. He and his four were the only vamps he permitted to live here . . . well, other than those creatures in the basement. But there are plenty of blood houses in the surrounding states. Not always houses, of course, sometimes clubs, like what Rajmund has up in Manhattan. About half as ritzy, though."

"I want a list of anyplace within . . ." Duncan thought for a moment. "Let's make it within two hours' drive from here. I suspect Victor's less savory entertaining was done somewhere other than this house. Not that he would have cared, but his guests might have. And Emma said Lacey talked about going to a party outside the city. How long will it take you to come up with that information?"

"No more than a few minutes, my lord. Victor kept lousy records, but I started building my own database a few weeks ago, pretty much as soon as I arrived here to start getting things ready for you."

"Excellent. I'm going to track down Miguel," Duncan said, "and you can meet us in the library once you have the list. The rest of you keep working on these files, and if you find anything noteworthy, call my cell."

Duncan found Miguel in the basement with yet another of the vampire crews that had come in last night. This one was very specialized and would only remain until their task was complete, which, from the looks of things, would be much longer than anyone anticipated.

"This is all shit, Miguel," a wiry, gray-haired vampire was saying. He slapped a beam of rotting wood and Duncan winced, hoping the entire house wasn't about to collapse on their heads. They'd probably survive, but it might take a while to dig themselves out.

Duncan grinned at the gray-haired vamp's back and said, "Think of it as a challenge, Alaric."

The vampire spun around with a bark of laughter. "A challenge is you trying to last the full five minutes in the ring with me, my lord. This . . ." He waved at the musty, dark basement around them. ". . . this is plain old shit. And I'm not even talking about the vamp dust left over from Victor's abomination experiment."

All laughter fled, and Duncan nodded soberly. "Louis cleaned most of it out," he said.

"And he did a fine job of it, too," Alaric agreed. "But I'll tell you, Duncan. I served in more than one war as a human and saw some pretty awful things. And God knows, I've seen my share of horrific sights as a vampire. But this? This place gives me the creeps. I wouldn't want to sleep down here, even if the foundation *wasn't* rotting and about to dump the whole house on my head."

Duncan regarded the other vampire thoughtfully. Alaric was the finest vampire contractor in North America. He'd built the daytime sleep vaults in every one of Raphael's personal residences and scattered headquarters, including the new compound up near Seattle. There were a couple of other crews doing similar work in the vampire community. They'd all trained with Alaric, and that let them charge a very pretty price for their services. But there was no substitute for having Alaric himself in charge of your project, and Duncan would have paid any price Alaric asked in order to secure the safest possible resting place for his people. A vampire was completely helpless during daytime sleep. The recent murders of two of Raphael's vampires, along with three more in Canada, had proved that beyond a doubt.

"So, what do you propose?" he asked now.

"It's going to take time and a lot of money to put in a decent underground vault," Alaric warned him immediately. "This whole city's built on a fucking swamp."

Duncan didn't miss the gleam in Alaric's eye when he said that, although it was probably as much from the challenge as the price tag.

"I don't care what it costs. If it can be done, I want it done."

The vamp shook his head, laughing softly. "I'll give you this, my lord. You do things right. Okay. Let me get the rest of my guys in here, and we'll do a full inspection." He gave Miguel a pointed look. "I won't be needing *you* for that part."

Miguel looked affronted, but Duncan intervened quickly and said, "That's good. I need Miguel with me tonight anyway."

His lieutenant gave him an inquiring look, but Duncan just signaled him to follow. Vampire hearing was entirely too good, and as much as he admired Alaric's skill, he had no desire to share the details of his personal affairs.

Miguel immediately took the lead, going upstairs ahead of Duncan, pausing to scan the hallway before stepping through the doorway. As if enemies were already lying in wait for them somewhere between the kitchen and the stairs. But Duncan didn't say anything. The situation was still too unsettled. Security was better, but not yet up to Miguel's— or Duncan's—standards. There were vampires working all over the house, and yet it was still more than half empty. Eventually it would feel like home and safety. But not yet.

Louis was already waiting for them in the library. "I e-mailed the data to both of you, my lord."

"What data?" Miguel asked, pulling out his smartphone.

"Victor was giving parties with guests who'd rather not be seen," Duncan replied. "Which means he was using a house that's at least private, if not isolated. He wouldn't have wanted neighbors seeing people come and go all the time; they might get nosey and see someone they recognize. But he wouldn't have been using some rundown cabin in the woods, either. Victor was a snob. The house will be elegant, expensive, very possibly in an exclusive area of homes, but with substantial acreage for privacy."

"Leesburg, Virginia, my lord," Louis said confidently. "Victor owned two properties there, both of which would suit, and there's a blood house nearby, too."

"How far?" Duncan asked.

"About thirty-five miles. This time of night, thirty minutes to an hour, depending on traffic."

Duncan nodded. It might be late winter, but the nights were still long. They'd have plenty of time. "Let's go, then. Unless you'd rather stay here and knock down some walls for Alaric." He started for the door, then glanced down at what he was wearing. Like the others, he was dressed casually, in jeans and a sweater. He hadn't planned on meeting any of his new subjects tonight, hadn't planned on even leaving the house, much less visiting any of the blood houses. But it would take time for him to change, and besides these clothes were warmer. That decided it for Duncan. He grabbed a leather jacket from the old-fashioned coat tree near the door, pulling it on over his sweater. There was a leather hair tie in the jacket pocket, so he finger-combed his hair back and tied it into a rough tail. It would have to do. Raj's Manhattan club might be tuxedo territory, but most blood houses were far less formal. And if not, well, he *was* their lord and master, and he'd wear whatever he damned well pleased. And if anyone had a problem with it, he wouldn't mind a good bloodletting either.

Chapter Seven

The blood house didn't exactly look like a hot bed of vampire activity. Located in a tony housing tract in an upscale suburb of Leesburg, it was a meticulously maintained contemporary home with a low-slung profile and pristine landscaping. The houses in this area were spaced far apart and surrounded by a broad swath of green forest, which gave the illusion of living amongst nature. The effect was lovely, and very private.

It was two a.m., or vampire high noon, but there were no cars in the driveway or in front of the house. Duncan could detect two vampires inside, however, both wide awake.

"Kind of quiet for a blood house, isn't it?" Louis asked, eyeing the house doubtfully.

Duncan nodded, agreeing with Louis. Something wasn't quite right here. "Well, someone's home. Let's be polite and ring the doorbell."

The door opened while they were still making their way down the paved walk to the flat front porch. Miguel and Louis both tensed and immediately formed a wall in front of Duncan.

By contrast, the slender, dark-haired vampire standing in the doorway gave them a big smile and bowed gracefully. "Welcome, my lord," he said, trying discreetly to catch a glimpse of Duncan behind the wall of vampire. "Please," he added, straightening to give a welcoming gesture, "come inside and get warm.

"Thank you, Brendan," Duncan murmured, stepping around his two bodyguards.

Since they'd never met, Brendan twitched at the sound of his name, but Duncan knew he was Brendan Folmer. He'd taken the knowledge from the vampire's brain before he'd ever opened the door.

"I am Duncan," he said, entering the house. He indicated the others. "My lieutenant, Miguel, and security chief, Louis."

Brendan closed the door behind them. "Erik will be down in a moment, my lord," he said, referring to the second vampire in the house, the one Duncan could sense upstairs. "We didn't expect you and—"

Brendan's worried explanation was cut off as the second vampire appeared on the landing. He raced downstairs and immediately knelt in front of Duncan. "My lord Duncan," he said reverently. "Thank you for coming."

With a look of dismay, Brendan dropped gracefully to his knees next to his partner and lowered his gaze.

Duncan brushed a hand over their bowed heads, acknowledging their submission. "I'm gratified by your welcome," he said.

Erik jumped to his feet as soon as Duncan's hand lifted. "You'll find no sorrow for Victor's passing here, my lord. Nor anywhere in the territory, I would imagine." He gestured at a matching pair of pale leather couches in front of the fireplace. "Would you like to sit? The fire is nice, especially on these cold nights."

Brendan laughed. "Erik thinks anything below seventy degrees Fahrenheit is freezing."

Duncan privately agreed with that assessment. Washington winters were going to take some getting used to after so many years in L. A.'s balmy climate.

"So this is your home, then?" he asked, settling onto the couch and stifling a sigh of pleasure at the fire's heat.

"Yes, my lord." Erik sat opposite Duncan and crossed his legs, propping an ankle on the opposite knee. "Bren and I bought this house several years ago from a vampire named Scovill. An older vamp. What would you say, Bren, two, three hundred years?"

"Oh, much older than that," Brendan said. "And not too pleased with how Victor ran things, either. He bought a house way back in the Blue Ridge mountains, I think." He shuddered discreetly. "Very unpleasant vampire, but powerful too. The locals probably think Big Foot has finally come home to roost."

Miguel had been prowling the downstairs, but now took up a position behind Duncan and said, "Victor had this place marked as a blood house. Why?"

"Oh, that," Erik said dismissively. "We have a small group of vampires who come together every weekend, my lord," Eric said, addressing Duncan. "Private affairs, very discreet. There is a blood house in this area, however. On the other side of Leesburg. Victor probably did own that one. And there's a second property, more in the way of an estate—big house, lots of property. I imagine it's all yours now, my lord."

Duncan nodded and signaled to Miguel. "I want to verify the addresses we have."

Erik pulled out his PDA and began conferring with Miguel. But Brendan gave Duncan a somber look. "What you really want to know about are Victor's parties, I imagine." He paused, waiting for a response. When Duncan simply looked at him, he hurried on. "That's what the estate was for. He used to come out here regularly with a bunch of big wigs. Senators, congressmen, even the occasional cabinet member, and a whole bunch of lobbyists. That was the real purpose of the parties. The lobbyists got unfettered access to policymakers away from the glare of the Washington press, and Victor got paid very, very well for making it possible."

"And what did the policymakers get out of it?" Duncan asked quietly.

Brendan looked away in obvious discomfort, glancing over at Erik and back again, clearly reluctant to continue.

Erik murmured something to Miguel, then nodded and dropped his PDA onto the side table. "Go ahead, Bren," he sighed. "You've gone this far, so you might as well tell the whole sordid story."

"The policymakers got different things," Brendan said evasively. "Some of our fine elected leaders got kickbacks in the form of soft money campaign donations. Others . . ." He tightened his lips in distaste. "Sex, I think."

Duncan frowned. Sex? That was the big secret? Men in power being offered sex in exchange for favors? That was so common it was almost trivial. There had to be something more to it, something the neatly pressed Brendan didn't want to talk about.

"Not just sex," Erik explained, with a sympathetic look in Brendan's direction. "Victor seduced women for these men, often very young women, and all of them very beautiful. He got them to do things that I'm quite certain most of them never would have done otherwise. Hell, he got them to do *men* they probably wouldn't have done either. I know power's an aphrodisiac and all that, but even that can only carry so far with most people."

"So, Victor was getting paid for these parties?"

"You mean were the lobbyists paying him directly?" Erik clarified. "Yes, I think so. More than one of them joked about it. Victor insisted some of us attend his sordid little affairs, even though we refused to whore for him. We were all professionals of one sort or another, and Victor thought his clients would respect him more if they saw the kind of vampires he controlled, if they saw how powerful he was."

"As if," Brendan muttered.

"Yes, well. He thought so, anyway," he continued. "And then there were the other parties, the *special* ones."

Duncan felt Miguel's attention sharpen behind him.

"Booze flowed freely at Victor's parties and his guests liked to talk. One of the things they loved to talk about was the special parties. That's what they always called them, 'the special.' Like, they'd point out a particular woman and say, 'Hope that one's at the next special.' Victor didn't have that kind of party often, maybe a couple times a year, but they were hard-core. If you can believe what the men bragged about—and I do—the women were flat out raped, and by more than one man. Some of them were even hurt pretty badly. The man who told me all this laughed when he talked about how Victor would heal the women afterward so they'd be ready to go again the next night. It made me sick, but I wouldn't be surprised if Victor or his henchmen have a website where you can download a video of his 'specials' for a price."

Miguel leaned forward. "Surely the men involved wouldn't want their identities revealed."

"So they film from the back," Brendan said, with a shrug. "The viewer gets a shot of a senator's pasty white ass while he whips some poor girl."

"Did you report this?" Duncan asked.

"To whom, my lord?" Erik asked mildly. "Victor was our lord. By rights, he was the one to whom we'd have reported such an abuse. And every vampire lord in the country would be after our heads if we went to the human police. We'd never live long enough to testify."

Duncan was forced to agree. Even if Erik or Brendan had complained to another vampire lord, Victor would have been told, and the two vampires would have been executed without anyone raising a word of protest.

And even now, hearing about it for the first time, Duncan didn't know what to say that wouldn't sound like a meaningless platitude. All they had was his word that he was different from Victor, that such things would never happen under his rule. Duncan stood, turning to face Erik and Brendan, who had jumped to their feet.

"If you ever need anything," Duncan said, "you may call me. If I'm not available, you may speak to either Miguel or Louis. They'll fill me in, and I will get back to you. I'm not Victor, gentlemen. You will see that in time."

He stepped around the couch, signaling Louis who was waiting by the front door.

"Thank you for the information, and for your hospitality."

"My lord," Brendan said when Duncan was halfway to the door.

Duncan turned and gave him a questioning look.

"Thank *you*, my lord. We knew you were different from the moment you claimed the territory. You cared more in those few minutes of terror and confusion than Victor had in his entire rule. Just by getting rid of him, you've done every vampire in this territory a service already. We'll talk to the others, too, and let them know."

Duncan nodded. "We'll see each other again, Brendan. I don't intend to be a stranger to my people."

* * * *

"Fucking Victor," Duncan swore as Louis steered the big SUV down the curving driveway. "I can't believe none of us realized how corrupt he was."

"How could you, my lord? He never let anyone but his guards live in the District, and anyone else who may have known was too frightened to take action."

"That's no excuse. I saw him every damn year at the Council meetings, and I never suspected any of this. Neither did Raphael, and it's not easy to pull one over on him."

Miguel shrugged. "Not if he's looking for it, but why would he have looked for any of this? I've never been to a Council meeting, but I know they don't last long. A few hours, maybe? It's not like they meet for cocktails and dinner afterwards. And when they're together, I imagine everyone has their shields locked up as tight as a virgin's knickers."

Duncan gave his lieutenant a sideways look. "You're not old enough to know about virgins or knickers, Miguel," he said dryly.

"Hey, we still have virgins!" Miguel protested with a smile.

"If you say so," Duncan agreed. He was grateful for the change of mood. "You checked the addresses with Erik?"

Miguel nodded. "It's the same two we have, though we didn't have a record of the one property operating as a blood house. From what Erik said it's pretty active, too. It's the only one for a hundred miles around here."

"I'm beginning to think this whole trip was a waste of time, but we might as well check it out next."

"We need to leave enough time to get back to the city tonight, my lord," Miguel commented. "And that blood house is a good hour's drive on the other side of Leesburg. I don't want you to end up spending a day unguarded in a strange blood house, or worse, that party place of Victor's. God knows what sort of people he let in there. We should head back tonight and get an early start tomorrow. Check them both out then."

Duncan frowned. The whole idea of Victor's parties made him want to kill the vampire lord all over again, but it also sounded a lot like what Lacey had described to Emma, and that couldn't be good. He wanted to see the house for himself, but Miguel had a point.

"All right," he said. "We'll do them both tomorrow. The blood house and Victor's party place, though I expect there's nothing left there but the ghosts of pain and old blood."

* * * *

The next night, as Duncan stood in the yard of Victor's Leesburg estate, he looked back and remembered those words. He remembered and thought how foolish he'd been to believe he'd already understood the full depth of Victor's depravity.

Chapter Eight

Emma found it nearly impossible to concentrate. Two days had passed since she'd spoken to Duncan at the vampire embassy, and she'd heard nothing back from him yet. She was so strung out with nerves that she'd skipped her morning coffee, figuring she didn't need the caffeine, even though she'd barely slept last night. But then she hadn't really slept since the first night Lacey had gone missing. And no matter what anyone else thought, Emma had never doubted Lacey was missing. They'd known each other since they were eleven years old, that horrible year when Emma's mother had died from the same cancer that had taken her Grandmama years before. Overnight, she'd found herself orphaned with no other family on her mother's side to take her in. She'd never known anyone from her father's family; didn't even know if there was anyone. So Emma had been left all alone in the world, shuffled into foster care along with the thousands of others just like her. And she would have stayed all alone, too, if not for Lacey.

By the time Emma arrived, Lacey had already been living with their foster parents for three years. Lacey's birth parents had been more interested in their drugs than their only child, bouncing in and out of jail until finally a half-starved and terrified Lacey had been taken away from them for good. But you'd never have known it from meeting Lacey. She was as sunny as her hair was blond, a cheerful little girl who'd taken the lonely Emma in hand and announced they were sisters. Just like that. As if deciding it somehow made it so.

But for Lacey it did, and eventually for Emma, too. They'd been inseparable ever since, sharing horrible apartments through college, squeezing the system for every penny of financial aid they could get, and working two and three jobs to make up for the rest. After college, Lacey had gone right to work, while Emma went to law school. And then had come their big decision to move to Washington, the center of power, the place where their fortunes would be made—or married into, in Lacey's case.

And now, as Emma sat at her desk, staring sightlessly at the computer screen in front of her, she wondered if Lacey would still be missing if Emma hadn't insisted they move here.

"Emma!"

She hid her grimace at the sound of her boss's voice—or rather her boss's wife's voice, which was the same thing.

"Sharon?" Emma said, looking up and over her monitor.

Sharon Coffer frowned down at her, every strand of her carefully tinted and styled hair in perfect alignment, her face almost immovable beneath a layer of makeup so thick that just looking at it made Emma's skin gasp for oxygen. What was it with so many of these political women that they felt the need to roll on the makeup? And she didn't *even* want to get started on that helmet of a hairdo.

"Have you finished the draft of that constituent letter yet?" Sharon demanded, which was pretty standard for Sharon. She never asked; she demanded.

Emma nodded. "I just finished. You want me to print it out?"

Sharon's scowl deepened further as she clearly tried to decide if Emma was mocking her or not. God forbid the woman have to read a damn one page letter on her computer monitor. That would mean she'd have to *wear* her glasses instead of hiding them in her purse like some sort of shameful deformity.

"Do that," Sharon said at last, then spun on her heel and stomped off to torment some other unfortunate.

"I don't think she likes you," Noreen whispered from the desk right next to Emma's. Noreen was Congressman Coffer's personal secretary, not that Sharon ever permitted her to meet with the congressman alone. Sharon didn't trust any female when it came to her husband. The all-American good looks and charm that had helped Guy Coffer get elected also made him far too attractive for Sharon's peace of mind. But Emma had never heard even a whisper of gossip about the congressman and another woman. And if there'd been something, she would have heard about it. The grapevine in these hallowed halls made the old ladies back home look like total amateurs in the gossip department.

"She doesn't like *anything* with a vagina," Emma murmured back to Noreen, and was rewarded by the sound of choking laughter.

Not that Emma gave a damn about Sharon or her handsome husband. Except that Sharon's insane jealousy was a major roadblock to advancement in the Congressman's office for anyone female and under sixty, and Emma had aspirations for her career that went well beyond dealing with constituent complaints. She had a law degree, dammit, and sometimes she doubted her decision in coming here at all, which brought her thoughts right back to Lacey.

"Em, there's a birthday party next door and I need cake. You want some?"

Emma looked up at Noreen and gave her a blank stare.

"Earth to Emma, you want cake? I bet it's cho-co-late." Noreen dragged the last word out tantalizingly, but Emma shook her head, glancing down at her watch. She couldn't do this. Couldn't sit here like everything was business as usual while she waited for the vampires to decide if something had happened to Lacey.

"I have to leave early today."

Noreen goggled at her. No one left early, not from this office, and pretty much not from anywhere on the Hill when Congress was in session.

Emma felt her face flushing, but she ignored her friend's disbelief to open her desk drawer and drag out the enormous bag she called a purse. She'd tried a million times to go with something smaller, but each time she invariably ended up back with the big one. She was closing the drawer when the staccato sound of high heels announced Sharon Coffer's return.

"Emma, the Congressman wants you in on this meeting."

Emma turned in disbelief. She was *never* invited into meetings, especially not meetings like this one. They were reviewing the Congressman's domestic priorities for the rest of the session, which meant every important piece of legislation likely to come up before the summer recess would be discussed and analyzed. It was everything she lusted after.

But why did it have to happen today?

"Emma, let's go!" Sharon's voice was sharp with impatience as she turned and headed back toward the Congressman's inner office.

Emma shoved her purse back into the drawer, grabbed a bottle of water, tucked her laptop under her arm and rushed to follow.

Chapter Nine

Emma closed her car door and staggered up to the house she shared with Lacey, thankful she'd managed to snag a parking space right out front. A sudden gust of wet air blew down the street, chasing the remnants of a newspaper someone had dropped or tossed aside. Its pages littered the gutters, rattling as they rushed ahead of the icy wind. She climbed the stairs, her fingers nearly numb as she inserted her key into the lock. The door opened to a cold, dark house, and Emma stood there for a moment, feeling lost.

She was lucky to be home before midnight. The way the meeting had dragged into the evening, she'd expected Sharon to order in some cots so they could have a sleepover. And Emma knew she shouldn't complain, even if the meeting *had* gone into the wee hours. Today was the first time she'd felt like she was actually doing the job she'd been promised when she came to work for Guy Coffer. And yet, it didn't feel like any kind of victory. There was no adrenaline rush and none of the excitement she would have expected. Somehow, with no Lacey to help her celebrate, it all felt empty.

She sighed and kicked the door closed, then dropped her keys into the ugly dish on the small table near the door. Walking across to the light switch on the living room wall, she thought again how stupid it was to walk through a dark room every night when she came home. She should get a small lamp for the table. Of course, she'd been telling herself that same thing for two years now. And usually, Lacey got home before dark, at least on weeknights, so most of the time it didn't matter.

But what if Lacey never came home again?

"No," she said out loud. "She *will* come home, and she'll be full of great stories about the hot, vampire lover who swept her away for—" *A whole week, Emma?*

Her throat closed up with fear, and she wanted to sit right down on the stairs and bawl her eyes out. But she refused to give into the urge. She was just so damn tired it was hard to think straight. The long hours at work, coupled with sleepless nights, were beginning to take a toll, and today had been the longest day of all.

Bracing a hand on the newel post, she lifted her feet one at a time and took her heels off, then walked up the stairs in her stockinged feet, shoes in hand. One thing about sitting in meetings all day, her feet didn't hurt nearly as much as they did when she spent the day running all over the Capitol building like an overpaid messenger. On the other hand, her ass hurt and her lower back was killing her.

By the time she reached her bedroom on the second floor—hers was the one with the big bay window sticking out over the small front yard like a turret on the old Victorian house—her blouse was unbuttoned and she was already yearning for the hot bath she'd promised herself all the way home.

She glanced down at the street before twisting the rod on the cheap blinds over the window and shutting out the night. The house she and Lacey had rented wasn't in the best neighborhood in Washington, but not the worst either. And it had been completely renovated before they moved in, including the bathrooms. Lacey had insisted Emma take the bigger bedroom, with the big window and the attached bath, because she paid the bigger share of the rent. In the months where she wasn't paying the whole thing, that is.

Dropping her shoes in the closet as she walked by it, she went directly to the tub and turned on the water, letting it run. It sometimes took a few minutes for the hot water to make its way up to the second floor.

She had pulled off the rest of her clothes, throwing the whole bunch into the laundry basket, and pulled on a warm robe, when she decided the long day warranted a glass of wine to go with the bath. Nothing was more relaxing than a good hot soak with a glass of . . . hmmm, white or red? She'd see what was open.

Thinking of the cold hardwood floors, she shoved her feet into a pair of UGGs, turned off the water and hurried down the stairs, not permitting herself even a glance at Lacey's empty room at the other end of the hall. A part of her still expected to come home and find Lacey wiped out and hung over, full of stories and apologies about her unexpected getaway in the arms of some rich guy she'd met. But too often these last few days, when Emma wasn't being run ragged by her job, her thoughts had turned to far darker imaginings, and she'd wonder if she'd ever see Lacey again.

"Stop it, Emma," she scolded again as she rounded the bottom of the stairs and headed for the kitchen. The wine would help that, too. Help dull the worry and shut down her brain for a few hours.

She was reaching for the kitchen light switch when a heavy car door slammed out front. Two more doors slammed hard after the first, and a deep, male voice said something she couldn't make out. She told herself it was one of her neighbors. Few of the houses here had garages, and most of the residents parked on the street, just as Emma had tonight. But something about the noise made her curious. She tiptoed—and why was she sneaking around her own house?—over to the window near the door and lifted the thin, fabric shade away from the edge so she could look onto the street.

She gasped, then immediately covered her mouth against the sound. Vamps supposedly had super hearing, and that was Duncan out there! Even worse, that Miguel guy was with him.

"Shit," she mouthed silently and backed away from the door. Were they coming here? Well, of course they were. Where else would they be going? She'd backed nearly to the kitchen when the doorbell rang, and she froze. Should she answer it? Maybe if she was very quiet, they'd think she wasn't home and leave.

But what if he has news about Lacey? she thought frantically, her tired brain finally clicking back into some semblance of reason. That had to be it. Why else would they be here?

She started toward the door, then glanced down at herself and froze once again. She was wearing a *bathrobe!* A purple, fuzzy bathrobe. And no underwear. Ah, hell, no bra, and Emma did not have the kind of bustline that could go braless without being obvious about it.

She blew out an exasperated breath.

"Emma?" Duncan's cool-water voice called her name, tinged with a little bit of worry.

He was worried? About her? That was nice, wasn't it?

Yeah, but, Emma, you aren't wearing any panties!

Right, right. Underwear first, then handsome vampires.

"Emma, I know you're there. Open the door."

He knew she was here? How'd he know that?

"Um, just a minute," she called out. She raced past the door, slowing long enough to flip the locks and yank the door open as she went by. "Y'all come on in. I'll be right back."

Before she'd gone halfway up the stairs, her house was full of vampires and one of them was standing in front of her, blocking her way. Her eyes widened in shock and her heart kicked in her chest. He'd moved so *fast*, and she hadn't sensed a thing, nothing more than a faint breeze passing her on the stairs. Her startled gaze took in his features in the dim light, and she frowned. It was Miguel. The growler. She backed down a step away from him.

"Where are you going, Ms. Duquet?" he asked.

"It's all right, Miguel," Duncan said from somewhere behind her.

Miguel didn't move, and Emma's frown deepened. She refused to hold her robe closed like some sort of maiden aunt, so she stuffed her hands in her pockets and turned to face Duncan. The door was partly open, and she shivered in the cold air.

"I was going to put some clothes on," she explained slowly, as if they were too dense to understand such a simple concept.

Duncan's gaze made a leisurely journey from her UGG-covered feet to the fuzzy bathrobe, hesitated a breath too long over her braless chest, and continued to what she knew was her pissed-off expression. But instead of showing even a hint of remorse, the bastard smiled. As if he found the entire situation amusing. Again. Emma was getting very tired of being the source of his entertainment.

Her eyes narrowed, but Duncan's smile only grew wider.

"It's all right, Miguel," he said again. "Let her by."

"Well, thank you very much," she said, letting the saccharine sweetness of her Southern upbringing flavor the words.

Duncan's eyes widened in appreciation, and Emma felt like snarling. That wasn't the reaction she'd been going for.

Determined to retain the little dignity she had left, she started up the stairs again. The growler got out of her way, but he only moved closer to the wall, so she had to squeeze past his bulk. Why were these vampires all so big, anyway? Drinking nothing but blood, you'd think they'd be skin and bones, pale and starved looking. Not these guys. Every one of them—and there were more than just Duncan and Miguel in her house, though she hadn't bothered to count—was awfully healthy looking. Maybe they dined on bloody steak every night? She frowned, thinking about where that steak might come from. What sort of *animal*.

Don't be ridiculous, Emma. She reined in her vivid imagination, stormed into her bedroom, closed the door with exquisite care, and began pulling on clothes.

* * * *

Duncan watched Emma Duquet's shapely bottom sway beneath the ridiculous purple bathrobe as she hurried up the stairs, edging past Miguel as if she feared he'd leap upon her at any moment. She disappeared into a room on the second floor without so much as a glance backwards, shutting the door with a firm click. Her footsteps clunked overhead in the ungainly boots before a pair of solid thumps told him the boots had been kicked off. He imagined the robe falling away next. She'd been naked under that robe. That much had been obvious, to him at least. Miguel had seemed to fear she was rushing upstairs to arm herself, but Duncan knew she'd simply wanted to get dressed. Too bad. He'd rather liked her the way she was.

Duncan strolled farther into the house, grateful when Louis finally closed the door, shutting out the cold air. He'd have to invest in a few heavy winter coats if this went on much longer. When did spring come to these parts anyway? It had been too long since he'd lived anywhere with a real winter. He couldn't remember exactly how long they lasted this far south along the Eastern seaboard. Not that Washington, D.C. was considered part of the South anymore. It was south of the Mason-Dixon line, but there were too many Yankees living here today.

He smiled, remembering the long, hot summers of the true South. His youth had been spent toiling the fields beneath the burning Tennessee sun. There'd been no long, lazy school vacations for him. No school, for that matter.

A door opened upstairs, and Duncan backed up several feet until he could see Emma emerge onto the landing above him.

"Good evening, Emma," he said, trying to pretend he hadn't seen her wearing that fluffy purple monstrosity of a robe.

She narrowed those violet eyes at him, as if judging his sincerity, and apparently decided he passed muster. "Good evening, Duncan," she said finally. "What's up?"

"Are we going to have this entire conversation with you standing up there?"

She blew out a flustered breath. "No, of course not."

She descended the stairs quickly, wearing the same clunky boots, but with a pair of jeans, a hooded sweatshirt, and, regrettably, a bra, as well. Although, he contemplated, perhaps it was a pretty bra, something lacy and feminine. He liked pretty bras. He liked taking them off pretty women . . . like Emma.

"Can I get you something to drink?" Emma asked politely. She switched on a pair of floor lamps, one at either end of an old overstuffed couch. A battered coffee table sat in front of the couch, both pieces looking as if their better days were long behind them.

"No, thank you. We can't stay."

Emma stopped halfway to the kitchen. She turned to study him nervously, her hands twisting the ties of her sweatshirt. "Did you . . . find something?"

"Nothing specific about Lacey yet, although we are making headway in retracing Victor's activities. He hosted a lot of parties, many of them in homes he owned out of town. It seems likely Lacey attended one of those parties, given what she told you. Unfortunately, it's unlikely the other attendees will volunteer any useful information."

"You're talking about people from the Hill," she said somewhat bitterly.

Duncan nodded. "And probably some others. The usual Washington assortment. You said Lacey worked for a lobbying firm?"

"She still *does*."

"Of course," he said, accepting her correction. There was always a possibility, however slim, that Emma's friend Lacey was still alive. He understood her need to hold on to whatever hope there was.

"There must have been other women at the parties," Emma said. "They might be willing to talk to you. Or to me."

Duncan nodded. "Victor had several favorites among his women. He kept track of who was invited when, but there were no names. We have photos, which is how I know Lacey was among them, but these women were not in the public eye. Even with photographs, locating them is difficult. If you wish to help, you could go through the files for us and see if you recognize anyone."

"Absolutely," Emma said eagerly. "Did you bring them with you?"

"Ah. I'm afraid we're heading out of town this evening. I wasn't certain you'd be home. We're still checking out Victor's—"

"You're going to one of those party houses, you mean?"

"Perhaps, but—"

"Take me with you."

Duncan regarded Emma silently. He wasn't used to being interrupted at every turn. Not many would have dared, not even in his years as Raphael's lieutenant, and he was somewhat surprised to discover just how much it irritated him. Emma, however, seemed blissfully unaware of both her transgression and his irritation.

"Well?" she demanded impatiently.

Duncan wasn't looking at Miguel, but he could feel his lieutenant's anger at Emma's rudeness, and it was like a fire burning hotter by the moment. As Duncan's child *and* his lieutenant, Miguel was instinctively protective not only of Duncan's person, but of his dignity.

"If I might finish," Duncan said gently.

Emma's pupils flared, her emotions signaling outrage and embarrassment in equal measure to his empathic senses. She blew out a calming breath, visibly trying to relax, and gestured for him to continue. Duncan almost grinned, his earlier irritation banished by the obvious effort it took her to remain silent.

"I told you we would look into Lacey's disappearance," he began, "and—"

He stopped. Emma had opened her mouth to interrupt him once again. Her mouth snapped closed.

"And I promised," Duncan continued, his gaze daring her to say a word, "that I would get back to you in few days. This is me getting back to you. We are making progress, but we have found nothing concrete. If you give us a call tomorrow evening, we'll arrange a time for you to come by and look at the photographs."

Emma stared back at him silently, as if waiting to be sure he had nothing more to say, then said in a rush, "Can I go with you tonight?"

"No," he said firmly.

"But—"

Duncan used his vampire speed to step very close to Emma, very fast. To her, it would seem as if he hadn't moved, that he was suddenly just *there*. He was close enough that her breasts brushed against his chest when she inhaled, close enough that he could feel the heat off her skin and hear the pounding of her heart. And he saw the flash of arousal in her eyes.

"Emma," he said softly. He brushed the back of his fingers against the velvet softness of her cheek, wishing he didn't have to leave her here. But there would be other nights. He would make certain of it. "It will not be safe for you where we're going," he said. "You'll have to trust me on this."

He leaned closer, barely touching her mouth with his lips before stepping back with a pang of regret. "Miguel," he said and turned, heading for the door.

Louis twisted the doorknob and stepped into the opening, pausing long enough to check out the street and get the go ahead signal from their security people by the SUVs before starting down the steps.

Duncan walked through the doorway. Behind him, Emma called out, "Hey!"

He didn't respond, knowing first that nothing he said would satisfy her, and second that there was no way he was going to let her go with them. Even if he didn't have plans to stop at the blood house, he agreed with Miguel's assessment from last night. He had a bad feeling about this Leesburg house of Victor's, and he didn't want Emma anywhere near the place. He frowned, wondering at this sudden protective impulse he had for her.

Emma's footsteps hurried across the wood floor behind him as he descended the stairs outside. Louis was already holding the SUV's door open while his driver, a vampire named Ari, stood in the open driver's door and confirmed that they were now heading for Leesburg. Miguel was close at Duncan's back, blocking Emma from trying to follow.

"Go back inside, Ms. Duquet," Miguel said impatiently. And then suddenly Miguel was swearing softly, and Emma was crying out in pain.

Duncan spun back, his anger flaring abruptly. Miguel stood next to Emma, his hands in the air, indicating to Duncan that he hadn't touched her. But Emma was rubbing her arm and there were tears brightening her eyes.

"What happened?" Duncan demanded.

"My lord—" Miguel began, but true to form, Emma overrode him.

"Your guard dog here is built like a brick wall. I tried to follow you and ran into him."

Duncan's anger cooled instantly. "Miguel is my lieutenant, Emma, not a guard dog. He is also very serious about my security and trusts almost no one. You cannot go with us this evening. As a friend of mine would say, deal with it."

He nearly laughed at her expression—she was gaping at him in outrage, speechless for a change. He and Miguel were down the stairs and inside the SUVs before she'd recovered her wits, and the last thing he saw as they pulled away from the curb was Emma standing on her porch staring angrily in his direction.

* * * *

Emma glared at the departing SUVs—two big, black monstrosities that looked like tanks driving down the narrow street of her old neighborhood. All they needed was a big woofer in the back and they'd look like every other pimp in this town.

Assholes.

She pursed her lips thoughtfully, and suddenly remembered the feel of Duncan's mouth on hers, the press of his hard chest against . . .

She shrieked angrily. He'd done that on purpose! He was trying to distract her, to lull her into being a good little human. An *obedient* human.

"We'll just see about that, vampire."

She rushed into the house, snagged her keys and her cell phone from the table, grabbed her bag, then turned around and raced back outside, delaying only long enough to lock her front door. It was cold, but she pulled her hood up and tucked her hands into the front pocket of the sweatshirt. Her car was right in front of house, and once she got inside, she could crank the heat as high as she wanted.

But she was *not* going to let them get away with this. She'd heard what that vampire had said, the one driving the SUV with Duncan in it. He'd called over to his buddies and said something about Leesburg, something like, "We're heading to Leesburg now?" Or close enough.

Well, it was a free country. She could go to Leesburg, too. Even better, she could find out if Victor had a house there. Did Duncan think he was the only one with connections? Well, think again. She worked for a damn congressman. Hell, her *job* was handling problems for constituents too lazy to do it for themselves; people who thought a few thousand bucks bought some help from their congressman . . . or his staff. And, come to think of it, they were right. But the upshot was that Emma had connections. And finding out who owned a piece of property pretty much anywhere in the country was a piece of cake.

She snapped her Bluetooth over her ear and was already placing phone calls by the time she turned toward the Beltway.

Chapter Ten

The Leesburg blood house was crowded when Duncan and his team arrived. This was no elegant house in the suburbs, like the one where Brendan and Erik hosted their tasteful weekend get-togethers. This was a blood house through and through. Backing up to a thick stand of trees and sitting on a wide open expanse of what had probably been farmland once upon a time, the house was a two-story red brick with white trim and an attached garage. It was a good-sized place, but dwarfed by the huge lot, making it seem smaller than it was. Cars were parked haphazardly all around the front, and Duncan couldn't help wondering what the neighbors thought was going on here. Not that they were close. The lights of the nearest house were barely visible in the distance, but the traffic of so many people coming and going from here should have been noticeable. Or maybe the people who lived on those comfortable estates didn't bother with what happened outside.

His driver, Ari, grunted unhappily at the mishmash of cars parked in front of the house. Jerking the wheel to one side, he cut across the field and pulled around back instead. Miguel and Louis both bailed from the SUV when it stopped, but Duncan sat and waited while the second vehicle parked behind them and his security team piled out and took up positions. He spent that time probing the crowded house, separating humans from vampires, or perhaps the other way around. Vampires burned so much brighter to his empathic senses than the humans did. And there were two or three very bright vampires inside this house. Interesting.

Miguel opened the door next to Duncan. "My lord," he said.

"Thank you, Miguel," Duncan said and stepped out onto the half-frozen ground. He studied the back of the house. There were low lights in every window, and this close, he could feel the deep thumping base of the music playing inside. The garage was off to the left. To the right was a small porch with a closed door.

Miguel signaled as Duncan started for the porch. One of his vampires went ahead, making quick work of the lock. Not that it was a bad lock, but his staff were very good at such things. He tamped his power down, wanting to size the place up before announcing his presence.

The music hit him as soon as the door opened, much louder than he would have expected from hearing it outside. Someone had invested in some serious soundproofing, because modern houses weren't usually built that way. The extra sound dampening was a good sign, however, telling him the house was well run, that whoever was in charge was paying attention.

Duncan entered the house with only Miguel and Louis, leaving the others to secure the outside perimeter. If he needed them, they could be at his side in seconds, but he was more concerned about someone coming up behind him than taking him down from the inside.

The house was as crowded as he'd expected, given the parking situation out front. The back door opened onto a long, narrow kitchen and den area, with a breakfast bar in between. The kitchen was nearly empty, but the room beyond was packed wall-to-wall with vampires and humans, some dancing to the music, and some only pretending to dance while they engaged in other pursuits. What furniture there was had been pushed up against the walls to make more room for the dancers. And he could both hear and sense more people upstairs, mostly having sex from the sound of it, which was perfectly normal for a blood house this big. That's what humans came here for, after all. They offered blood from the vein in exchange for a sexual high like no other. A hundred years ago, vampires hunted and took what they needed. Today the humans lined up for the privilege of opening their veins.

A pair of vamps were deep in conversation as Duncan came through the door. They glanced up, and one of them automatically straightened into an aggressive posture, but he took one look at Duncan and dropped his eyes, backing away until his ass hit the kitchen counter. The other vamp only stared, eyes wide.

"Who runs this place," Miguel snarled.

"Otis," the wide-eyed vamp offered eagerly. "He's in there. I mean, through the next room and past the stairs. That's his place."

Miguel glanced over at Duncan, his expression somewhat troubled. Duncan was sure his lieutenant and he were sharing the same thought. Why had the vamp been so *happy* to give up Otis's name?

Only one way to find out. They started forward. The music was blaring as loudly as ever, as Duncan stepped into the room. He stood still for a moment, simply observing, and then he released his power. It rolled across the crowded room like a wave. One by one the dancers turned to stare, their eyes wide with recognition. They shrank back, pressing against the walls and taking their humans with them. Some fell to their knees, others whispered, "Master," as Duncan passed, following the suddenly wide open path through the crowded room.

He proceeded past the stairs, where a few more vampires froze in mid-step, staring at their new lord, and strolled into the high-ceilinged room beyond.

Otis, at least Duncan assumed this was Otis, was ensconced on a big, black leather sectional in a corner. The room was no doubt intended to be a formal living room, with its tall windows, elaborate chandelier and elegant stone hearth. Otis had made it his throne room. He sat in the light of a brightly burning fireplace. *Holding court.* There were no other words to describe it. His arms were stretched out to either side of the couch, while a human woman knelt between his wide spread legs performing oral sex. Thankfully, she was finishing her performance right about the time they walked into the room. She tucked Otis's cock gently back inside his jeans, then zipped him up with agonizing slowness, clearly terrified of making a mistake.

"That's good, pet," Otis said lazily, closing his knees and trapping the woman between them. "But don't go far. I might need you again."

The woman, who'd been poised to stand, closed her eyes in resignation and slumped back to the floor, resting her head on the sofa cushion between Otis's legs.

Another vampire approached Otis, this one wearing neatly pressed khakis and a button-down blue shirt, his dark hair cut short. He was holding a clipboard in one hand, a pencil in the other.

"Lance is here, Otis," he said, reading something on his clipboard. "It's been three weeks, and I think it's time—"

"On your knees when you talk to me, Nelson."

The dark-haired vamp stiffened, and Duncan could see every muscle tightening as he tried to resist the order, but eventually he surrendered. His knees hit the carpeted floor with a dull thud.

"That's a good boy," Otis drawled. "Now, what was it you wanted to ask me?"

"Lance," Nelson repeated sharply. "It's been three weeks—"

"Fuck that bastard. Tell him to go someplace else."

"There *isn't* anyplace else, Otis. You know that. He's been traveling over a hundred miles just to feed. That's not—"

"I don't care how far he's fucking traveling," Otis roared, sitting up and knocking the woman out of the way. "Let him hunt! I don't want that bastard in my house or even my line of sight." He smiled then, and ran a casual hand back through his long hair, as if aware his outburst had made him seem out of control. And Duncan knew that control would be everything to someone like Otis.

"Some vampires just aren't worth the effort, Nelson. You understand," he said with a sickening smirk. He started to lean back against the sofa, but caught sight of Duncan and his people. He sat up straight, his dark eyes skimming over each of them in turn, resting finally on Duncan.

"Well, looky who's here, Nelson," he sneered. "It's our new lord come calling."

Nelson, still on his knees, twisted around to stare at Duncan. His face registered first surprise, and then a fierce satisfaction. He grabbed the woman, dragging her with him, as if clearing a path between Otis and their new vampire lord.

"Feel free to help yourselves, boys," Otis said, waving a casual hand at the crowded house. "We've a full house tonight."

Miguel stiffened, a growl rumbling in his chest. Duncan rested a hand on his forearm.

"Well, hell, Nelson. Get these boys a room. It's okay, gents. We're an equal opportunity establishment, if you get my drift. Maybe a nice boy for dinner?" Otis laughed loudly, amused by his own pathetic wit.

"Miguel," Duncan said. "Get rid of the humans."

"Hey!" Otis shot to his feet. "This fucking house is mine! I give the orders, not you."

The woman broke away from Nelson to stagger over to the door, and Miguel shoved her out of the room as he muttered orders into his Bluetooth mike. Several more of Duncan's people slammed into the house and began scouring it from room to room, racing up the stairs to clear the second floor. Humans screamed and vamps roared, but the noise quickly abated as the local vamps realized what was happening and helped herd the humans out of the house. Within moments, the only hearts that could be heard beating were the vampires'.

"Nelson," Duncan said, drawing the startled attention of the preppy vampire with the clipboard. "Come here."

"What the fuck?" Otis demanded. "I don't care who you are! Nelson belongs to *me*."

Duncan ignored him, turning his attention instead to Nelson, who had scrambled over on his knees and was now gazing up at Duncan with unconcealed longing.

"Nelson? Is that your full name?"

"Nelson Conway, my lord. But everyone calls me Nelson."

"You know who I am?"

"Yes, my lord. You're our master, the new Lord of the Capital Territory."

"Do you run this establishment, Nelson?"

"No, he does *not!*" Otis roared, jumping over the glass coffee table to confront Duncan. "This is *my* house and he's *my* fucking child. I turned him to handle all this shit."

Duncan shifted his gaze to Otis, but didn't waste any words on him. With a silent exertion of his will, he drove the angry vampire to his knees and choked away his voice. Otis's face twisted with rage as he crashed to the floor at Duncan's feet.

"Nelson?" Duncan prompted, bringing the other vampire's attention back to him.

"Yes, my lord, I run the house. Otis makes policy. He decides who gets in how often, and who doesn't," he added with a dark look in his Sire's direction. "But I'm the one who manages everything."

"And did you volunteer for this job? Did you ask to be made Vampire?"

Nelson stared up at Duncan, as if trying to figure out the right answer to the question.

"The truth will do," Duncan prompted quietly.

The preppy vampire glanced away, as if ashamed or embarrassed, then lowered his eyes, speaking to the floor. "No, my lord. I was in Leesburg visiting some friends. That was more than two years ago, though it seems even longer. We all came to this blood house together, on a stupid dare. When Otis found out I had graduated from business school, he started hitting on me, even though I told him—"

The young vampire broke off, his face heating, and his embarrassment now obvious. Duncan could easily imagine how someone like Otis would have single-mindedly pursued the young human, seducing him into sex not because he wanted him, but because it suited his need at the time. If Nelson had been drunk, which seemed likely, it would have been easy for Otis to seduce him. And once he'd bitten the young man, the powerful euphoric substance in his bite would have wiped away whatever was left of Nelson's will. Until he woke the next night and remembered what he'd done.

"I'm sorry, Nelson," Duncan said. "If I could reverse it, I would."

Nelson looked up and shook his head. "That's all right, my lord. I still hate what he did to me that night, and I was shocked to discover what I'd become, but . . . it's not so bad now. And I don't mind running this house, it's just—" He shot a hate-filled glance at Otis, but didn't say anything else.

"Very well," Duncan said into the silence. "Miguel, if you would?"

Miguel produced a four inch switchblade as Duncan drew his leather jacket off and threw it onto the coffee table. He shoved up the sweater sleeve on his left arm.

"Nelson Conway, do you come to me of your own free will and desire?" he asked formally.

Nelson's eyes widened in surprise, then he turned sharply, staring in fear as Otis began thrashing like a fish on a hook. But the vampire was unable to speak or to rise from his knees.

"Don't worry about him," Duncan said dismissively. "Unless you'd rather remain his?"

Nelson's head swung back around to Duncan. "Hell, no," he growled. "Er, my lord."

Duncan nodded. "Then let us begin again. Nelson Conway, do you come to me of your own free will and desire?"

"I do, my lord," he said fervently.

"And is this what you truly desire?"

"Yes, my lord, it is my *truest* desire."

Duncan sliced open a clean line between the tendons, from the middle of his forearm down to his wrist. Blood swelled from the wound in round droplets, turning quickly to a slow, steady rush of red.

Nelson stared, his breath coming in pants, tongue poking out to lick his lips hungrily.

Duncan didn't taunt the young vampire by holding back. There was no need. Nelson had been his from the moment he'd walked into this house.

"Drink, Nelson," he said softly. "And be mine."

Duncan gazed down at Nelson's bent head and felt the tug deep in his chest as yet another soul became his to guard, his to care for. Nelson didn't gulp, but he didn't waste a drop either. There was a precision to his drinking, the way some people eat an ice cream cone by constantly licking all around, keeping the cone neat and tidy, while others end up with a big mess. Nelson was a tidy drinker. It was probably the same quality that made him a good house manager.

"Enough," Duncan said gently. Nelson lifted his head at once, settling back on his heels with a glazed look. Miguel produced a handkerchief for Duncan's arm, and Duncan figured he must have a goodly supply of them somewhere. Boxes of plain, white handkerchiefs for the too frequent times when his master slit his own wrist. He smiled at the idea, wiping the kerchief up his arm before wrapping it carefully and snugging his sweater sleeve down. Duncan's blood was powerful enough that the wound would begin to close in minutes, and would heal completely in a hour. There was a healing property in Nelson's saliva, as in every other vampire's. But it only worked on humans, not on another vampire.

"This house is yours, Nelson," Duncan said as he pulled his jacket back on. "It has only one purpose, and that is to feed my vampires. *All* of my vampires. If you see someone you don't know, you may request identification. If you have doubts, you will call Miguel or Louis." He nodded at his respective aides. "But no one is to be turned away unless they break the rules. And there are only two rules. No drugs. No violence. And we observe human laws within the limits of our needs. Do you understand?"

"Yes, my lord," Nelson said, still breathless from the effects of drinking Duncan's potent blood. His eyes opened wide suddenly, and he leaned forward to whisper, "What about *him?*" His gaze shifted slightly toward Otis.

Duncan turned to regard the former house manager. "Otis, I'm afraid your services are no longer required," he said, baring his teeth in a predator's grin. "Some vampires just aren't worth the effort. You understand."

Otis's eyes bulged even further, if such a thing were possible, his throat working as he fought to scream. Duncan's power reached out and simply stopped his heart from beating.

Nelson scooted aside, brushing his khaki pants fastidiously as Otis crumbled into a pile of greasy dust. "Uh, shall I—" he fumbled to say. "I mean is it okay—"

"By all means, Nelson," Duncan said cheerfully. "Feel free to vacuum, and remember, if you need anything, call. But, know this. I keep track of my people, and I know what's going on in my territory."

"Yes, my lord. I won't disappoint you."

"I know. One last question, did Victor come here often?"

Nelson gave him a blank look. "Victor, my lord? He was *never* here, that I know of, and I've been at this house almost every night for two years."

Duncan nodded. "As I suspected. Thank you, Nelson. Miguel, we're leaving."

With the humans gone, it took far less time to get out of the house than it had to get in. Someone snapped the music off as Duncan made his way through the den, and the silence was deafening. The house was still crowded, but with kneeling vampires who inched aside, clearing a path with bowed heads, murmuring their allegiance as Duncan walked past.

At some point in the future, he'd come back here, more than once if he lasted that long—and he had every intention of lasting a very long time. He wanted to know the vampires in his territory. Wanted to know the lives he held in his hands. But tonight he had other, more pressing business.

Duncan stepped out of the overheated house and lifted his face, welcoming the brush of cold air over his skin as he drew a deep breath. His security people waited, standing all around him with infinite patience.

"How far to Victor's house, Louis?" he asked.

"Half an hour, my lord. No more."

"Then, that's where we're going next."

* * * *

The SUVs raced down the dark roads, the people of Leesburg safely tucked away behind the walls of their houses, not knowing that vampires were speeding by in the dead of night. The convoy turned off the main road and passed through a well-lit neighborhood of neat, modern homes before leaving the lights behind once again. Victor's house— now Duncan's—was a few miles beyond, down a two-lane road with wide, grassy fields to either side. A spacious home was perched in the middle of each of those fields, well away from the road and up on a low hillside, as if to better gaze down upon their less fortunate neighbors.

The address Duncan and his people sought was down a sharp turn to the right, and then a long driveway ending in a square of neatly trimmed spruce trees, growing tightly together to create a barrier against casual observation. The driveway split through the trees to reveal a sprawling white clapboard house, with an old-fashioned covered porch along the entire front face. A single chimney and multiple peaked roofs made it look like a farmhouse on steroids.

Duncan had no sooner taken in the sight of the house, than Louis was jumping from the still-moving vehicle, snapping commands into his headset. The trailing SUV raced past, leaving muddy tracks on the perfectly maintained green lawn as it swerved around and back onto the driveway, tires squealing as it skidded to a stop in front of Duncan's SUV.

"Miguel, what—" Duncan started, then saw the car parked to one side of the huge house. *Damn her.* "No one touches her, Miguel," he said tightly. "Let me out of here."

"My lord—"

"Out, Miguel. Now."

He heard her voice before he saw her. Standing on the front porch, waiting for them like she owned the place, was Emma, the thorn in his side. Despite himself, he grinned, thinking it might well be worth a few scratches for a taste of Emma Duquet.

His people ushered her off the porch and away from the house, surrounding her with a wall of impenetrable vampire bulk. Obedient to his orders, no one touched her, but they didn't give her a choice, either. She either moved, or she would be crushed.

Duncan gestured, telling his vamps to fade back, and then he waited, knowing she'd never be able to remain silent.

"What?" she demanded, meeting his calm stare.

"Why are you here, Emma?"

"Probably the same reason you are," she snapped.

"How did you know where we were going?"

"Hey, I work in this town. I have sources, too." Her lips were pinched defiantly as she glared up at him, her violet eyes silvering in the new moon's light. She shuddered suddenly, and he realized she wasn't wearing anything but the hooded sweatshirt she'd put on back home.

"You're cold," he murmured and shrugged off his leather jacket, wrapping it around her shoulders before tucking her against his body and rubbing his hands up and down her back. She shivered again, almost violently, burying her face against his chest.

"Emma," he said quietly against her ear. "What if someone had been waiting for you here?"

She spoke without raising her head, clutching his jacket closer. "The house is empty. I already checked it out through the windows."

"You couldn't have known it would be empty," he said, exasperated. "And you still don't. Just because you didn't see anyone—"

"But you said," she shuddered once, hard, then grew still, as if her body had expressed its displeasure with the cold temperature one final time before admitting it was now warm. "You said Victor was gone."

"He is, but there were others involved, and we know nothing about them yet. It's not safe for you to be here, certainly not alone."

"But *you're* here now." She looked up, giving him big eyes, as if that could fool him into believing her innocent. "You'll keep me safe, won't you?"

"You'd have been safe if you'd stayed home, as I asked."

"Well, I'm here now." Her voice sharpened, and he almost smiled.

He'd known she couldn't keep up the wide-eyed façade for long.

Duncan ran his hands up and down her arms, as if still trying to warm her, using it as an excuse to delay—and to think. He didn't want Emma anywhere near whatever Victor may have done in this house. The knowledge alone could be dangerous. But he understood all too well her need to know the truth about Lacey's disappearance, her need to do *something*.

"You know, Emma," he whispered, feeling her grow still as she listened to him. "I could take away your memories of this entire evening and send you home none the wiser."

She drew back from him with a jerk, searching his face. "I'd never forgive you if you did that."

"You'd never know. There'd be nothing to forgive."

"I'd know," she said firmly.

Duncan did smile then. She was stubborn as a mule, this one.

"I'll be perfectly quiet. I promise," she wheedled, clearly sensing his weakening resolve.

Duncan sighed. "Very well. But you will remain right by my side. And you will do whatever I say when I say it, no arguments."

"As long as it's nothing ridiculous," she muttered.

"Ridiculous?"

"You know what I mean. If you tell me to bark like a dog or something, I'm not doing it."

Duncan laughed and hugged her tightly before letting her go. "Very well. No barking."

"Do you want this back," she said, making a halfhearted move toward pulling the jacket off.

Duncan stopped her with a hand on her arm. "Keep it. You should have worn something warmer."

"I didn't have time. I wanted to get here before you guys, so I grabbed my keys and ran."

"Maybe you should keep a jacket in your car. You know, for your next close pursuit."

She gave him a quizzical glance, as if trying to figure out if that was a joke or not.

Duncan let her wonder. He took her hand and headed for the front door. "Remember your promise, Emma. What I say, when I say it."

"Yeah, yeah. Your wish is my command and all that."

"If only it were that simple."

Miguel sent two of the security detail around to check the house from the outside. The others accompanied Duncan, most of them going in ahead of him.

Duncan scanned the front of the house as he approached, searching the many windows, although he wasn't certain what he was looking for. That bad feeling Miguel had talked about was getting worse by the moment, and he already regretted letting Emma stay. He should have wiped her mind and sent her home. Forget what she'd said about remembering. He was very good at what he did, and she wouldn't have remembered a thing. The problem was it felt wrong to do that to Emma. That didn't make any sense to him, but something in his mind— or his heart—told him to be honest with her, or he'd regret it later.

Miguel held back a few moments, letting the security team go ahead. Lights soon came on inside, dimmed severely. It was the kind of lighting a vampire would prefer, and the hell with whatever human guests might be joining him. Typical Victor. But Duncan was glad for it, because he could already detect the unmistakable scent of old blood. A lot of it. And if that much blood had been spilt in this house, he didn't want the glare of bright lights distracting him from whatever his other senses might have to tell him.

He walked through the doorway with Emma, who squeezed his hand tightly despite her earlier brave words. He took three slow steps and stopped, nearly crushed as his empathic senses were inundated by the pain and fear saturating every wall, every floorboard, every damn inch of this house.

"Emma," he said in a strained voice. "Go back to your car."

Her head whipped around. "Duncan?"

"Now, Emma, please. Miguel, have someone stay with her." His lieutenant moved to take Emma's arm, and Duncan added, "Gently, Miguel."

"Duncan?" Emma repeated, her voice trembling with uncertainty. She might not have his exquisite sensibilities, but she wouldn't need them to know something was wrong.

"I'll be out soon. Don't worry."

He heard more than saw Emma leave the house, heard Miguel order one of the vamps to stay with her at the car. And then his lieutenant was back.

"Do you feel it, Miguel?" Duncan whispered, and sent a fraction of what he was sensing down the link he shared with his vampire child.

Miguel sucked in a breath. "Sick fuck," he hissed.

"Not sick," Duncan corrected softly. "Evil." His gaze traveled up the wide staircase. It would be worse up there. So much worse. "Upstairs," he said.

Miguel sent one of his vampire guards up ahead of him, but Duncan knew they'd find nothing. There was nothing to see any longer, only to feel. He tightened his shields down hard, needing to know what had happened, but unwilling to let the full measure of Victor's corruption swamp his senses. What he was feeling was horrific enough. He didn't need to drown in it.

He climbed the stairs slowly, reluctantly, for all that he was determined to do it. At the top of the stairs, he turned unerringly to the right, the waves of pain and terror like the fingers of a ghost, tugging at his clothing, drawing him closer.

They passed the first room, and the second. Duncan paused, looking ahead. Every one of the rooms up here reeked of lust, of a hunger that would never be satisfied. But the worst of it, the true depths of depravity that had been perpetrated here . . . that had happened in the room at the end of the hall. The door was closed. Duncan wished it could stay that way.

His fangs emerged, sliding over his lower lip unbidden, as he stared at that closed door—as he stalked down the hall to that nightmare chamber. Next to him, Miguel gave him a startled glance, his own fangs appearing in response to Duncan's obvious anger. Duncan almost staggered when it finally hit him, a red haze filling his vision. He opened the door and halted there, unwilling to cross the threshold. He heard the voices of men laughing, swearing, grunting in release. And he heard the terrified cries of women begging for mercy, screaming in agony.

He swallowed a furious howl, biting down so hard that his fangs sliced his lip. Blood dripped down to his chin, warm and thick. He licked it up without thinking, lost in the memory of what had been done here, of how far they'd gone to satisfy their perverted need to inflict pain on the helpless.

Duncan spun on his heel, unable to bear another moment within that agony-soaked room. It ran in invisible rivulets down the walls, rotting the boards, the carpets; everything it touched was fouled by what had happened there.

He strode back toward the staircase. He needed to get outside before the leftover emotions destroyed what was left of his shields. He shuddered at the thought of facing the searing pain of that house without even a shred of protection.

Miguel hurried next to him, his worried gaze searching every room they passed, not knowing what he was looking for, but feeling the tiniest part of what Duncan was drowning in. Duncan started down the stairs, forcing himself to take them one at a time, when all he wanted was to jump the banister and race outside.

"My lord, what did you find? What should I tell the others to look for?"

They reached the first floor. The nightmare lifted enough that Duncan felt as if he could breathe again. "Tell them to search—" He paused, detecting a fresh sense of alarm from . . . was it Ari? "Is Ari outside?" he asked Miguel quickly.

"Yes, my lord. The backyard."

"Let's go."

Miguel pointed through an arched doorway on their left. They raced through a huge dining room to a wide open kitchen with two sets of French doors that opened onto a covered patio. Miguel snapped the handles down hard, not bothering with locks, and Duncan strode outside, quickly finding Ari where he stood head down, staring at the ground, tension radiating from every muscle. Duncan frowned. There was nothing here, except—

It hit him then, a whiff of decay on the night breeze, growing stronger the closer he got to Ari. When Duncan finally reached his side, the dark-haired vampire looked up, his coffee brown eyes gleaming with wild power that yearned for an enemy to strike down. But there was no enemy here. There was only the dead their enemy had left behind.

Duncan reached out to his vampire—and Ari was his, not a child of his own, but sworn to him in blood—and calmed Ari's rage with the touch of his power.

Together they studied the minuscule disturbances that spoke loudly to those who knew what to look for, even without the smell of death to guide them. To the untrained eye, there was nothing to see but dirt and a little bit of grass that was dry and brown from the winter. No one had bothered to lay down green turf, as they obviously had in the front yard before Victor's last party. Had that been the one Lacey attended? If Duncan had still believed in a merciful God, he would have offered a prayer that it not be so. He didn't want Emma to lose her friend that way, didn't want her search to end here in this house of horrors. But the world had proven to him long ago that faith had no place in this world.

He sighed. "I have to talk to Emma first. Then I'll make the call."

Chapter Eleven

Emma was sitting in her car, the engine running to keep the heater blowing, because despite Duncan's jacket, she was freezing. It was more than the winter temperature making her cold. She was scared. More scared than she could ever remember being. More than when she'd been forced to kiss her dead grandmother as she lay in the casket. Even more than when her mother had died and left her all alone. She'd been too young then to appreciate all the things that could go wrong, and young enough to believe she'd be fine on her own.

But not anymore. She knew exactly how the world delighted in fucking with her by taking away everything. Everything but Lacey. If she lost Lacey, too . . . She convulsed in a fresh round of shivering, and turned the heater up another notch.

Something awful had happened in that house. Duncan was a master at keeping anything from showing on his face, but his very stillness told her it was bad. If he was working that hard at keeping it inside, it had to be very, *very* bad.

And she was terrified.

The vampire standing guard on her stiffened abruptly, his gaze riveted over the top of her car, around the right side of the house. Emma stared through the windshield. Was something coming? Was it whatever awful thing lived in that house?

She caught a flash of movement, and saw one of Duncan's vampires racing around the house and into the backyard. Curiosity won out over fear, and she opened the car door enough to put one foot on the ground.

"What is it?" she asked her guard. "Have they found something?"

The guard didn't respond right away, his attention wholly focused on whatever was happening beyond the house. Emma was about to ask him again when he turned and urged her back into the car. "You should stay inside," he said tightly. "It's warmer."

"Why? What did they find?" she asked, searching his face, knowing somehow that she was right. They'd found something. Not in the house, but behind it. She'd been back there before Duncan arrived, and there was nothing there except a strip of covered patio. Beyond that was a wide patch of dead lawn and then open field. What had they seen that she hadn't? What could there be—

Emma's breath caught as pain squeezed her chest. She must have made a noise of some sort, because the guard reached out to her, the look of sorrow on his face confirming her worst fears.

"No," she whispered. "No!" she screamed and shoved the door wide open, knocking it into the guard and throwing him off balance. She raced for the backyard, knowing she'd never make it, that the guard's vampire speed would catch her and stop her, but she ran anyway. She had to see, had to know . . .

The guard grabbed her before she'd gotten two steps down the side of the big house, scooping her up and wrapping her tightly in iron hard arms. "You don't wanna do that," he whispered against her ear. "Trust me, Emma. You don't wanna see."

"Let go of her, Baldwin." Duncan's voice was hard as he walked toward them.

Her guard, Baldwin, released her immediately. "Forgive me, my lord," he said.

Emma didn't know what he was apologizing for—letting her get away or holding her too tightly, but whatever it was, she didn't care. "Tell me what you found," she told Duncan. "And don't lie to me."

Duncan closed the distance between them, his hands coming out to take hers and pull her into a rough embrace. "Emma," he started, but she pushed away from him.

"No. Don't do that. Don't coddle me like some fragile flower who can't handle life. I've been taking care of myself since I was eleven years old, so don't you do that. Tell me what you found," she insisted.

Duncan sighed. "A body. We're—" Emma made a pained noise in spite of herself, her fist coming up to her mouth as if to trap the sound inside. Duncan paused. "Emma, Baldwin's right. You don't—"

"Don't tell me what I want! Is it a woman?"

He studied her a moment, then turned his head slightly, as if listening to what was happening in the yard. When he turned back and met her gaze, she knew. "Yes," he said unnecessarily.

"I want to see. If it's—"

"No. That's not necessary. We have a picture of Lacey, and they've buried her things with her. We can identify—"

"I want to see," Emma repeated in an uncompromising voice that she barely recognized as being her own. "It's my right, Duncan. She's my—" Emotion stole her voice, and she drew a breath, turning away for a moment. "Lacey's *my* friend," she continued, ignoring the hot tears rolling down her cheeks. "Mine."

Duncan clearly didn't want to give in, but he just as clearly believed that what Emma was saying was true. It was her right to be the one, her right to lay claim to Lacey, and no one else's.

"Very well," he said unhappily. "You may view the body. But, Emma, decomposition has already begun. You may no longer recognize Lacey even if it's her."

"I'll recognize her," Emma insisted stubbornly.

Duncan frowned and shook his head slightly, as if already regretting his decision. "You will tell me if you think it's Lacey or not," he said finally. "And then you will leave. Baldwin will drive you home."

"But if it's Lacey—"

"Take it or leave it," he said, his voice every bit as uncompromising as hers had been.

Emma nodded once. Duncan reached for her hand, but she pulled away, choosing to proceed under her own power.

She moved in a blur, her eyes so filled with tears she could barely see. Her mind kept whispering denials, kept telling her it didn't have to be Lacey, that there'd been other women at the parties, that this house and Victor had been around for years, and that the land around here was riddled with old burial grounds. But in her heart she knew what she'd known ever since Lacey hadn't come home Sunday night. She'd known that something awful had happened, because nothing else would have kept Lacey from calling her. And now . . .

"Emma?" Duncan's voice next to her was gentle, full of compassion. But she didn't want his compassion, couldn't afford it. She had to stay strong. She looked around and realized Duncan's vampires were all looking at her expectantly. They were standing in a circle around something, and now had opened the circle as if to admit her. She looked down and her heart began to pound.

"Emma, you don't have to do this."

She brushed away Duncan's hand and stepped between two of the vampires, nearly tripping on a pile of dirt. One of the vamps caught her arm, and she looked down into a big hole in the ground. No, not so big. Just big enough for . .

A cry of denial was torn from her throat, a wordless, animal sound of grief. Emma stumbled as she backed away, suddenly wishing she hadn't insisted on being here. She didn't want to see what was in that hole, didn't want to see that dead thing wearing a grotesque caricature of Lacey's face, her blond curls limp and tangled, her limbs twisted in death as they'd never been in life. She wanted to rewind her life and keep Lacey home from Victor's party. They'd eat popcorn and drink bad wine and watch cheesy horror flicks until neither one of them could sleep. And they'd never have to worry about anything worse than movie monsters under the bed.

"Emma." She hadn't even seen Duncan move, but suddenly he was there, wrapping her in his arms. And she knew the monsters were real this time.

She shoved away from him. "Don't touch me," she hissed. "If not for you—" She knew she was being unfair, that it wasn't Duncan who'd put Lacey in that grave. But it was his people. Vampires. Monsters who preyed on humans, who seduced Lacey with their promises of wild parties and high living. She stumbled down the side of the house, bracing herself against the wall, determined to get back to her car. She had her cell phone there. She'd call the police and—

Duncan's strong arms scooped her up. She fought against him, but he only tightened his hold and ordered, "Stop it, Emma."

"Put me down," she demanded, pounding on his shoulders, hearing herself sob with grief and not recognizing it as coming from her own throat. "I don't need—"

Duncan's arms were like steel bands as he carried her to the front of the house, anger radiating off of him in waves, though somehow she knew the anger wasn't directed at her. Emma saw her car, saw Baldwin rushing ahead to open the door. Duncan lowered his head to her ear and whispered something.

And then there was nothing at all.

Chapter Twelve

Duncan watched Emma's car until it rolled beyond the line of spruce trees and he couldn't see it anymore. She was in the backseat, sleeping deeply, and she'd stay that way for several hours, until Lacey's body had been recovered and the scene processed. He and his team had a few hours left, but they would have to return to D.C. before morning. There was no way he'd ask any of his people to spend a single day sleeping in this nightmare of a house. When they were finished here, when the forensic people had recovered every last bit of evidence they could find, he'd have the whole damned building razed to the ground. After that, the land could sit fallow. Maybe in a century or three, the horror would fade.

He'd already called the experts in to deal with this. If there could be any good fortune in this tragedy, it was that it had happened in Virginia, with the FBI's Quantico facilities so close by. Several vampires worked in the labs there, although their identities were known to only a select few in the vampire community. Raphael, of course, knew who they were, which meant Duncan did, too. The death he and his vampires had discovered here tonight couldn't be covered up completely, but it could be managed. How well depended on Emma. If she went to the human authorities and demanded an investigation . . . Well, he wouldn't let it come to that. He didn't want to replace her memories, but he would if necessary, knowing that if she ever found out, he would lose her trust, and might very well lose *her*. But he could not jeopardize the whole of vampire society for the sake of his affection for Emma Duquet.

That didn't mean he discounted the crime committed. He might cover up the specifics, but he wouldn't forget the offense. Victor was already dead, along with his four vampire guards, all of whom had no doubt participated in the violence and blood fest. But there were others still out there, humans who had willfully, joyfully, joined in the torture of young women for sexual gratification. He would hunt them down and destroy them every bit as permanently as he'd destroyed Victor.

"Sire."

Duncan turned. "Yes, Miguel?"

"In the house, my lord. In what we believe is Victor's safe room. There are videos."

Duncan met his lieutenant's carefully shuttered gaze, and knew the night was about to get worse. He sighed wearily and placed a comforting hand on Miguel's shoulder.

"At least now we'll know who to kill next, Miguel."

"We'll hunt, my lord?"

Duncan nodded. "We'll run them to the ground and listen to them beg as we shred their beating hearts."

Miguel bared his teeth, growling his approval, and Duncan braced himself to enter that house of evil one more time. As he crossed the threshold and the horror pierced his soul, he had only one thought—despite the agony of his last breath, Victor had been granted far too gentle a death.

An hour later, he sat on the front porch, taking in some much needed fresh air, when an unfamiliar truck rolled up to the house. He stood, eyeing it warily. As if by magic, several of his vampires appeared, taking up positions between him and the approaching vehicle. It rolled to a stop and Duncan watched as a small, dark-haired vampire dropped first to the running board and then to the ground. Her mane of bushy black hair had been pulled away from her face and forced into a severe bun at the back of her head, and she wore a plain, dark pantsuit and black cotton blouse. Together they made her appear older than she was, or rather, older than she'd been when she'd been turned over a century ago.

"Phoebe," Duncan called out, sending a mental command to his guards that this was the forensic expert he'd been expecting.

Phoebe Micheletti had never been an FBI agent herself, but she'd trained with one of their finest investigators, a human male who'd later become her husband and mate. After years of sharing the mate bond, and blood, with Phoebe, Ted Micheletti had been forced to retire early from the FBI when it became too obvious that he wasn't aging. The two of them now ran a consulting business of their own, offering their investigative services to law enforcement agencies around the country, many of whom couldn't afford to keep a full-time investigator on staff. Duncan was sure business was booming in these difficult economic times, and he knew that sometimes Phoebe and her mate worked for free. They simply enjoyed their work.

"Duncan." She started to kneel, but Duncan stopped her. Phoebe lived in Virginia, which meant Duncan was officially her master now. But, though they'd never met in person before, they'd known each other for years, and he was too weary tonight for meaningless ritual.

"It's good to see you," he said.

"And you, my lord. Congratulations on your ascension."

Duncan nodded, and Phoebe looked beyond him to the open back of a cargo van where two vampire forensic techs were loading a black body bag. There'd been no need to leave Lacey's body in situ, no need to preserve the grave site. They already knew who'd killed her.

"Do we know who she is?" Phoebe asked.

"Lacey Cray," Duncan said somberly. "Twenty-seven years old, and a secretary on K Street."

"How did she end up here?"

"Victor."

"Fuck," Phoebe swore viciously. "I hated that bastard."

"Surely, he didn't mistreat you or Ted?"

She shook her head swiftly. "He wouldn't have dared. Victor was a typical bully. He only picked on people who couldn't fight back. So how do you know the girl?"

"Her roommate came to the house in D.C. the night after I disposed of Victor. Ms. Cray was missing. She'd apparently partied with Victor before, but she told Emma this was a big one. A weekend in the country."

"Emma?"

"Emma Duquet, the roommate. *She* works for a congressman."

"Well, that's a complication. Does it get any worse?"

"Brace yourself," Duncan warned her. "Victor was quite the voyeur. We've found video records of what went on here and in D.C. I don't know if he was blackmailing anyone, or if he just liked to watch. We're still working on identifying everyone, but Lacey's is the only body we've found—and the only woman from his files who *isn't* in any of the videos, which is telling in and of itself. I'm assuming at this point that the other women are still alive. If so, their memories have probably been wiped, which is a blessing, because the things that were done to them—" His mouth twisted and he looked away, unwilling to go on.

"What about Lacey?"

"It was probably an accident. Given the level of depravity we've found here, nothing would surprise me, but burying her in the yard like this . . . it has an unplanned feel to it."

Phoebe nodded. "He had time to take care of the videos, but not enough to do a better job of losing the body."

Duncan shrugged. "He probably meant to come back and take care of it, but then I showed up."

"Any files in the D.C. house?"

Duncan nodded. "Hidden and encrypted, but my people are good."

Phoebe tilted her head, studying him. She gave him a crooked smile. "I'm glad you're here, my lord. We needed you." The smile fled as she turned her attention to Lacey's still form. "I only wish you'd had a better greeting than this."

"*I* wish I'd arrived a week earlier. Lacey might still be alive. We need to keep this quiet, Phoebe."

"Does she have family?"

"Just Emma. They've been friends since childhood."

"Is this Emma going to raise a fuss?"

"No." When Phoebe's curious gaze met his, he added, "I'll take care of it." He let a touch of power chill his voice to remind her who he was.

Phoebe lowered her eyes briefly. "How can I help?"

Duncan nodded. "My security chief, Louis, is upstairs, along with a couple of others. We'll take the computers and files back to D.C. with us, but in the meantime, he's made a composite file of every face visible in the videos. Some of them we think we know, but I want you to help track down the others."

She stiffened, then bowed formally from the waist. "I am yours to command, my lord." She spun around and headed into the house. Duncan watched her go, then walked over to the forensic tech who was closing the doors of the cargo van.

"You've a place to store the body?" Duncan asked.

"Yes, my lord. One of ours owns a funeral home right outside Falls Church. We can leave her there for now."

"Make sure Miguel has the information on the funeral home before you leave, but you should go soon." Sunrise was only a couple hours away, and they'd need that time to get Lacey's body properly stored before going home to sleep through the day.

"Yes, my lord." The vampire pulled a sheet of paper from the bottom of his clipboard, wrote briefly and handed the sheet to Miguel, who'd followed Duncan like a shadow ever since they'd found the body.

"We should leave, too, my lord," Miguel said quietly as the vampire tech climbed into the van and drove away.

Duncan looked over from his contemplation of the departing van. "I need to stop at Emma's on the way home."

"My lord, the time—"

"Miguel," Duncan said softly. "I will stop and speak with Emma."

Miguel nodded sharply. "We'll leave at once then. Ari can drive. I'll have the others finish up here and lock the house. They can take the second truck back to D.C."

Duncan nodded. He didn't look forward to telling Emma what had to be done, but he couldn't let her go to the human authorities. Somehow he'd have to persuade her to let him handle it, and if he couldn't . . . Well, then he wanted one last time with her before she hated him forever.

Chapter Thirteen

Emma's car was parked a few doors down from her house when they arrived. Duncan sent a thread of power into the house, searching. Baldwin was there, and aware. Baldwin was one of those who'd been with Duncan the other night, which meant he'd already been invited into Emma's house. That was important since Emma had been deeply asleep and would remain that way until Duncan woke her. He sighed, hoping she was having sweet dreams, because when she woke the nightmare would become real.

He would have preferred to put this off until tomorrow night. The horrors of Victor's playhouse had left him riding the very edge of violence, and he wanted nothing more at this point than to pound someone to a bloody pulp. Not that he would ever harm Emma. But his temper was definitely frayed, and she was bound to argue with him.

Duncan knew his reputation, what some considered his uncanny ability to remain calm in the face of even the worst provocation. It was why Raphael had decided he'd be perfect for dealing with the human charlatans who masqueraded as leaders in Washington, D.C. And there was truth to Duncan's reputation, too. But it was a hard-won truth, and tonight his reserve had been severely tested.

Unfortunately, he couldn't keep Emma asleep until he woke tomorrow night, and he definitely did *not* want her waking up during the day without talking to him first. Knowing Emma, even as little as he did, he knew she wouldn't hang around waiting for sunset. Even if she didn't call the police, she'd drive herself back to Leesburg, where she would find nothing at all. The body was gone, as was all evidence that anyone had been buried there. Everything in the house that could lead back to Victor or vampires in general was likewise gone. It was already on its way to the residence in D.C., where Duncan's people would scour it for information and then destroy it. At this moment, even the title to the Leesburg house was being altered, with documents put in place that made it appear the house had changed ownership some months ago. Not even Emma's inside sources would be able to find anything to indicate otherwise.

But that wouldn't stop Emma. Her next step was likely to be the human police, and that was the worst possible outcome for everyone involved, including Emma herself.

So, Duncan had to talk to her tonight.

He drew a deep breath, burying his rage and papering over his more aggressive instincts. It didn't have to last long, no more than an hour or so. Long enough to settle Emma, then return to the D.C. house to sleep. And when he woke tomorrow night, he'd carve out some time in the gym to work off the worst of his anger.

The house door cracked open silently as he and Miguel started up the walk. There were no lights on inside. Baldwin's silhouette was a short, square block of darker shadow as he stood there, holding the door open.

"Anything I need to know?" Duncan asked him.

"No, my lord."

"Join Ari in the truck, then. You, too, Miguel."

Miguel stiffened immediately, his mouth open to protest, but Duncan just looked at him. His lieutenant scowled, but he gave a sharp nod and followed Baldwin back to the truck.

Duncan sighed in relief. It would be hard enough to maintain his composure with Emma tonight. He didn't need the additional aggravation of his vampires' emotions beating at his shields. They didn't have his sensitivity to the nightmare of that house, but they had picked up enough of it that their instinct was to close the circle around him. Which left *him* at the very center of their storm of outrage.

He needed this small space of time alone, without his vampires hovering, to restore his own calm center before talking to Emma. He crossed into the living room, circling the ancient couch. Emma lay on her side, beneath a crocheted blanket that Baldwin must have thrown over her. She was curled into a protective ball, knees drawn to her chest, arms held tightly in front, hands fisted as if against the blow that was coming.

He sat down next to her, and the couch sagged beneath his weight. She couldn't be comfortable sleeping here. Maybe he should take her upstairs first. He smiled slightly, recognizing the thought for what it was—a way to delay the inevitable.

Her dark hair had fallen forward, covering half her face. He brushed it away and whispered, "Emma."

Her eyelashes fluttered, dark against her fair skin, and her breathing became less regular. Duncan ran the backs of his fingers down her silky cheek. "Wake up, Emmaline."

* * * *

Emma felt Duncan's presence before she heard his voice. She thought it must be a dream, but it felt real. It felt like Duncan always did, a blanket of calm that was the opposite of how most people seemed to put everyone on edge, at least at first.

Whatever it was, she knew she had to wake up because there was something she needed to remember. Something about why Duncan was here.

"Emma." His voice penetrated her sleep, urging her to wake. But suddenly she didn't want to wake up anymore. It was nice in her dream. Safe. And there was something awful waiting for her when she woke up.

His hand stroked her cheek. "Wake up, Emmaline."

The last vestiges of sleep fled before the unexpected use of her real name, and she moaned softly. She tried to roll over, to turn away from him, but Duncan wouldn't let her. His strong hand on her shoulder held her in place, gentle but unyielding.

"I know you're awake, Emma."

Emma's eyes flashed open. She stared at Duncan, barely able to see him in the dim light.

"Would you like me to turn on a light?" he asked. He always seemed to know what she was thinking. He said it was skill at reading faces, but she wondered if it was something more.

"No," she said, her voice rough with sleep. She knew why he was here. It was about Lacey. And she wanted the darkness. She sat up. She was still wearing Duncan's jacket, and she pulled it around herself as she pushed her grandmama's afghan down to the foot of the couch. She didn't remember coming home, didn't remember falling asleep.

"Would you like some water?" Duncan asked. He was sitting on the side of the couch, and she swiveled around him to sit up, dropping her feet to the floor.

She leaned forward, hugging herself, and shook her head. "No, thank you."

She heard him sigh as he moved from the couch to sit on the sturdy old coffee table she and Lacey had rescued from the curb when they first moved to this house. Someone two blocks over had put it out for the trash, but Lacey had seen it on her way home and dragged Emma back with her to pick it up. The damn thing was so heavy that they'd struggled to force it even halfway into Emma's trunk, and then they'd barely gotten it up the stairs into the house. The two of them had been grunting like rooting pigs, stopping every five minutes to rest. She smiled at the memory, and was horrified to feel tears burning the backs of her eyes.

Emma bit her lip as she fought for control. She wasn't going to cry. Tears wouldn't bring Lacey back. Nothing would. Emma's job now was to see Lacey properly buried. Then she'd find whoever had done this . . . and kill him. She had a gun and she knew how to use it. You didn't grow up where she had and not learn how to shoot. She even had a membership at a shooting range in Virginia. No sense having a gun if you couldn't hit anything with it. She didn't get out to the range as often as she would have liked, but her aim was good enough. And up close and personal, it wouldn't matter.

Either way, Emma wasn't going to wait for the police. Police were too easily bought off in this town. Besides, if they'd taken her more seriously when she reported Lacey missing, maybe her best friend wouldn't be dead right now. Who knew how long she'd been buried in that—

But, she wasn't going to think about that. She was going to hold it

together long enough to convince Duncan she was okay, and then the
killer had better start looking over his shoulder, because she was going
to make someone pay.

"Emma?" Duncan said softly.

Emma raised her eyes to his. He looked worried, but there was no
need. She was fine. Finer than fine. She was cold purpose.

"Duncan," she said, proud of how even her voice was, how calm.
Duncan appreciated calm. "You don't need to worry about me. I'm
fine."

Duncan's watchful gaze seemed to freeze, and for a moment Emma
thought she saw a deep bronze glow replace the warm brown of his
eyes. In that moment, she was convinced he knew what she was doing,
what she *planned* to do tomorrow and the next day. But then he blinked,
and she persuaded herself it was impossible. A figment of her always
vivid imagination.

"I'm sorry, Emma."

"You're very kind," she said, drawing on Grandmama's teachings.
A platitude for every occasion. Anything to cover up what you're really
feeling, so no one ever has to suffer the embarrassment of a genuine
emotion.

Duncan's eyes narrowed into a scowl. "Stop that."

She glared at him. "Stop what?"

"Stop shutting me out with your proper Southern manners."

"I don't know what you're talking about."

"I'm a vampire lord, Emma. You can't fool me."

"Good for you," she shot back. "I'm a human, and I'm doing the
best I can." Who the hell did he think he was anyway? If she wanted
to pretend her heart wasn't breaking, if she *needed* to believe it, who
was he to tell her she couldn't?

"Fine." He stood, shoving the heavy table out of his way as if it
weighed nothing at all. He turned his back, ignoring her for a moment.
She could tell he was angry and trying to control it. Some men would
have slammed a fist into a wall, or maybe thrown something. Duncan
was too controlled for that, but there were still signs. He wasn't the
only one who could read body language. She and Lacey had survived
seven years in foster care. She was a damn expert at reading body
language.

"There are some things you need to know," he said finally, but
without turning.

"Where's Lacey's body?" she asked instead.

That brought him around to stare at her. At first she thought he
wouldn't answer her question, but then he said, "At a funeral home in
Falls Church."

She frowned. "Why there? Won't the police—"

"There won't be any police."

Emma stood, abruptly just as angry as *he'd* been a moment ago. Forget that she'd been planning to shut out the police and pursue her own revenge. She wasn't going to let him cover this up and pretend nothing had happened.

"What do you mean *no* police?" she demanded. "You and your vampires murdered Lacey. The police will make Victor come back and—"

"Victor's dead."

Emma froze, suddenly confused. "But, how? I mean, when?"

"Four nights ago."

She frowned, counting back. "But that means the first night I came to see you at the embassy—"

"It's not a fucking embassy," he snarled, "and yes, he was already dead. That's how it works with vampires."

"How what works?" she insisted, not at all put off by his mood. She wanted answers.

He started to respond, then caught himself and said, "It doesn't matter. What matters is that vampires were involved in this crime, and vampires will take care of it."

"What does that mean?" she persisted, feeling like snarling herself. "So Victor's dead. Great, fantastic. That's one down—"

"Five down," he interjected. "He had bodyguards."

"Five then," she snapped. "I don't care. If they had anything to do with Lacey's—" She choked on the word, and had to force herself to keep going, stoking the flame of her anger to keep moving forward, to get it done. "—with Lacey's death," she continued calmly, "then they deserved to die. But they weren't the only ones."

"You're right. They weren't. But I know who was, and I'll take care of it."

Emma gazed at him, struck dumb for the first time. He already knew who killed Lacey?

"I'll take care of it, Emma. I promise."

"I want to be in on whatever you're going to do."

"Absolutely not."

She raised her chin defiantly. "Think again, vampire. You don't want me to go to the police? Then I want on the inside. You give me what I want, you get what you want."

Duncan was suddenly right in front of her, towering over her, crowding her with his sheer size and strength. That cool reserve of his was gone, and in its place was something ice cold and deadly, and absolutely lethal. This was the real Duncan, the vampire powerful enough to command others, and she knew instinctively that he could kill her with a thought.

"You have no idea what I want," he said deliberately. "Be very careful, Emmaline."

She swallowed hard. Her heart was tripping so wildly it was climbing up her throat. "Okay," she whispered, then steeled her courage and glared back at him. "But I still want in."

He stared at her a few seconds longer, and then a tiny smile curved his lips upward, there and gone almost before she could see it.

"Very well," he agreed.

Emma couldn't have been more shocked. He was agreeing?

"You have a deal," Duncan continued smoothly. "I'll expect you at the embassy, as you call it, one hour after sunset every night until this is finished. And I'll expect you to work just like the rest of us."

"All right," she said, her thoughts stumbling as she tried to switch gears. He was going to help her find Lacey's killer. Or rather she was going to help *him*, but what mattered was that he could do it much faster than she could alone. And once he pointed her in the right direction, she'd take matters into her own hands. After all, vampires slept all day long. There'd be nothing he could do to stop her.

Duncan was studying her closely, and she quickly blanked her thoughts, busying her mind with efforts to remember when the sun went down and how she could convince Sharon to let her leave work early every day for a while.

"When do we start?" she asked

Duncan's gaze softened. "Take a few days. Bury your friend. The men we want, the ones responsible, won't know that we found Lacey's body. There's no reason for them to be suspicious, no reason for them to run. And even if they do, I'll find them."

Emma stared up at him, believing him, knowing he would help her get justice for Lacey.

Lacey. Grief swelled inside her without warning. She wanted to be alone. She *needed* to be alone, to bury her face in a pillow and keen the pain of her loss where no one could hear it. Duncan's face blurred, and she blinked away her sudden tears. There was one last thing she needed to know.

"Could you give me the name of the funeral home, please? I need to make arrangements for my Lacey."

* * * *

Duncan closed the door behind him, listening as Miguel and the others settled down for the day. Doors slammed and voices quieted until there was only silence. He stripped off his clothes, letting them fall to the floor. They held a reek of death that would never come out. He'd have them burned with the trash tomorrow.

Crossing the room, he checked the windows automatically, making certain the blinds were drawn, the heavy drapes closed tightly. He was tired tonight, both body and mind anguished by the atrocities he'd uncovered, but even more by the weight of Emma's grief. It had touched a place in his soul, an old wound that was so scarred over it was barely there anymore. It was that gut-wrenching loss of someone so dear, someone you'd have gladly given your life for. A pain he'd buried so long ago, he'd persuaded himself it was truly gone.

But Emma's grief had brought it all back . . .

* * * *

1862, Stones River, Tennessee

He lay in the mud, listening to the screams of the men dying all around him, and the soft moans of the ones too far gone to scream. The sun had set some minutes ago, though it seemed much longer than that. He'd watched the red glow on the horizon, and wondered how much of that color was the sun and how much a mist of blood from the day's brutal fighting. God knew there'd been enough blood spilled today to color a thousand sunsets. His only consolation was the knowledge that the dying had been on both sides of the battle line, and that was small consolation indeed. More comforting was the certainty that at least *his* fighting was over.

He wasn't screaming, not yet, but he feared he would be before long. He lifted his hands, daring to look down at the blood-soaked tatters of his filthy uniform, and groaned at what he saw. He was no surgeon, but he'd seen enough slaughtered animals to know what he was looking at. He'd been gutted as surely as a pig in summer. His skin was sliced open, his intestines bulging outward in great loops of gray, grayer than the uniform he'd been given only weeks before. The coat had come from a dead soldier, someone he'd never known. He'd shivered when they'd handed it to him, wanting no part of a dead man's clothes. But these were troubled times. If you rejected the gray, no matter the reason, people looked on you with suspicion in these parts. This was Tennessee where there were nearly as many for the Confederacy as not, and it didn't matter what you said. It mattered what you did. So Duncan had taken the gray jacket and shrugged it on, feeling as if death itself was settling into his bones. And he hadn't been far wrong.

He lowered his hands over his belly once again, ignoring the slimy push of his guts against his fingers. He wanted to howl to the heavens. Not with pain, although it felt like a hot poker had been stuck in his belly to be stirred around every once in a while. But that wasn't what made him angry enough to curse God, his generals, and all those other men in suits who sent farmers like him to fight. It was death itself that made him angry. Not that he feared it. He figured he'd lived a good enough life that the heavenly reward the scriptures promised would be his eventually. It was what he was leaving behind that made him angry, the things left undone—even though he knew some of those things were not Christian-like and would probably send him straight to hell. But even lying here on the edge of death, it would have been worth it. He'd have given up heaven itself to revenge the wrongs done to those he loved.

He sighed and lay back in the mud, no longer caring about the filth or even the stench. It didn't seem so bad anymore, and he reckoned he'd either gotten accustomed or his senses were dying. Either way, he didn't have it in him to care.

The soldier closest to him fell abruptly silent and Duncan closed his eyes in prayer for the man's soul. He only hoped there'd be someone left to pray for him when the time came.

A shadow darkened the moon's light behind his closed eyelids, and his heart kicked up a bit. Maybe this was it after all.

"You aren't hurt so bad, boy," a deep voice said, the accent one he'd never heard before.

Duncan's eyes flashed open and he stared at the man crouched over him. No one had spoken to him since the surgeon who'd come by earlier, and he'd only shaken his head sadly and moved on. Duncan didn't blame the man. No point in wasting skills on those who couldn't be saved. And that included Duncan and every other man whose guts were fouled. They'd be picked up eventually by those tasked with collecting the dead and dying. But Duncan wasn't dead yet, so who was this stranger and what did he want?

The man raised his eyes, and Duncan wondered if maybe God had judged his final thoughts of vengeance and sentenced him to hell after all. Because this was no ordinary man. His eyes were the black of midnight, with an unholy silver gleam about their edges, as if something peered out from behind. And he was bigger than any man Duncan had ever seen before. Bigger than Duncan, and he was counted a big man.

The stranger smiled and his teeth were clean and white. "I'm not your Christian devil. And this isn't hell." He looked around with a frown. "Or not the one you're thinking of anyway."

Duncan stared. "How do you know what I'm thinking?" he whispered, his mouth almost too dry to form the words.

"I know many things," the stranger said, turning that black gaze on him once again. "I know you don't have to die today." He studied Duncan intently. "Unless you wish to."

Duncan felt a surge of hope, quickly followed by fear. He wanted to live, at least long enough to seek his vengeance, but what price would this devilish man demand of him? Men like this gave away nothing for free. But then, some things were worth any price.

"I want to live," he said, taking a chance.

"No questions, no negotiation?" the man mocked lightly. "Are you so quick to deal with the devil, Duncan Milford?"

"How do you know my name?" Duncan asked, swallowing hard.

"I told you. I know many things. But let us discuss our deal first. I *will* save your life tonight, but in exchange, I want your service."

Duncan blinked. Was the stranger a spy for the Union then? Did he think Duncan had some useable information? Because he surely did not. "What sort of service?" he asked, curious despite himself.

The man shrugged. "I'm a traveler to this place. I need someone who knows local customs, even language. Though I thought I spoke it well enough before I got here," the man added in an aside.

Duncan examined the man's words. He actually spoke well enough, though perhaps a bit too well. The very correctness of his speech gave away his foreign roots, that and the accent which Duncan still couldn't place.

Duncan shifted, trying to ease the renewed pain in his gut. "You want me to—" He gasped as that hot poker started jabbing and stirring again. He fell quiet, willing it to be gone for a few more minutes. Closing his eyes, he tried to remember the faces of his children, pictured his son running to greet him at the end of a day. He smiled, but their faces began to fade as a wave of fresh agony seared his guts and blackness stole his memories along with his thoughts.

When he opened his eyes again, he knew time had passed. "How long?" he asked the stranger who knelt next to him in the mud. "How long was I out?"

"Long enough," the man growled. "How do you feel?"

Duncan licked his dry lips, grimacing. There was a strange taste in his mouth. Not bad, better in fact that the bitter tang of bile which was all he'd tasted since being wounded. He drew a cautious breath, not wanting to awaken the pain, and realized his gut hurt no more than a mild ache. He looked down in shock. His trousers were still torn and bloody, but his stomach was whole, the skin puckered with raw, red scars instead of split and spilling shiny gray intestine. Duncan stared, then looked up in sudden terror. This was surely unholy.

The man made an impatient noise. "Enough, Milford. I've already told you, I'm not the devil. Doesn't your God heal as well? Now, do you want my bargain or not? You live, and in return, you serve as my aide."

Duncan stared. "But you've already healed me."

The man smiled gently. "So I have."

Well, this was vexing, Duncan thought. For this was no trick. The worst of the pain was gone. And not only the pain from the wound which would most certainly have killed him, but the ache in the leg he'd broken as a child. The break had healed poorly and had pained him every day since. And yet, lying here in the mud and blood, he felt better than he could remember since childhood. And perhaps this *was* a gift from the heavens, for the stranger did not bear the likeness of any of the demons Duncan had seen in the good books, nor did he carry himself like one in the way the ministers warned of in their sermons. Even more, he gave no indication he would take *back* his healing if Duncan refused the bargain, which a servant of the devil surely would have done.

But at the same time, Duncan could not, in all good faith, refuse the bargain since the stranger had in truth healed him. Vexing indeed.

"For how long?" he asked suddenly.

The man raised a fine brow in question.

"How long would I have to serve you?"

The man shrugged. "For the rest of your life or mine," he said, and turned to survey the battlefield once again.

Duncan sighed. He'd expected as much. Not that it mattered. He had nothing and no one to go home to anymore. He doubted his home was even there any longer.

"Very well," he said. "I agree to your bargain."

"One more thing," the stranger said, turning toward Duncan with a wide grin.

Duncan froze beneath the sudden weight of that black gaze. His heart began to pound and his breathing became short, as if his body already knew something that his mind had not yet grasped. Some part of him knew he should be gibbering in fear, crawling on hands and knees, if that's what it took to flee this inhuman monster before him. Instead, he lay and stared, almost in wonder, as the man's grin grew fangs as long as any red wolf's, and as the silver light of his eyes began to glow like the stars themselves. Perhaps the stranger had bespelled him somehow, or perhaps he was dead after all, and this entire conversation was nothing but a dying fancy.

"What are you?" he heard himself ask.

"I am Vampire," the man said. "And if you choose to remain with me, you will be, too."

"I don't know what that is," Duncan said, amazed at his own calmness.

The man—no, the *vampire*—laughed. "It is a wondrous thing," he said, then lowered his head, staring intently at Duncan once more.

"Are you . . . human?" Duncan asked.

The vampire lifted one shoulder. "I was born human. I still am, in a way. But becoming Vampire changes you. Makes you more of whatever you were. You will still be Duncan Milford, but you will be more, as well. Stronger, sharper, more powerful."

Duncan thought about that. "Could I ask a boon of you?"

The stranger seemed surprised by this, but he nodded. "You may ask."

"If I go with you, if I become this . . . vampire as you are, I would ask that you permit me one final task before we leave."

The vampire tilted his head in curiosity. "What task is that?"

"Vengeance," Duncan said softly.

The silver in the vampire's eyes gleamed so brightly Duncan feared it would bring others running. "Done," the vampire said. He stood and offered his hand.

Duncan grasped it and felt himself pulled to his feet as if he weighed nothing at all. "What do you I call you, sir?"

"Raphael," the vampire said. "My name is Raphael." He stepped back and made a sweeping gesture. "Lead the way, Duncan Milford. Your vengeance awaits."

They walked most of the night. Duncan had worried at first about sentries, about being labeled a deserter or worse. But Raphael had assured him they would not be seen, and they weren't. Several times they passed within feet of a sentry, once walking past the command tent itself. And yet no one seemed aware they were even there. Animals were a different matter entirely. The horses sensed them, moving about and snorting restlessly when they slipped through the picket lines, but Raphael and Duncan were long gone before anyone came to check the animals, assuming anyone had bothered.

As they walked, Raphael told Duncan something of who he was, of what it meant to be Vampire.

"As your Sire," Raphael said as they traveled down an abandoned country road, "I will teach you how to survive, how to use whatever gifts the rebirth bestows upon you."

"Rebirth?" Duncan repeated.

The big vampire nodded. "That's what we call it, for that's what it is. Everything you were before will change. You'll leave everyone you know behind, even family. Do you have family, Duncan?"

A wave of grief swept over Duncan, nearly drowning him, and it was several steps before he could speak again. Raphael kept his silence, and Duncan was grateful for it. Finally, he said, "I did once. No longer."

Raphael said nothing at first, as if pondering the many ways a man could lose his family. "This vengeance you seek, it's for your family." He said it as fact, not in question, but Duncan answered anyway.

"Yes." He swallowed the hard knot of loss clogging his throat. "My wife and children."

It was several minutes before Raphael spoke again. "That's a heavy burden for any man to bear."

Duncan nodded, then studied the vampire closely, wondering if he, too, had lost someone. "Did you leave family behind, sir?"

A fierce look crossed Raphael's face, and Duncan thought perhaps he'd gone too far, presumed too much. He opened his mouth to apologize, but Raphael spoke first. "My parents," he said abruptly. "Though my father was no loss to me, I grieved for my mother. My sister, too, or so I thought for a time."

Duncan was curious about that last bit, but decided against pressing his luck any further. "You said you're newly arrived in this country, sir? You picked a bad time for it."

"In truth, we arrived a few years past. It's taken this long to get settled and decide to move west."

"We?" Duncan questioned somewhat nervously. "There's more of you?"

Raphael must have heard the nerves. He grinned down at Duncan, his eyes going that strange silvery color again. "If you mean vampires, there's more than a few, though humans are largely unaware of us. My own group is small, just those I brought with me from the old country. You needn't worry, though. They're completely loyal to me."

"Might I ask where they are, sir?"

"Stop *siring* me, boy. If you must, my title's lord, for that's what I am, a vampire lord."

"Yes, my lord," Duncan said dutifully, though it seemed odd to say it. There were no such titles in this country. The founders had left behind that sort of thing, but perhaps vampires were different. "Do you have many land holdings, then, my lord?" he inquired.

Raphael barked a laugh. "And there you've pricked my pride but good, Duncan."

"I didn't mean any—"

"Don't apologize. You've the right of it. I've nothing but a few loyal men and a purse filled with coin. The men were carefully chosen, and the coin comes easily. For the rest of it, be assured, Duncan Milford, I will rule an empire before I'm through."

Duncan nodded in agreement, and the two of them continued for some time without speaking. The moon had set and the night had begun to take on the stillness that precedes the dawn, when Raphael verged suddenly from the road, heading deep into the trees. Duncan followed, not knowing what else to do. He'd chosen the route they were taking back to his home, but they had many miles to go yet, and he wasn't familiar with the lands they were passing through. Raphael seemed to know where he was going, however, weaving his way through the thick forest until they reached a small hut. Hidden beneath some low-hanging branches, it was a rough-built structure of unfinished logs and mud, but it looked sturdy enough and was most likely used by hunters in summer. Since it was winter now, the place was empty as far as Duncan could tell, and the sturdy lock on the door didn't invite visitors. But Raphael didn't hesitate. He walked right up and twisted the thick metal lock as if it were paper, then tossed it aside.

Duncan stared from the now useless padlock to Raphael and back again.

"You'll do the same soon enough," Raphael assured him, then pushed the door open and stepped inside. Duncan followed more slowly and found Raphael giving the place a critical survey. "I've slept in better," he said. "And worse. This will do."

He closed his eyes briefly, then opened them and said, "We've just enough time. Have a seat, Duncan." He didn't wait, but dropped to the floor, pressing his back up against the wall.

Duncan shrugged and sat beside him, wondering what was coming next.

"There are things we must discuss before going forward," Raphael began. "I was made Vampire unwilling, or at least unknowing. No one inquired as to whether I wanted it or not, but I tell you this, I do not regret it. It is an incomparable gift. I have lived nearly three hundred years, Duncan. I have power that you would not believe if I told you, but that you will understand when you join us. There are many things you will have to learn about being Vampire, but the most important is this. In order to survive, you will need to drink human blood."

Duncan's eyes widened in horror. "My lord! I have fought in war, as you well know, but I've no desire to survive by killing innocents!"

Raphael shook his head. "It is not necessary to kill the humans you choose to drink from, Duncan. Moreover, once you become Vampire, your bite itself will become enjoyable to them. Some will actually invite you to drink their blood in exchange for this pleasure, though there will be times you will have to take what you need. But you will never *have* to kill for it."

Duncan looked away, mulling over what he'd just heard. This certainly cast a fresh light on the decision he'd made. Could he do this? Could he bite another human being and drink his blood?

"Again, I will not make you Vampire without your willing consent, Duncan. You may still, with my blessing, consider the healing a gift and return to whatever waits for you. Or you can go forward with me and the others. The choice is yours, but you must make it now."

Duncan stared through the same empty doorway Raphael had, seeking his own past and his future . . . and found nothing at all. His past had been stolen when his family was killed, and his future had died along with them.

"I'll do it, my lord," he whispered, then repeated more strongly, "I'll do it."

"Then we must begin, for the sun is not far off. An important lesson, Duncan. The sun is our enemy. It traps us in slumber through the day, and if we are exposed to its light, we will burn unto ash if left there. It is perhaps our greatest vulnerability."

"Can we be killed otherwise, my lord?"

Raphael nodded. "A stake through the heart, or a sword, if wielded properly. Fire, if the damage is too great to be healed. And no one, not even a vampire, can survive having his head removed."

Duncan laughed nervously. "Good to know, my lord."

Raphael clapped him on the shoulder, then stood and looked around. "Lie over there," he said

"My lord?" Duncan asked, looking up at him in confusion.

"Lie down," Raphael repeated. "It will be easier for both of us."

Duncan's heart stuttered a bit, despite his earlier words. "Now?"

"Now, Duncan," Raphael said gently.

Duncan rose to his feet. It was nearly too dark to see, but he could make out a lone cot against the far wall. It was little more than a wood frame and slats, not even a straw mattress. Whoever used the place in summer would have known better than to leave such a thing behind. It would have been crawling with vermin by the next season. He shuffled over to the cot, then reached down with one hand, putting weight on the slats to test their sturdiness. They gave a bit, but held, so he lowered himself down, thinking even this was better than the cold ground he'd slept on for the weeks since he'd been swept up by General Bragg's march through Tennessee. He let out a weary breath and thought he could probably sleep, except—

"Comfortable, Duncan?"

"Er, yes, my lord."

Raphael loomed over him in the dark. "I'm going to bite you," he said as he knelt next to the cot. "On the neck, because it's fastest."

"Will it hurt?"

"Only at first," Raphael said with surprising honesty. "But after that, you'll experience the pleasure of a vampire's bite for the first and last time. Vampires cannot feed from each other, nor does their bite have the same effect as on a human."

Raphael turned Duncan's head firmly to one side and held him there. His breath was hot as he drew closer, and Duncan's heart kicked furiously in his chest. There was the touch of something hard and pointed, and then a pain as sharp as a knife slicing into his neck. He had one moment to think perhaps he'd been played for a fool, and then his blood heated and his body stiffened in a way it hadn't in the months since his wife died. Some small part of his brain was telling him this was wrong, but it didn't feel wrong. It felt . . . wondrous! And then he felt nothing at all.

When Duncan woke, he lay still for a moment, listening, astonished at the multitude of sounds all around him. He turned his head at a scratching noise and knew there was a mouse scurrying along the wall, though he couldn't see it. Outside, an owl swooped overhead, its wings a hard flutter of sound. Duncan smiled. It was as if he'd lived in only half the world until now, with the other half beyond his pitiful senses. But no longer.

He stretched, feeling strong and limber, marveling again at the lack of pain or soreness. His grin stretched wider, and he wanted to throw his head back and laugh with a joy he hadn't felt in years.

"You're awake." Raphael ducked as he stepped through the doorway, and Duncan realized it was still night. Or was it?

"How long did I sleep?" he asked.

"Just the one day," Raphael said. "You'll sleep later into darkness than some of us at first, but my blood is powerful, and your strength will build up fast enough. After that, it's up to you. No one can predict what gifts Vampire will bestow. We have to wait and see."

"This is gift enough," Duncan said enthusiastically. He stood, testing his legs one at a time, twisting from side to side, and gave in to the urge to laugh.

Raphael grinned back at him. "We've got to get going. There's your vengeance to see to, and then we must rejoin the others."

Vengeance, Duncan thought. He straightened and faced his new master. "I'm ready, my lord."

* * * *

Washington, D.C., present day

Vengeance. It was the first thought Duncan had as he woke the next night. He couldn't bring Lacey back for Emma, couldn't take away the pain of her death. But he could bring vengeance against those who had wronged her.

Chapter Fourteen

Falls Church, VA

Emma sat perfectly straight, hands folded together in her lap. It had taken two days to get everything ready. Two days to arrange a proper farewell for the only person in the world who'd really mattered to her. The funeral director had been very kind, but there were so many decisions to make, things she'd never have thought of on her own.

But despite the rush, despite the stress of arranging the funeral so quickly, it was all beautiful. And perfectly Lacey. The music, the flowers, even the casket with its bronze embellishments and beautiful mahogany wood.

The soft swell of some of Lacey's favorite music muted the murmur of whispered conversations all around her. It had been difficult to find the right songs for tonight. Lacey had always been a rock and roll kind of girl, her music better suited to roaring down the highway with the windows open and music blasting.

Emma smiled sadly at the memory, and smoothed her skirt with nervous fingers. She'd worn her best black suit, her gray silk blouse, even the black Jimmy Choo pumps she'd bought on a dare from Lacey and then never worn, because they were too nice for work. And since Emma never went *anywhere* except work, they'd sat in her closet, still in the box, never worn until tonight. Lacey would have loved that the Jimmy Choos had been broken out for her funeral.

Emma closed her eyes, unable to bear the sight of the casket any longer. She'd half expected Duncan to show up, but she was glad he hadn't. She didn't think she could deal with any vampires right now. Even knowing it wasn't his fault, that blaming him for what Victor had done would be like blaming the guy next door for what someone across town had done. She still wasn't ready to face him. Not yet.

The burial wasn't until tomorrow; that would be private, just between her and Lacey. But Lacey had so many friends, and they'd all called Emma, wanting to participate somehow, to say good-bye. So, the funeral director had suggested this memorial. He'd called it a viewing, but Emma had refused to permit an open casket. Lacey would have hated that.

Emma had arrived early and stood by the door at first, shaking hands, staring at faces she didn't know as they said all the right things. They were Lacey's friends, not hers. Lacey had always been so much more social than Emma. She'd made friends so easily.

And one of those friends had helped kill her. Actually, probably more than one, from what Duncan had said.

But the people here tonight didn't know that. They all thought it was an accident. That Lacey had lost control of her car and spun off the road on her way to visit someone back home. Of course, Lacey didn't have anyone back home. There *was* no back home. But these people didn't know that either.

Emma opened her eyes and stared straight ahead, sitting on the bench in the front row where she'd taken refuge, unable to cope with anymore well-meaning strangers. She couldn't take one more understanding smile, one more delicately dabbed tear, not even one more gentle handshake.

She wanted to die. She couldn't imagine living with this pain, this horrible emptiness. Lacey was gone, and Emma was left horribly, impossibly alone. The weight of her grief bent her back until she was bowed in half, until she thought it would crush her. She'd lost before— her grandmother, her mother, even the father she'd never known.

But Lacey wasn't supposed to die. Not Lacey. Emma studied; Emma worked. But Lacey *lived*. It never mattered where they found themselves or how little money they had, Lacey had always found something to celebrate, to laugh about, to dance for. She was the sister Emma had never had, the only friend she'd ever needed, her *family*.

And she was gone.

Emma closed her eyes again, afraid if she moved, if she so much as blinked an eyelid, she'd fall apart, scattering into tiny pieces that no longer knew how to put themselves together. How could there be an Emma with no Lacey to make her whole? She choked back a sob and wondered if this night would ever end.

She knew the moment *he* arrived. Felt the warm blanket of comfort reach out to her frozen soul, felt the safety of his presence long before he made his way down the aisle to sit next to her. He didn't reach out, didn't touch her. It was almost as if he, too, knew she might shatter and disappear.

A single tear slid out from under her closed eyelids, and she reached blindly for his hand. He took her hand and more, gathering her close, his arms coming around her warm and strong as her head sank onto his shoulder, as her tears finally came, soaking the wool of his fine suit.

He whispered meaningless words as she cried, holding her together as she shuddered with grief. He was an island of calm in a world she didn't understand anymore.

She couldn't say how long they sat there. She'd long ago stopped crying; her body had no more moisture left for tears. Finally, she lifted her head, brushing aside her tangled hair. She should have been embarrassed, but she wasn't. He offered her a perfect, white handkerchief. She stared at it, then raised her eyes to his. Who carried a handkerchief anymore?

He looked back at her. "I'm old-fashioned," he explained, seeming to know what she was thinking, as always. But for some reason, the idea no longer bothered her. It was simply who he was. He was Duncan, and vampire or not, he was a very good man.

He kissed her forehead, his lips warm and firm. "They'll pay, Emma," he murmured. "I promise you."

Others had offered sympathy, had told her what a great person Lacey had been, how much she'd be missed.

Only Duncan had offered her the one thing she needed. Vengeance.

Chapter Fifteen

Emma unlocked her front door and pushed inside. It was dark. She still hadn't remembered to leave a light on, still expected Lacey to be home first. She sighed and started across the room to the light switch, but Miguel beat her to it.

"Thanks." She ducked her head, a little embarrassed at his kindness after she'd thought such terrible things about him.

Duncan lifted his chin in the direction of the door, and Miguel left, pulling the door closed behind him, although Emma was sure he wouldn't go far. He might no longer believe that she had dastardly plans for Duncan, but he didn't completely trust her either. Or maybe it was like Duncan said; he just didn't trust anyone. That was something she could understand.

"Emma," Duncan said with barely controlled impatience. "I want you to come home with us. You shouldn't stay here alone."

Emma turned to him with a rueful smile. He'd made the same argument to her all the way home, but her answer hadn't changed.

"I appreciate that, Duncan. Honest. But . . ." She gazed around the softly lit room. It looked so inviting, comfy almost. She and Lacey had thought themselves incredibly lucky to have found this place and they'd been happy here. But Emma knew she'd be moving as soon as possible. There was no way she could stay in this house with Lacey gone.

She sighed. "I have to get up early tomorrow. There's so much to do, and the burial—"

"So, reschedule the burial for tomorrow night, and I'll go with you." He cupped her cheek in one hand and lifted the other to brush a lock of hair from her eyes. "You don't need to do this alone."

That was the rest of the argument he'd made on the drive from the funeral home. Actually *argument* wasn't even the right word. He'd simply told her how it was going to be. Or he'd tried to, at least. Emma had a feeling Duncan wasn't used to being told *no*. But he was going to hear it this time. Because burying Lacey was something she *did* need to do alone.

"I'm sorry," she said gently, "but no. I'm going to say good-bye to Lacey in my own way. Then I need to go to work. I haven't been there since—" She broke off, not knowing what words to use to describe the events of Lacey's death. She shut her eyes as a newly familiar pain squeezed her heart. Would the day ever come when she wouldn't feel this terrible ache at the thought of her murdered friend? Would she someday be able to remember the joy they'd shared without being forced to remember how it all ended?

"I haven't been to the office in a few days," she amended, meeting

Duncan's narrowed gaze. "I need to find out when they expect me back, and make some excuse for leaving early so I can work with you every night until we find Lacey's killer." She linked her fingers with his and held on tightly. "You haven't changed your mind, have you? You're still going to let me help?"

Duncan tilted his head in assent. "I keep my promises, Emma. All of them."

Emma blew out a relieved breath. "I'm counting on that."

"But you won't change your mind and come home with us— reschedule the burial."

She gave him a lopsided smile. "No. But I'll come to the embassy, I mean the house, tomorrow night, and I'll be ready to work."

He frowned, clearly unhappy, but then gave a minimal shrug that was more an expression than a movement on his part. "As you wish. I'll expect you tomorrow evening, then. One hour after sunset."

"I'll be there, boss."

Duncan didn't smile. He was staring at her intently, his eyes flaring with emotion. Emma leaned closer, drawn to his raw power, to the danger concealed beneath that civilized exterior. His gaze skimmed her face, settling on her mouth, and she surrendered to the sudden, burning need to lick her lips. He took a half step forward, and her heart began to pound. His big hand curved over her hip possessively, tugging her closer still, as he lowered his head. And Emma forgot how to breathe.

His mouth touched hers in a chaste kiss, his lips warm and surprisingly soft. Emma opened her mouth, wanting more, wanting to taste him. Her tongue slid along the seam of his lips, and Duncan's fingers dug into her hip, pulling her flush against his body as he lifted his other hand and threaded his fingers through her hair.

His body was hard, her breasts crushed against his chest as she tilted her head back, opening her mouth in invitation. Duncan responded with a low growl, deepening the kiss, his tongue delving into her mouth, twisting around her tongue, sending shivers of desire racing through her body. She lifted up onto her toes, wanting more, curling her arms around his neck with a hungry moan.

Duncan's arms tightened around her, and she felt the unmistakable press of an erection against her belly, a long, thick column of hard flesh that made liquid heat swell between her legs. Sudden images of Duncan naked, gleaming with sweat, his arms corded with muscle as he rose above her, his hips pumping—

Duncan broke the kiss with a groan, his breath hot against her neck as he held her close, his hands flexing against her back.

"Emma," he gasped warningly, breathing hard.

Emma heard him, but she didn't answer, couldn't find the *breath* to answer. He was trying to protect her, she knew. Trying to be sensible, to be sensitive. But Emma didn't want sensible. She wanted to lose herself in the heat and passion that was buried beneath that cool, Duncan exterior. Wanted to warm herself at the fire that he kept so carefully banked and hidden from view.

"Emma," he repeated, more softly this time.

She sighed regretfully, knowing he was right. He eased away from her enough that their bodies were no longer touching.

"I apologize," he said. "This isn't the time or place."

"Will there be one?"

Duncan's brown eyes heated, glowing with that same bronze fire before he brushed her ear with his lips. "There will be a *time*, Emmaline," he whispered. "And when the time comes, the *place* will no longer matter."

He straightened and kissed her lips one more time, a gentle touch there and gone.

"Sleep well," he said. "And if you need anything, call. I have people on staff around the clock."

"Okay," she said, already missing him. "I'll see you tomorrow night."

Duncan's arm snaked around her waist, pulling her close, his head dipping until she felt his lips on her neck. She gasped at the hard scrape of his teeth—his fangs!—against her skin. He breathed deeply, as if inhaling her scent, then lifted his head with a growl.

"Don't be late."

And then he was gone, leaving the door rattling in its frame.

Emma stood in the dim light of her foyer, heart thumping as she raised shaking fingers to her neck, feeling the heat of her skin where his lips had touched her. She hugged herself, wondering what it would be like to make love to a vampire, to feel the scrape of his fangs against her tongue or . . . she shivered remembering the brush of his mouth against her neck. And she knew it wasn't fear making her shiver.

She chided her overactive imagination. She was overloaded emotionally, that's all this was. She was drained and exhausted, and Duncan had been there to hold her when she needed it. He'd been so kind, the perfect gentleman, and she'd all but assaulted him when he'd tried to help her, to comfort her. And, okay, he'd been interested, but only because she'd thrown herself at him, rubbing herself against him . . . She nearly groaned aloud, remembering the feel of his cock against her belly, the heat in his eyes.

She squeezed her suddenly aching breasts, rubbing the flat of her palms over her nipples, gasping with pleasure as she sank to the stairs. She was in *so* much trouble.

Chapter Sixteen

Duncan stormed into his office, furious with himself, with the entire situation. He hadn't wanted to leave Emma alone, despite her insistence. But he certainly hadn't helped matters when he'd all but attacked her. It had taken all his considerable will power to break away from her seductive warmth. What he'd wanted to do was to push her against the wall, shove that tight skirt up to her waist, and take her right where she stood. She'd been ready for him, her breasts swollen, her nipples so hard he'd felt them against his chest despite the layers of clothing between them. And her scent! God, the sweet scent of her had driven him mad with desire.

Thankfully, he'd come to his senses in time. By all that was holy, the woman was in mourning, emotionally vulnerable, her feelings raw and wide open. Only an animal would take advantage of her in that state.

He unbuttoned his suit jacket and yanked his tie loose, disgusted. Despite all of that, he still wished she'd come home with him. He was worried about her. Whoever had killed Lacey would be desperate to make certain no one ever found out about it, and they'd be nervous once word got around that Victor had left town. At least that was the story Duncan and his people had put out about the late vampire lord, that he'd been called away without warning.

And that was a timely reminder for Duncan, too. Instead of seducing vulnerable young women, he should be taking up his duties as representative of vampire interests in the capital. Those duties included figuring out what Victor had been up to, but there was more to it than that. He had to become part of the Washington social and diplomatic circuit. He grimaced with distaste at the thought, but there was no alternative. Before he took that up, however, he had to make arrangements for Emma's safety.

Miguel strolled through the doorway, having delayed downstairs to double check the daytime guard deployment. The routine here was still new enough that it didn't hurt to be sure everyone knew their assignments.

"Set a guard on Emma Duquet," Duncan told his lieutenant without preamble. "Day and night. I don't want one of Victor's former clients getting nervous and going after her."

"Yes, my lord." Miguel made a quick call on his cell and it was done. They'd let go the security company Victor had employed, and replaced it with the men and women Miguel had trained personally for this job. Duncan trusted these humans with his life—quite literally until they got the basement vault constructed and functional.

"How's Alaric progressing downstairs?" Duncan asked.

"Excellent, my lord, but, as he keeps telling me, he has to rebuild

this *ancient and rotting* foundation before he can add anything to it."
He grinned. "The old man loves a challenge."

Duncan pulled off his jacket, throwing it on a chair as he settled behind the desk of his new second floor office—an office which looked very much like the library downstairs, and for a good reason. While it had been necessary for Duncan to move away from the library—for security reasons, if nothing else—he'd liked the ambience of the old room—the books, the furniture, even the wainscoting. So Alaric's crew had moved everything up here. It was quite remarkable, really. Every book, shelf, table and lamp had been moved. Now if they could just provide him with a decent place to sleep. And a gym.

"How are we doing on the videos from Leesburg?" Duncan asked. He refused to refer to the house itself anymore. He wouldn't rest until it burned to the ground.

"There's still no video of Lacey Cray, my lord. Not there, and not on any of the ones we discovered here, even though she's in Victor's files and, according to Ms. Duquet, was a regular at Victor's parties."

"I'm surprised he didn't delete her from his files altogether."

"He probably would have eventually. He expected to be around a lot longer than he was."

Duncan nodded in satisfaction. That much at least had gone right. Victor was gone, and Duncan had been the one to destroy him.

"There's still plenty of incriminating video, my lord," Miguel said. "Enough to destroy more than one political career, even if the men involved could prove it was consensual. Victor hedged his bets, and I'm sure he made sure they knew about it."

"Except there are no faces on the video. All we have are Victor's files, and even those don't name names."

"Phoebe's working on that. We can probably get some IDs by combining what we do have—the video and Victor's paper files—with what Brendan and Erik and their friends know. They talked to some of the men involved, after all. We can at least identify those."

"What about the women?"

"It's more complicated with them. The men are public figures for the most part. The women . . . who knows?"

"Emma can help with that tomorrow night. Even if she doesn't know the names, she may be able to tell us possible workplaces, or even other people to check with."

"Yes, my lord."

"And it's time I introduced myself to those powerful circles of Victor's, too. Something casual where I can talk to people." Duncan thought for a moment. "Check Victor's calendar. See if there's anything already scheduled. If so, have someone contact the organizers. Give them the line we agreed on, Victor's been called away and I'm the new ambassador."

Duncan didn't like to use the pretentious title, but apparently he'd have to get used to it. "In the meantime," he continued, "contact every senator and congressman from Virginia, Maryland and Delaware. Let them know I'm taking over and I'd like to meet with them. See if they have any events coming up and get us invited. Fundraisers, especially. Make sure they know we're good for a donation. Maybe Emma can help with that, too. She works in a congressman's office, after all. She knows how all of this works."

He thought for a moment while Miguel took feverish notes.

"Put California's senators on the list, too," he added. "I voted there last election, and Raphael's a big contributor. Which reminds me, we need to establish a legal residence for me outside the District, so I can vote in my own territory."

"Victor owned a house in Annapolis," Miguel offered. "I can send some people to check it out. If nothing else, you can use the address."

"Good." He frowned as he watched Miguel tap the information into his PDA. "We're going to need more people, Miguel. You're my lieutenant, not my admin, and this enormous house will need a housekeeper and staff, too. How did Victor handle that?"

"Humans, my lord," Miguel replied, looking up with a disapproving scowl. "He had a crew in once a week."

"Well, we won't be doing that. Put the word out, you know the routine. Give preference to vampires within my territory, but anyone from outside who's willing to swear fealty in blood will be considered. Appoint someone to do the initial screening, but you or Louis handle the final selection personally. And I'll want to choose the housekeeper myself."

"Yes, my lord."

"Do you have the photos?"

"My lord?"

"The composites from the videos. I'd like to take a look."

"They're on your computer, my lord, along with Phoebe's preliminary report."

Duncan swung his chair around to the computer, which sat on an L-shaped extension to the desk. Pulling up the relevant file, he scanned Phoebe's report quickly, then brought up the grainy images. Only the women were shown in full-face; the best Louis had managed of the men was the occasional partial profile. But profiles gave away more than people knew. That one, for example, had a very distinctive beak of a nose, and the next one a crude, almost primitive brow combined with the collapsed nasal bridge of someone whose nose has been broken too many times. It wasn't much, but he'd remember these men. They might not know him when they met at a party or a fundraiser, but he'd know them. Their emotions, even more than their words, would give them away. The only challenge would be waiting until the evening was over to rip out their throats.

Chapter Seventeen

Emma walked down the familiar hallway to Guy Coffer's congressional office. She passed a few people she knew and there was sympathy in their gazes. But there was a morbid curiosity, too, as if they feared—or maybe hoped—she'd break down weeping right here in the hallowed halls. That wasn't going to happen.

Oh, Emma still grieved. She would mourn Lacey every day for the rest of her life, but her grief was private, just as her final farewell this morning had been private. Mr. Pettry, the funeral director, had been there, but he'd remained discreetly in the background. There'd been no prayers, no stranger from the cemetery's list of convenient clergy to mumble a pro forma eulogy over a woman he'd never known.

Just Emma and the two workers who'd lowered Lacey's casket into the ground and then slowly, shovel by shovel, buried her.

Emma had stood there through the whole thing, her tears hot despite the icy drizzle which had begun to fall, freezing every inch of exposed skin. She'd waited until the last shovel full of dirt had been thrown, the earth packed down again, and the neat squares of sod replaced. The two diggers had straightened then, glancing from her to the funeral director, accustomed, she supposed, to the irrational behavior of grieving families.

Mr. Pettry had finally approached slowly, his footsteps crunching on grass that had already begun to ice over.

"Ms. Duquet?"

Emma hunched her shoulders, knowing it was time. She nodded, and looked up at the two graveyard workers.

"Thank you," she told them.

They nodded solemnly and hurried off, eager, no doubt, to be out of this awful weather.

"May I walk you to your car?" Mr. Pettry inquired, hinting gently that it was time for her to leave, as well.

Emma had forced a smile and taken his proffered arm, grateful for the support. She'd worn the Jimmy Choo pumps again, and the heels were too high for the uneven grass.

She glanced down at the black pumps now, as she hurried along the marble floored hallway. She'd been right after all, about not wearing them to work. If she made it to the office without twisting an ankle, she'd count herself lucky. She probably should have followed her first instinct and buried the damn shoes with her friend, but Lacey never would have forgiven her. Lacey had taken her designers very seriously. Yet another reason she'd never had the rent money.

Emma sighed and wished she didn't have to go to the office at all today, but there were too many people eager for a job like hers. If she stayed out too long, Sharon Coffer might very well use it as an excuse to hire someone old and ugly, or at least male. And Emma needed the money. She couldn't afford to lose her job, especially now. The lease on the house she'd shared with Lacey had two more months on it, and then there'd be the expense of securing a new place and moving. Besides, if she went home, she'd be surrounded by memories of Lacey. It was better to stay busy until tonight, when she could finally get down to the only thing that mattered to her . . . helping the vampires track down her friend's killer. And the irony of that last thought wasn't lost on her, since it was vampires who'd been responsible for Lacey's death. It was like asking the fox to figure out who ate the chickens. But Duncan wasn't going to let the human police get involved. She had no doubt he'd do whatever was necessary to keep that from happening. So, if the vampires were the only game in town, then Emma intended to make sure they played by the rules. Because if they didn't, then she'd do whatever she had to do to find justice for Lacey.

She finally reached the hallway outside Guy Coffer's office and paused to catch her breath before going in. Coffer had been in Congress for enough years that he had one of the more decent office suites. Not as grand as others, but nowhere near as tiny as the ones she'd seen some of the freshman legislators squeezed into. She smoothed her skirt and pulled open the big wooden door, steeling herself against the expected wave of curious attention. She stepped inside and, for a brief moment, everyone seemed to stop what they were doing. Then, as if they'd all become aware of it at the same time, the noise returned in a rush and everything was normal again.

Emma felt her face heat with embarrassment as she crossed the outer reception area. She'd never liked being the center of attention. Open double doors led into the second office. Everyone pretended not to notice her as she hurried into the third office of the shotgun styled suite and over to the corner she shared with Noreen. Her friend was at her desk, her back to Emma as she pecked furiously at a computer keyboard. The typing stopped, and Noreen turned as Emma slid into her chair.

"Hey, Emma. I wasn't sure you'd be here today. How're you doing?" Noreen's big, brown eyes were wide with concern. She'd been the only one from the office who'd come to Lacey's memorial last night.

"I'm fine," Emma said, the lie rolling off her tongue. People really didn't want to know how she was. Death was too terrifying. Everyone knew it happened, but they were almost embarrassed to ask about it.

Noreen studied her for a moment. "You won't believe it now, hon, but time really does heal."

Emma nodded. It wasn't time that would heal in this case; it was revenge. But she was sure Noreen didn't want to hear about that either.

"Thanks, Noreen," she said, meeting the other woman's gaze. "And thank you for coming last night." She opened a drawer and threw her bag inside. "So," she said, wanting to change the subject, "what have I missed?"

"Oh, not too much. The subcommittee rescheduled at the last minute, something about a pipe leak in the meeting room, if you can believe it, so everything—" Noreen's voice trailed off as her gaze fixed over Emma's shoulder.

"Emma," Guy Coffer said from behind her.

Emma spun her chair around and tried not to jump as Congressman Coffer took her hand and cradled it in both of his. "Sharon and I are so sorry for your loss, Emma. All of us are."

Emma blinked in surprise. Those were the most words Coffer had said to her since she'd been hired. Usually her instructions came through Sharon or one of the senior staff. The Congressman's handsome face was creased with sincerity, his eyes meeting hers unflinchingly. It was such a perfectly political moment that she was amazed she'd never noticed before how phony he was. Or maybe it was just that he usually never bothered to wear his campaign face in the office.

"If there's anything we can do . . ." he said, tightening his hold on her hand just the right amount to indicate his concern.

"Thank you, sir," she finally managed. "You've already been very kind." He seemed taken aback by that, and she added, "Letting me take so much time off, for the funeral and everything."

"Well, of course," he said, seeming genuinely surprised that she would mention it. "It's the decent thing to do."

Emma smiled. "I appreciate it anyway, Congressman."

"You've worked here for two years, Emma. Call me Guy."

He knew how long she'd worked for him? She was mildly surprised he even knew her name, much less how long she'd been in his office.

"Guy," Sharon Coffer's sharp voice cut into the moment, and Emma would have sworn she saw the Congressman wince briefly. "You have people waiting."

"Yes, of course," Coffer said quickly. He patted Emma's shoulder awkwardly. "If you need anything, Emma, let me know."

"Thank you, sir."

He smiled, his face smoothing out into its usual bland good looks. The mask was back so quickly that Emma doubted it had ever been gone. She watched as he trailed dutifully behind his wife to the innermost private office. Sharon stepped in after him and closed the door, but not before giving Emma a long, considering look. Like it was Emma's fault Guy Coffer had done the decent thing and offered his condolences. If she got fired over this, she was going to be well and truly pissed.

"What was all that about?" Noreen whispered.

"I have no idea," Emma muttered.

She buried herself in work the rest of the day, trying not to count the minutes until sunset, which was at 5:37 precisely. She'd checked online to be sure, before driving to the cemetery and then to the Capitol. She didn't usually drive to work. Parking was a pain in the butt, and public transportation was quite good. But it would save her time getting to Duncan's tonight. Her biggest problem would be getting out of the office that early, but she'd already decided she wasn't going to ask anyone; she was simply going to leave. Let them think whatever they wanted, that she was overcome with grief, that she still had business to take care of regarding Lacey's death. She didn't care.

So, when the discreet clock on the office wall clicked over to 6:00 pm, Emma straightened her desk, shut down her computer, stood and pulled her purse out of her desk drawer.

Noreen looked up at her in surprise, but Emma simply said, "There are some things I need to take care of." Then she slipped the strap of her purse over her shoulder and walked out of the office as casually as if she left this early every day. Once outside the building though, she picked up the pace, moving across the crowded parking lot as quickly as she could in the ridiculously high Jimmy Choos. Duncan had promised her she could help, and she wasn't going to give him any excuse to go back on that promise.

Traffic was its usual snarled mess, but less than an hour later, Emma drove right up to the gate of Duncan's house—he'd made it clear that it wasn't an embassy—no parking down the block and sneaking past a dump truck. Not that it would have been possible. It was obvious there was new management in town. The gate was not only securely closed, but there were two burly and well-armed men— or maybe vampires—standing in front of it. When she pulled closer, she could see even more armed guards prowling around inside the grounds.

She pulled up to the closed gate and stopped, rolling down her window.

"Hi," she said, handing him her driver's license. "Ambas—er, that is, Duncan is expecting me."

The guard—and oh, yes, he was a vampire. He made no attempt to conceal his fangs as he looked from her license to her face and back again. He didn't say anything, but turned away from her long enough to hand her license to a second guard who had remained in the small gate hut. That one studied her license for himself, entered something into an unseen computer, then pulled out a cell phone and hit a speed dial number. He glanced up and saw her watching, then gave her his back while he spoke to whomever he'd called. Emma could hear his voice, but not make out the words. She was pretty sure it was English, but wouldn't have sworn to it. And all the while the first vampire guard stood right next to her car, his arms resting on a big, black gun slung over his chest on a sling of some sort, while he watched her unblinking.

Emma wanted desperately to *move*, to tap her fingers or pound the steering wheel and give a good scream to release some stress. She always got twitchy when she was nervous or excited, and tonight it was a combination of both. But with the unfriendly vamp standing right outside, that probably wasn't a good idea. So instead she focused on what she could see of the house through the iron bars, trying to spot all the security people who had sprouted up from seemingly nowhere in the few days since she'd last been here. She jumped when the gate suddenly began sliding open.

"They're expecting you," the first vampire said in a flat voice. He handed back her license. "Park in the area to the right." He pointed to a small paved area about twenty yards from the front door. "Someone will meet you at the door."

Emma took her license, proud that her fingers remained steady. Rather than sit under his scrutiny while she put it away, she dropped it into the center console and pulled slowly forward, feeling a sharp double bump underneath as her car rolled over the gate's thick metal tracks. She took the right hand arm of the curved driveway and parked near the big house, sitting there a moment and looking around. Hers was the only sedan in the parking area, but there were quite a few trucks of various sizes. Most of the trucks were either piled high with construction material, or looked like they'd recently been emptied of the same. Their tail gates hung open, and ropes and bungee cords were lying in the truck beds like forlorn snakes. Obviously, there was some remodeling going on inside the house. She didn't see any of Duncan's SUVs, though, so she figured there was a garage around back, or maybe a separate parking area.

Emma breathed out a nervous laugh and decided she'd wasted enough time worrying about where other people were parked. She opened her car door and swung her legs out, which was made more awkward than usual by the stiletto heels. She had some more practical clothes with her and had actually intended to change before she left the office, but when the time came, she'd been too worried that Sharon or someone else would drag her back to her desk for one last question or phone call. So she still wore the somber dark gray suit she'd worn to the cemetery this morning, with its snug skirt and tailored jacket, and still wore the ridiculously high heels. But at least she looked good. Er, professional. It wasn't as if she cared whether Duncan found her attractive or not. She merely wanted him to think of her as a professional, someone he could rely on to get the job done.

Oh, who was she kidding? She hoped she knocked his socks off. That kiss last night had only made her want another taste of the delectable Duncan. She appreciated his sensitivity in not wanting to take advantage of her vulnerability, but she'd spent the night wide awake, trying not to think about Lacey and thinking about Duncan instead. She knew it was part of the grieving process, the desire to lose herself in the physical as a way of forgetting the emotional. But whatever it was, she wanted more of him, and if his body had been telling her anything last night, it was that he wouldn't object.

She hefted the purse with her laptop over her shoulder and grabbed the gym bag with her change of clothes from the backseat. Beeping her car locked, she headed for the fan-shaped brick stairs, but before she'd put her foot on the lowest step, someone opened the door.

Emma looked up, her heart spiking in anticipation. But it was only . . . Louis, that was his name. He stood in the open doorway, smiling pleasantly and without even a glimpse of fang.

"Good evening, Ms. Duquet," he said politely, standing back so she could enter. "Lord Duncan is expecting you."

Lord Duncan?

"Um, thank you," she said, trying not to fidget. "Is there somewhere . . ." She held up her gym bag, silently asking if there was somewhere she could change. Apparently she should have been more explicit, because Louis took the bag from her and walked over to the room where she'd met Duncan the other night, the room with the books. Emma followed him, but stopped in the doorway to stare. The books were gone and so was the room. Well, not precisely, the room was still there, but it looked completely different. The walls were bare and painted a bland, soothing warm beige, and the furniture looked like something you'd find in a nicely appointed dentist's office.

"What happened to the books?" she asked. "And the Tiffany lamps?"

Louis gave her an infectious grin. "My lord liked the room, so we moved it for him."

Emma blinked. "The entire room?"

He nodded. "Close enough." He dropped her gym bag on the floor of the newly refurbished waiting room and indicated the purse over her shoulder. "You can leave that here for now, too."

"It's got my laptop in it."

He winked. "It'll be perfectly safe here. Honest."

Emma scowled as she felt embarrassment heat her cheeks. She let the purse slide down her arm and rested it carefully on top of the gym bag.

Louis nodded and gestured down the hall behind the stairs. "They're in the gym. Come on, I'll show you."

Emma opened her mouth to protest—she was hardly dressed for the gym—but Louis took off so quickly that she found herself hurrying to keep up. She followed him down a dark hallway that passed right under the stairs. It intersected a brightly lit corridor that seemed to run the length of the house in either direction. Louis turned right and kept going, glancing once over his shoulder to make sure she was still with him.

Emma was struck by the change from her first night here, when it had been so quiet and empty. She'd only seen Duncan and Miguel that night, and it had been like whispering in a church. But now the house was filled with noise. For one thing, it sounded like someone was tearing down the walls upstairs, and she could hear shouts and thumping sounds emanating from below her feet, presumably in the basement. Clearly, the former library wasn't the only room being renovated. She caught the startled glance of a big black guy who was working over a drafting table in one of the rooms she passed. And another man—or a vampire?—this one shorter than she was, and wiry, nearly bowled her over as he raced out of a doorway right in front of her and headed back the way they'd come. Emma was still catching her breath from that encounter, when a huge crashing noise echoed from the general direction of the front door.

She jumped at the sound and looked anxiously over her shoulder, but Louis merely grinned as he spun to face her and walked backwards a few steps. "Don't worry, Ms. Duquet. It's just a bit of remodeling. Come on, we're almost there."

"There" turned out to be a large, wide-open, high-ceilinged room, which she was certain had originally been a banquet room, not the gym it currently was. The vampires had stripped it bare and laid down some padding on the floor, but they hadn't had time to paint. She could still see the discolorations on the walls where huge artwork of some sort had once hung. And then there was the giant medallion embellishment in the center of the high ceiling, which certainly had never been intended to witness sweaty vampires working out. Incongruously, there were still heavy, gold brocade drapes pulled over every window, with velvet swags and twisted gold rope tiebacks.

"Stand over here," Louis said quietly, and Emma realized there was a fight going on out on the mats. Four other vampires stood against the wall on the sidelines. They studied her distrustfully until Louis did some sort of intricate sign language thing, and they all turned their attention back to the center of the room. Emma followed suit and blinked at what she found there. Two males, stripped down to nothing but loosely tied gi pants, their feet and chests bare, were engaged in a blazing martial arts battle that moved back and forth across the room so fast they were almost a blur. One had short dark hair, she could see that much, and the other . . . Emma caught her breath.

It was Duncan. And the other fighter was his lieutenant, Miguel. And to call what they were doing a fight didn't do it justice. It was more of a dance, although no doubt it would have been deadly if they'd wanted it to be. The two of them were pure, lethal grace, as they snapped out kick after kick, seeming to defy gravity as they twisted in midair, then changed tactics to meet in a whirlwind of fists and grunts, each blocking as many hits as he took. Emma winced as the sound of flesh hitting flesh echoed off the bare walls, some of the hits so powerful she knew a human would have been down and screaming long ago. She stifled a gasp, hand over her mouth, when Miguel connected with a hard fist to Duncan's jaw, his head twisting with the force of it. But it didn't stop him. Duncan flowed with the hit, ducking low and spinning around and up into the air, one leg flying out like a battering ram, striking the side of Miguel's neck. Miguel hunched under the blow and staggered briefly, then came up again as the two of them fought face-to-face once more, moving back and forth across the floor, neither of them appearing to be superior to the other.

Suddenly, Duncan went low, digging his shoulder into Miguel's gut and plowing over and under. He tossed Miguel over his back and sent him at least ten feet into the air. Miguel landed with a hard crack of wood, despite the heavy mats. Impossibly, he was on his feet in an instant, charging back as the two of them went toe-to-toe like two heavyweight boxers with no survival instincts. Fists clenched, they exchanged blow after blow until they were both bloody, until Miguel suddenly grabbed Duncan's arm, dipped and spun, tossing him over his shoulder.

Duncan came up grinning, mouth dripping blood, fangs gleaming as he took several running steps and flew into the air, his feet hitting Miguel's chest in a one, two, three pattern that sent the dark-haired vamp flying backwards to land flat on the mat with another backbreaking thud. Or maybe not backbreaking for a vampire, because Miguel came to his feet again, laughing like a lunatic.

"You've been practicing, old man" he said, assuming a defensive posture once again.

"That's *lord old man* to you, youngling. And maybe you're getting lazy," Duncan taunted.

"Words are cheap, *my lord*," Miguel growled. And it was Duncan's turn to laugh.

He was still laughing when he happened to glance over and caught sight of Emma. He lifted a hand, palm out, to stop Miguel, then tilted his head slightly as he took in the unlikely sight of Emma standing in his gym wearing her somber gray suit and high heels. He grinned at her, his hard muscled chest heaving, gleaming with sweat, drawstring gi pants hanging low on narrow hips to reveal a hard, flat abdomen and just a glimpse of that sweet narrowing of muscle into a man's groin.

Emma stared, her mouth dry and her heart twisting oddly in her chest. She *wanted*. And if the hunger on Duncan's face was anything to go by, he wanted her right back.

Or maybe he was just hungry. As in blood. She watched warily as Duncan prowled over to her, his hips rolling bonelessly like a big cat's, his gaze raking up and down her form before settling on her face with a lazy, slow blink of his eyes.

"Emma." His voice was a seductive purr that turned her name into a caress.

She wet her lips nervously, and then caught herself, refusing to give him the satisfaction of knowing he'd rattled her. "Hey," she said, pleased by how normal her voice sounded. "You wanted me here an hour after sunset. Here I am."

"Here you are," he repeated, his eyes dipping to scan her figure once more. "You look very lovely this evening."

"Oh. Well, thanks." It was such a Southern gentlemanly thing to say, the kind of thing young men of breeding learned in cotillion class. Emma didn't know if he really meant it, or if he was only being polite. Although, *polite* wasn't the word she'd have used to describe the way he was looking at her. No, nothing polite about that at all.

"I brought clothes to change into," she told him, determined to take control of the conversation again . . . if she'd ever had it in the first place. "I wore these to the burial this morning and—"

A look of genuine dismay crossed Duncan's face, and he took a sudden step closer, brushing the backs of his fingers down her cheek. "Forgive me," he murmured. "I was thoughtless. How are you?"

Emma blinked up at him, feeling the heat of his big body, inhaling the clean, masculine scent of his sweat. He was so close and her heels were so high that if she raised up the tiniest bit, their lips would touch. "I'm fine," she whispered. "Mister Pettry was very kind."

"If you need more time, this can wait. You needn't—"

"No," she said immediately, cutting off the rest of his words. "I want to do this. I *need* to do this."

His full lips curved slightly, and she thought she saw something like respect in his eyes. "Very well," he said. "Louis will show you to a room where you can change."

He looked beyond her to where the other vampire waited. "One of the guests rooms, Louis, with a bath. You know better than I do what's available. And then get Ms. Duquet set up in the security center with the headshots and a computer. Phoebe will be by later to work with her."

"Yes, my lord."

Duncan stepped back, turning away from her to catch a towel that Miguel tossed at him. He rubbed it over his face and neck, and she noticed a very slight pink tinge to his sweat.

"I've got to shower and change myself," he said, then lifted her hand, barely touching the back of it with his lips. "We'll see each other again soon."

Emma tucked her hand in the pocket of her jacket to keep it from trembling as she watched Duncan stroll from the room, followed by

Miguel. The other vampires had moved out onto the gym floor and were engaged in more rapid fire bouts of fighting. She couldn't have said what the particular discipline was. She didn't know enough about any of them. Her only experience with martial arts had been two weeks of a disastrous class she'd taken in college. Every inch of her body had ached—no, *ached* was too kind a word for how she'd felt. Her body had *hurt,* and she'd finally decided there had to be a better way of staying fit.

"You ready, Ms. Duquet?"

Emma jerked her head around to stare at Louis. Apparently, she'd been daydreaming. *Gosh*, she thought. *I wonder why?*

"Thanks, Louis," she said out loud. "And please, call me Emma," she added as she followed him back down the hallway. After about ten steps, she thought to ask, "Who's Phoebe?"

"A friend. She works with the FBI. Duncan called her out to Leesburg the other night. I isolated some video composites, and Phoebe's running them through some identification software she has access to.

Emma didn't remember seeing a woman among Duncan's vampires, but there was a lot about that night that was a blur. "I didn't meet her, did I?"

Louis stopped long enough to give her a weirdly intense look. "No," he said finally. "She arrived after you were gone."

He started walking again, and Emma frowned at his back. Was there something she'd missed? Maybe Duncan and Phoebe were *more* than just friends. And maybe Louis was close to Phoebe and resented the obvious sexual tension between Duncan and Emma. Or maybe Emma was letting her imagination run around in her head like a schizophrenic yappy dog.

Yeah, that was probably it.

After going back to the waiting room to retrieve her things, Emma picked up her purse and laptop, while Louis carried the gym bag upstairs for her. It wasn't all that heavy, and Emma could have done it herself. She'd learned long ago, however, to let guys carry things if they wanted to. Truth was, she kind of liked men who were still gallant, who opened doors and who offered their seats to women. She drew the line at car doors, because she felt too silly sitting there like a lump while the guy ran around the car. But she didn't mind the other stuff. It was nice. So, she let Louis carry the gym bag to a bedroom on the second floor. He dropped it at the foot of the bed and backed quickly out of the room.

"We're working right down there," he said, pointing. "Join us whenever you're ready. You can't miss it."

"Thanks," Emma said. "I won't take long."

"No rush." He gave her a toothy grin. "We'll be here all night."

Emma chuckled dutifully, waiting until he had disappeared down the hall before closing the door. She looked around. It was a nice room.

Sort of dated and frilly, and not really to her taste, but the furniture was beautiful and everything was clean. And there was an en suite bathroom. She hurried in that direction, having been in such a rush to make it out of the Capitol building before anyone stopped her, that she'd ignored that particular necessity.

Washing her hands afterward, she stared at her reflection in the mirror over the sink and wondered why any man, much less one with Duncan's looks and sheer masculine charisma, would give her a second glance. She looked awful. Too many nights with too little sleep had put circles like dark, purple bruises under her eyes. And they were all the more obvious because her skin was pale and drawn. She hadn't bothered with mascara this morning. She'd known it would just be cried off, but she had naturally thick eyelashes, so that part wasn't too bad. Even her lipstick was gone, probably chewed off on the way over here. Her face was one big, pale blotch with tired eyes, and it was topped off by a dark tangle of messy hair. Lovely.

She sighed and turned away. She had a hair brush in her bag, and a bit of lip gloss couldn't hurt either.

It was only a matter of minutes before the Jimmy Choo pumps had switched places with her Nikes in the gym bag, along with her neatly folded office clothes. She finished tying her shoes and crossed to the bathroom to study her reflection once again. She looked better. Not great, but definitely better. She wore a faded pair of denims, loose enough to be comfortable, but tight enough that she knew they looked good on her. Emma worked hard to keep in shape and didn't mind letting it show. What was the point otherwise? Along with the denims, she wore a white, long-sleeved, cotton t-shirt, and a zippered hoodie to keep her warm just in case. She tucked the tube of lip gloss in the side pocket of her hoodie and left the rest of her stuff where it was.

She opened the door and turned in the direction Louis had indicated. She could already hear a steady buzz of conversation and clicking computer keys, occasionally punctuated by vicious swearing in a variety of languages. She followed the noise about halfway down the hall to another bare-walled room, this one much smaller than the gym downstairs. It was probably intended as a bedroom, but it now held a mishmash of tables and desks set at haphazard angles with no obvious pattern. Computers and other equipment sat everywhere, and the various kinds of cables slinking between them were a disaster waiting to happen as they snaked and twisted from desk to desk and all over the floor. Although, maybe vampires didn't have to worry about falling on their asses like she did.

She frowned. If this was their security center, she wasn't that impressed. She'd expected something more professional from Duncan's team, or at least more orderly.

Louis came up to her and must have seen the doubt in her expression, because he said, "It's temporary until we get the new room outfitted downstairs."

Emma forced herself to smile. "As long as it all works, that's what matters," she said.

"Oh, it works," Louis assured her. "They may not look like much, but—" A chorus of growls greeted this assessment and he laughed. "But they're some of the best operators in the world. Between us, there isn't a code we can't crack, or a system we can't hack."

Emma chuckled at both his lame rhyme and his enthusiasm. It was contagious, and she found her own eagerness growing. Finally, she was doing something positive. Taking care of Lacey, arranging her funeral and laying her body to rest . . . that had been absolutely necessary, and it was a duty Emma had lovingly fulfilled. But it had done nothing to see that justice was served on those who'd killed her. Tonight, at last, Emma would begin the most solemn duty of all, and that was finding whoever was responsible and making them pay.

Of course, the first steps down that road involved sitting at a computer and doing some basic research. Emma took the photos Louis had grabbed from the videos and cropped them onto a single page, with the idea of deleting them one by one until there were none left. An hour later, she'd managed to identify only two of the women, and those were only because she'd met them at a birthday party for Lacey last year. Even then, she had only their first names and no idea where they worked or lived. But the rest of them . . . She shook her head. There had to be a better way to do this.

She pushed back from the computer and took a long drink of water from the bottle Louis had dropped on her desk sometime ago. She squinted thoughtfully at the pictures. There were tens of thousands of young, professional women living or working in Washington, D.C. Too many. So she had to narrow it down somehow. First question, how did Victor meet these women? From what Duncan and the others had said about the dead vampire lord and his habits, she deduced he'd had limited social interaction with humans. He'd gone to the occasional fundraiser, but he'd attended only those social gatherings where scoring an invitation was a coup of sorts. He *had* given parties of his own, but it appeared he'd only invited legislators and lobbyists. None of the usual society doyennes were ever invited, no Hollywood stars, or even the big name media types.

Emma frowned. So maybe most of the women were drawn from that same pool. Not legislators themselves, and not lobbyists, either. But their secretaries and assistants, young women eager for a chance to mingle with power. Women like Lacey.

Emma sat up straight. That was it! And she had a much better way of identifying them if she was right.

"I'll be right back," she said to no one in particular, and rushed down the hall to the room where she'd left her things, including her purse and laptop. Hurrying into the frilly bedroom, she dropped to her knees and dragged her enormous purse from under the chair where she'd shoved it earlier. She pulled out her computer and opened the lid, waiting impatiently while it woke up and searched for the house's Wi-Fi connection. It asked for a password, and she swore in frustration. She should have thought of that.

She shoved her purse out of the way again and had gathered her legs beneath her to stand when someone tapped lightly on the door and pushed it open.

"Emma?"

She looked up at the sound of Duncan's voice, her smile freezing as he stepped into view. She could only stare. Sweaty, bare-chested Duncan was gone, and in his place . . . she sighed with pleasure. Emma loved a man in a tux, but Duncan in a tux took her breath away. Lacey would have known which designer was responsible; Emma only knew that Duncan should have graced the pages of the most exclusive fashion magazine. He had a body made for formalwear, with broad shoulders and narrow hips, and the tux was tailored to emphasize that perfection. It was simple and black, with narrow, notched lapels and a hint of white cuff. His long, blond hair had been pulled tightly away from his face, so that his hair looked almost short from the front.

"Emma?" he repeated, holding a hand down to her.

She sighed and tucked the computer under her arm, holding her other hand up so he could pull her to her feet. This was really too much. It was as if the Fates had figured out the perfect man and said, "*Here, Emma, he's all yours.*" Except he wasn't. He was a powerful vampire and probably had all sorts of beautiful women vying for his attention. She stifled the irrational surge of jealousy that thought evoked, and managed to meet his gaze with a mischievous grin.

"You look very lovely this evening, Duncan," she said, emphasizing her own accent and letting him know he wasn't the only one who knew proper cotillion-speak.

His brown eyes crinkled in amusement. "Why, thank you, Miz Duquet. You're very kind."

She pursed her lips thoughtfully. "But, obviously, you're not helping out in the research department tonight."

"No, I'm afraid not. Although honestly, I'd rather be doing that. Unfortunately, I've a fundraiser to attend. Black tie," he added, gesturing dismissively at his tux. "It was on Victor's calendar, but they'll be getting me instead. I confess I'm hoping to meet someone useful to our current investigation."

Emma sobered immediately. "You need to be careful, then. Is Miguel going with you?"

His eyes warmed briefly with humor. "Miguel and Ari both. I'll be quite safe. I'm more worried about you. By now, the men who killed Lacey will know her body was found. The story you put out, that she died in an auto accident has most likely put them off until now. But after tonight, they'll know for certain that Victor is gone, and they'll get nervous again. Especially if there's any hint that you're checking into Lacey's activities before her death."

"No one knows I'm even here, much less what I'm doing. I told them at the office that I had some things to take care of. They'll assume it has to do with Lacey's death, but nothing unusual."

Duncan tipped his head in acknowledgment, but said, "Still, I'd feel better if you weren't all alone in your house. We've plenty of room here, you know, and no one would bother you."

Emma hoped Duncan truly couldn't read her thoughts right about then, because she wouldn't mind at all if *he* bothered her. His expression changed, becoming suddenly more intent, and Emma blushed, convinced that, once again, he did know what she was thinking. He touched his fingers to the heat of her flushed cheek and leaned a little bit closer.

"I wouldn't want anything to happen to you, Emmaline," he murmured, and brushed his lips against hers in a soft, too fleeting kiss.

Emma stared up at him. "Why do you call me that?" she whispered.

"Because it's your name and I like it. It's old-fashioned."

"You're the only one who uses it."

"Good." He kissed her again, longer this time, but not nearly long enough. "We'll talk later."

And just like that he was gone. Emma stared after him in frustration. When he did stuff like that, she was sure he wanted her, just like she'd been sure in the gym when the heat sizzling between them had all but burned her skin. But then he'd step back or get called away, or who knew what else, and he'd disappear, leaving her hot and bothered and wondering.

Or maybe she was putting too much into what was for him nothing more than a mild flirtation. Maybe he wasn't looking for anything more than a few hours of sexual gratification. Several hot, sweaty, satisfying hours.

Emma laughed quietly. Yeah, she could go for that. But then she sighed, knowing herself too well. What she felt for Duncan was more than simple lust. Maybe not a lifetime commitment, not yet anyway, and maybe not ever, but it was more than what a few hours of sweaty sex would satisfy. Of course, that didn't mean she'd turn down the opportunity if he offered. Especially since she had a feeling they'd be the best few hours of her life.

She shook herself out of the fantasies flashing across her brain and hurried back to the computer room. She couldn't do anything about Duncan and his damnable appeal, but she could definitely make a difference in identifying some of the people on Victor's list. She gripped her laptop more securely. She wasn't a computer hacker like Louis and the other vampires, but she *was* a compulsive collector of information. And the information on her computer might be exactly what they needed.

* * * *

Duncan climbed the aged brick stairs of the private home where Senator Max Grafton was holding a fundraiser. Strictly speaking, of course, it wasn't the senator holding the fundraiser, but one of his supporters. Someone wealthy enough to afford this Georgetown townhouse which made up for its tiny lot by climbing four stories above street level. Miguel walked beside him, and Ari would remain with the SUV. He'd ignored the valet service, but he probably wasn't the only one. This kind of affair drew nothing but wealthy guests, people who could help the senator get reelected by writing a check and/or coaxing others to join them. Duncan also knew from personal experience that, despite official protestations to the contrary, money talked. If you donated enough money to the right politician, you bought that politician's ear and often his vote as well. It had been that way for as long as some humans had been raised into positions of power, and it always would be.

A discreetly colored awning had been stretched above the stoop in front of the townhouse, and two security types were stationed on the small square landing to screen guests. Their glances skated over Duncan, but lingered on Miguel who made no bones about what he was—a highly trained and motivated bodyguard. He was also armed, but that, too wasn't unusual. At a gathering like this there would be other private security, and they would all be armed. They couldn't do their job otherwise. The men guarding the door didn't know it, but Miguel could probably have done his job just as well without the gun. For that matter, Duncan could do Miguel's job. Until a few days ago, a great part of *his* job had been to protect Raphael. But that was before he'd become a vampire lord himself, and now his world had forever changed. He was not yet certain if he preferred it this way, but it was too late for regrets.

Miguel sized the guards up as they did the same to him. None of them gave any indication of their thoughts, not even a twitch of a muscle. But Duncan knew the two human guards were both troubled and puzzled by Miguel, sensing there was something different about him, but not knowing what. They didn't know yet that Miguel and Duncan were both Vampire. Not yet.

Miguel handed over Duncan's invitation—well, Victor's invitation, but it was Duncan's now. He smiled grimly at the thought, even as he watched the guard's eyes widen when he read the name. The human stiffened, did a quick reappraisal of Miguel, then shot a glance at Duncan who met his gaze calmly.

"Gentlemen," Duncan said finally. He put a little punch of power into it, tired of being forced to wait on the porch like an unwelcome solicitor.

The guard nearest the inside door jumped at the reminder. Regardless of his feelings about vampires, Duncan was an invited guest at a party where only the most powerful were welcome. The guard pushed the door open and stepped aside, pressing himself against the wall to avoid accidentally brushing against Duncan as he went by. Duncan smiled in amusement, wondering what the man feared. Did he think vampirism was contagious? That if he touched Duncan, he'd turn into a slavering animal? But, no, the guard was broadcasting his emotions like a brass band. He was terrified, but not of catching a disease. He was afraid of Duncan himself, as if Duncan was a wild animal who could turn at any moment and rip out his throat for no reason. Duncan sighed inwardly. The man was a fool, but educating misinformed humans wasn't his purpose here this evening.

He entered the crowded townhouse, and immediately winced at the level of noise. Directly in front of him was a dark hallway, and to the right of that a narrow staircase that twisted up beneath the low ceiling. A few people lingered on the stairs, as if caught going up or down, but most of the guests he could see were in a drawing room to one side. A fireplace gave the room a welcome feel, but it was hardly necessary to add any heat. Not with all those people standing about and talking nonstop. There were more people upstairs; he could hear them talking and laughing. More oppressive than the noise, though, was the press of emotion from too many minds in a singularly confined space.

Duncan kept his face carefully impassive, but it was an effort. This was a large home, as such things went, and perhaps with fewer people it would have seemed more spacious. But as it was, Duncan felt as if he was being squeezed from all sides by humans who maintained a steady stream of dialogue, but had very little to say.

"Ambassador Milford?" A woman's voice calling his last name drew him out of his thoughts. He looked up to see an elegantly dressed matron coming his way, her very high heels making tinny tapping noises on a checkered marble floor that reminded him of the courtyard in front of what used to be Alexandra's house in Malibu. The human woman drew closer, her curious gaze never leaving his face. She was attractive for her age and fashionably thin, with the perfect smile of a professional hostess.

"We received word you would be joining us, Ambassador."

Duncan inclined his head. "Madam . . ." he said leadingly.

"Forgive me," she said, and laughed as she drew close enough to extend a hand. "Margery Whitlow. I'm delighted to meet you."

Duncan took her hand and squeezed carefully, feeling the movement of fragile bones beneath his fingers. "Mrs. Whitlow, of course," he said, remembering the name of the hosting couple from Victor's invitation.

"Oh, call me Margery," she said, and laughed again. She had a refreshingly genuine laugh, not something one usually encountered at parties like this, Duncan thought.

"Mrs. Whitlow is so stuffy," she added. Her glance strayed to Miguel, but she didn't say anything, clearly dismissing him as one more bodyguard. "Senator Grafton was most intrigued when I told him your staff had called. None of us knew Victor was leaving. It must have been quite sudden."

"It was," Duncan said noncommittally.

Margery paused for a moment, probably expecting him to offer an explanation. When none was forthcoming, however, she recovered deftly. "You have your work cut out for you, settling into a new post on such short notice. It was good of you to make time for us."

"On the contrary, Margery," Duncan said. He deliberately laced his words with a touch of seduction, and sensed the little rush of excitement she felt when he said her name. "There *is* a lot to do at the house, but houses can always wait," he said smoothly. "I'm very pleased at this opportunity to meet Senator Grafton—and yourself, of course."

Margery flushed with pleasure, and Duncan smiled.

"Margery!" An over-perfumed woman emerged from one of the side rooms, her arms held out in embrace. "I missed you when we came in."

Margery pulled away from Duncan with obvious reluctance, her gaze lingering on his face even as her body turned to greet the other woman. "Gloria," she gushed with totally faked enthusiasm. "How long has it been, darling?"

Duncan took advantage of the distraction to move in among the other guests. Miguel lingered near the doorway as Duncan glided from cluster to cluster of humans, picking up names and tidbits of gossip, introducing himself, and charming the locals. He was good at this sort of thing, much better than Raphael, and his Sire would be the first to admit it. Raphael at his most humble and charming was still massively intimidating. He couldn't help it; it was simply who he was. Duncan, on the other hand, had the ability to lull the humans into forgetting *what* he was.

He was deep in conversation with the wife of a famous French author, modestly accepting her compliments on his impeccable accent, when Margery touched his elbow.

"Ambassador," she said eagerly. "I've been neglecting you. Come. You must meet Senator Grafton. He's in the main room upstairs."

She laced her arm through his and pulled him toward the stairway. Miguel stiffened, but Duncan caught his eye and waved him off. With some vampires, her familiarity could have been fatal, but Duncan was too used to humans to be offended. Besides, Margery wasn't a bad person as far as he could tell. Her strongest feelings toward him were curiosity laced with lust, which was partly his own fault.

She released his arm when they reached the stairs, which were simply too narrow for such intimacy. Duncan followed her at a discreet distance, Miguel ghosting behind him like a shadow. He had reached the twist in the staircase when another man came into view, heading the opposite direction. He had a ruddy face that spoke of too much booze on too many nights, and he was carrying a crystal tumbler of amber liquid that sloshed recklessly as he started downward. Duncan could smell the peaty scent of Scotch beneath the stink of sweat. The man looked up and saw Duncan coming towards him. He nearly stumbled in such obviously shocked recognition that there was no doubt he knew who Duncan was. Duncan studied his face in return, noting the crude features and scarred visage of an athlete whose best years were behind him.

"Miguel?" He queried his lieutenant on a narrow telepathic thread. Miguel was his child. This close the other vampire was like an extension of Duncan himself.

"Congressman Dean Kerwin, my lord."

Interesting, Duncan thought. And the man was nervous at seeing Duncan. He nodded at the Congressman, as if he knew who he was, more for the pleasure of seeing the man's nervous jerk of surprise than anything else.

"There you are," Margery caroled as he stepped onto the second floor. "I keep losing you." She hooked her arm through his again and drew him over to one corner of yet another narrow room, this one with thankfully far fewer people in it.

"Max," she said, closing in on a pair of men deep in conversation. "This is Ambassador Milford."

Max Grafton was a small, compact man with a sharp-featured face and intelligent eyes. And unlike Congressman Kerwin, Grafton was completely sober. The champagne flute in his left hand was artfully drained to half-full, but there was not a hint of alcohol scent about him. He turned away from his companion and extended his right hand to Duncan in greeting.

"Ambassador," he said smoothly, his voice surprisingly deep for a man his size.

"Senator," Duncan replied, giving him the requisite hardy handshake.

"Thank you, Margery," Grafton said in obvious dismissal of their hostess.

Margery made a slight sound of protest that no one but a vampire would have heard, then smiled brightly and turned to Duncan. "I hope we'll speak again later, Ambassador."

On a whim of gentility, Duncan took her fingers and lifted them to his lips, lightly kissing the back of her hand. "It would be my pleasure, Margery," he said letting the slow honey of his Southern upbringing flavor the words.

Margery raised the hand he'd kissed to her flushed cheek. "Oh, my," she said. "You're one of those charming Southern boys. I'll have to warn the ladies." She laughed again in that delighted way, then hurried off on her high heels.

Duncan turned in time to see a sour look flash across Grafton's face, before it was quickly erased. "Brad," Grafton said to his companion. "Give us a moment, will you?"

"Of course," the man said and wandered across the hall to yet another drawing room filled with people.

"So," Grafton said, drawing Duncan's attention. "Duncan Milford, is it? I don't think Victor ever used a last name."

Duncan couldn't think of anything to say to that rather inane comment, so he remained silent, studying the human in front of him and wondering at the hostility he could feel rolling off the good senator. He decided on a frontal assault. "Victor spoke highly of you, Senator," he said. It was a lie, of course. Victor hadn't spoken to Duncan about anyone, nor would he ever again, but Duncan was curious to see what Grafton's reaction would be.

The senator grew very still, those intelligent eyes searching Duncan's face as if hoping for a clue of some sort. Not that he'd find one.

"Did he?" he said finally. "I wouldn't have expected my name to come up at all."

Duncan smiled knowingly, as if amused. "Come, Max, we both know—" Grafton's emotions shot into something very close to panic before Duncan finished his sentence. "—that Victor was a supporter of yours. A whale I believe you call someone like that, a person who is capable of delivering bundled donations of considerable sums."

Grafton's breathing slowly settled into a normal rhythm and he smiled. "Ah, that, of course. Victor was very generous." Grafton took a long sip of his champagne, though it had to be quite warm by now. When he lowered his glass, the mask was firmly back in place. "So, Milford, you're from the South?"

"Originally," Duncan agreed. He nodded at a server who appeared with a tray of fresh champagne and took one of the glasses. Grafton's eyes watched carefully as he took a tasting sip.

"I didn't think you pe—that is, vampires ate regular food."

"We don't. But we do drink." Duncan didn't bother explaining that while some vampires enjoyed the taste of alcohol, and others the burn, it had no effect whatsoever on their minds.

"Victor doesn't. At least not that I've ever seen."

"No? I'm surprised."

"What happened to Victor, anyway?" Grafton demanded. "I saw

him less than two weeks ago and he said nothing about leaving. I do hope he's well," he added, as if to soften the demand in his earlier words.

Duncan met the senator's gaze evenly. "Perhaps he didn't want to trouble you."

Grafton studied him a bit longer, then drew closer, as if in confidence. Miguel tensed slightly where he stood near the room's open archway, but Duncan shot him a quick glance of reassurance. Max Grafton was no danger to Duncan, at least not in the middle of this civilized gathering. Max struck him as more the type to lie in wait with a big gun. Or rather to hire someone else to do it, while Max himself established a credible alibi.

"Tell me, Milford. Will you be assuming . . . *all* of Victor's responsibilities?"

"You mean the parties," Duncan said negligently. "Of course. I have all of Victor's files."

Grafton froze and his heart rate soared once again. "I have no idea what you're talking about."

Duncan nearly laughed out loud, but settled for a grin that made his amusement plain. "Grafton, please. A man of your sophistication and . . . tastes? You must have known Victor was taping everything that went on at that house. You preferred blondes, didn't you? You and the drunken Congressman Kerwin, both. In fact, I believe you shared one or two."

Grafton stared at Duncan, his face pale and his breathing so rapid that Duncan feared the man would pass out. He swallowed hard once, twice, and then his lips tightened in anger and he snarled, "I don't know what you're pulling, Milford. But I will not be harassed in this—"

"Harassed," Duncan hissed, leaning right into the good senator's space. "You're confusing me with Victor, Grafton, and that would be a mistake. I don't *harass* my enemies. I eliminate them. Remember that."

Duncan stepped back and signaled to Miguel, who waited until Duncan had walked past and then followed him. The stairs were empty as they headed straight for the door, their mission, such as it was, accomplished for the evening. He heard Miguel calling Ari on the radio, telling him to bring the SUV around, and by the time they were once again out of that claustrophobic house, the familiar vehicle was rolling up to the curb. Ari powered down the window so they could see him, but remained behind the wheel as Miguel opened the back door for Duncan, then followed him inside.

Duncan had felt Miguel's anger growing all the way out of that house and onto the street, and he suspected it was directed at him. Once they got underway, he placed a casual arm over the back of the seat and glanced at his lieutenant sitting next to him.

"What is it, Miguel?"

Miguel shot him an angry look. "You all but invited him to come after you, Sire. You've set yourself up as bait."

Duncan shrugged. "Perhaps. But it seemed the fastest way to flush them out. Kerwin looked familiar, didn't he? He certainly knew who I was. And I'd lay good money that Kerwin and Grafton were conferring before I showed up and ruined their party. Emma needs to see Lacey's murder avenged, Miguel, and I want this matter done with. It isn't what we came to this city to accomplish."

"I understand that, my lord. But the job will proceed *much* faster if you're alive to do it," he growled.

Duncan sighed. Miguel had a point, but he knew men like Grafton. Unless Duncan pushed and pushed hard, they could dance around each other for months. Emma deserved better than that. She'd never be able to get on with her life until this was resolved.

Next to him, Miguel clicked the receiver on the Bluetooth device in his ear, answering a silent call. Duncan frowned. As far as anyone knew, they were still at the fundraiser, which meant no one would call unless it was urgent.

"What is it?" Miguel snapped into the phone. "Who is— Where are you now? No. No! Don't call anyone. We're on our way. Five minutes." He leaned toward Ari before he'd even clicked off. "Emma Duquet's place, Ari. *Fast.*"

Chapter Eighteen

After Duncan left, Emma hurried back to the security center and plugged in her laptop. No sense in draining the battery if she didn't have to. Louis glanced over when she returned, but he kept working on his own computer, fingers flying at a remarkable speed. The vampires were all happy to let her do the grunt work of wading through photos, trying to figure out who was who. That was okay with her, as long as they let her do *something*. Pulling up her database, she scanned the information and sorted out the fields she thought would help.

Part of Emma's job at Guy Coffer's office had been filtering the daily requests from lobbyists who wanted to see the Congressman about one thing or another. Sometimes, they wanted a face-to-face, sometimes they only wanted to invite him to a cocktail party or other glad-handing social event. The thing was, there were something like eleven thousand lobbyists in Washington, D.C., and every one of them thought their particular issue was *the* most important thing on the planet. She didn't fault them for that; it was their job to feel that way. But Congressman Coffer sat on a couple of very influential committees whose influence went beyond any one issue. And that meant a whole lot of lobbyists were after his vote. Emma's job was to weed through the requests and provide a daily report as to who wanted what and whether they were worth the Congressman's time. The deciding factor was usually money in the form of campaign donations, but since she was a government employee, her time couldn't be used for any fundraising purpose. So her reports had to be couched in other terms, like importance to a particular constituency or public awareness of an important issue. It was all bullshit. But money won elections, and publicity provided sound bites so the people back home felt like their congressman was doing something once they elected him.

Emma, being the hyperactive Energizer Bunny she was, had built up a database of information on the various lobbyists—names, affiliations, contact info—along with information on the assistants and secretaries she dealt with at least as often as their bosses. She pulled up the list of initials they had from Victor's files and started working, trying to match them with her various contacts. It took far longer than she expected and was ultimately disappointing. There were too many women with the same initials, and no way of sorting them by likelihood. If she'd had marital status in her database, for example, she could have eliminated the married women, at least on the first cut. Some of them, she knew, were too old to match any of the photographed women, but for most she had no idea if they were the ones she was looking for or not.

"Emma," Louis said from behind her.

She straightened and turned around, rubbing her back, which had gone stiff from sitting hunched over the computer.

A woman stood next to Louis. She was petite, with a wild mane of curly dark hair, and she had to be a vampire. Either that or Duncan was employing teenagers now, because this woman looked about nineteen in her tight, faded jeans and bright red sweater.

"Emma, this is Phoebe Micheletti. She's the one I told you about, with the FBI."

Okay, definitely a vampire. But it was kind of unsettling to know the FBI had vampires working for them. The conspiracy theorists would go nuts if they knew!

"Former FBI, and only a consultant," Micheletti corrected, and smiled as she held out her hand.

Emma stood, automatically taking Micheletti's hand, feeling the strength in those delicate fingers. "Emma Duquet," she said. "Louis mentioned you'd be coming by."

"And here I am." She made a shooing motion at Louis and said, "Run along, Louis, I'll take it from here."

Emma blinked, waiting for Louis to react to the female vamp's dismissal, but he laughed. "You can't have her, Pheebs. If Emma wants a job, Duncan has first dibs."

"I have no idea what you're talking about," Phoebe said innocently.

Louis gave her a skeptical look, but strode back to his computers.

Phoebe continued to watch as Louis sat down and bent to work once again. "He's one of the best hackers alive, you know. I tried to recruit him for my firm, but he's Duncan's down to the bone." She looked at Emma. "If Louis wants you, you must be good."

Emma shrugged uncomfortably. "I haven't done anything yet. I think he's just happy someone else is doing the grunt work."

Phoebe had been reading over Emma's shoulder, her eyes switching between Emma's computer with its database and the list of initials. "What's this?"

"It's my own database of lobbyists and their affiliates. I work for Congressman Coffer."

"Ah," Phoebe said. "That explains it. Louis is a compulsive collector of information. He has database envy."

Emma laughed. "It hasn't done me much good yet. I never thought I'd say this, but there's too much information."

"No luck, then?" Phoebe murmured, sitting on the chair next to Emma's and paging through her notes. The action irritated Emma for some reason. Those were *her* notes. The female vamp could have at least *asked* before she started snooping through them.

She realized Phoebe was waiting for her to say something. "No luck," she said, remembering the question. "Not yet. But I'm still working."

"How about the men?"

"Louis said you were working on that."

"I am," Phoebe said, flashing a smile. "But like you, I haven't had any luck yet. You have what, hundreds of entries in your database?"

"Thousands," Emma corrected, feeling insulted and fighting the urge to snatch her database away from the *former* FBI consultant. Hundreds of entries, indeed. And was there any such thing as a former FBI consultant? She wasn't sure she wanted anyone in government seeing the information on her computer, much less the FBI. Forget that she herself worked for the government. It wasn't the same thing at all.

"Thousands," Phoebe allowed. "But there are millions in our facial recognition database, and as brilliant as Louis is, those composites were . . ." She shrugged without finishing her thought, but it was obvious she didn't think they were very useful.

Emma sat back down at her computer, feeling an irrational need to defend her methods. "I was thinking about this before you came in. If I could identify even one of these women, it would lead to the rest of them."

"How do you figure that?"

"Because they all know each other. They all go to the same parties, and I'm not only talking about Victor's. The people who work inside the Beltway are like a small town. Everyone knows everyone, or knows someone who does."

"So, maybe we go to a few of those parties ourselves," Phoebe mused. "You can get us in?"

"Sure. I get invitations every day in the Congressman's office. It's just a matter of picking the—" She froze as a thought occurred to her. "The women all knew each other which means they probably all knew Lacey, too. Lacey's funeral," she finished on a whisper.

"Pardon?"

"Lacey's funeral," she repeated more certainly. "There were so many people there, but I only knew a few of them because they were all *Lacey's* friends."

"But you have the pictures from Victor's files. Wouldn't you remember if any of these women had been there?"

"No," Emma said. "I was pretty much in shock that whole night. If not for Duncan, I don't know what I would have done. I don't remember anyone, *damnit*." She thought furiously. "Wait, there was a—"

"Glen Pettry handled the funeral?" Phoebe interrupted.

"Yes, he was the one who told me—" She stopped speaking because Phoebe had pulled a cell phone out of her pocket and was already punching in a number.

"Glen," she said pleasantly. "Phoebe Micheletti. How are you? He's good, grumpy as ever. Listen, do you have security cameras at your place? No. I understand. It's something we're working on, but we'll figure it out. Thanks anyway."

She clicked her phone off and dropped it into her pocket. "No joy. He has video, but only at the back entrance where the bodies come in because they arrive at all hours. The front entrance is more sensitive. No one wants to think they're being recorded at Aunt Tessie's funeral, and the funeral home's in a good neighborhood. Besides, Glen does a lot of business with vampires, and none of us want a record of our comings and goings."

Emma remained silent. There was another way of identifying who'd been at the funeral, but she wasn't inclined to share it. She'd already decided she didn't want to work with the pushy vampire anymore than she had to.

"It was a good thought, though," Phoebe said. She stood and looked around. "Listen, if you do find these women, you need to let me deal with them."

"I think I should call—"

"I'm not trying to steal your thunder, Emma," she interrupted. "We're all after the same thing. Besides, Duncan wants you safe, and he's pretty bossy. He'll want one of us to follow up if you get a lead, and I can get a lot more information out of those women than you can."

"I wouldn't be too sure—"

"It's likely Victor messed with their memories," Phoebe interrupted again. "No matter how persuasive or sympathetic you are, they can't tell you what they don't remember. I'll be able to undo whatever Victor did and help them recall things they don't even realize they know."

Emma frowned. "If you say so," she agreed flatly.

Phoebe laughed again. "You haven't been around us long enough yet, but you'll be a believer soon enough. All right, I'm out of here. It's a long way home for me. Louis has my number if you come up with anything, and I'll let you know if we get any hits on the facial recognition." She smiled and patted Emma's shoulder. "Don't look so discouraged, Emma. It always starts this way."

She pushed her chair back into the table and looked over to where Louis was typing furiously. "Louis," she called, waiting until he looked up, his expression a little vague, as if not quite in the now with the rest of them. "I'm out of here. I'll call if anything pops." He nodded and went immediately back to whatever he was doing, slapping away the hand of another vampire sitting next to him.

Phoebe smiled. "Chin up, Em," she said. "I'll be in touch."

Emma watched her go with a sour look. "Chin up, Em," she mimicked. She *hated* being called Em.

She waited until the annoying vampire was gone, even sticking her head into the hallway to be absolutely sure. And then she picked up her own phone and scrolled through the numbers. Pettry's was right on top since she'd called him more than anyone else in the last few days. He answered after the second ring.

"Mister Pettry," she said, "it's Emma Duquet."

"Ms. Duquet," he said warmly. "How can I help you?"

She noticed he didn't ask her how she was. That particular social convention probably didn't work well in his business, since pretty much everyone he dealt with was miserable or they wouldn't be calling him.

"There was a mourner's book for Lacey's funeral, wasn't there?"

"Yes, of course. I'm sorry I didn't give it to you, but you left rather suddenly, and there were still a few visitors for Ms. Cray—"

"That's fine, Mister Pettry. I understand. Thank you for keeping it for me. I am sort of anxious to get a hold of it now, though. Do you suppose I could pick it up?"

"Certainly. At your convenience," Pettry said.

"I know it's late." She glanced at her watch. "Very late," she amended. "And it's asking a lot, but I really need that book. Do you think I could pick it up tonight?" She felt guilty even asking, but if Pettry did a lot of business with vampires, he must be used to having customers drop by in the middle of the night. And sure enough, her request didn't even faze him.

"Certainly, I'm here quite late every night. Just come around back and ring the bell."

"Thank you, Mister Pettry, and thank you again for all your kindness during Lacey's service."

"I was pleased to be of assistance during this difficult time."

Emma disconnected. "Louis, I need to run an errand," she said, already gathering her things.

Louis jumped up and came over. "Where are you going?"

"The funeral home. I need to pick up the mourner's book. I think it'll help with this." She indicated her scattered notes.

"That's not necessary. I'll send one of our guys to pick it up for you."

"No, thank you," Emma said pleasantly, unplugging her laptop and tucking it under her arm. "I'd rather do it myself, and I'll go straight home after that. I need to get up early tomorrow."

"Duncan won't want you doing that."

"Good thing Duncan's not my boss, then," she said matter-of-factly.

Emma picked up her notes and left before Louis could argue with her any further, stopping only long enough to gather her things from the frilly bedroom before heading downstairs. She glanced at her watch again, nearly groaning at the late hour. By the time she got out to Pettry's and back home again, it would be another night without much sleep. But a few cups of coffee would take care of that in the morning, and she figured she could sneak in some research in the office.

With the gym bag in one hand and her laptop back in the purse slung over her shoulder, she headed out to her car, only to find Baldwin waiting for her. He was a good-looking guy, or vampire. Shorter than

she was by an inch or so, but he had scruffy dark hair, a five o'clock
shadow and probably outweighed her by fifty pounds, all of it muscle.
He straightened as she came down the front stairs and immediately
reached for her bags.

"I'll take you home, Emma."

"I've got my car. Thanks."

"Then I'll follow you."

Emma stopped and regarded him curiously. "Why?"

He shrugged. "Boss's orders."

"Am I in danger?"

He grinned. "Not with me around."

Emma grinned back and informed him cheerfully, "I'm not going
straight home. I need to stop at Pettry's Funeral Home outside Falls
Church."

"That's not a stop, that's a detour. We'll drop off your car first."

Emma shrugged. She didn't feel like fighting, and besides, it was a
long drive. "Whatever you say."

He carried her bags to her car, waiting while she got settled behind
the wheel, raising his eyebrows pointedly when she didn't immediately
fasten her seatbelt.

"Geez, Baldwin, you're like a mother hen."

"I like my job, Emma. I don't want anything happening to you on
my watch." He closed her door and sped back to his SUV, then tailed
her through the front gate and onto the street.

It was a short and uneventful journey back to her house. She didn't
live that far away in simple distance. It was traffic and street closures
for the constant VIP convoys that made the trip longer during the day
and evening. But this late at night, the streets were nearly empty. There
were parties going on, but not in her part of town, so once they left
Duncan's neighborhood, there wasn't even that to consider.

But when they got to her house, there was nowhere to park. With
the end of winter, the street sweepers were back and everyone had
moved their cars to one side of the street for the next morning's cleaning.
She had to park a block over and two blocks down, and even then the
space was barely large enough for her car. Good thing she was a good
parallel parker.

Baldwin pulled up next to her and reached across to open the
passenger door on his SUV. "Get in," he called.

Emma grabbed her bags, tossed them into the SUV's backseat,
and climbed in, gazing around happily. She liked riding in big trucks.
She would have bought one for herself, but it wasn't practical in D.C.
Maybe someday she'd have a house in Virginia or Maryland, and she'd
have two vehicles—a practical sedan for the ride into work, and a big
ass SUV like this one for zooming around the countryside on weekends.
She smiled, liking the idea.

"What're you smiling at?" Baldwin asked.

"I like your truck."

"Not my truck. I'm only the driver."

"Well, I like it anyway."

"I'd let you drive, but Duncan wouldn't like it."

"Why not? I'm a good driver."

"Yeah, but what about the other guy? My reflexes are faster than yours."

As it turned out, Baldwin's reflexes were good for more than avoiding accidents. He drove like a bat out of hell, switching lanes and zooming into tight spaces that had Emma reaching down to check her seatbelt more than once. But they made terrific time, getting there much faster than she would have on her own.

Pettry was busy when she arrived—she didn't want to inquire doing what this late at night—but he'd left a maroon, linen-covered box for her that held a similarly covered bound book with the words *In Loving Memory* gold-stamped on the front. Tears sprang to her eyes, and she closed the box quickly. This was going to be harder than she thought.

"Is that everything, Emma?" Baldwin asked quietly.

She nodded, not trusting her voice.

"Come on, sweetheart. Let's get you out of here."

Emma clutched the box to her chest and followed the vampire back to the truck. He helped her up onto the high bench seat, not saying anything when she refused to let go of the box.

The drive back was just as fast, but much quieter. Emma was tired. She'd been going all day, and it was nearly one o'clock in the morning. She might even have dozed off a bit, because suddenly they were in front of her house. Emma blinked, then straightened and reached for her door handle, still clutching the memory book to her chest.

"Wait," Baldwin said. He double-parked, turned off the engine and climbed out of the truck, circling around to her side to open her door. "Get your keys out," he ordered.

Emma didn't argue. She handed him the book, then twisted around to the backseat and shoved a hand into the zipper compartment on her bag. She dug out her keys and raised her hand, jingling them in the air where he could see them.

"Okay," he said and held out a hand to help her down. He gave the book back to her. "Give me a minute to get your other stuff."

He closed her door and had reached for the back door of the SUV when his phone rang. He raised a finger, telling her to wait, and answered the phone. Emma could only hear his half of the conversation, but it was obviously one of the other vamps looking for something at the house. Everything was such a mess there. She didn't know how they kept track of it all. Baldwin tucked the phone between his chin and shoulder and opened the truck door. Emma shivered. There was a slight wind, and she was cold, despite her warm jacket. With a glance at Baldwin, who was reaching across the backseat, she went ahead and climbed the stairs to her house, thinking about nothing but getting inside and into her warm bed.

She slipped the key in the lock and pushed the door open. She heard Baldwin call, "Emma, wait!" And then several things happened all at once.

The shadows of her living room belched forth a big man, his eyes twin ovals of white in a dark-bearded face, his hands hard as he closed the few feet between them and grabbed her arm with one hand, while the other closed over her mouth.

In the same instant, her front door crashed open to slam against the wall, and Baldwin was there, twisting her away from the stranger and stepping between them so quickly that Emma stumbled and nearly fell. The man squawked as Baldwin's hand closed on his throat.

A gunshot rang out, and then another, startlingly loud in the confines of her small house. Baldwin grunted, staggered through the open doorway, and literally threw the invader away from the house, sending him flying past the SUV and into the street. The attacker shrieked, the sound cut off abruptly when he hit the hard pavement and rolled into the opposite gutter.

"Emma," Baldwin rasped urgently.

She spun toward Baldwin, struck by something in his voice. He was slouched over, barely standing, one hand clutching his chest where . . . "Oh my God, you're bleeding! Are you shot?" She grabbed him before he could fall over, slipping her shoulder under his arm and puffing out a gasp of air as his full weight fell on her all at once. With her arm around his waist, she gripped him tightly and all but dragged him out of the doorway and into the living room. She tried to get him to the couch, but he pushed away from her and dropped to the floor with a moan of pain, rolling over onto his back and staring up at her.

"Computer," he wheezed. "Get your bags in here."

"My—" Her eyes widened, and she raced back to the open SUV, grabbing her gym bag and purse with the laptop inside. She closed the truck door, then lugged her bags into the house, and slammed and locked that door, as well. Taking her phone from the table, she rushed over to Baldwin, falling to her knees next to him.

"Should I call nine-one-one? Do you need an ambulance?"

"Miguel," he whispered. "My phone."

Emma nodded as the blood in her body finally started routing to her brain once more and she could think clearly. Of course. Baldwin was a vampire. He wouldn't want the usual medical help. She put her phone aside. "Is your phone in the truck?"

"Pocket."

Emma looked down. He was wearing jeans and a pullover hoodie which was soaked with blood. She clenched her jaw, determined not to fall apart. Baldwin needed her. She patted his pockets rapidly, ignoring the blood, and found the phone tucked into the kangaroo pocket of his hoodie. She lifted it so Baldwin could see.

"Okay," she asked. "How do I get Miguel?"

"One," Baldwin managed.

Emma did a quick survey of the phone and hit the first speed dial. It rang twice, and then an angry voice said, "What is it?"

"Baldwin's been shot," she said urgently. "Twice, I think. He's bleeding—"

"Who is—"

"Emma. You've got to hurry."

"Where are you now?"

"My house. Should I call an ambulance or—"

"No. No! Don't call anyone. We're on our way. Five minutes."

Miguel, or at least she thought it was Miguel, hung up, and Emma scooted closer to Baldwin. Yanking her grandmama's afghan off the couch, she tucked it around him, then leaned forward, trying to share the warmth of her body, the comfort of her presence.

"Hang in there, Baldwin. Miguel's on the way."

But Emma was worried. He didn't look good. She didn't know much about vampire physiology, but she figured any creature with blood couldn't afford to lose too much of it, and he was losing a lot. His eyes were closed, his chest barely moved when he breathed, and . . .

"Baldwin?" she said urgently. No response.

She tightened her arms around him and started counting the seconds, waiting for each new breath, holding her own and hoping help arrived soon.

* * * *

The slamming of heavy car doors, loud in the night, alerted her. Her head came up. She had time to remember that her door was locked and they couldn't get in, and then they burst into the house, breaking through the lock as if it was made of paper. Miguel was first, and Emma knew it was because he didn't trust her enough to send Duncan into an unknown situation on her word alone. And then Duncan was there, his eyes meeting hers, holding her gaze briefly before doing a quick scan of her body and back up again, as if to make certain she was okay.

Ari came in last. He closed the door and pulled the hall table in front of it. It wasn't a heavy table, but at least it held the door closed.

Miguel dropped to the floor, lifting away the afghan and tearing open Baldwin's clothes so he could see the vampire's chest. Emma moved aside, pulling the rest of the afghan with her.

"Emma." Duncan's voice was steady and reassuring, calm despite the obvious crisis. She looked into his warm brown eyes, hoping to see something that would tell her Baldwin would be okay.

"I need you to move," he said gently. "Baldwin needs me."

She realized he'd taken off the tuxedo jacket he'd been wearing and was rolling up the sleeve of his white shirt. She scooted back, then stood, wanting to be out of the way, but also wanting to know what they were going to do. Why was Duncan baring his arms? If there was surgery to be done, wouldn't Miguel be the one—

Her thoughts stuttered to a halt when Duncan produced a small, sharp knife and sliced into his forearm. Emma had never been one to faint, and she wasn't about to start now. But she'd never seen a man cut open his own arm either, and it made her feel queasy. She leaned against the wall, but her gaze was riveted on the blood welling from Duncan's arm, an arm he now placed . . . Oh, of course. Baldwin needed blood to replace what he'd lost, just like a regular human would. The difference was he could suck it through his fangs instead of needing an IV. Okay, no surprise there.

She drew a deep breath, and then held it, her eyes growing wide, as Miguel took the knife from Duncan and cut into Baldwin's chest. There was so much blood already that it hardly mattered, but it still made her lightheaded if she thought too much about actually sticking a knife into a man's chest and slicing him open like that. She shuddered and closed her eyes against the sight.

"Miguel needs to get the bullet out," Duncan explained calmly. She opened her eyes and found him glancing back at her. His arm was still latched over Baldwin's mouth and the vampire was sucking noisily on it like a child with a pacifier. "It would work its way out by itself," Duncan continued, "but it's very close to his heart and we don't want to take that risk. The healing will also go much faster with it gone."

Emma swallowed and took a careful step closer, curiosity winning out over squeamishness. She had a million questions she wanted to ask, but didn't want to disturb Miguel's concentration.

Duncan glanced back again and gave her a quick smile of approval that made her warm all over. Her reaction irritated her because she didn't need anyone's approval, but she couldn't deny the way he made her feel either. She sighed inwardly and saw a smile cross Duncan's face. Since she knew he couldn't be smiling at Baldwin's open chest, it had to be something she'd done. Which irritated her all over again.

"The bullet has damaged his lung," Duncan explained, focusing his gaze on the ongoing surgery. "But my blood can heal that. The heart is another matter. Too much damage can be fatal."

Miguel's gaze shot up to Duncan almost unwillingly, as if he was too shocked to control his reaction, and then his attention went right back down to the operation he was performing. Interesting. Maybe vampires didn't like to reveal the vulnerability Duncan had just admitted to her.

Suddenly Miguel stopped cutting and dug his fingers into Baldwin's chest, eventually coming up with a bloody bullet. Ari squatted down next to him and held out a hand for the slug, waiting until Miguel fished around and came up with a second one before wrapping them both in a piece of cloth and tucking them into his pocket.

"Do you have a first aid kit?" Miguel muttered without looking up.

"Yes," Emma said quickly. She ran into the kitchen, dropping the afghan on the washing machine. She'd have to soak it or the blood would never come out. She reached up to the cupboard over the machine and drew down the metal lunchbox-shaped first aid kit she'd put together when they first moved in. She hurried back and knelt next to Miguel, placing the open kit between them.

"What do you need?" she asked with some pride. She'd never used the kit before, but it was fully stocked.

"Antibiotic spray if you have it, liquid if you don't."

She popped the top and handed him a fresh spray bottle of Bactine, thinking it would numb the pain, too. But then she glanced down at the gaping hole in Baldwin's chest and decided it would need a whole caseload of Bactine to numb it. Besides, Baldwin didn't seem to be in any pain. He was sucking happily on Duncan's arm, eyes closed, his expression showing no stress. He hadn't even groaned once, now that she thought about it.

"Can he still get infected?" she asked curiously, watching. "I mean if Duncan's blood can heal all of this, can't it heal infection, too?"

"Yes, it can," Duncan replied. "Vampires in general are almost completely resistant to all types of infection. But with a wound this size, if we minimize the contamination, that's one less problem his vampire physiology will need to deal with and the wound will heal more quickly."

Miguel sprayed thoroughly, then handed the bottle back to her. "Bandages," he said. "Big gauze pads or gauze wrap of some kind."

"I have both," she said immediately, knowing exactly what was in her kit.

Duncan and Miguel both gave her an odd look, probably wondering why a congressional legislative analyst would need such a complete first aid kit, and she obviously didn't. But when it had come time to buy one, the ready-made kits had seemed so puny that she'd made her own and prepared for the worst. And maybe went a little overboard.

She unwrapped several large nonstick gauze pads and handed them to Miguel.

"Tape," he said, not even bothering to ask if she had it. "Cut me several pieces, eight or nine inches long."

Emma nodded and began cutting tape, glad she'd gone for the full size scissors instead of those crappy things that came in the regular kits. As she and Miguel taped up Baldwin's chest, Duncan finally pulled his wrist away from the vampire's mouth. Ari whipped out a clean white handkerchief and handed it to Duncan.

"Do you need a bandage, too?" she asked, giving Duncan an inquiring look.

He smiled. "No, thank you, Emma."

She frowned, her eyes going wide as he wiped the blood from his wrist and she could see that it had already begun to heal.

"Tape!" Miguel snarled.

She jumped, muttering, "Sorry," before handing him the next piece of tape.

"All right," Miguel said finally, sitting back on his heels. "That'll do it."

Duncan ran a comforting hand over Baldwin's forehead, brushing back his hair.

"Ari," he said, "Get Baldwin back to the house. Miguel and I will follow with Emma."

"My lord," Ari acknowledged. He and Miguel lifted Baldwin carefully and took him out to the car, Miguel shoving the table aside while Ari carried him through the door.

"Emma," Duncan said.

They were both still sitting on the floor, and she looked up from where she'd been repacking her first aid kit.

"Tell me what happened," he said.

Her eyes filled with inexplicable tears, as if now that the crisis was over, her body was giving her permission to react. She rubbed a hand over her eyes tiredly, brushing the tears away. "There was a man waiting for us, for me. He was already in the house when I opened the door. Baldwin was getting stuff out of the car and he told me to wait, but I was so cold. He, the attacker, I mean . . . he came at me the minute I opened the door, and he must have thought I was alone. But Baldwin . . ." Her eyes widened suddenly. "Is he still there? In the street? Baldwin threw him—"

She stopped talking because Duncan was up and out the door. She heard voices and ran over to the doorway to see what was happening. Ari was already driving away, but Duncan and Miguel were hunched over something in the street. Miguel stood, and she realized he was carrying her attacker over his shoulder. They walked over to a big, black SUV. Duncan pulled the hatch open and Miguel threw the man into the back, then reached in and did something to him. The man made no noise through all of this.

Miguel closed the hatch quietly and Duncan came back inside.

"Is he dead?" Emma asked.

"No," Duncan said. "But he may soon wish he was. Put your things together, Emmaline. You're coming back to the house with us.

It's not safe for you here."

Emma gave him a narrow look. "I'll be fine," she said. "I have to work in the morning."

"Then you can leave from my house," Duncan said evenly.

"I'd rather stay here. All of my things are here."

"Then bring your things with you," he said deliberately. "You are not staying here alone."

"I *am* staying here," she insisted. The truth was if he had *asked* her, she would have agreed to go with him, because she really *didn't* want to stay here all alone, not when some new gun-toting asshole might show up at any minute. But he hadn't asked, had he?

"Emma," Duncan snapped. "Someone broke into this house and nearly killed Baldwin. You're being unreasonable."

"So I'll go to a hotel." She saw a flash of hurt in his eyes, and her stubbornness drained away. "Fine," she snapped in turn. "I'll go with you. But you have to stop ordering me around, *damnit*."

"I'll remember that," Duncan muttered. "Where are you going?" he asked as she started past him toward the stairs.

"I'm going to pack my things," she said impatiently.

"Oh." He smiled, and she couldn't help it. She smiled back. "I'll help."

"I really don't need—" But he was already past her and up the stairs, heading for her bedroom.

"Wait," she called, racing after him. She came around the corner as he was reaching for her top drawer.

"Stop," she said and hurried across the room. "I'll pack myself, thank you."

"What's in the drawer?" he asked innocently, but his eyes were dancing.

Emma regarded him carefully. "You're trying to distract me."

He gave her a puzzled look.

"You're worried I'm going to freak out about what happened and you're trying to distract me by threatening to play with my underwear."

His eyebrows shot up. "Is that what's in here?"

"Yes, it is, and you're avoiding the issue."

The grin vanished. He was suddenly perfectly serious as he reached out and rubbed his knuckles down her cheek. "You could have been killed."

Her chest tightened with emotion, her heart racing faster than it had all night. "I didn't even see the gun. I just heard it when—"

Duncan closed his eyes briefly, as if the thought of that bothered him even more. He pulled her gently into his arms. "Are you all right, Emmaline? Really?"

She put her arms around his waist and held on, relishing the feel of his big body surrounding her, feeling safe and secure again. She nodded against his shoulder. "I wasn't hurt. Baldwin saved me."

"I'm glad," he murmured, his hand rubbing up and down her spine in a comforting rhythm.

Emma could have stayed there all night, but Duncan touched his lips to her hair and said, "Pack enough for several days. It's not safe for you here until we find out who was behind this."

She nodded and stepped back reluctantly. "I won't take long," she said without looking at him.

He put a finger under her chin and lifted her face. "Take as long as you want," he said seriously, then gave her a sly look. "Are you sure you don't want help with that drawer?"

Emma chuckled weakly. "No, I can handle it."

"Then I'll be downstairs. I have to talk to Miguel. Let me know when you're ready and we'll help with the bags."

* * * *

Duncan was controlled fury as he strode down the front steps of Emma's house and over to the SUV where Miguel waited with the dead man. Of course, the human wasn't dead *yet*, but he would be. As soon as he told them everything he knew.

"Sire," Miguel said formally as Duncan approached.

"Did Ari check in?"

"Yes, my lord. He just arrived at the house. Baldwin woke up when they carried him inside. He's not happy, but he's well."

"Good." Duncan glanced through the back window at the unconscious human. "If he'd wanted to kill her, he had the chance."

Miguel nodded. "Maybe he was only supposed to scare her. Or maybe he had a message that he never got to deliver because Baldwin was there."

"If there's a message, we'll know it," Duncan said darkly.

"If they know she's working with us, my lord., they'll come after her."

Duncan's rage soared and he fought to keep it from showing, but Miguel was aware of it anyway. He could tell from the watchful look on his lieutenant's face, the careful formality. The idea of anyone laying hands on Emma made him want to rip out the throats of every human in Victor's files, whether or not they'd had a hand in Lacey's death. None of them were innocent, as far as he was concerned.

He forced himself to think calmly, something he found increasingly difficult when it came to Emma Duquet. But he couldn't afford to run around killing humans, whatever the reason. That was the very opposite of why he was in this corrupt city in the first place. Not that the men responsible for Lacey's death would be permitted to live. Oh, no. They were all going to die. Maybe not tonight, maybe not even soon. But eventually. And he would make sure they knew it, too. Every one of them would live the last few months of his life looking over his shoulder, waiting for death to find him.

The thought pleased him and he smiled slightly. "Have someone set up a secure room at the house for the prisoner for when we get there," he said gesturing at the truck. "Somewhere far from where Emma will be sleeping. The basement. Comfort isn't important. And brief the daylight guards, as well. I don't want a bungled rescue drawing in the human police, and I don't want him killed under our noses, either."

"Yes, my lord."

They both turned when Emma appeared in her doorway, lugging a suitcase and carrying a garment bag over one shoulder.

"Emma," Duncan said impatiently. "Let us help with that."

She pushed the suitcase in his direction. "You take that and I'll—"

He lifted the suitcase and whipped the garment bag from her shoulder, handing them both to Miguel.

"Okaaay," she drawled. "What do I do about this door?"

Duncan frowned, then studied the doorframe. "The lock is broken, but the frame is sound. I don't suppose you have a hammer and nails . . ." His voice trailed off as Emma disappeared back inside her house. "Of course, you do," he amended.

She reappeared with the requested items and a smug grin.

"Nobody likes a know-it-all," he teased as she strolled past him.

"Oh, I don't know it all," she replied breezily. "I'm just prepared for it all."

Duncan laughed and picked up a hammer for the first time in more years than he could count.

* * * *

Emma sat inside the warm SUV and watched as Duncan nailed her front door shut. It wasn't every day she saw a man in a tuxedo wielding a hammer. Of course, it wasn't every day some wacko tried to assault her in her home. Except that maybe the guy hadn't been a wacko. In a weird way, it would be reassuring if Lacey's killers *had* sent someone after her. It would mean she was on the right track.

She frowned. But, if that was the case, why didn't he kill her outright? He could have. Maybe he'd planned something else entirely for her. Duncan and his vamps hadn't let her see all the details of what had gone on at Victor's so-called parties—they were protecting her, which was infuriating in its own way—but she had a good sense from what they *had* let her see, and the things she'd overheard. It broke her heart to think of Lacey involved in all of that, and she shuddered for herself, thankful that Baldwin had been there tonight.

Duncan dropped the tools on the floor of the front seat, then joined Emma in the back. Miguel was driving since Ari had taken the smaller SUV with Baldwin in it. "We'll get a locksmith out here as soon as possible," Duncan said, as he closed the door. "I'll have one of my people meet him here."

"What if it's not until morning?" she asked. "I can—"

"I have human guards for daytime, Emma. They can handle it."

"My car's around the block," she said, raising her voice to include Miguel, so he'd know they had to stop. "Left here, then the next right," she added, then said to Duncan, "I have to go to work tomorrow, er, I mean this morning. I have meetings, besides—" She stopped herself, thinking it would probably be better if Duncan didn't know about her plans to continue tracking down the women from Victor's parties during the day tomorrow.

"Besides what?" Duncan asked, eyeing her curiously.

"I can't afford to lose my job," she said lamely. She blushed with the lie, but hoped he would assume she was embarrassed because of her implied money shortage. Besides, it really wasn't a lie. She couldn't afford to lose her job.

Duncan looked at her, his expression carefully blank, and she knew he sensed something was off. He couldn't know precisely what she was lying about, but she was pretty sure he knew she wasn't telling him the whole truth either.

When they reached her car, Emma started to jump out, but Duncan put a hand on her arm to delay her. "I'll ride with Emma, Miguel."

Up front, Miguel's head snapped up and he twisted around to give Duncan a sharp look.

"You can drive behind us," Duncan said. "It's not that far."

Miguel stared at Duncan for a heavy moment and then he nodded. "Yes, Sire," he said, the respectful words tight with anger.

Emma glanced at Duncan, hoping she wasn't going to get stuck between two angry vampires, but Duncan's expression was as calm and controlled as ever. He held Miguel's stare until the other vampire looked away, then he turned that cool gaze on her and gestured to the door. "If you would, Emma," he said.

Emma scrabbled for the door handle, shoved the door open and stepped out into the cold air. It should have been bracing after the warmth of the SUV, but she shivered, and exhaustion rolled over her like a thick blanket. God, she was tired. How long had it been since she'd slept? And she had to go to work in a few short hours, had to make it look as if she was moving on from Lacey's death, doing her job, maybe finding a smaller place to live. But certainly not spending her nights wide awake and searching for the killer, who might very well have an office in the next building, or even just down the hall.

Duncan's hand came over hers, slipping the keys from her numb fingers. "Get in the car. I'll drive."

"I can—"

"Of course, you can. But I'll drive anyway."

"Bossy," she muttered, stomping around to the passenger seat. "Phoebe said you'd be bossy."

"Yes, well—" He slid behind the wheel and started the car. "Phoebe isn't exactly a pushover herself."

Emma turned the heat on its highest setting, and Duncan immediately adjusted the vents in her direction.

"Is her husband a vampire, too?"

"No. Most vampire matings are with humans. Sharing blood is intensely sexual. I've seen one or two ménage à trois that worked, two vampires and one human, but that's rare."

Emma felt her own blood heat as she pictured Duncan's mouth on her neck, his upper body naked, gleaming with sweat the way he'd been in the gym earlier. She reached out and turned the heat down, unzipping her jacket.

Duncan glanced at her. "Too warm?"

"Yeah, I think—" She coughed slightly. "This heater starts slow, but once it gets going, it's a bit much."

Duncan's sinful mouth curved slightly, but he never took his eyes off the road.

What she wouldn't give to see him rattled, to break that ever-present cool of his. Just once. She didn't want anything awful to happen. She just wanted to shake him up a little and see what tumbled out. She had a passing thought, wondering if he was in control in bed the way he was everywhere else. And then her eyes went wide, shocked at her own thoughts. Obviously, she'd been working too hard for too long. All work and no play apparently made Emma a very horny girl. She swallowed a laugh, biting the inside of her cheek so the all-seeing Duncan wouldn't notice.

When they pulled through the gate of the vampires' big house, it was nearly four in the morning. Emma considered not even going to sleep, but there wasn't enough coffee in the city to keep her awake all night and all day, too.

They didn't park out front, but drove around to the back of the house. Several motion detector lights flooded the area as soon as they pulled into it, making it almost as bright as daylight. Vampire guards appeared out of the shadows, some of them whipping sunglasses on to shield their eyes. Miguel did the same, his eyes covered by nearly black wraparound lenses when he emerged from the SUV. He spoke to one of the other vampires, then strode over and opened the driver's door of her sedan, which looked small and tattered next to the line of gleaming SUVs.

"The prisoner will be secure in the basement, my lord," he said as Duncan slid out from behind the wheel. "Alaric has constructed a stockade."

"And enjoyed doing it, no doubt."

"Yes, my lord. He did comment that it had been years, and he hoped he remembered the proper ratio of bar tension."

"I want the prisoner alive, Miguel, not strangled to a slow death. Not until after I question him anyway."

Emma gave him a startled look. What *would* they do with their prisoner after they'd questioned him? The vampires seemed to avoid any contact with human police, but they couldn't just let the man go, either. She frowned. For that matter, what would they do with Lacey's killer when they found him—or them?

"What are you thinking, Emma?" Duncan asked, his voice right next to her ear.

She jumped, scowling at him. "We need to put a bell on you."

Duncan simply smiled and placed his hand at the small of her back, urging her toward the door. "You could try. I'd probably enjoy it . . . the trying part, that is." He opened the door and held it for her.

"So," he continued, as they walked through a large kitchen. "What had you frowning so?"

"You mean besides you?"

He nodded easily. "Besides me."

Emma considered making something up, but she really needed an answer on this one. "What will you do when we find them? The men who killed Lacey?"

They had reached the foyer below the stairs by then, and Duncan stopped, turning to face her. "It is the policy of the vampire community to work with the human police and authorities at all times," he said blandly. It sounded rehearsed and Emma knew she was hearing the party line.

She met his perfectly human-looking eyes. "I didn't ask what the policy was, Duncan. These are powerful men. If you turn them in to the authorities, they'll be back on the streets in hours not days. I want to know what you'll actually *do* when you catch them."

He studied her for a long moment, then said, "The interests of the vampire community always come first." She opened her mouth to demand he answer her question, but he forestalled her, saying, "There are some secrets we vampires never share. I have reason to believe Victor was . . . indiscreet, shall we say, with regard to certain of these secrets. Such knowledge, particularly in the hands of men such as these, represents a threat to my people, and I do not tolerate threats to my people."

Emma listened, hearing not just the words, but what he was trying to tell her. She nodded. "So you'll eliminate the threat," she said, wanting to be perfectly clear.

"Yes."

"I have no problem with that," she said firmly.

His brown eyes sparkled. "I am relieved."

Emma rolled her eyes, then gazed up in dismay at the many stairs between her and a comfortable bed.

"I could carry you," Duncan said seriously.

She smiled regretfully. "Thanks. But I have a feeling I'd never live it down."

"I wouldn't tell anyone," he said, placing a hand under her elbow and lending his considerable strength as they started up the stairs.

"I was talking about you."

Duncan laughed out loud, then swept her into his arms and raced up the stairs. Before she'd even caught her breath, they were in the bedroom she'd used earlier and he was setting her on the floor, sliding her down his body so she felt every inch of hard muscle in his chest, his thighs. She caught her breath. His muscles weren't the only thing that was hard about him.

Emma glanced up and found her gaze caught by the bronze glow of his eyes.

"Your eyes," she whispered, raising her hand to trace the curve of his brow. "They're glowing."

"They do that," Duncan murmured, his strong fingers flexing over her hips.

"But not all the time," Emma said softly.

"When I use my power," Duncan explained, one hand swooping almost to the curve of her ass as he tugged her closer. "Or when strong emotion comes into play."

"Emotion," Emma repeated softly, her fingers now playing along the softness of his mouth. "Like . . . desire?" She raised up and planted a quick kiss on his mouth. "Lust?" Another kiss. "Want?"

She again raised up, intending to give him another quick kiss, but he growled, holding her in place as he deepened the kiss into something hot and demanding. One hand rode up her back, his fingers twisting in her hair as he shifted the angle of their kiss, going deeper as his tongue delved into her mouth.

Emma moaned softly. He tasted of hot nights and dark secrets, though she couldn't have explained what that meant. She just knew it was true. She wanted more. She wanted to bite his lips, to taste more of him. She reached behind his head and tugged the tie off his blond hair, shoving her fingers into the warm thickness of it, scraping her nails along his scalp.

Duncan snarled against her mouth, and Emma felt something hard and sharp. Her heart raced as she realized what it had to be. Fangs. She ran her tongue along their slick smoothness, and Duncan's answering groan shivered through every cell of her body. Emma pushed harder, crushing her mouth against his. It was as if she couldn't get close enough, couldn't—" She felt a sharp prick on her tongue, tasted her own blood, warm and coppery.

Duncan's fingers clenched in her hair, holding her so tightly it brought tears to her eyes, but she didn't cry out, didn't move as his tongue swept over hers, licking up every last drop. His erection, already a long, hard presence against her belly, grew impossibly harder, straining against the clothing that separated them. Emma fisted a hand in Duncan's shirt when he broke their kiss, pulling him back to her with a small, hungry moan as she took his mouth once more.

"Emma," he murmured, then swore softly when she nipped his lower lip angrily. She didn't break the skin, but it had to hurt anyway.

"What?" she snapped, her body screaming at her to get him naked now!

"It's late," he said, his strong hands on her arms holding her away from his body when all she wanted to do was rub up against him like a cat.

"Late?" she repeated. "Late for what?" she demanded.

Duncan laughed, twisting away when she punched his gut in retaliation.

"Stop laughing and tell me what's going on, you stupid vamp—" Realization struck. "Oh."

Duncan rubbed his abdomen, as if her fist had actually done any damage to those rock hard muscles of his. He played it for all it was worth, though, until she rolled her eyes in mock disgust.

"So, how long is it until sunrise?" she asked, staring up at him and letting her desire show in her eyes.

Duncan groaned softly. "Don't look at me like that," he said. "This is hard enough."

Emma grinned wickedly at the probably unintended double entendre, but, of course, he knew what she was grinning at.

"You're bad," he said. He let his hands run down her back to cup her ass, pulling her close enough to feel precisely how hard it was. "Just over an hour," he murmured against her ear. "And Emmaline, my sweet, when I finally get to make love to you, I'm going to need much longer than that."

Emma was suddenly glad he was holding onto her, because the wave of lust she felt at those murmured words would have knocked her off her feet. This was so unfair.

"What are you—" Her voice broke and she coughed slightly. "What are you doing tomorrow? I mean at night?"

"I'll be here all night," he whispered, his breath warm against her skin as he kissed the tender spot just in front of her ear, then deposited a line of soft kisses over to her mouth.

Emma stretched upward, but he placed one final, hard kiss on her lips and stepped back. "You be careful today, Emma," he said seriously, brushing her hair behind her ear.

"Promise me."

"I will," she said breathlessly.

"Don't trust anyone," he continued, then pressed a chaste kiss against her forehead. "And you should get whatever sleep you can. You're going to need it later." He winked, then spun around and strolled out to the hall and away.

Emma stared at the empty doorway, her body thrumming with unmet need. "Dammit," she whispered, then reached out and closed the door firmly. The only lock was the one on the knob, which wouldn't keep out a vampire. But she didn't really expect anyone to disturb her. She glanced around the room restlessly, then checked her watch. If she went to sleep immediately, she could manage two hours at the most before she had to get up and go to work. But the odds of falling asleep right away were zero point zero thanks to a certain vampire. What was the male version of a cock tease anyway? She'd have to look that up later. For now she resigned herself to a caffeine fueled day and opened her suitcase.

* * * *

A few hours later, Emma was wearing her uniform of power suit and heels, strolling down the marbled halls of Washington. Well, okay, she wasn't actually strolling; that would have been too obvious. She hurried, just like everyone else did in this building, rushing about, sometimes with a pack of reporters and cameramen trailing after them, as if the fate of the world rested on their shoulders. She supposed sometimes that was true, but it was nowhere near as often as the politicians liked to think it was.

It was crowded this morning. Yet another congressional meeting on something earth shattering like baseball players using steroids. People starving all over the world, dying on battlefields, hacked to death by their neighbors, and the most pressing thing the leaders of the free world could think of was a bunch of big-headed, small-balled athletes using steroids. Who cared? Not Emma, although her male colleagues had insisted it mattered. She was just glad Congressman Coffer wasn't on any of the relevant committees. She didn't think she could have kept a straight face, or kept her mouth shut.

She desperately grabbed a cup of coffee on her way to her desk, and managed not to spill it while juggling her bag with the laptop and Lacey's memorial book inside. She'd left the box in her room at Duncan's. It was too bulky for even her giant purse.

She'd barely managed to take a few sips of precious caffeine and skim over the relevant files for the morning's meeting, when the Congressman's door opened and her colleagues jumped up to head into the office. Emma followed more slowly, marveling that only a few days ago, she would have been every bit as pumped up as the others about tomorrow's hearing. But this morning it was nothing but a distraction. What she wanted to do was sit down with her computer and follow up her new idea about how to identify the women from Victor's parties.

It was past noon when she had the chance, however. The meeting had run long, and then there'd been a pile of constituent requests for her to wade through. Most had been shuffled to other staff members right away, but a few had been of a more serious nature and she'd had to deal with them herself.

But finally the office was nearly empty, with everyone off to lunch somewhere. Washington took its lunches very seriously, seeing them as one more opportunity to court votes or raise money or sometimes just to have a couple of martinis and stop the shaking for an hour or two. Emma grabbed a leftover muffin from the morning. It was cranberry, the runt of the litter, crushed and disreputable looking, which was probably the only reason it was still there. She took it and yet another cup of coffee back to her desk, pulled up the list of women's initials from Victor's files and began going through Lacey's mourner's book looking for names. She was initially surprised at the number of people who had signed the book. She'd been in such a fog, and she'd had no idea that many people had come. Some had simply signed their names, but most had written at least a few words of condolence, and a very few had done more than that. It was an effort not to get lost in their remembrances as she read the words of people she didn't know, but who had known Lacey and would miss her. It reminded her of why she was reading the book at all, so she wiped away her tears and began searching the pages more methodically.

She was bent over trying to decipher some of the handwriting when a door opened and Guy Coffer's surprised voice said, "Emma?"

Emma jumped, nearly choking on a piece of muffin. She grabbed her coffee and took a long sip, thankful it had sat there long enough to be only warm.

"Congressman," she managed finally, coughing.

Coffer gave her a worried look, his hand outstretched, as if he was thinking about patting her on the back. "Are you okay?" he asked, concerned. "I didn't mean to startle you."

Emma took another sip of coffee and waved a hand dismissively. "I'm fine," she said, setting the cup down. She spun her chair around, bracing a hand on her desk and surreptitiously hitting the hot key on her laptop which would shut down her files.

"I didn't realize you were here," she said cautiously.

Coffer gave her his handsome politician's grin. "I walked through earlier. You were hard at work."

Emma was slightly alarmed by the idea that he could have passed by without her noticing. Then she glanced around and felt a new kind of worry. The phones were ringing almost constantly, as usual, and she could hear people in the outer office, but other than that she and Coffer were alone. If Sharon walked in right now, she'd stroke out, and maybe fire Emma. Shit.

"I'm sorry. I didn't hear you. Was there something—"

"Don't apologize. You're entitled to lunch just like the rest of us. I came out to get a cup of coffee."

"It's pretty low. Let me make some fresh." Emma closed the cover on her laptop and jumped up, hurrying over to the coffeemaker on the side cabinet. There was a bigger setup out front, but venturing to the outer office sometimes meant being ambushed by someone wanting something, so the analysts working in this part of the office tended to use this one. Everyone was supposed to do their part to keep the pot full, but as always, there were those who shirked the duty, thinking it beneath them. Emma wasn't one of those. She valued her coffee too much.

"What are you working on?" Coffer asked, glancing at the mourner's book which lay open on Emma's desk.

Emma forced herself to stay calm, waiting until she'd filled the coffeemaker and flipped the switch, before turning to face him. "That's the condolence book from Lacey's funeral," she told him, letting her real emotions flavor her words. "So many friends came to say good-bye to Lacey, people I didn't even know." She paused, glancing out the window, noticing the winter's accumulation of dirt on the glass.

"Were you and Lacey very close?" he asked, and his eyes were so sad that Emma stared at him for a moment before nodding.

"Lacey was like a sister to me. The only family I had."

"I'm sorry," he said.

Emma knew Coffer was a skilled politician, but he seemed so sincere that she couldn't help giving him a reassuring smile. "Everyone tells me it will get better with time. I'm not sure I believe that, but—"

"They're right, you know," he interrupted intently. "The day I learned my brother had died overseas was the worst day of my life. One moment he was here, and the next he was gone. The pain of losing him . . . it's still there, but not as much as it used to be. Sometimes I feel guilty about that, but I think it's the way our minds cope with such a terrible loss. Otherwise, we'd go mad."

Emma didn't know what to say. She was quite literally overwhelmed by his kindness. "Thank you," she managed. "That was very kind."

Coffer ducked his head, smiling. "I didn't mean to get so serious. If that coffee's ready—"

"Of course," Emma said, thankful for the break. Things had gotten a little too intense there for a moment. She fixed a cup for him, two sugars the way everyone knew he liked it. Just like everyone knew Sharon always made it with a sugar substitute instead.

"Thanks," he said, giving her a conspiratorial wink. "I'll get out of your hair now. Finish your . . ." He glanced around her at the remains of her muffin. "Muffin?" he said, then smiled and strolled back to his office.

Emma practically fell back into her chair, her nerves still jumping at the shock of having Coffer walk up on her like that. Sure, her desk was in the distant corner and when she was working, her back was to his office, but even so . . . She shook her head. She might make a great investigator—no, she *was* a great investigator. Give her a problem, she worked it like a dog with a bone. It was what made her a terrific legislative analyst, too. But apparently, she wasn't cut out for sneaking around. Shaking her head, she opened her computer and went back to work, making a point of angling her chair so her back wasn't entirely to the room. She didn't want any more surprise visitors.

She was actually down to the last few pages of condolences. She'd been so certain it would be the definitive data source, that all of the women would somehow magically appear within its pages. But so far, she had only one possible name, and that one was doubtful. Victor's files had listed a V.S. as one of his women, but the only matching entry in the book was a V. Slayton. No name, just the initial, and the handwriting gave her no clue as to whether it was a man or a woman. Discouraged, she turned to the last page and saw the name Tammy Dietrich. And Victor had a T.D. on his list. Her stomach tightened with excitement. Maybe she'd been right all along and this was the break she'd been looking for.

A cluster of voices sounded in the outer office, announcing the return of at least some of her colleagues. She closed the mourner's book, her fingers rubbing the soft cover thoughtfully. Ever since they'd found Lacey's body, she'd had this feeling that there was a big clock ticking away the seconds and very soon it would be too late. The powerful men involved were already working to cover their asses so thoroughly that no one would ever see those pale, white globes again. She wrinkled her nose at the image her own thoughts conjured up, but it was a halfhearted reaction. Because the truth of that thought was undeniable. They needed some progress on this investigation before the men responsible erased every hint of their involvement. Emma only needed to ID *one* of Victor's women, someone who'd been there, who could name names.

She didn't give herself any time to change her mind. She grabbed her notes, shoved her laptop into her purse and left the office before anyone who mattered was there to notice. She wanted to follow up on Tammy Dietrich and the V.S. person, too, and was pretty sure she knew someone who could help her.

She rushed out into the chilly afternoon of the Capitol parking lot, tugging her coat closed. Last year, it had been warm by this time of year. People had even complained about the mall's famous cherry blossoms peaking too soon. Not this year. She gave the gray sky a wary glance. It couldn't actually snow anymore, could it?

She unlocked her car and slipped inside gratefully, turning the heater on full blast. While she waited for the car's interior to warm up, she called Lacey's old office, breathing a sigh of relief when the voice that answered was one she knew well.

"Betty," Emma said. "It's Emma Duquet."

"Emma," Betty Napoli responded, her smoker's voice warm with sympathy. "How are you, hon?"

"Okay, I guess. It's been rough."

"Of course, child. We all miss Lacey. She was such a lively little thing."

"Thanks," Emma said quietly. "She was special."

"She sure was. How can I help you?"

"I'm writing thank you notes. You know, to the people who sent flowers, the ones at the memorial service, too. I have the book you all signed, but I don't know some of these people, and I thought maybe you—"

"Well, you know me, and I know everyone else. Who do you need?"

"Just two right now. A ..." she paused as if checking her list. "Tammy Dietrich? I think that's right. It's hard to read some of these signatures."

"Well, Tammy Dietrich I know right away. In fact, let me give you her address."

Emma scrambled to find a pen as Betty rattled off the office address of a law firm she'd never heard of. Not that this was a great surprise. Lawyers littered the capital like trash after a parade, and she ought to know since she was one of them.

"And what's the other?" Betty asked.

Emma had found a pen, gotten it to work and was trying to catch up with Betty's recitation of the address. "I'm sorry?" she said absently.

"The other name," Betty said patiently. "You said there were two."

"Oh, right. I'm sorry. The damn pen didn't work right away. Yes, the other one is something Slayton, I think. The first initial is V, as in . . . Victor."

"Slayton," Betty repeated thoughtfully. "Slayton. You know, I think she worked here for a bit. Only a month or two, which is why I'm not sure she's the one. I don't know that she and Lacey would have met, but . . . yes, here she is. Violet. That's a lovely name, isn't it?" Betty mused briefly. "Violet Slayton. I don't know where she went when she left here, though."

"Do you have a home address?" Emma inquired, knowing that even if Betty had it, she couldn't give it out.

"Well, now, I do. But you know how they are about things like that. I'll tell you what, though. We were talking, and I think she mentioned her family was from Springfield, Virginia. Had a place on Donset. We remarked on it, because I have some friends out that way. Might be a place to start."

Emma wrote down the city name and smiled. Without actually

telling her anything, Betty was saying that Violet Slayton was living with her parents in Springfield. With that plus the street name, she could find Slayton easily.

"Thanks, Betty," she said sincerely. "I really appreciate this."

"Well. It was a terrible thing what happened to Lacey. So young . . ." Her voice cracked a little and she sniffed discreetly. "You let me know if you need anything else, you hear, Emma?"

"I will," Emma said, feeling her own chest tighten with emotion. "Thanks again."

Not wanting to dwell on the reminder of how much she missed Lacey, Emma clicked off and immediately opened her laptop. Still sitting in the parking lot, she was close enough that she could access her office Wi-Fi. She checked out Tammy Dietrich first, because that was easiest. The address Betty had given her was in Alexandria, Virginia, but chances were Dietrich was a member of the D.C. bar, as well. Even Emma was licensed to practice in D.C., and she had no intention of ever standing before a court here. It was just something one did if working in or near the District, especially if one was as compulsively organized as Emma. If nothing else, it gave her access to things like the bar association membership directory, which came in handy at times like today. She typed in Dietrich's name. There was no picture, which wasn't that unusual. Emma didn't have one with her listing, either. There actually wasn't much information for Dietrich at all, just her law school alma mater, which was Georgetown, and the business address that Betty had already given her. Dietrich's was the only name listed for the firm, which probably meant she had a private practice, maybe with one or two other lawyers.

Still, the Alexandria address was very pricey. She was either doing very well for herself, or she came from money.

Emma called up a map and decided to at least drive by and check out Dietrich's office. Maybe she'd walk in and ask for directions, just to get a look around. Chances were that since she didn't know Dietrich, Dietrich didn't know her either. Besides, she probably wouldn't get past the front desk anyway.

Alexandria was close enough that under normal circumstances, it would have been faster to take a cab, or even the bus. But Emma still hoped to get out to Violet Slayton's house this afternoon, and she couldn't afford to waste the time it would take to track back to the Capitol parking lot for her car. She sighed. It was going to cost a fortune to park in Alexandria.

* * * *

Emma lucked out and caught a parking space a couple doors down from Dietrich's office. It was only a ten minute slot, but she already knew it wouldn't take any more time than that to check Tammy Dietrich off her list. For one thing, Dietrich was listed as a partner on the discreet plaque outside the door of the office building. Victor's taste in women for his parties leaned more toward secretaries than law partners. And for another, the law offices were located in an Old Alexandria brownstone, which screamed money and lots of it. This was almost certainly a dead-end, but since she was already here, she would check it out anyway.

The receptionist looked up when Emma approached the desk. The woman was maybe ten years older than Emma and dressed far better. She was doing her best to look down her nose, even though she was looking up through a pair of very traditional tortoiseshell glasses.

"Hi," Emma said, pretending to read the several pieces of paper she'd folded and now carried in her hand, as if for reference. "I'm supposed to meet some friends at . . ." she peered at the papers, "Waterfront Park, and I can't seem to—"

"It's on the water," the receptionist said frostily, with a heavy dose of *my God you're stupid* thrown in for good measure. "The water is *that* way," she added, pointing with one perfectly manicured finger in a direction that just happened to be out the office door.

Emma gave her a friendly smile. "Well, of course it is. Where's my brain this afternoon? You've been very kind," she added, although it wasn't true. Robots had more human kindness than this woman. But Emma didn't need any warm fuzzies. She'd already gotten what she came here for. On the wall behind the frigid receptionist's desk were professional portraits of Tammy Dietrich and her law partner. And Tammy Dietrich was most definitely *not* one of Victor's playthings. Emma didn't have names for the women in Victor's peep show videos, but she definitely had faces. And Dietrich wasn't one of them.

Emma didn't waste any more pleasantries on the unfriendly receptionist. She left the office and hurried back to her car with two minutes to spare on the meter. It hadn't been a total waste of time. She hadn't found one of the women on Victor's list, but at least she'd eliminated Dietrich. That was something. Not *much*, but something. And she still had Violet Slayton, who definitely *had* worked with Lacey.

Emma pulled her laptop over and piggybacked onto someone's unsecured Wi-Fi connection. She logged onto her office network and accessed a listing of households in the Springfield, Virginia area. Using Slayton's last name and the street name Betty had given her, she soon had the address of Violet Slayton's parents. She clicked over to her favorite map site, typed in the address, and scrutinized the directions. She nodded to herself. She could definitely get out there and back to Duncan's place before his one hour after sunset deadline.

She had a fleeting thought that Duncan wouldn't be too happy about her going to see Slayton without him. Especially after her armed intruder last night. But they didn't know for sure yet that the guy last night had anything to do with Victor. He might simply have been a burglar caught in the act. And, even if someone *was* keeping track of her investigations, they'd hardly be following her every move. She hadn't known herself that she'd be driving out to Virginia this afternoon, so how could anyone else know? Besides, Violet Slayton could turn out to be as big a dead end as Tammy Dietrich. The men responsible for Lacey's death were probably sitting back and laughing as Emma raced around, chasing shadows.

She sent the directions to Slayton's house to her cell phone, then started her car and pulled away only seconds ahead of the parking meter guy.

Chapter Nineteen

Violet Slayton was as nervous as a cat in a room full of rocking chairs, as Emma's Grandmama had been known to say. Slayton was pale and too thin, but Emma had the impression these were both recent developments. Her clothes were too big, and her skin had that parched look of someone who wasn't eating or hydrating properly. But none of that, not the clothes and not her pallor, could conceal the fact that she was beautiful. Her eyes were deep brown and luminous, surrounded by long, black lashes, and her dirty hair was thick and wavy. Violet reminded Emma of the women she'd met while doing an internship at a rape crisis center during law school. The thought of what could have made Violet react that way had Emma's blood running cold, and she knew she'd done the right thing by coming out here.

"I was sorry to hear about Lacey," Violet said, settling into the corner of a large, overstuffed couch. She spoke so quietly Emma had to lean closer to hear. It was as if Violet was afraid someone would overhear, even though Emma knew there was no one in the house but the two of them. Slayton hugged herself, wrapping her too big sweater nearly double around her body. "Lacey was a good person. Brave. I felt I had to go to the service, had to pay my respects, even though—" She stopped abruptly, and her beautiful eyes were filled with fear when they flashed up to stare at Emma.

"Even though what, Violet?" Emma asked gently.

Violet looked away. "I haven't seen anyone since I left the firm. I left kind of suddenly. I didn't give them proper notice, and they weren't happy with me. I didn't know if I'd see anyone I knew at the funeral. I didn't *want* to see anyone, but . . . Lacey was kind. I couldn't let them . . ." Her mouth tightened, her lips rolling under until they disappeared entirely.

"You said Lacey was brave," Emma said quietly. "Why would you say that?"

Violet stared down at her fingers, which played with a leather button on her sweater, rolling it first one way, then the next. "She wasn't afraid of anyone," she whispered. "It was as if she didn't believe the world could hurt her." Violet looked up suddenly, meeting Emma's gaze. "But she was wrong, wasn't she?"

Emma nodded, letting her own sorrow show. "Lacey was the only family I had," she said, without knowing why. "There's a place inside of me, right next to my heart, that hurts all the time since she's been gone. I don't think it will ever stop hurting, but I *know* it won't until I find out what really happened to Lacey."

Violet gave her a startled glance. "But I thought—" Realization bloomed in her eyes, and she lost what little color she had. "No," she whispered, shaking her head.

"You went to the parties with Lacey, didn't you, Violet?" Emma asked softly.

"I can't talk about this. I won't." Violet shook her head, once again refusing to look at Emma. "I don't remember anything anyway."

Emma watched the other woman, hating herself for being here, for forcing Violet Slayton to relive even the smallest part of whatever had happened to her. But those men were still out there. And they deserved to pay for what they'd done, to Lacey certainly, but to Violet and the others as well. And to some other woman in the future if they weren't stopped.

"Lacey was murdered," she told Violet bluntly, taking a huge chance. "I let everyone think it was a car accident because I don't trust the police to handle it. The men who killed her have too much money and power, and those things talk in this town."

Violet was staring at her again, shaking her head. "I can't help you. He did something so I wouldn't remember. It's the one decent . . ." She laughed bitterly and ran a hand back through her dirty hair. "As bad as this looks, it's better than the alternative."

"Are you having flashbacks?" Emma asked, remembering the rape victims she'd talked to back in college. "Nightmares? Bits and pieces of things that make no sense, but terrify you anyway?"

"Worse," Violet whispered. "It's worse *because* they make no sense. Sometimes I think if I could only put the pieces together and make sense of it all, it would finally go away. But then I'm afraid of what I'll discover if I ever get that far."

"Let me help you," Emma said. "Let my friends help you."

"Friends? What friends?" Violet said, suddenly suspicious. "Not one of them?"

"Them?"

Violet's breathing shallowed until she was almost panting. "Vampires," she breathed. "They exist, you know," she said defiantly, as if assuming Emma wouldn't believe her.

Emma nodded. "I know."

Violet blinked. "You believe me?"

"Of course. I've been to the vampires' residence, the embassy. I know about Victor, and I know what he did." Emma leaned forward earnestly. "Victor is dead, Violet. He can't hurt you anymore."

"Dead?" Violet whispered in disbelief. Her eyes filled with tears and she raised a trembling hand to her mouth. "Dead," she repeated. Her gaze flashed up to meet Emma's. "Then you don't need me."

"But I do," Emma said softly. "I need you to tell me what happened. I need to know who the men were, so I can make them pay."

Violet closed her eyes, as if in pain. She sat that way a long time, and Emma thought she'd failed. But then Violet spoke in a surprisingly strong voice. "I don't want my family to know. They've suffered enough with this."

Emma thought quickly. She needed someplace to meet with Violet, someplace where she'd feel safe. Duncan's estate was probably the most secure, but it was clearly out of the question. Even if Violet had never been to the house, there were too many vampires. And Duncan would never agree to do it at Emma's house, not after the other night. *Damn.* Well, they'd work something out. Duncan and his vampires probably had houses all over the place. They'd simply have to be sure the one they chose wasn't someplace Victor had used for his perverted games.

"If you agree to help me, I'll pick you up myself," Emma assured Violet. "You can tell your parents I'm a friend. They'll be glad you're getting out," she said, knowing it was true.

Violet nodded tiredly. "Fine. I just want this over with. I want my life back."

"I'll do my best," Emma said and meant it. She'd started this to find justice for Lacey, but they couldn't hurt Lacey anymore. They were still hurting Violet Slayton, though, and Emma was going to make them stop.

She traded phone numbers with Violet, promising to get back in touch with her first thing in the morning to set up something. She was nervous about leaving Violet alone, afraid something would happen. Afraid, frankly, that she'd change her mind and run. But Violet flatly refused to go with her, so there was nothing Emma could do. She'd just have to trust.

It wasn't until she was in her car and heading back to the District that she realized how late it had gotten. In retrospect, she was kind of surprised that Duncan or one of his guys hadn't called to find out where she was. It actually concerned her a little. Had something else happened? Something that had them all so busy, they didn't have time to worry about her whereabouts?

At the next red light, she picked up her cell phone and scrolled through to Duncan's number. It was the first time she'd called him since he'd given her his business card a little over a week ago. She was startled to realize it hadn't been any longer than that. So much had happened, it didn't seem possible so little time had passed.

The light turned green and she tucked the phone between her ear and shoulder as Duncan's number went straight to voice mail. Maybe it was too early to call. After all, the sun was barely down, the sky still light on the horizon. Maybe vampires weren't early risers or whatever you called someone who woke with the sunset.

Duncan's voice mail beeped, inviting her to leave a message. She dropped the phone into her hand and held it to her face.

"Hi, Duncan, Emma here, calling to let you know I'm on my way, and I've got news. I'll tell you when I get there."

She paused, suddenly unsure how to sign off. The usual *okay, bye* didn't really cut it, and the *mwaah* of a phone kiss seemed trite, given the heat between them. She took the coward's way out and simply disconnected, tossing the phone onto the passenger seat.

She and the too sexy Duncan were going to have a heart-to-heart very soon. Maybe tonight after he heard about how she'd found Violet Slayton. This was good news for their investigation, really good news. A little celebration wouldn't be out of order. And what better way to celebrate than finally getting naked together?

Her stomach tightened as the image of a half-naked Duncan flashed in her mind. She zipped up the ramp onto 95 and hit the gas. It was going to be a very good night.

Chapter Twenty

Duncan stared at his prisoner, the unfortunate who'd attacked Emma and nearly killed Baldwin, as difficult as it was to kill a vampire. It was just good fortune that Duncan and Miguel had been so close, and that Baldwin had been alert enough to get Emma to call them. A few more minutes and he'd have bled out, despite their best efforts. And apart from the threat to Emma—which Duncan wasn't likely to forget—the attack on one of his own was something he couldn't forgive.

Except that this man truly was an unfortunate who, if he could be believed, had chosen the wrong house to burgle. And Duncan had no reason not to believe him. As far as he could determine, the man was telling the truth. And there were damn few vampires more skilled at detecting lies among humans than Duncan was, especially once he'd slipped into the human's mind and made him all comfy and relaxed. At that point, there was no deception left in the man.

"I'm telling you the truth, man," the prisoner whined for the umpteenth time. "I don't know nothin' about nothin'."

"So you say," Miguel snarled.

"'Cuz it's the truth, man. I saw the funeral notice and checked out the house."

"So, you steal from the dead, is that it?"

"I ain't ashamed of it. A body's dead, what does it matter who gets their stuff? Might as well be me. Nice place like that, I figured there'd be something worthwhile, so I kept an eye on it, and when nobody comes home, I made my play. Two minutes later, this bitch shows up and all hell breaks loose."

"And you shot my man," Duncan said tightly.

"Yeah, well, shit happens. He startled me is all. Shouldn't startle a man like that."

"I see. So it's his fault he got shot."

"Well, yeah, sort of."

Duncan studied the man, wondering if he shouldn't return a good dose of fear to the human, if for no other reason than to punish him for being such a worm.

"Is it possible someone got to him, Sire?" Miguel asked softly.

Duncan had already considered, and rejected, the possibility that another vampire had manipulated this pitiful excuse for a man and sent him to kill Emma.

"There's no sign of tampering. The problem is," he admitted, "that this creature really does prey on the dead. If someone knew that, it would be simplicity itself to direct him to Emma's and let him do what he does best. The necessary suggestion would be so mild that unless the vampire was a total idiot, the result would be all but undetectable, even to me. Especially since the human honestly believes what he's telling us."

Miguel frowned. "So what do we do with him? He nearly killed Baldwin."

Duncan agreed. He couldn't simply let the man go. He hadn't killed anyone last night, not that Duncan knew of anyway, but it was probably only a matter of time before he did. On the other hand, it wasn't Duncan's responsibility to protect the human race from itself, either.

"I don't believe our friend here fully appreciates the dangers of his chosen profession. I think a small lesson is in order, after which you can send him back into the wild and let nature take its course."

Duncan released the human from the hold he had on his brain, and watched fear reassert itself as all the appropriate chemicals filtered back into the man's bloodstream.

"What the fuck?" the human said, staring around with wide, terrified eyes as he took in his predicament. "Who are you people?"

Miguel bared his fangs and grinned at the struggling human. The man was still screaming when Duncan left the basement and headed for his office, wondering idly where Emma was. It was well past the one hour after sunset time they'd agreed upon. He could always call the guard he'd assigned to her and find out what she was doing. But if anything significant had happened the guard would have called *him* by now. Perhaps she'd had to work late or perhaps . . . His phone rang as he sat behind his desk. Glancing at the caller ID, he saw that it was Jackson Hissong, the human in charge of his daytime guards. Duncan frowned. It wasn't usual for Jackson to be around this late.

"Jackson," he said, answering. "You're here late."

"Yes, my lord. I'm about to head out, but the guard assigned to follow Emma Duquet today just reported in."

"Emma?" Duncan said, alert but not yet alarmed, since there was no tension in Jackson's voice. "Did something happen?"

"She was never in danger, my lord, but she didn't exactly sit in her office all day, so I thought you'd want to know where she went."

"Why, yes," Duncan agreed. "I'd be *very* interested in knowing that, Jackson."

* * * *

Emma waved at the guard as the gate opened and she drove onto the estate. She parked in her usual spot to the right side of the front door and got out of the car, slinging her purse and laptop over her shoulder. Still riding the high of having found Violet, she practically skipped up the stairs.

She opened the front door and stepped inside, blinking in surprise. The big house was even noisier tonight. It sounded as if they were tearing the place down from the inside out, and not trying to be neat about it, either. Ducking her head against the possibility of flying debris, she skirted a pile of . . . what *was* that anyway? Walls, maybe. Walls that had been torn apart and—

"Look out below!" the warning shout sounded from above, and Emma quick-stepped into the former library barely evading the new layer of debris which plummeted down the open stairwell and landed on the growing pile.

"Good God," she muttered, and peered back into the entryway.

"Emma! There you are."

Emma did a double take as Baldwin joined her in the small room. "Baldwin," she said, examining him up and down. "You look . . . healthy."

He laughed at her surprise. "Vampire, sweet thing. We heal like crazy, especially when someone like Duncan does the honors."

Emma remembered Duncan opening his wrist for Baldwin to drink. "Duncan's blood did that?"

Baldwin nodded, suddenly serious. "Duncan's über powerful, you know."

She nodded slowly. Baldwin had been dying on her floor last night. This was beyond powerful. This was fucking incredible. "I'm glad you're okay," she managed.

He grinned. "Me, too."

"I, um . . ." Emma searched for something to say. "I parked out front. Should I move around back?"

"Nah. Give me your keys. I'll do it."

"You sure?"

"Sure thing. You're working with Louis, right? I'll bring the keys up, but the big man wants to see you first. He put out the word and didn't seem too happy about it either"

"He didn't?" Emma asked, more curious than worried.

Baldwin gave her a sympathetic look. "Don't worry, sweetheart. He likes you, so it won't be too bad. You got those keys?"

She dug out her keys and handed them over. "Thanks," she said faintly.

He took the keys, giving her a wink before disappearing outside. Emma stood in the relative safety of the former library for a moment, mulling over Baldwin's warning. So, Duncan was unhappy with her? Okay, so she hadn't gone to work and rushed right back here, like a good little worker bee. And maybe she was a little late, and maybe he'd been worried, but she *had* called. And she'd found Violet Slayton, which was huge, if only anyone would listen. Wasn't this what she was supposed to be doing? Wasn't that what this was all *about*?

Mentally squaring her shoulders, and kind of pissed that her good news was being trampled on by Duncan's ego, she took a single step out of the former library, looked up carefully, then dashed up the stairs.

Duncan was on the phone when she stuck her head around the half-open door of his office. She had already started to step back into the hallway, when he caught her eye and pointed at the chair in front of his desk. Not that she had to obey him, but it would have been too cowardly to pretend that she hadn't seen nor understood his gesture. And what was she worried about anyway? She sat on the designated chair and wished she'd changed clothes before coming here. At least then she could have slumped casually instead of sitting up straight in her pencil skirt and heels like little Miss Priss.

Duncan ignored her once she was in the chair. He was sitting sideways to the desk and speaking to someone about what sounded like the house renovations. Something about the basement and a vault and the water table. She yawned pointedly. A point which Duncan obviously got and didn't appreciate, if the look he gave her was any indication. Gee. Too bad.

Emma was feeling more belligerent with every moment she waited for Duncan to get off the phone. Who did he think he was anyway? She didn't work for him. Here she'd managed to find their biggest break yet, and she was being made to feel like a misbehaving school girl. And all because she'd taken the initiative instead of waiting hours for Duncan's permission. Like she needed that? She'd built up a fine, righteous anger by the time Duncan disconnected and tossed the phone to his desk. He stood and strolled over to the door, closing it quietly.

Emma followed him with her eyes as far as she could, but refused to feed his ego by twisting around in the chair to watch him close the door at her back. She was exquisitely aware of him, though, especially when he came up right behind her and said, "How was your day, Emma?"

"Busy," she said briskly. "How was—" She jumped as he placed his hands on her shoulders, slid them down her arms and covered her hands, trapping her in the chair.

Duncan leaned in close, his lips nibbling at her ear before he said softly, "Busy doing what?"

Emma sat perfectly still. She could feel the strength of his hands over hers, the muscles in his arms and chest as he surrounded her. His hair was loose, and it brushed against her cheek like strands of warm silk. He was the sexiest, most gorgeous man she had ever met, and if they'd had an extra hour late last night, they'd have been fucking like bunnies. But there was something about him tonight that made her primitive, animal brain sit up and scream *danger!*

"Duncan?" she said.

"Yes, Emma?"

"Are you upset with me?"

His lips touched her temple in a soft kiss. "Why would I be upset?" he murmured. His lips roamed down along her jaw, skimming the edge of her mouth before moving back up to the soft skin beneath her ear.

Emma was having trouble breathing, and her heart was pounding so hard she was pretty sure he could see it thumping up and down beneath her clothes. As if he'd heard her thought, Duncan lifted one of his hands from hers and slid his fingers beneath the collar of her shirt and along her clavicle, teasing downward until his touch grazed the top of her breasts. Emma closed her eyes and let her head fall back against his chest.

"Tell me, Emma," Duncan said, his voice a midnight whisper against her ear, promising all sorts of sinful delights. "Did you enjoy your visit to Alexandria?"

Emma froze. "What?"

"And Violet Slayton, that was very clever of you, except—"

"Except what?" She snapped upright, her body abruptly torn between the desire still thrumming along her nerves and anger that he somehow knew every step she'd taken today. She tried to pull away from him and found herself lifted out of the chair, the hold on her arms careful but unbreakable as he spun her around and glared at her. His brown eyes were no longer just warm; they were burning hot, with that bronze glow lighting them from within.

"Except that Tammy Dietrich works for Max Grafton," he growled. "The same Max Grafton who we *know* was connected to Victor and his filthy parties."

Emma hadn't known about Dietrich's connection to Grafton. Her own checking hadn't turned up any obvious link between them, but if there was one, it was significant. He was right about that much. Not that she was going to admit it. "That doesn't mean anything," she argued defiantly. "A guy like Grafton has tons of lawyers doing work for him. She could—"

"She's his fucking sister, Emma. And he's her *only* client. What does that tell you?"

"Wait," Emma said, trying to focus when Duncan was still holding her as close as a lover, even though he was well beyond upset with her. Something didn't add up about all of this. If she could only—

It suddenly clicked. "How did you know about Dietrich? I didn't even know about her until earlier today when I went through the mourner's book and called . . . Are you tapping my phone? Is that it?"

"Don't be ridiculous."

"Then how—"

"I didn't need to tap your damn phone. I had a guard on you."

"You had me *followed?*" She pushed against his chest, but he still wouldn't let go.

"Of course, I did. Someone nearly killed you last night," he growled.

"You don't know that," she insisted. "He didn't pull the gun until I—"

"Jesus Christ, Emma," he exploded. "Do you have to be dead and bleeding before you'll let me help you?"

Emma stared at him in shock. She'd never seen Duncan lose his cool like this. Not when they'd found Lacey's body, not even when his own man was bleeding out on the floor of her house. "You *have* helped me," she said quietly. "I wouldn't have survived any of this without you."

Duncan sighed and loosened his grip at last, rubbing the knuckles of one hand over her cheek. "I don't want to lose you, Emmaline. Not like that."

"You're not going to lose me." She rested her forehead against his cheek, breathing in the scent of him. "Besides," she added softly, and looked up to meet his eyes. "You owe me hours of incredibly hot sex."

Duncan grew still, his gaze hot and intent, but not with anger this time. "What I promised was hours of making love, not simply sex," he murmured, brushing his lips over hers, before his teeth closed gently on her lower lip. "There is a difference, darlin'."

Then he kissed her, and Emma discovered there was indeed a difference. His mouth was soft at first, his lips barely brushing hers, as if seeking entry. Her lips parted on a sigh, and he moved in for the kill, his mouth coming down hard and demanding as his arms tightened around her.

Emma met his demand with a ferocity all her own, her tongue meeting his in a twisting dance for dominance as she raised her arms around his neck and raked her fingers beneath his long hair and up against his scalp. He bit her lip again, harder this time, and laughed against her mouth when she bit him back with a low growl.

"Vicious woman," he murmured, pulling her shirt out of her tight skirt and running his hands up her bare back to her bra, which opened to a deft twist of his fingers.

Emma groaned as her breasts were freed from their confinement, rubbing herself against his chest, relishing the hard planes of muscle against her sensitive nipples. She grabbed the bottom of his sweater and yanked upward, wanting some skin. He swore softly, but let go of her long enough to tug the sweater over his head and toss it aside. Emma shrugged out of her jacket and shirt all at once, letting them fall behind her as her bra slid down her arms.

"Beautiful," Duncan whispered, and covered her breasts with his big hands, his thumbs stroking her nipples until they were firm and dark and begging to be suckled.

But Duncan had other plans. Emma whimpered when he abandoned her breasts, his hands reaching instead for her butt as he pressed her up against his erection, squeezing the globes of her ass as he pumped against her. His mouth was all over her neck, licking and sucking until she thought she'd go mad. What was it she'd thought of calling him the other night? A pussy tease? Clit tease? Whatever it was, he was still doing it—and still trying to drive her crazy.

"Duncan," she panted.

His only response was a humming noise as he bent to take a taut nipple into his mouth at last.

Emma groaned, fisting her fingers in his hair and holding him against her in case he thought to escape. She struggled to catch her breath, wishing she'd worn a different skirt, or no skirt at all, so she could wrap her legs around his hips and feel that long, hard erection between her thighs. She would climax from just the feel of it against her swollen sex. She knew she would.

"Duncan," she said again, sucking in a sharp breath as he scraped his teeth over her nipple and she felt the sharp points of his fangs against her tender flesh. She breathed out on a sigh of pleasure. "You know those hours you talked about?"

His tongue lapped at her breast, soothing the sting of his fangs. "Mmmm," he said as he moved to her other breast, his fingers continuing to stroke the one he was leaving behind.

"Do you think . . . Oh my God," she gasped as his mouth closed over the second swollen nipple and he sucked hard, pulling half of her breast into the warmth of his mouth. She almost orgasmed right then as pleasure shot along her nerve endings like lightning. It arrowed straight to her clit which she swore could feel every ridge and vein of Duncan's cock despite the two layers of clothing between them. Emma moaned in frustration and gave his hair a firm tug.

He looked up at her, his eyes so hot with color she was amazed he could see anything at all.

"Can we fuck first?" she heard herself say. "And make love later? Please?"

Duncan stared at her for all of ten seconds, and then bared his teeth in a slow, wicked smile. Faster than Emma would have thought possible, he grabbed her skirt and shoved it up to her waist, his fingers gliding along her bare thighs before shifting to rip away her panties. Just as quickly, he lifted her to his waist, wrapping her legs around his hips as he pushed her against the wall. She felt the brief touch of his hand between them, and then his cock was free, sliding along the soaking wet folds between her thighs, tormenting her already begging clit. Another touch of his hand as he positioned himself, and then one long, steady thrust, and he was balls deep inside her. Emma's entire body shuddered with such intense desire that she bit into his shoulder to swallow her screams. Duncan pumped once, twice, and then Emma was coming harder than she ever had before, her head thrown back, teeth buried in her lip to keep from letting the entire household know she was being fucked against the wall and loving every minute of it.

Duncan held onto her as she trembled in the aftermath, jolts of sensation continuing to shoot along every nerve. His hands were cupping her bare ass, his chest crushing her breasts as he held her against the wall. And then he started moving again—long, slow thrusts of his thick shaft that left the walls of her vagina shivering with delight, rippling along his cock as he lifted her higher and drove even deeper inside her. Emma tightened her inner muscles, squeezing and caressing him, welcoming his delicious penetration.

Duncan hissed as her sex clenched around his erection, and then groaned as he began to pump faster, his hips slamming into hers with the slap of bare skin, his mouth moving over her neck until she felt the nip of his teeth over her jugular. Emma's heartbeat soared with equal parts fear and excitement as she felt the dull scrape of his fangs, and then fear and every other emotion fled as a sudden heat seared the blood in her veins, as raw ecstasy shot along every nerve in her body, all of it coming together in the tiny nub of her clit. Her vaginal walls convulsed around the thickness of Duncan's cock, and she heard a high keening noise coming from her own throat as she struggled not to scream, trapping the sound in her chest where it took on a life of its own fighting to get out. She gasped for air as Duncan continued to pound into her, until finally she felt a rush of wet heat and he roared his completion.

They hung on to each other, panting for breath, hearts pumping in a single beat. Emma's legs were still locked around his waist, her arms cradling his head as he nuzzled her neck where Emma was pretty sure he hadn't bitten her yet. He'd nipped at her skin, but she didn't think he'd actually drawn blood. He'd told her that vampire sex was addictive because their bite felt so good, but she couldn't imagine sex with Duncan being anymore intoxicating than what she'd just experienced. She'd never want to let him out of bed. Come to think of it, she thought with a smile, she already didn't.

The rush of blood faded enough that Emma could hear again, and she became aware of the construction noise outside Duncan's office— the shouts of his men, the crash of materials as they tore the house apart. She groaned, realizing they'd probably heard everything.

Duncan chuckled, his mouth nibbling her neck one last time before he lifted his head and met her gaze. Blond hair hung over his forehead and his eyes gleamed with smug good humor. "They didn't hear us, Emma. This room is insulated for privacy, and besides, you were too busy biting me to scream."

Emma's face heated with embarrassment, but then she said, "But . . . you didn't bite me?"

"I didn't," he said, confirming her suspicions.

Emma frowned. "Why not?"

When Duncan gave her a puzzled look, she said, "I mean, you said sex and blood were connected for you all, and that—"

"I would never take blood from you without asking first, Emma. And since you demanded that we fuck immediately," he added, with a grin, "I had no time to ask."

Emma blushed at the reminder, and was suddenly aware that he was still holding her against the wall and that she was more than half naked. Her blush deepened. "Um, you can probably put me down now."

"I don't think so," Duncan said. Instead of releasing her, he tightened his hold and, without warning, turned away from the wall and started across the room.

Emma shrieked in surprise, her arms clutching his neck. "What are you doing?" she demanded.

"I'm keeping my promise," he said carrying her around his desk and over to another door, which she assumed was a closet until he bent his knees slightly and opened it with one hand.

"What—"

Duncan stepped into the adjoining room and kicked the door shut behind them. Emma looked around as soft lights came up. They were in a bedroom. A *huge* bedroom, with heavy drapes covering the windows and an enormous bed. Oh my.

Duncan set her in the middle of the big bed and immediately began stripping away what was left of her clothes. Her jacket and shirt were gone, as were her shoes, and her panties were nothing but shredded lace on the floor in his office somewhere. He unzipped her skirt, which was bunched around her waist, then tugged it off and eyed her thigh-high stockings thoughtfully.

"I like those," he said, then kicked off his shoes and shoved his faded denims down, stepping out of them to reveal two things . . . one, he wasn't wearing underwear—and wasn't that just the sexiest thing. And two, vampires didn't need recovery time between erections. His cock was long and thick and beautifully aroused, stiffening even further when she stared at it, as if it enjoyed the attention.

Duncan knelt on the bed and ran his hands up her legs, caressing her calves beneath the silk of her stockings, pressing her thighs open as his touch moved to the delicate skin between her legs. Emma felt her face heat as he spread her thighs even wider, as his hot gaze settled on the swollen folds of her sex. He raised his head to meet her eyes, then licked his lips slowly, deliberately.

Emma gasped, feeling her face get even hotter when he stretched out between her legs and palmed her butt, his thumbs coming up to open her wide. Her breath caught as he ran his tongue through the folds of her slit. She was already wet and slick from the thundering orgasms Duncan had given her, and he lapped it up like cream, his tongue dipping into her shivering core, gliding along every crease and fold until he finally licked her so sensitive clit. Her muscles jerked in reaction and he did it again, circling around and over that tight bundle of nerves in an unpredictable pattern, tormenting her.

Emma fisted her hands in his hair, her need so overpowering, she forgot to be embarrassed, too focused on deciding whether she wanted to hold him in place or pull him away. Her head was thrown back, her eyes closed, as she struggled to process the overload of feelings. Not only his mouth on her pussy, or his wicked tongue teasing her clit, but the press of his big shoulders against her thighs, the silken slide of his hair against her belly. But even more was the simple fact that it was *Duncan* doing these things.

"Duncan," she whispered, wanting to tell him it was too much, that she couldn't handle so many different sensations all at once. But as if anticipating her protest, he suddenly sucked hard on her clit, taking it into his mouth like a juicy morsel of fruit.

The orgasm rocketed through her without warning, her abdomen clenching tightly as her inner muscles rippled, trying to hold onto a cock that wasn't even there. He'd brought her to a climax with just his mouth, and unbelievable ecstasy speared her through and through. Emma screamed, unable to hold it back, no longer caring if anyone heard.

* * * *

Duncan gripped the firm globes of Emma's ass, drinking in the sweet nectar of her orgasm as she convulsed beneath him. God, she was wet. And she tasted so good. Her cream was almost as good as the tiny taste of blood he'd had from her breasts earlier. It had taken supreme self control to satisfy himself with only the scent of her blood, with nipping at the skin above her vein and knowing that soon he would have Emma's blood rolling like liquid velvet down his throat.

And she'd been so ready for him. When he'd brushed the dull edge of his fangs against her skin, she hadn't pulled away, hadn't shrieked in fear. He'd sensed the rush of excitement as her heart sped up, as her blood pumped harder, plumping her vein in anticipation of his bite.

She would come so beautifully when he finally bit her. Just as she was coming for him now.

He stroked his tongue over her clit a final time, then came up on all fours, prowling up over her body until his shaft was nestled between her legs. He bent over and sucked the tip of one full, tender breast into his mouth, and Emma's violet eyes flashed open. They were glazed nearly lavender with lust as she smiled up at him. And he was gone.

He reached down and positioned his cock against her opening, then thrust once hard with his hips, burying himself deep inside her. Her inner walls, still throbbing with her climax, pulsed along his length, surrounding him in liquid heat. He lowered himself over her, taking her mouth as he began flexing his hips, reveling in the friction of her satiny channel against his cock as he moved in and out of her, the feel of her full breasts, her nipples big and swollen—hard like velvet-covered pebbles against his chest.

Emma wrapped her arms around his shoulders as he kissed her, her legs crossing behind his back as she began to lift her hips up to meet him. He growled and began to thrust harder, wanting to make her climax again, wanting to feel her body clench around his shaft as her juices flowed hot and wet.

"Emma," he whispered against her neck, breathing in the tantalizing scent of her blood so very close. He stroked his tongue over her vein, feeling the blood straining against its confinement, begging for his fangs.

"Emma," he repeated intently.

Emma moaned, then licked her lips slowly. Her eyes opened and met his directly. "Do it," she whispered.

Duncan gave a hard thrust of his cock. "Are you sure?"

"Yes. Please, Duncan." She turned her head to one side, baring her neck, stretching it taut in invitation.

Duncan hissed, his eyelids drooping heavily as lust-fueled hunger roared along every nerve and into every muscle. He bent his head to her neck, his mouth going unerringly to the thick swell of her jugular. Using only his lips, he sucked hard on the vein, plumping it further, drawing it into his mouth without breaking the skin. Emma gasped, and he smiled. He rubbed the blunt surface of his fangs along her neck, gliding them back and forth, teasing her. Emma's fingers dug into his biceps and her already pounding heart began to race. A sudden tremor of excitement tightened her inner muscles, rippling along his cock, still sheathed deep inside her.

He lifted his head and sank his fangs into her vein, groaning at the rush of thick, sweet blood, fragrant with arousal, as rich as honey. Emma's hands moved from his shoulders to grip his nape, holding his mouth against her. She cried out in surprise as the euphoric in his bite hit her bloodstream, as if she was stunned by her own body's response. The ripple of muscle along his shaft quickened, and Duncan began thrusting harder, faster, driven as much by Emma's need as by his own. Her beautiful violet eyes opened and she stared up at him.

"Oh, my God," she whispered, and then she was pushed over the edge as her hot, little body clenched, grabbing his cock so tightly he could barely move. Emma screamed as the orgasm rolled over them both, as his own groans mixed with her cries of pleasure, and he shot his release deep inside her womb.

Duncan lay on top of her, breathing hard, knowing he should move. He was heavy, and for all her height, Emma was delicate. But he couldn't find the strength to lift himself. He lay there a few moments longer, Emma's arms still holding him, her ankles still locked over his ass. Finally, he reached back and lifted one of her legs. Her thighs fell open as if there was no strength left in her muscles. Duncan smiled and shifted to one side, taking her with him so she lay against his chest, in the curve of his arm.

They stayed that way for a long time, silent, breathing, their hearts slowly returning to normal.

"You okay, Emmaline?" he asked, rubbing his chin over her fragrant hair.

"Okay?" Emma murmured lazily. "Okay doesn't even come close. Blissed out, maybe." She lifted her head enough to lick his nipple. "Tell me something," she said. "Am I allowed to bite you, too?" Her teeth closed over his nipple, emphasizing her words.

Duncan growled, reaching down to squeeze her ass in warning. "Just remember, my fangs are sharper, and you're very tasty."

"Hmm. Well, I'm not complaining. As long as I get to bite back."

Duncan shuddered with pleasure. "Feel free, darlin'. I'm all yours." He realized as he said the words that it was true. Emma Duquet had somehow managed to do what no woman had since his wife had died nearly two hundred years ago. She'd gotten inside his heart.

Emma gave his nipple another playful lick, then sat up and, humming softly, straddled his hips. The wet heat of her sex teased the base of his cock as she rocked back and forth above him, her hands braced on his chest, her breasts swaying tantalizingly out of reach. He leaned up and caught one in his mouth, sucking hard before she swayed away from him again.

"You're pushing your luck," he warned, his gaze heavy as he watched her.

"Sauce for the goose," she murmured.

Duncan frowned briefly, but decided he didn't care what she meant. All he cared about was getting his mouth on those beautiful breasts and his dick inside her one more time.

"Come here," he said, gripping her hips.

"Nuh uh," Emma replied, continuing to rock, but leaning back so he couldn't reach her breasts.

"Emma."

"Yes?" she said sweetly.

In a single move, he flipped her over and under him, driving himself deep inside her, exactly where he wanted to be. Emma gasped in surprise and then groaned as he began to move, grinding against her clit every time he plunged into her tight pussy.

"I did warn you," he murmured, then lowered his head and bit the tip of one swollen nipple, letting his fangs scrape against the soft skin of her breast until blood welled. He licked the blood away, and Emma shivered with a pleasure that matched his own as he tasted her sweet blood on his tongue. He began to thrust harder, wanting to feel her hot and tight as she came around his cock one more time, to establish once and for all that she was his and no other's. Her stomach muscles trembled as the orgasm began to rip through her, the convulsions shivering down through her womb to race along the slick walls surrounding his shaft. Her sex tightened around him, alternately squeezing and releasing his cock as he continued to slide in and out of her, grinding against her swollen clit.

Emma cried his name when she came this time, her nails drawing blood along his back, her legs crushing the breath from his body. Duncan felt his own release building as his sac tightened and his balls grew heavy. Suddenly, Emma bit his shoulder hard enough to draw blood, and with a shout he crashed over the edge as the orgasm took him.

Duncan didn't think he could move. A hundred and fifty years of making love to some of the most beautiful women in the world, and for the first time he actually felt drained. Not that he'd have any trouble getting it up again if Emma was so inclined. He lifted his head and gazed down at her, brushing a lock of hair away from her sweaty cheek. He smiled and figured she wouldn't be demanding a repeat performance for a while at least. Moving carefully, he slid to one side, pulling her with him. She sighed and nestled against his body, her head on his shoulder.

A powerful surge of protectiveness flooded his senses and he had to fight to keep his muscles loose and relaxed so she wouldn't notice. The urgency to mate, to make her his, had eased now that he'd taken her body and blood. She might not know it yet, but Emma Duquet belonged to him. No other vampire would dare touch her, or they would face his wrath. And his wrath would be a terrible thing when it came to Emma.

* * * *

The ringing of his cell phone stirred Duncan to alertness sometime later. Emma had fallen asleep and he hadn't wanted to disturb her, so he'd held her while she slept and let his mind continue working over the many details demanding his attention these days. Everything from the continuing construction, to the question of Lacey's killers, to the all important issue of Emma's safety. If it was up to him, she wouldn't leave the residence until he knew that all of those responsible for Lacey's death had been dealt with and were no longer a threat. His preferred mode of ensuring her safety was the most permanent one, although rationally he understood it would raise a few flags if several elected officials died all at once. So he'd kill the worst of them and ensure the others left town. For now.

Emma stirred at the sound of the phone, her eyes fluttering open slowly. She stiffened, probably realizing she wasn't in her own bed. And then, to his great pleasure, she relaxed against him. It did something to his heart to know that waking next to him made her feel secure enough to relax.

"It's probably Miguel," he said, kissing the top of her head. "I should talk to him."

Emma sat up, then leaned over to give him a thorough kiss, her naked breasts swaying close enough that he cupped one in his hand, smiling when her nipple immediately hardened in response. She hummed with pleasure and pushed against his hand before pulling away. "Tell Miguel he has lousy timing," she said, then slipped out of bed and headed for the bathroom.

Duncan watched her shapely ass until she closed the door, then padded out to the other room to retrieve his phone from the desk. He didn't actually have to answer to know it was Miguel calling him. The connection between a Sire and his vampire child was very strong, especially when the Sire was as powerful as Duncan.

"Miguel," he said, answering the phone.

"Sire," Miguel said cautiously. "I don't mean to interrupt—"

"You're not," he assured his lieutenant. If it had truly been an interruption, Duncan wouldn't have answered at all.

"My lord, the guard we had on Ms. Duquet today tells me she spent a great deal of time with Violet Slayton."

"So I understand," Duncan said. "Emma and I will join you in the computer room shortly."

"Thank you, Sire."

Duncan disconnected, smiling at Miguel's discretion. What he'd told Emma about the room being soundproofed was true. None of his vampires would have heard what was going on. But that didn't mean their brains stopped working. Even without their blood link to him, they would have detected the strong emotions being generated. When one added that link into the mix, they knew very well what Duncan had been up to this evening.

Emma emerged from the bathroom, her beautiful breasts and everything else on full display. She glanced up to see Duncan watching her hungrily.

"Stop that," she chided him. "Or we'll never get out of this room."

"Would that be a bad thing?"

Emma laughed. "Eventually you'd get tired of me."

Duncan crossed to her in two long strides, sliding his arm around her waist and pulling her firmly against his body. "Never," he whispered in between nibbling kisses to her ear and throat. Emma wrapped her arms around him with a hungry little cry of her own, and tilted her head against his shoulder, giving him full access to her neck. She shivered when he bit the lobe of her ear, and her nipples poked his chest.

"You're a very bad man, Duncan," she whispered, her breath hot against his skin.

"I'm not a man at all, Emma. And while some may consider me bad, I'm very good at what I do."

"And what's that?" she asked, kissing his shoulder before pulling away to give him a curious look.

"I take care of the people who matter to me, and especially those I consider mine." He kissed her soft mouth. "And you, Emmaline, are most definitely mine."

Chapter Twenty-One

"I don't want her badgered," Emma said for what felt like the hundredth time. She was sitting in the makeshift computer room along with Duncan and several of his vampires, including Phoebe. The chair was hard and uncomfortable, the room was cold, and she was bone tired. She'd been up most of the previous night, had worked a full day today, driven out to Violet Slayton's home and back again, and *then* spent a vigorous couple of hours with Duncan—not that she'd give back one minute of her time with Duncan no matter how little sleep she had. But it was beginning to look as though she wouldn't get much sleep tonight either. That was the problem in working with vampires. They were fresh and raring to go, just getting started on their day, so to speak, while she wanted nothing more than to sleep for about eight hours straight.

Except that they were discussing their approach to Violet Slayton, which was something Emma cared a great deal about. She was *not* going to let them badger the poor woman into telling them what she knew, no matter the stakes.

"Emma," Duncan said patiently. "She's probably our best source for getting the identity of the men involved in Lacey's death."

"She doesn't remember anything."

"But she *will*," Duncan insisted, also for the hundredth time. "The very fact that she's as spooked as you say she is, that she *knows* something happened and is having nightmares about it, tells me that whoever messed with her head did a piss poor job of it. I can fix that and get what we need at the same time. You say you care about her, then let me repair the damage they've done to her mind."

Emma regarded Duncan steadily. He was leaning back against the table across from hers, long legs stretched out in front of him and crossed at the ankles. He looked his usual cool and studly self in black jeans and t-shirt, his hair pulled back in a neat tail. And she was pretty sure he could lie his ass off and she'd never know the difference if he didn't want her to. But she trusted him. God knew he was wicked in bed, but he was also a good man out of it.

"All right," she agreed. "But no one else, Duncan. If you all show up en masse, she'll freak out and we'll never get a word out of her."

"Agreed," he said, nodding.

"And I go with you." When Duncan frowned, she added, "I don't think she'll see you otherwise."

"All right, then," he said reluctantly. "But you said she didn't want to meet at her home."

"Right. So we'll have figure out someplace neutral. Not here," she said immediately. "For all we know, this is one of the places Victor and his buddies assaulted her."

"Miguel," Duncan said, shifting his gaze to his lieutenant. "We'll need someplace private, but not so isolated that she feels threatened. And none of Victor's properties. We can't know which ones he used."

"You can do it at our house," Phoebe offered from her seat next to Emma. "It's close to where Slayton lives, and we have plenty of privacy. Plus with Ted living there, it has a messy, lived-in feel to it," she added dryly.

"Are you sure, Pheebs?" Duncan asked, frowning.

"Absolutely. Our offices are on the same property, so we have people in and out all the time, but I'll make sure you have the place to yourself for this."

He nodded. "Thank you, then. Miguel, we'll do it tomorrow night. You can check out the property tonight. Do whatever you need to do to feel secure about the setup. Emma and I will pick up Violet—"

"No," Emma interrupted. "I'll pick up Violet alone and take her to the house. Once we're there, you can join us. She won't want a stranger in her house, Duncan," she insisted when he looked as if he'd argue. "You can have someone tail me if that makes you feel better, but I'll bring her to Phoebe's house alone. I'll need the address and everything so I can map it out ahead of time."

"We'll program the GPS for you," Duncan said. "You'll be driving one of our SUVs. They're safer."

Emma nodded, privately hoping she'd get one of the big V8 SUVs, not some smaller, punier version. Maybe if she asked nicely. Behind Duncan, Baldwin was giving her a thumb's up, and she fought back a grin. Duncan narrowed his eyes at her suspiciously, but she gave him an innocent smile, which she was sure didn't fool him for one minute.

"Very well," Duncan said, clearly calling an end to the meeting. "Louis, you and the others keep working. Miguel, you and I need to talk to Alaric. He's waiting for us in the new wing. Emma, a moment of your time, please."

Uh oh, Emma thought. *Busted.*

She followed him down the hall, barely making it through the door of his office before he had her up against the wall and was kissing her. She reacted without thinking, going up on her toes and rubbing her breasts against his chest, kissing him back for all she was worth. He growled and crushed her lips beneath his mouth, his fangs fully in evidence as he bit down hard enough to draw a small taste of her blood.

Emma gasped and bit him back, tasting the thick honey that was his vampire blood a moment before it hit her bloodstream and sent a jolt of lust spearing right between her legs. She moaned into his mouth, hooked her leg over his hip and began grinding herself shamelessly against him, needing to release the heat building there like a volcano about to blow.

Duncan swore softly, ripped her jeans open and shoved his hand down into her panties, hissing when his fingers slid into the already wet folds between her legs. "You're so damn hot," he whispered and plunged two fingers up into her hungry pussy, tipping her over into a searing orgasm that slammed her into the wall and left her shuddering and clinging to his shoulders while small jolts of pleasure fired along her nerves at random.

Duncan carried her to the bedroom and threw her on the bed, his gaze liquid fire against her skin as he stripped away first her pants and then his, not even bothering with the rest of their clothes before he lifted her legs over his shoulders and plunged deep inside her with a single, strong thrust, his sleekly muscled arms braced to either side of her.

Emma wanted to stroke him, to glide her palms over the smooth muscles of those powerful shoulders, that firm chest with its light dusting of golden blond hair. He was so beautiful stretched out above her, his cock filling her so completely as he pumped in and out, her body closing eagerly around him with every thrust. She brushed a hand over her nipple—swollen with desire, aching for attention—and gasped at how very good it felt. Duncan's gaze riveted immediately on her breasts, and Emma smiled, caressing them, squeezing them together, rolling her nipples between her fingers and pinching them hard enough that they grew flushed with blood.

He snarled, his gaze flashing up to hers and back to her breasts as he began to pump harder. Emma cried out, feeling the pressure growing between her legs, the first tremors of climax tightening her belly and sending shivers of pleasure coursing along her inner walls with every thrust of Duncan's cock. She closed her eyes against the overwhelming flood of sensation, rubbing her hand down her abdomen and over her mound to her clit which was begging for release.

Realizing what she was doing, her eyes flashed open in guilt and she looked up to see Duncan watching her hungrily. "Do it," he demanded. "Come for me, Emma."

Embarrassment heated her already flushed face, but she began to fondle herself, feeling the weight of his stare with every stroke of her fingers. The lips of her sex were swollen and puffy as she rode the tight nub between them, her vagina stretched tight around the thickness of Duncan's cock.

"Look at me, Emma."

She looked up at him, and he began to pump even faster, his powerful arms holding her in place as he fucked her, as she began to rub her clit harder, desperate now for release. It hit without warning, going from a thrilling ripple to a full blown tidal wave of incredible sensation that roared through her, jumbling her senses until she could only scream and hope she wouldn't explode from the raw power of it. Some part of her registered Duncan's triumphant shout as his release flooded inside her, filling her with heat before he collapsed on top of her and scooped her into his arms.

* * * *

Duncan tightened his hold on Emma and smiled against her warm, silky hair. She was curled up against him, her lips nuzzling his neck, one arm draped tightly over his chest. She was still trembling from the force of her climax, and he reached down, tugging the coverlet over her body so she didn't cool down too quickly. Not that he worried for her health, not with all the biting she was doing. He grinned, thinking of the blood she'd taken from him. He could already sense it inside her and knew it would serve as a beacon between them. No matter where she was he would find her. It was a connection which would only get stronger the longer they were together, the more blood she took from him, and he from her.

The thought of her blood made his cock twitch, despite the fact that he'd barely recovered his breath. He hadn't bitten her this time, though he'd wanted to. It had been an effort, but he'd already taken quite a bit from her vein earlier and he didn't want to weaken her. Not when things were so uncertain, when their enemies could be waiting at every turn to take them down. He made a mental note to be sure there was sufficient regular food in the kitchen for her. Eventually, things would normalize, but for now, it was only him and his vampire staff, and they'd barely begun to stock the kitchen with enough blood for all of them.

Emma stirred and yawned delicately.

"You should sleep," he murmured.

"I can still work—"

"There's no point until after we speak with Slayton tomorrow. And you need to sleep. I've exhausted you." He heard the smug flavor of his own words and wasn't surprised when she slapped his chest lightly.

"Braggart."

"It's not bragging if it's true, darlin'."

"Oh my God," she said in disbelief. She laughed in a way that sounded suspiciously like a giggle before she clapped a hand over her mouth to cover it.

He grinned. "Well?"

"Oh, fine," she agreed, as if doing him a favor. "You were magnificent."

He slapped her ass playfully. "Remember that the next time you think about flirting with Baldwin."

"Flirting?" she sputtered. "I was not— Is *that* why you went all caveman on me? Because of Baldwin?"

"I did *not* go *cave*man."

"You certainly did. I expected you to start peeing on me or something, marking me with your scent."

"I can still do that, if you'd like," he growled.

"Not if you value your dick," she said dryly. "Remember who sleeps all day and who doesn't."

"You wouldn't do anything to my dick. You like it too much."

She was quiet for a thoughtful moment. "Well, that's true. But you're totally off-base about Baldwin. I wanted to drive the SUV the other night and he wouldn't let me. He said you'd kill him if anything happened to me and his reflexes were faster."

"Why'd you want to drive?"

"I like driving fast, and I especially like driving fast in big trucks with muscle engines. So when you said I'd be driving one of the SUVs tomorrow night, Baldwin thought it was funny. So did I."

"Well," Duncan said, realizing he may have overreacted just a tad, not that he was going to tell Emma that. "You need to realize that vampires are extremely territorial, and none more than a vampire lord, which is what I am. It's why I rule this residence and this territory. And you belong to me, Emma."

Emma pulled back and gave him an appraising look, her violet eyes like gleaming amethysts in the dim light. "If I belong to you," she said, watching him closely. "Does that mean you belong to me, too?"

Duncan didn't even blink. "Body and soul," he said, almost daring her to accept it.

Emma smiled slowly, beginning with a curve of her lips, then lighting up her entire face. "Then I'm yours, my lord."

* * * *

Duncan pulled the covers over Emma, then leaned down to leave a gentle kiss on her cheek. She was deeply asleep, as he'd known she would be. Earlier he'd seen the circles under her eyes, the lines of weariness in her face. And it really wasn't necessary for her to remain awake tonight. Louis and his team would continue digging through Victor's files, but the truth was they weren't even looking for data on the illicit parties anymore, or the men who'd killed Lacey. Everything there was had already been found. As he'd told Emma, if they were going to make any immediate progress on that front, it would have to come from Violet Slayton.

Duncan was confident of his skill when it came to manipulating a human mind. He'd learned from Raphael and there was no one alive who was better. But he couldn't know until he met Slayton how much damage Victor had done. He knew he could at least give the young woman some peace and relieve her of the nightmares and flashes of unknown memories. But whether he could do more than that remained to be seen.

He closed the bedroom door and let himself out of the second floor office, heading downstairs to the east wing. Alaric was there, and so was Miguel. At Duncan's request, Alaric had pulled everyone off the other projects to focus on this one. More than anything, Duncan wanted his people safe, and they wouldn't be until the new vault was completed.

He strode down the back hallway, following the sound of construction and male laughter. Their enemies were closing in. He could feel it. It wasn't specific. Not like a scout warning, "They're coming over the hill at dawn." It was more of an amorphous and vague sense of danger that filled his lungs with the first breath he drew every sunset and didn't stop until it was choking him with its urgency.

He only hoped he would be ready when it finally broke over them all.

Chapter Twenty-Two

"Whose house is this again?"

Emma swallowed her instinctive burst of irritation at Violet's question, which she'd already asked at least three times since they'd arrived.

"A friend's," she said evenly. "Husband and wife, actually. They're both FBI, so you know it's a safe place." It was pretty much the same answer she'd given every time, too. Fortunately, Phoebe and her husband had enough pictures and memorabilia of his days in the FBI—hanging on the walls and sitting on virtually every flat surface—that it was completely believable. Of course, it was also true that the pictures featured much younger versions of well-known FBI directors and various politicians, including one former president. But that worked for them in this case, because it had led Violet to assume they were a comfortably retired couple instead of an eternally young vampire and her mate.

"Nice house," Violet commented. "Two government pensions," she added, as if that explained the nice house.

Emma nodded. It *was* a nice house. Violet was right about that much. Emma had followed the instructions from the pleasant lady on the GPS, and pretended she didn't see the vampires following to make sure she and Violet got here safely. Phoebe and Ted Micheletti's place was actually an old Virginia farm, with a broken-down barn still standing in postcard perfect disrepair about a hundred yards from the house. Unfortunately, the only thing Emma could think of when she looked at that rickety old barn was rats. The thing had to be crawling with them. She only hoped it was far enough away that they didn't travel between there and the house. She hated rats.

"They don't mind you using their house?" Violet asked.

"They travel a lot, and they're gone for a few days. I figured it would be better for you if we met outside the city, and this isn't that far from your parents' place."

Emma had rationalized the nighttime meeting to Violet by pleading her work schedule. With the funeral and everything, she'd told her, she couldn't take off any more time from work. And it wasn't far from the truth, either. Sharon had been downright nasty when Emma showed up at the office this morning. Fortunately, Congressman Coffer had been in committee meetings all day, and of course Sharon, as his Chief of Staff, had been with him. That had pretty much prevented Emma from crossing paths with either one of them for the rest of the day. The explanation had touched the right note for Violet, too. She came from a decidedly working class family and understood the importance of a paycheck.

"Would you like a cup of something hot?" Emma asked Violet. "Or maybe a soft drink?"

"A diet Coke would be good, or—" Violet stiffened as the sound of an engine announced someone's arrival out front. She raised wide eyes to Emma and looked as if she were trying to decide whether or not to bolt. A single car door opened and then closed after a brief delay.

"That will be Duncan," Emma said reassuringly. Emma and the others, including Duncan, had agreed it would be best to use his real name. It was unlikely, but if Violet ever happened on his picture somewhere and remembered him, she'd know they'd been honest with her. The most probable outcome of today, however, was that Violet wouldn't remember ever having met Duncan or any other vampire. Ten days or ten years from now, she could bump into him on the street, and he'd be a complete stranger to her. But just in case something went wrong, they were giving her his real name as a sign of faith.

Duncan knocked on the screen door instead of using the doorbell. Emma figured it was intentional, more like a neighbor come calling than a stranger. She strolled over to greet him, moving slowly and casually, trying not to let Violet see any of the stress she was feeling about tonight's encounter.

Duncan smiled at her through the screen's mesh, and Emma nearly staggered as a punch of sheer lust hit her. She'd left the residence only a few hours ago, but it was as if she hadn't seen him, hadn't touched him, in ages. He winked at her and she blushed, feeling like a schoolgirl with her first crush.

"Good evening, Emma," he said, his gaze never leaving hers, his voice stroking her nerves with velvet sheathed fangs. He was looking very handsome this evening, but then when didn't he? Tonight, however, he'd dressed very intentionally, balancing trusted professional with sympathetic listener. He was wearing dark tan khakis that fit far better than those she'd seen on other men, and hugged his tight rear end wonderfully. A black turtleneck and wool blazer topped off the look, with his neatly tied back hair adding a touch of Bohemian free thinker. No stuffy, unimaginative drone here. You want to talk about vampires? This is a man who will not only listen, he'll believe you.

"Duncan," she said, feeling wicked and wanting to be sure he was experiencing the same tug of desire she did. "Good of you to . . . come." His eyes filled with heat and Emma's body responded instantly, making her wish they had ten minutes to themselves. That's all it would take. Up against the wall, just a taste to slake her thirst. But, no. She banked her lust, storing it for later, when they'd be alone again in that big bed.

In the room behind her, Violet coughed softly, and Emma nearly jumped at the timely reminder of why they were all here. She opened the screen door and said, "Come in," not knowing whether the invitation was necessary or not. Phoebe was a vampire, after all, so maybe the restriction didn't apply. But she'd forgotten to ask earlier if a vampire's residence was sacrosanct like a human's. Darn. If she was going to hang around with vampires, she'd have to start making a list of things she needed to know.

* * * *

Duncan stared at Emma through the open door. The scent of her arousal filled his senses and he was instantly hard. He forced his body to relax, using every bit of control learned in over a century and a half of living. Still, to make things interesting, he let his arm brush against Emma's breasts as he went by her. He heard her sharp intake of breath and smiled to himself. She wasn't the only one who could tease.

"Duncan," Emma said, somewhat breathlessly, he was pleased to note. "This is my friend Violet." She walked over to stand next to the other woman who was seated. "I told you about her."

"Yes, of course," Duncan said. He didn't offer to shake hands immediately, but slipped off his blazer and tossed it onto a nearby chair. He took the chair closest to where Violet sat on the sofa, near enough that he could reach out and touch her, but not so near that she would feel overwhelmed by him.

"A pleasure to meet you, Violet," he said, finally offering his hand. "I hope I can help."

Violet didn't move at first. She was a pale little thing. Pretty underneath all that stress, and a complete submissive. He knew what Victor had seen in her, knew why she'd been chosen. He didn't like it, but he understood. She sat there, frozen, like a soft, gray mouse beneath the eye of a predator, although she couldn't possibly know how apt that description was. Duncan remained still, not wanting to spook her, letting her do this her way and take her time. She studied him for a few minutes, her gaze going from his offered hand to his face, where it lingered to search his eyes, and then back to his hand. She reached out slowly and let him wrap his much bigger fingers around hers. He didn't shake her hand, but held it loosely, radiating safety and warmth through that connection, gently persuading her that he meant her no harm.

Silent tears filled Violet's eyes as she relaxed for what was probably the first time since Victor had messed with her mind. Even a cursory probe told Duncan that the dead vampire lord had been crude in his effort to wipe the young woman's thoughts. Maybe he'd been in a hurry. Maybe he'd intended to come back and do a more thorough job of it. Or, more likely, he'd simply been a butcher who hadn't cared what damage he did to the humans he toyed with.

Duncan reached out and brushed away a tear that had escaped to roll down Violet's cheek. "It will all be well, Violet. You'll see."

She nodded and bent her head, wiping her eyes quickly before raising her head and firming her chin defiantly. "What do you need me to do?"

Duncan smiled at her courage. When Emma had first told him about Violet, he'd assumed she was a broken woman, someone cast off because Victor had found her wanting. But that wasn't true. She might be naturally submissive, but that didn't necessarily mean weak. It was far more likely that she'd survived as well as she had because she was stronger than Victor expected. Her mind had refused the old vampire lord's manipulation and clung to the truth, despite the cost to her sanity.

Duncan squeezed her fingers slightly. "Just tell me what you remember," he said gently. "I'll do the rest."

Violet drew a deep breath through her nose, her mouth tight with determination. "Is this like hypnosis or something?"

"Or something," Duncan agreed easily. "But you won't lose consciousness and you'll remember everything."

She studied him again for a long moment, then said, "I don't remember that much about what happened."

"Tell me whatever you recall," Duncan said, and sent her mind a mild suggestion to *remember*.

"Okay." She paused for a moment, as if deciding where to start. "The first party I ever went to," she began, "was with Lacey."

With every word she spoke, Duncan wove himself deeper into her memories. He was appalled at the mess Victor had left behind. Knots and tangles of memory and half-truths, all jumbled together with things that had no bearing on what Victor had been trying to hide. Duncan was ashamed on behalf of his kind that a vampire lord as powerful as Victor could have been so incompetent, or so cruel. Slowly, he teased out bits and pieces of truth, each new revelation freeing Violet to remember more. He kept a firm hold on her emotions while working, not wanting to cause her any more psychological distress than she'd already endured.

Violet smiled when she spoke about Lacey. "She was so pretty, so full of life. All the men loved her. I used to watch them watching *her* at the parties. When she crossed a room, heads turned as if she was iron and they were magnets. Or maybe it was the other way around. It never affected her, though. Not like some of the others who got all bitchy and looked down their noses. Lacey thought the whole thing was a game." She frowned briefly. "But it was definitely a game she wanted to win. She was looking for something at those parties. A husband maybe, or maybe just a rich lover. I never knew her well enough to ask what it was."

"You're talking about the parties at Victor's house?" Duncan clarified quietly.

Violet nodded. "The one in the embassy district, the big white one. Nice place, but the inside was more like a fraternity house than an embassy. It was odd."

"What happened at these parties?"

She shrugged. "Nothing at first. They were typical Washington stuff. The men were all grabby, especially the married ones, and most of the women didn't care. Not the young ones anyway. It wasn't until Victor invited us to the other house, the one in Leesburg that I felt . . . uncomfortable."

"Why?"

Violet tensed up, and Duncan reached out, soothing her with both his hand and his mind. "No one can hurt you here, Violet. You know that, don't you?"

She nodded quickly. "Yes. I believe you."

Her words of trust added a fresh burden of responsibility to Duncan's soul. It was minuscule compared to that which he already bore, but he felt it nonetheless.

"Thank you, Violet." He waited a moment, then said, "Why did you feel uncomfortable at the Leesburg party?"

"It was my first time at one of the weekends. Lacey had told me about some other house, in Annapolis, I think, but that had been only one night and everyone left before dawn. The party at Leesburg was supposed to be for a whole weekend. I didn't want to go, but I remember feeling like I had to, like I'd be disappointing someone if I didn't. It didn't make sense, but the closer I got to the date of the party, the more I felt like I *had* to go." She shrugged, as if even now she couldn't understand it. But Duncan did. Victor had clearly planted the suggestion in her mind and let it run.

"I drove down with Lacey, and when we got there," Violet continued, "there were only a few men—two or three that I ever saw, plus Victor and his guards. I assumed more people would be coming, but except for three other women who arrived right after me and Lacey, no one else came. And when I realized it was just us and those men, I knew what they wanted us for." Tears began rolling down her cheeks again, but that was the only sign of her distress as she kept talking.

"Victor did something to me, to all of us. I did . . . awful things for those men. Disgusting things. Even when I was doing them, I knew something was wrong. It was like my mind was screaming at me from somewhere, but I couldn't make my body listen. And it went on forever, not just with one man, but with all of them."

"Did Victor participate in—"

"Not with me," she said quickly. "I don't know about the others. His guards did, though. When the clients—that's what Victor called them, like we were whores." She swallowed hard, revulsion for the men and maybe for herself, too, written on her face. "When the clients were finished with us, Victor's guards took over. And they wanted more than sex, or more than *just* sex, because they took that, too."

"Blood?" Duncan asked, careful to keep the anger from his voice.

Violet nodded. "And the next night, it started all over again, but the men were worse than before. More violent. I thought they were going to kill us all," she whispered. "But they only killed poor Lacey."

Duncan's eyes flashed immediately to Emma who sat next to a cluttered dining room table behind Violet. She met his gaze, distress in every nuance of her body. He wanted to tell her to leave, that she didn't need to hear this, but he knew she wouldn't go. And he wouldn't ask her to.

"Did you see what happened to Lacey?" he asked, returning his attention to Violet and making the question sound only mildly curious.

Violet shook her head. "I was next door. But I heard them. I think . . . I heard one of the other men shout at someone else, saying they'd killed her. He said something like, 'You've strangled her, you fool.' And then the man who was with me—I'm ashamed to say I don't know who he was—anyway, he jumped up and ran into the hallway and everyone started yelling, and then someone punched someone else and I could hear them fighting. And then one of Victor's guards ran into my room and grabbed me." She rubbed her arm, as if she could still feel the grip of his hand.

"He dragged me down the hall and threw me into this tiny room with all the other women and locked the door. Lacey was the only one missing. We were all naked, but there was a bed there so we grabbed the sheets and blankets. Two of the women . . . I don't know their names. Lacey was the only one I knew from before, and none of us used our real names. I think we all knew this was something we wouldn't want anyone to know about. Anyway, two of the women were unconscious, or at least they weren't moving anymore. So, I and the other girl wrapped them in the blankets, figuring they needed the extra warmth, and we took the sheets. And that's all I remember. It's like there's a big black spot in my brain, and no matter how hard I try, I can't put anything in it. I woke up in a car driving back to the District. I was wearing clothes, but they weren't even mine. One of Victor's guards dropped me off at my apartment, handed me my purse, and that was it. I went upstairs and . . ."

Violet bent her head, hiding behind her hair as her eyes closed, her throat working as she struggled to contain her emotions. Duncan felt dirty prying into her heart and soul like this, but he couldn't help her, couldn't *fix* her any other way. And because he was trying to fix her, because he was so tuned in to what she was feeling, he knew her emotions were very much like the ones experienced by women who'd been raped. He'd felt that before, too, in other women he'd rescued over the years. It was combination of shame and guilt, of helplessness, and at the same time, pure, unadulterated rage, sometimes at themselves as much as their rapist.

"I showered," Violet whispered. "I showered until every inch of my skin was raw from scrubbing. And then I crawled into my bed and slept. And I never really woke up." She looked up, meeting Duncan's gaze. "Until today."

"I'm sorry to make you relive all of that," Duncan said, meeting her eyes and letting his own sorrow show. "But it's necessary. I wouldn't ask it otherwise."

Violet nodded. "I know. And I feel better simply knowing it was real, that I'm not losing my mind."

"Did you know any of the men, other than Victor?"

"Not then. But one of them was that senator you see on the news all the time now, Grafton. My dad's always saying how the name fits, because politicians are always on the take. I remember two others, but I don't know their names. One was the creep with me when Lacey died. I'd know his face if I saw it, but I don't know his name. He was kind of beat up looking, and he drank a lot. He had that smell that alcoholics get. I don't know what it is, precisely, but I had an uncle who was an alcoholic and he always smelled that way. The man couldn't . . ." Her face heated with embarrassment, and she looked away.

"The man couldn't get an erection," Duncan provided. "Is that it?"

"Yes," Violet said, still not looking at him.

"What about the third man?"

"I don't know his name either, but if I had to guess, I'd say he was a politician of some sort. He had that slick, captain-of-the-football-team personality. He looked like one, too. I remember wondering why a guy that good-looking would need someone like Victor to pimp for him."

That description fit too many of the glad-handing politicians in town to be useful, but the alcoholic she'd described . . . *that* matched the appearance of Congressman Kerwin whom Duncan had last seen at Grafton's fundraiser, flushed with too much alcohol and staring at Duncan like he'd seen a ghost.

"But I never saw the woman," Violet added unexpectedly.

Duncan and Emma both stared at her. "Woman?" Duncan said, puzzled. "You mean one of the other women who were there with you?"

"No," Violet said, shaking her head. "There was a woman there with Victor. I never did see her; I only heard her voice. She came later, at the end, after Lacey . . ." She frowned and bit the inside of her lip unhappily. "She was yelling, I mean *really* angry, like she was in charge or something. It surprised me, because I'd never heard *anyone* talk that way to Victor before."

* * * *

They took Violet home after that. Emma drove the same SUV, with Violet in the passenger seat up front, but Duncan rode in the back this time. He didn't say much, but Emma could feel the comfort of his

presence behind her, like a banked fire on a cold night. She knew he
was probably doing it for Violet's benefit, but she enjoyed it anyway.
And she wondered if he knew what it felt like when he did whatever
that was. Had he ever been on the receiving end of it? Had someone
taught him how to project that overwhelming sense of safety and
security? Or was it instinctive, just a part of who he was?

Violet's parents were home when they got there. The porch light
was on in welcome, and Emma could see the flickering of a television
screen behind the sheers on the front window.

"Will your parents be worried?" Emma asked, not knowing what
Violet had told them. They had to wonder why their daughter, who'd
been all but homebound for the last two weeks, would suddenly be out
late at night.

Violet shook her head. "I told them I was going out with a friend.
They were thrilled."

Emma could understand that. "You want me to walk in with you,
then?"

"No, it's okay." Violet turned in the seat and addressed Duncan.
"Thank you, Duncan," she said somberly. "I don't know what you
really did today, and I don't care. You saved my life and that's all that
matters. To me, anyway." She opened the door and climbed out, then
stopped and looked at Emma. "I hope you find whatever you're looking
for, Emma, and I hope it brings you peace." Then she slammed the
door and ran up the stairs, moving with an energy and grace that had
been totally lacking a few hours earlier.

"Will she remember any of this?" Emma asked, watching as Violet
disappeared into the house.

"No," Duncan said. "She'll wake in the morning and remember
being ill, and now she'll get better."

Emma sighed. It was a bittersweet victory. They'd given Violet
her life back, but Lacey was still gone. And her killers were still out
there. But at least Violet had given them something to go on. Grafton
for sure, which they'd already suspected, and the drunk who couldn't
get it up, probably Kerwin. And then there was the woman. Grafton's
wife? Or maybe Tammy Dietrich? Emma sighed. The more they
learned, the more complicated everything became.

Duncan's warm hand touched her shoulder. "Pull over, Emma."
She did so, not even questioning why. Their escort pulled in behind
them, and a minute later Ari was knocking on her window. He took
over the steering wheel, while Miguel claimed the passenger seat.

Grumbling all the way, Emma climbed into the backseat with
Duncan, but consoled herself by snuggling up close to him. Duncan put
his arm around her and gave her a warm kiss that made her hope Ari
made Indy 500 time on the drive back to the house. But he was quiet
after that, leaving Emma to her own thoughts. Towns and neighborhoods

flashed by outside. Ari was driving much faster than she would have dared, especially since a light rain had begun to fall. Apparently he didn't worry about being pulled over for speeding. Could a vampire talk his way out of a ticket if he did get pulled over? Or maybe they had some sort of diplomatic immunity? And were girlfriends included? That could come in handy.

They arrived back in the District with hours to spare before sunrise. Ari pulled in behind the house, maneuvering around construction equipment and piles of supplies, gleaming wetly in the headlights. Emma scrambled down from the SUV, frowning at the abundance of construction-related materiel. She knew there were more people, more vampires actually, working on the house than what she saw. She'd seen evidence of the remodeling and sometimes heard them shouting back and forth. But this seemed like an awful lot of stuff. Duncan joined her, his gaze raking over the house and back to her. He smiled, then put a hand low on her back.

"Let's get inside before it starts raining again," he said, and started walking toward the kitchen door. "Ask Alaric to leave an update for me, please, Miguel," he called without looking. "And tell him I'll meet him tomorrow night."

"Yes, my lord."

"You must be tired," Duncan said at her ear.

"Not that tired. Besides, you did all the work," she murmured back to him.

"Did I? Perhaps."

Emma frowned, but didn't say anything else until they had reached Duncan's suite and closed the bedroom door behind them.

She unbuttoned her blouse and stepped out of her heels, watching him covertly, admiring the graceful way he moved, even when it was something so prosaic as taking off his jacket and stripping away his sweater. Although, granted, there was nothing prosaic about Duncan's bare chest. Or his back, either. He was all smooth muscle, long lean stretches of it that came together over broad shoulders and powerful arms. Unable to stop herself, she slipped out of her blouse and crossed the room to him. All of her senses seemed suddenly more concentrated, as if being this close to Duncan brought everything into hyperawareness. The thick carpet was like silk beneath her stockinged feet, her hair almost unbearably warm on her bare shoulders, and the satin of her bra an exquisite torment over her breasts.

Duncan turned and watched her come toward him, his body perfectly still in a way that was his alone, his eyes glowing a soft bronze in the dim light. He held out a hand when she drew close enough. She placed her fingers in his, feeling the slight roughness of his skin as he closed his hand and drew her into his embrace, circling her waist with his arm and bending his head enough to touch his lips to hers.

"Emma," he said softly. Just that. Just her name, like a promise.

Emma stroked her hand down his face. "What Victor did," she told him quietly, guessing at the source of his discontent from this evening. "That's not you. You know that, right?"

"Of course," he said too quickly.

"But you still feel guilty."

He sighed. "Victor was one of ours. We should have known what was going on and stopped it."

"You *did* stop it," she reminded him. "And now he's dead." She held his gaze. "Victor really is dead, isn't he?"

Duncan studied her for a long moment, as if deciding whether to trust her. Emma held her breath, not only because she wanted Victor to be dead, but more importantly, because she desperately needed Duncan to trust her enough to tell her the truth.

"He's really dead," Duncan said flatly. He met her gaze for a moment, then tugged her against his chest. Emma wrapped her arms around him, her eyes filling with tears of relief.

"I want you to move your things in here, into this room," Duncan said softly. "From the other bedroom."

"I don't have that much here, it's—"

"It doesn't matter. *This* is your room now."

Emma rubbed her fingers up and down his spine absently. Was it simply that Duncan was used to giving orders? Or maybe it was that vampire possessiveness he'd warned her about? And did she really care? After all, it wasn't like she was moving in lock, stock and barrel. He wasn't even asking her to do that. It was only a few changes of clothes. She'd done as much with boyfriends in the past, when they'd each kept a few things at each other's apartment. So why did this time feel different? *Stupid question, Emma*, she scolded herself. It was different because this time she was in love with the guy. And she had no idea how he felt about her. Oh, sure, he lusted after her, and, yeah, he was possessive as hell. But was that love?

She sighed. Duncan heard her, obviously. He could hear a pin drop at twenty paces, but more significantly, he understood the emotion behind her sigh.

"You're mine, Emma," he said softly, but in a voice that brooked no argument. "I want that clear. As long as you're in this house, as long as we're together, you're mine. And no one else's."

Emma leaned back enough to see his face. "That goes both ways, vampire. I don't share either."

A slow grin spread over Duncan's face, and he drawled, "I've barely enough strength for you, Emmaline."

Emma laughed softly, letting him distract her. "Oh, you'll manage somehow," she murmured, then reached behind his head and tugged the leather tie off his hair.

"I keep losing those," he complained.

"You have an entire drawer full of them," she scoffed, threading her fingers through his hair. "Don't be such a girl."

Duncan's brow arched in disbelief. "Girl?"

"Um, well, it's just a—" She shrieked in surprise as he spun her around and threw her on the bed. In a flash, he had her bent over the edge, her skirt up around her waist, her panties on the floor. Emma started laughing, but then groaned as his cock pushed past her tender folds and deep into the hungry wet depths of her sex. She hissed in pleasure at how good he felt, how completely he stretched her open and filled her as he began pumping in and out of her with long, graceful strokes. He unclasped her bra and ran a long-fingered hand up her bare spine and she arched her back languorously, opening herself even more to his invasion. He leaned forward over her back and brushed her hair aside as he nuzzled her neck.

"Let this be a lesson to you," he whispered flush against her ear. She groaned again as her vulnerable position let him go deeper than he'd ever gone before. He stopped moving abruptly, still buried inside her, nothing but the slightest flex of his hips slipping fractionally back and forth as he held her motionless. "This, my darling Emmaline, is a cock filling your sweet little pussy. *My* cock."

Emma giggled. "Okay, I—"

"And do girls have cocks?" he interrupted. "No, they don't."

Emma rolled her hips gently against his, loving the smooth glide of his thickness inside her.

"I don't think you're taking this lesson seriously," Duncan scolded. Emma yelped a surprised laugh as he slapped her ass smartly and began fucking her in earnest. She closed her eyes and went with it, loving the scrape of the velvet comforter against her hard nipples, the heated friction of his shaft, the zing of blissful sensation as he held onto her hip with one hand while the other reached around to toy with her clit. He bent over her again, his chest to her back, and she felt the warm caress of his tongue along the side of her neck. She shivered expectantly, and everything below her waist began thrumming with eager anticipation. The smooth, firm surface of his fangs brushed against her neck and she shuddered, her heart filling her throat and making it hard to breathe. But who needed to breathe? She only needed Duncan.

His fangs slipped almost painlessly into the taut skin of her neck, puncturing her vein like the pinch of a needle, quickly forgotten in the rush of exquisite pleasure that roared through her blood. The velvet beneath her breasts became a warm, seductive caress against her swollen nipples, clenching her abdomen and making her pussy shiver in anticipation. Without warning, she exploded in a climax that convulsed every muscle in her body, even as Duncan continued to pound into her, his hips grinding against her ass as he held her open to him. Somewhere in all of that, she was aware of the soft pull of his fangs against her vein, of his deep growl as she bucked beneath him, and then his head lifted and, with a roar of release, he filled her with the hot wash of his climax.

Emma no longer felt like laughing. Actually, she might have laughed with sheer joy if she'd been able to feel any part of her body, but she was so completely satiated, she couldn't feel anything at all. Duncan's cock flexed inside her, and she moaned as her clit sparked an answer. Okay, so not *every* part of her was numb, after all.

She felt the warm drizzle of blood slide down her neck a moment before Duncan gave her a sensuous lick and belatedly sealed the twin puncture wounds. He kissed them afterwards, murmuring a quiet apology, but Emma didn't care. She loved the way he came, loved the feel of his cock pumping inside her, loved that he was so lost in his climax that he forgot to lick the wounds closed. What was a trickle of blood compared to that?

He straightened, then lifted her from the waist and pulled both of them fully up and onto the bed. Emma sat up enough to peel off the remains of her thigh-high stockings, then collapsed against him, her cheek resting on his muscled shoulder. She flattened her palm over the ridges of his abdomen, stroking with possessive pride. Duncan's rumble of laughter vibrated beneath her ear.

"I hate when you do that," she muttered.

"Do what?" he asked innocently.

"Oh, please. You read me like a book. Besides, I was just admiring your muscle tone."

"All right."

She lifted her palm and slapped the muscles she'd been admiring, but he only laughed harder. Emma smiled. At least he wasn't sad, like he'd been earlier.

"Duncan?"

"Emma."

"*Do* you actually read my thoughts? I mean, can you?"

He squeezed her closer and touched his lips to her forehead. "It's not that simple. I can easily read the thoughts of any vampire sworn to me, and especially those of my own children, like Miguel and Louis. With humans, it's the difference between listening to your neighbor's music, or walking over and turning on your own. I don't hear every thought, but if necessary, I can delve into almost any human's brain and know what they're thinking. I'm also capable of manipulating a human's thoughts and memories. It can be something as simple as dissuading a cop from giving me a speeding ticket, or as complex as what Victor did in making those women forget. Though I like to think my own manipulations are far more skilled and far less malicious than anything Victor did."

He reached down and lifted her chin to look at him. "I would never probe your thoughts without permission, Emma, but you should know that the more blood we exchange, the closer our thoughts will become, and the more open your mind will be to me."

"But you already know what I'm thinking!"

"I don't. Not really. I'm a fairly strong empath. I read emotion. I've always had some ability along those lines, even when I was human. But with becoming a vampire, my ability to read the emotions of others is nearly perfect. And, as I told you when we first met, I have decades of experience reading the human body language that goes *with* those emotions." He shrugged. "It's only the words that are missing."

His fingers were still playing along her upper arm, but she felt the rest of him go still, as if waiting for her reaction. She frowned, thinking about what he'd told her, about what it meant. He knew her emotions, her feelings . . . about him. That she loved him. Emma knew she should be embarrassed, but on the other hand, he knew she loved him, and he wasn't running away screaming. So, okay, then.

"Hardly seems fair," she muttered, pulling the small hairs on his chest.

"Ow! What's not fair?" he asked, rubbing his abused follicles.

"That I can't tell what you're feeling, too."

"You know how I feel, Emmaline. You're mine."

Emma sighed softly. Maybe it was a vampire thing, this whole *mine* hang-up. "So, who do you think the woman was?" she asked, changing the subject. "The one Violet heard yelling that night."

"Tammy Dietrich seems likely," Duncan said. "Powerful men always call their lawyers first when they get into trouble. And it might explain why she was at Lacey's service. Grafton would have been too obvious, but Dietrich could show up to check things out, and no one would notice."

"But why would she sign the mourner's book? It would have been smarter not to leave a record like that."

"Who knows? Force of habit? Maybe there was someone who knew her and she thought it would look odd if she didn't sign it. Besides, who looks at those things afterward? She probably didn't give it a second thought. They had to have known by then that Victor had disappeared, or at least couldn't be reached. And with Lacey's body being found, I'm sure they were eager to know what story was being given for her death, and whether the police were involved."

"Well, that's one thing we all agree on. No police."

"No police," Duncan confirmed. "I'll take care of this myself."

"*We'll* take care of it," Emma said firmly. "Lacey was *my* friend."

"And you're not a killer, Emma."

"But you are?"

"When I need to be, yes."

Emma considered all the years Duncan had been alive, and how different justice might have been back . . . She frowned. Back when?

"How old are you, Duncan?" she asked, wondering if he'd tell her. "I mean how old are you *really*?"

"I was born in 1836."

The unreality of that took Emma's breath away for a moment. Duncan was nearly two hundred years old, which meant that even when he'd been human, he was already old enough to be married, to have children, especially back then.

"Did you have a family? I mean before you became a vampire. Were you ever married?"

He didn't say anything for a moment, then he got up and left the bed. Emma thought she'd gone too far, that she'd touched on another vampire taboo, or maybe something that was too painful for him to think about. Duncan crossed over to a tall dresser, opened the top drawer, and removed a wooden box about the size of an old cigar box. Emma watched curiously as he lifted the lid and took something out, then stood staring down at whatever it was before finally turning and coming back to the bed.

He held it out to her, and she saw it was an old-fashioned photograph, the kind they called a daguerreotype. It was a portrait of a young woman and two small children—a boy somewhere around four years old, and a second child of indeterminate sex, maybe a year old, sitting on the woman's lap. Emma stared at the photograph, then looked up at Duncan.

"My wife and children," he said simply. "They died while I was at war."

Emma's heart clenched in sympathy. "I'm sorry," she whispered. "What happened?"

"They were murdered."

She stared at him in sudden understanding. All along, Duncan had been the only one who understood her need for revenge, her need to be a part of the search for Lacey's killer. And maybe that was because he knew firsthand the thirst for justice, not at the hands of the law, with its process and protections for the killers, but up close and personal. The biblical, eye for an eye, cold-blooded vengeance.

"What did you do?" she asked.

* * * *

1836, Nashville Basin, Tennessee

Duncan stared at the ruin of what had once been his family home. It looked old and tired, despite the cover of night. It had never been a grand building, but it had been filled with life once upon a time. No more. He was the last of his line, and now that he was Vampire there would be no one after him. And no one to care either way.

It had taken him and Raphael several nights to get this far. Raphael had told him that their ultimate path was westward, all the way to the western ocean. The journey back to what had been Duncan's home was a detour, but Raphael had never voiced a word of protest. He'd seemed to accept Duncan's need for vengeance as if it were his own. At first, Duncan had thought it was simply the bond between a vampire and his child, but he'd soon realized it was more than that. It was a measure of the man Raphael had been and the vampire lord he had become. He would stand shoulder-to-shoulder with those he took for his own. And Duncan felt the ties of loyalty growing stronger with each step he took beside the vampire who was now, and forever would be, his Sire.

"What happened?" Raphael asked quietly, staring at the abandoned house.

"This infernal war happened," Duncan said. He walked over to the tall chestnut tree in the front yard, bent over and picked up the torn remains of a thick rope. It had adorned the tree once upon a time, a swing fashioned anew every spring for his children to play on. He dropped the rope into the dirt and turned away, heading back toward the road and the nearby town.

Raphael kept pace with him without comment, though Duncan could feel his Sire's curiosity through the bond they now shared. It was a strange feeling to be so tied to another man, but there was nothing sexual about it. If anything, it made him stronger, as if Raphael were a reservoir of strength that Duncan could borrow from at will. Or perhaps it was the certain knowledge that Raphael would always stand with him against his enemies. And those enemies were in the town a few miles down the road.

"I didn't join the army at first," Duncan said as they kept walking. "The people around here were as content to remain with the Union as not, and many of us felt it wasn't our battle. But then the Confederacy came looking for troops and we had to choose." He shrugged. "We voted and the Confederacy won, or so the town fathers told us. I've no idea if they were truthful in that, or if it simply suited their interests better to have it so. In any event, those of us young enough and strong enough were recruited and sent off to be soldiers. And we were given assurances that our families would not suffer, that the town would stand together."

Duncan bent and picked up a rock, bouncing it in his hand as they walked.

"And did they?" Raphael asked.

Duncan considered the question. "They stood together. But not in the way I expected. My wife was a beautiful woman and I was a poor farmer. She married beneath her station in taking me for a husband, but she loved me, and God knows I loved her. There are times I think she'd

still be alive if she'd married someone wealthier, or just someone else."
He sent the rock arching into the moonlit darkness of the surrounding
field. "Before we married, she had a suitor. The banker's son, a young
man of money and privilege whom she rejected in my favor. He was
offended, of course, and while I was gone to war, he came to our
house, drunk and angry at what he considered her humiliation of him."

It was not necessary to spell out what had happened next. Any
man would know without being told what would have come of such an
encounter.

"Your children?" Raphael asked.

"My son tried to protect his mother and was clubbed aside. My
daughter was a baby, little more than a year old, not even walking yet
when I saw her last. She lay next to her mother for days before anyone
discovered what had happened. My wife's father came looking for her
eventually and found them like that. The children were dead, my wife
nearly so. But before she died, she told him what had happened, and
who had done it. He went to the town law, but the brute was long gone,
sent off to the war before his crime could be exposed. I was sent for,
of course, but returned only in time to visit their graves."

"And is this killer still alive?" Raphael asked in a cold voice.

"He is. But not much longer."

Raphael grunted his agreement. They walked another mile in
silence, until the buildings of the town came into sight, candlelight
flickering in distant windows. They stopped on the outskirts of town,
and Raphael did a slow turn as he surveyed the cluster of buildings.
"His house is here somewhere?"

"His father's house. That one, near the stand of hickory trees. You
can't see it from here, but there's a small lake, too. It's quite lovely in
the summer, though the common folk are discouraged from using it
now. It was open for all before he built his house there."

The banker's house was brightly lit, lanterns burning on the porch,
candles glimmering in every window. Duncan started for the steps,
Raphael beside him. They reached the front door and rang the small
bell hanging to one side. This was the part of their plan that had Duncan
most concerned. The banker's house was a private residence, which
meant, as vampires, he and Raphael would need to be invited inside.

A uniformed maid opened the door. She was young and pretty, and
African, which meant she was probably a house slave. She stared up
at them, her gaze going from their faces to their dusty clothes.

"We're invited guests, child," Raphael said. "Invite us in."

Duncan jerked in surprise, but the slave continued to stare up at
the big vampire lord, her eyes blank and unfocused, until she smiled
and said, "Come in, gentlemen. I'll tell the master you've arrived."

"Master indeed," Raphael muttered, but he smiled at the young
slave. "Thank you."

She blushed, ducking her head with pleasure as they walked past her into the house.

"Where is your . . . *master*?" Raphael asked smoothly.

"In the library, sirs. Shall I show you?"

"That would be most kind. Duncan?"

They followed the slave down a short hallway to the back of the house. She stopped in front of a pair of doors and was about to knock when Raphael took her hand. "There's no need to trouble yourself, child. Go back to your chores."

The young slave's eyes took on that unfocused look again, and then she turned and walked away, as if they weren't even there.

Raphael watched her go, then caught Duncan's gaze. "The banker is alone in there, but there are others in the house."

Duncan wiped his hands nervously on his filthy pant legs and tried to calm his galloping heart. He wanted to do this right, not just for his own vengeance, but to prove to Raphael that he hadn't made a mistake in choosing Duncan out of all the dying men on that battlefield. Earning Raphael's respect had somehow become the most important thing in his life, and he couldn't help wondering if these new feelings were part of the bond of which Raphael had spoken.

Raphael pulled open the doors and stepped into the library. He radiated strength and confidence, dominating the room not just with his formidable size, but with the power that fairly poured off of him. It was so strong that Duncan thought he would see the glow of it if he concentrated hard enough. But then the banker spoke, and Duncan had eyes for only the man whose son had killed his family.

"Milford?" the banker said, his thick body almost vibrating with its outrage. "What is the meaning of this?"

"Your son killed my family," he told the banker calmly. "I want to know where he is."

The banker leaned back in his chair, full of confident disdain. "You want money, is that it?" He stretched forward again and opened a desk drawer, pulling out a metal lockbox. The key was in the lock and he turned it, flipping the lid back to reveal a considerable amount of gold coin. "How much, Milford?"

Duncan stared at him. After months on the battlefield, he thought he'd seen the deepest depths to which a man could sink. But this . . . this *cur* thought gold could compensate him for the loss of his family?

"Come on, boy. Everyone has a price. What's yours?"

"I do have a price," Duncan said, enunciating each word with precision, so there could be no doubt. "And that is an eye for an eye. I want the life of your son."

The banker flicked his hand at Duncan in dismissal. "Don't be absurd. Besides, he's not here. He went off to the army like everyone else. I have no idea—"

Raphael made an impatient gesture and the banker stopped talking mid-sentence, his eyes bulging from his head as he struggled to speak. Fear sent rivulets of sweat dripping down his face, staining the starched collar of his shirt, which he wrenched open in his fruitless efforts to free his voice. His gaze switched frantically from Raphael to Duncan and back again.

Duncan could hear the man's labored breath sawing in and out of his lungs, the squeak of his fingers on the wooden chair arms. He could smell the rank odor of sweat, the stink of garlic on the banker's breath as he panted in fear. But more than that . . . he tilted his head curiously.

"I can feel his fear, my lord," he whispered to Raphael. "It's almost as if my own heart is racing, my gut churning with terror. But . . . there is no guilt. He feels only a righteous anger, as if he is the one being wronged."

Next to him, Raphael nodded. "Empathy. You must have experienced it as a human, but your rebirth has expanded it. It is an excellent talent to have, Duncan. It will serve us both quite well in the future."

Duncan bared his teeth at the banker. His brand new fangs slid into view, and he felt the man's fear intensify in a most satisfactory manner. Duncan had never been a particularly violent man. Always willing to defend what was his, he'd nonetheless found it easier to persuade rather than fight, and he'd always been able to find the words to work things out.

But right now, seeing this man he'd once thought powerful tremble in fear at the sight of Duncan himself . . . it felt good. It felt right.

"He's lying," Raphael said casually, reaching across the desk to help himself to the money box and all its gold. "His son is in the house." His gaze shifted to the right, staring at the wall as if he could see through the intervening wood and plaster. He smiled slightly. "Right down the hall, as a matter-of-fact." He snapped his gaze back to the banker. "Sleep."

The banker fell forward, his head hitting desk and bouncing once as he fell into unconsciousness. Duncan looked up at Raphael. "You learned of his son's presence from his thoughts, my lord?"

"I did," Raphael agreed. "The thoughts of sniveling men are easily spied upon. This way, Duncan."

They hurried back to the hallway, back the way they'd come only a short time ago. They met no one, not even the maid, as Raphael turned down yet another hallway, this one narrower than the first, and went directly to a closed door. There was a sputtering candle in a single hurricane lamp on a shelf opposite the door, but other than that, the hallway was barely lit.

Steeling himself for a confrontation, Duncan pulled his knife and opened the door. He ducked as he entered, expecting a rifle blast to greet him, if indeed this was the killer he sought. But the room was completely dark and nothing but a surprised grunt greeted his arrival.

Duncan felt a wave of Raphael's power roll past him. Candles flared, and the man he sought was revealed, hiding in the dark. He was in bed, covers drawn up to his chest, propped up on his elbows as he squinted at the intruders.

"Milford," the man said. "I'd hoped you were dead." He sighed, then pushed himself up higher against the wall behind the bed, and asked wearily, "What do you want?"

Duncan stared at the killer, his gaze taking in the man's well-muscled shoulders beneath his nightshirt, then down to his legs still covered by the blankets. He raised his eyes to meet those of the killer who was staring back at him defiantly.

"That's right, I'm a cripple now, but I'm still ten times the man you'll ever be."

"You're a killer and a rapist, lower than the cockroach that lives in shit."

The killer shrugged. "Are we finished here then? Because I'm tired." Raphael stepped into the light, and the killer looked up at him. "Brought someone to do your dirty work for you? It figures."

Raphael took in the killer's shriveled legs beneath the blanket and laughed. "I've seen this before, Duncan. His cock's probably as useless as his legs now. There's a certain justice in that."

Duncan fingered the blade in his right hand. He nodded. "Justice, my lord," he agreed, then took two quick steps forward and stabbed the killer in the chest, the narrow blade of the knife slicing easily through flesh and into the man's heart. Red blood bloomed on the white linen of his nightshirt, and the man howled, staring in shock from Duncan's hand, still fisted around the blade's hilt, to his face.

"But it's not justice I'm looking for," Duncan growled. "It's vengeance."

He waited until life left the killer's eyes, until his body slumped heavily against his hand, then pulled the knife out and lifted the sheet to clean the blade. Sliding the knife back into its sheath, he realized he'd just killed a man in cold blood, and yet he felt nothing but satisfaction. Surely he should feel some guilt, some conflict at least between his desire for vengeance and this blunt execution? Was this what it meant to be Vampire? Was he truly human no longer?

"We're still human after a fashion, Duncan," Raphael said, as if reading his mind. "But we're more, as well. For a vampire, there is no gray, only black and white. If a man takes something that is mine, if he harms someone I care about, or steals something I value, he dies. It's a simpler life, but more brutal as well. Some of us revel in it; others choose to live much as humans do. There is no way of knowing before a person's rebirth how things will turn out, but I am pleased to see that

I was right about you. You have power and talent, and you do not flinch in the face of your enemy.

"That's good, Duncan, because I intend to rule this continent someday. I'll need someone like you at my side."

Duncan turned to face his Sire. He heard the sincerity in the vampire lord's words. More than that, he *felt* the emotion that went with it and knew Raphael was speaking only the truth. He took a step back and gave a courtly bow from the waist.

"I am honored to serve you, my lord."

Raphael grinned and slapped Duncan on the shoulder. "Then let's get out of this place. The sight of a dead enemy is satisfying, but the stink is less welcome."

They were both laughing as they started down the road, breathing in the fresh, night air. Duncan strode proudly next to his Sire, and for the first time since his family had died, he knew he had something to live for.

* * * *

"Did you ever look back and regret it?" Emma asked. They were lying side by side again, and she raised herself up on one elbow to look into Duncan's face when he answered her.

He shook his head, meeting Emma's clear violet gaze head-on. And he told her the same thing Raphael had told him as they left that house all those years ago. "There are some things that cannot be forgiven if a man is to live with himself, some actions that define who we are. That man raped my wife, murdered her and my children. I could not let him live and consider myself a man."

Emma nodded, then rested her head on Duncan's shoulder once again. She placed her hand over his heart. "That goes for a woman, too, you know. I can't forget that Lacey's killer is out there. I can't live with that."

"You won't have to, Emmaline. Neither one of us will."

Chapter Twenty-Three

Emma went to work the next day, although she was no longer sure why she bothered. She was there in body, but that was it. Every time someone asked her a question, she had to play back in her head whatever it was they'd said, then remind herself of where she was before answering. That left her staring blankly at either her computer or the person who'd spoken while she tried to catch up. So it didn't even surprise her when Sharon Coffer stopped by her desk and asked her to step into the Congressman's office. Although *asked* was a polite way of putting it. It was more of a command performance.

Guy Coffer was out, so Emma and Sharon had the spacious office to themselves. Emma knew she was in trouble when Sharon closed the door deliberately before walking over to sit behind the desk. That was something even the most senior staffers would never have dared, but it had been clear to Emma from the beginning that Sharon considered this as much her office as her husband's, that Guy Coffer's election was as much about Sharon as it was about Guy. He just happened to have the more photogenic face, and more charisma in his little finger than existed in Sharon's entire body.

"Emma," Sharon said, indicating the chair in front of the desk. Emma sat dutifully. "We were all very sorry to hear about Laney—"

"Lacey," Emma corrected.

Sharon's expression tightened, her eyes narrowing to slits, but her voice was all smoothness and light when she continued, "Of course. Lacey. We were all sorry about her death, and we all know the strain you've been under." Sharon paused as if expecting Emma to say something, but Emma didn't know what that something should be, so she remained silent.

"Unfortunately," Sharon went on, her tone making it clear she didn't consider it unfortunate at all, "the business of this office must continue. And I'm afraid you're not keeping up. I'm sure you understand. Once you've packed your things, someone will have to escort you out of the building and, of course, confiscate your ID."

Emma blinked, not certain she'd heard that right. "Are you firing me?" she asked in disbelief.

"We're letting you go, yes. The Congressman will, of course, provide you with a letter of reference, and I'm certain you'll have no difficulty finding another position once your personal situation clears up. But until then—"

"You're *firing* me?" Emma repeated, still not believing what she'd heard. "My best friend dies, and you're firing me because I'm distracted?"

Sharon's mouth pursed in distaste. "Really, Emma, there's no need for hysterics." But she couldn't conceal the hint of satisfaction in her expression. This was a day Sharon Coffer had probably dreamt of. The day she finally got rid of Emma Duquet, who clearly had designs on Guy Coffer, and whose biggest sin was being better looking than Sharon. By a fucking mile.

Emma stood, refusing to give the bitch any more pleasure than she was already getting from this. "You have my address," she said flatly, then turned and walked out of the office. Noreen watched with wide eyes as Emma went directly to her desk and began gathering up the few personal items she kept there.

"Emma?" Noreen asked.

"The bitch fired me," Emma said, through gritted teeth.

"Are you kidding me? Why?"

"Apparently having my best friend die is too inconvenient. Business must go on."

"Oh, honey, I'm sorry."

Emma looked up and gave the other woman a smile. "Don't worry, Noreen. I've faced worse than this and come out okay. I'll do it again."

Brave words, she thought to herself as she stashed her stuff in her oversized purse. Jobs like hers were hard to find and nearly impossible to get, and Sharon knew that. All that bullshit about a letter of reference . . . Oh, sure, there'd be a letter, and it would say all the right things. But behind Emma's back, Sharon Coffer would be poisoning the well.

She pulled out all the drawers one last time, then slung her bag over her shoulder and grabbed her laptop and her jacket. She gave Noreen a quick hug, took a final look around, and walked out the door for the last time. If Sharon wanted someone to escort her out of the building, they could damn well catch up.

No one came after her, so Emma kept walking, all the way out of the building and into the parking lot. She threw her purse across the seat, and her laptop followed albeit somewhat more carefully. Emma got behind the wheel and twisted the key. Still no one in sight, and she wasn't going to wait.

She pulled out of the parking lot and drove through the snarl of D.C. traffic, trying to decide where to go. Her heart wanted to rush back to Duncan, to rant and rave until the calm that surrounded him penetrated her anger and made her see that the world wasn't going to end because she'd lost a job. Rationally, she already knew that, but she was so damn angry. Anyway, it was daytime and Duncan was sound asleep. She thought about joining him, but she hadn't slept through the day with him yet. It seemed even more intimate than what they had done together in his bed. It was probably silly, but she felt as if he needed to invite her to sleep next to him when he was that vulnerable. Not that she couldn't be trusted. Hell, he was probably safer with her there with him than not, but she had a gut feeling that he needed to be the one to take that first step.

So where to go? She was too tired to sleep, even if she used the other bedroom, and besides, the residence would seem far too empty without any of the vampires around. There were human guards on the grounds during the day, but from what she'd seen in the morning as she left for work, they stayed outside the house. For that matter, she wasn't even absolutely certain the guards would let her back inside before sunset.

So she turned away from the vampires' residence and headed for her own house instead. Duncan wouldn't be happy that she was going there alone, but he'd admitted that the guy the other night had been a common burglar, not some assassin sent to take her out. And there were practicalities to deal with. Her mail, and Lacey's, too, would be piling up, and there were bills to pay. And now that she didn't have a job, she needed to update her resume and start looking for something new. It was also time to let her landlord know that she wouldn't be renewing the lease on the house. Even if she'd been able to get past Lacey's absence, she simply couldn't afford the place on her own. Especially not if she had to go a few months without income.

Emma found a space on the street right in front of her house with no problem, because unlike her, most of her neighbors still had jobs. She had turned off the ignition and was pulling her keys out, when a familiar looking SUV parked right behind her. It was one of Duncan's. He'd had someone following her the other day, and apparently he still did. So much for going it alone. She sighed and glanced in the rearview mirror, but the SUV's windows were tinted. She couldn't see the driver, but didn't expect to recognize him anyway. She was more familiar with the vamps than the human guards. Grabbing her stuff, she walked back to the driver's side of the SUV and waited while he slid down the window.

"Hey," she greeted him.

"Ms. Duquet," he said.

"I'm going to pack some boxes and things. You want to come inside?"

He turned off the truck's engine. "I'll walk in with you, make sure everything's okay."

"Oh, I'm sure everything's—"

"All respect, ma'am," he said. "I don't work for you."

Emma blinked and thought it was too bad Baldwin wasn't around. At least he was fun. "Okay," she said, and walked away, pulling out the key to the new lock that Duncan had ordered installed. Mr. Grumpy could follow at his own pace.

As expected, there was a pile of mail on the floor inside the front door. She dropped her keys in the dish, set her bag and laptop on the stairs and gathered up the whole mess. Shuffling it into a more or less neat stack, she headed for the kitchen. Duncan's guard came in behind her and went immediately upstairs to check everything out. Emma rolled her eyes and stopped long enough to grab the remote and turn on the TV, more for company than anything else. She had a feeling her bodyguard wasn't going to be too chatty.

She dumped the mail onto the tiled countertop and noticed the message waiting light blinking on her answering machine. The machine itself was a leftover from when she and Lacey had lived together in college, before they'd been able to afford cell service. When they'd moved to D.C., they'd both gotten cell numbers, but their Internet service had been provided over a landline, so they'd automatically hooked up the machine. No one had ever called the number except telemarketers, and even they stopped calling after the first year.

So now Emma stared at the blinking light for a few seconds before she registered its significance. Someone had called her home phone. It was probably nothing but a junk call triggered by Lacey's funeral notice, except that the phone was in her name, not Lacey's, and she'd automatically used her cell number on all the required forms.

"Only one way to find out," she muttered and punched the button. The machine's mechanical voice confirmed that there was a single message and gave the date and time of the call, then the message began to play.

"Ms. Duquet," a woman's husky voice said. "We've never met, but you came by my office in Alexandria two days ago." Emma snatched her hand away from the machine, as if the caller had reached out and zapped her. Alexandria. That had to be Tammy Dietrich. There must have been video monitoring in the reception area. How else could Dietrich have known she'd been there? More importantly, why was she calling Emma, and why on this number?

"I tried calling you at Guy Coffer's office," Dietrich continued, "but you were out, and they couldn't . . . or perhaps wouldn't . . . say when you'd be back. I didn't leave a message with them for reasons . . . well, for reasons I'd rather not discuss on an answering machine."

Dietrich inhaled deeply, and Emma realized she was smoking a cigarette. That explained the rough quality of her voice, but not perhaps the tension that underlay every syllable she spoke.

"Call me, Ms. Duquet," Dietrich said bluntly. "But use a phone you can trust absolutely. Don't use your personal cell, don't use this line either. I'd recommend a pay phone, if you can find one, or a prepaid cell phone. I'm leaving you a number, but don't bother trying to track it. I've taken my own advice and will dispose of the phone if I don't hear from you within forty-eight hours. Call me. You'll be glad you did."

The machine beeped loudly, announcing the end. Emma stared, then scrambled frantically to replay Dietrich's message. She hadn't paid any attention to the date and time stamp, didn't know for sure if the clock was even set on the machine. *Damnit!* Why hadn't the woman called her cell? Okay, fine, she didn't want it traced, but couldn't she at least have given Emma a head's up? Her fingers were shaking as she found the right button and hit replay.

"What's that?"

Emma shrieked and spun around, having forgotten all about Duncan's guard.

He frowned at her. "Is something wrong?"

"Do you have a cell phone?" she demanded.

"Well, yeah, don't—"

"Give it to me," she said, punching the replay button on the answering machine, which dutifully informed her that Dietrich's lone message had come in last night. While Emma and Duncan had been with Violet. Did Dietrich know about Violet? Was that why she'd called? To warn them away from the young woman? Was Violet in danger because of what they'd done? No, that didn't make sense. If she'd already talked to them, there was nothing to gain by getting rid of her. The smart move now would be to get rid of Emma and Duncan. Maybe that's what Dietrich was doing. Setting Emma up to be eliminated.

The message wound down to the phone number Dietrich had left and Emma wrote it down, then turned to the guard who eyed her as if she'd lost her mind.

"Phone?" she asked impatiently.

He studied her for a minute, then handed it over. There was no way her enemies could know to monitor this particular guard's cell phone, so it should be safe. She punched in the numbers quickly, then waited while it rang and rang. She'd almost given up when Dietrich's raspy voice answered. "About time, Duquet."

Emma's stomach sank. "How'd you know it was me?"

"You're the only one I gave this number to," Dietrich said dryly. "That was the whole point."

Right. "I got your message," Emma said tightly. "What do you want?"

"You came to see *me*," Dietrich reminded her. "As it happens, however, I have some free advice for you. Get out of town. You and your boyfriend both. Go as far and as fast you can."

"Look, Dietrich. This *is* Tammy Dietrich, right?"

"Got it in one, sweetheart."

"Well, *sweetheart*, I don't know what game you're playing, but I'm not leaving until—"

Dietrich laughed bitterly. "This is no game. Max doesn't play games. He never did. He simply clears the board until he gets his way, and you, Duquet, are in his way."

"Max Grafton? Your brother?"

"Half brother, but who's counting. I don't have time for this. I called to give you a warning and I've given it. I wanted to talk to you at Lacey's service, but there were too many people around. So I'm telling you now. Your life is in danger, and dying won't bring Lacey back. That's it, Duquet. That's all she wrote."

"Wait! How do I get in touch with you?"

"You don't. I told you, I'm taking my own advice. I'm going to dig a hole somewhere far away and crawl into it, and hope to hell Max never finds me. Good-bye, Ms. Duquet."

"Wait!" Emma cried again, but Dietrich was gone. Emma gave a wordless shout of frustration and spun on the guard. "What's your name?"

"Marlon."

"How long 'til sunset, Marlon?"

He glanced at his watch. "Two hours, give or take, probably less."

Emma thought for less than a minute. Getting out of town wasn't even a consideration, especially without Duncan. And she would bet a year's salary that the vampire lord had absolutely no intention of leaving, not because of Max Grafton or anyone else. But as powerful as Duncan was, he bled and he could die.

"We're leaving, Marlon. Duncan's in danger."

Marlon didn't waste words. He grabbed her arm and hustled her out of the kitchen and through the living room, where the local TV news was covering a story about an explosion and fire somewhere in the District. They were calling it terrorism, which was the first thing everyone thought of these days, whether or not it was. Emma reached out as Marlon dragged her past, intending to turn off the TV, when she recognized . . .

"Marlon," she said breathlessly.

Something in her voice stopped the hard charging guard. He turned to stare at the same horrifying image on the television screen that had caught her attention. It was Duncan's house. And it was on fire.

Chapter Twenty-Four

Emma felt like she was dying. If she had gone directly to Duncan's after leaving work, maybe she'd have been there in time to have stopped whatever this was. She needed to get to the house, needed to see for herself what was going on and how bad it was. Duncan and his vampires were all there, helpless in sleep. Was the house burning around them? Were they dying as she and Marlon raced through the D.C. streets? She didn't believe it, couldn't believe it. Deep in her heart, she was sure she'd *know* if anything had happened to Duncan. He was too important, too *alive,* to die without causing even a ripple in reality, certainly in *Emma's* reality. But what if he wasn't dead, but badly injured? What would she do then? Every vampire she knew was with him. Whom could she call for help? When Baldwin was shot, it was Duncan who brought him back with his blood. But who would be there to bring Duncan back?

She gripped the padded handle of the door as Marlon sped down side streets to avoid traffic, taking every turn with a squeal of tires. Emma had the local news channel up on her cell phone, the same one they'd watched back at her house. The station was running a live feed from the scene, but it didn't show her enough. She needed details, closeups. She screamed at the screen every time they broke away to the useless news anchors, who did nothing but repeat what she already knew. The authorities were on the scene and refused to speculate on the cause, but that didn't stop information from leaking. This was Washington, after all. The leading theory was a gas explosion of some kind. But was it an accident or intentional? Speculation was running wild. All the embassies in the area had shut down tight.

There was no mention of anyone being hurt, but there wouldn't be. Duncan and his vampires could all be dead and no one would know it until sunset. Emma swallowed hard, refusing to give in to the terror screaming at the back of her brain. She squinted at the tiny images on the video, comparing what she was seeing to what she knew of the house and its layout, trying to determine which part of the house was burning. A gas explosion could be anywhere, and the house was half-empty. But the images she saw were from the street, and the flames and destruction were very visible, which meant the front of the house was involved. And Duncan's bedroom looked out over the green expanse of the front lawn. Emma turned the phone face down on her thigh and looked away. She couldn't watch it anymore. She needed to see for herself.

She closed her eyes and half-listened to Marlon, who was on the phone, trying to reach his supervisor, the guy in charge of the daytime guards, but so far he'd had no luck. The guard commander was far too busy dealing with the emergency to worry about Marlon and Emma. But then she heard Marlon tell someone they were on their way back.

"She's here with me. Yeah, five minutes tops." He paused, then, "Why the fuck not?"

"What?" Emma demanded. "Put it on speaker, *damnit.*"

Marlon gave her a harassed look, but said, "Wait. I'm going to speaker. It's my boss," he added for Emma's sake.

"Ms. Duquet?" The voice that came out of the speaker was deep and controlled. The voice of authority.

"Call me Emma. What is it?"

"Well, Emma, the fire department wants to enter the residence, and I can't permit that."

"Wait. Say that again? Are you telling me no one's fighting the fire?"

"No. They're on the scene and they've got hoses going full-bore, but they want to get inside the house. Lord Duncan himself has given me very specific orders that no one, under any circumstances, is permitted inside the house during the day."

Emma listened with half an ear, her brain racing. It had to be an embassy thing. Embassies were considered the foreign government's sovereign territory and everyone treated the vampires' residence like an embassy. She could see why there might be some confusion, but . . .

"Okay, I understand that," she said out loud. "But this is an emergency. Surely—"

"No one, under any circumstances," he repeated firmly. "Except you."

"Pardon?"

"You're the only one allowed inside during daylight. Even I'm not allowed to go in there."

"Well, but that's—"

"Standard procedure, ma'am. And the press is all over this. I'd rather not say more until we can speak in person."

Emma looked up as they finally made the turn onto Duncan's street and the house came into view. "Oh, shit," she breathed. Then to the guard captain, "We're coming up on the gate now, can you get us inside?"

"Definitely. But, Marlon, you'll have to park outside." His voice started jumping, as if he was running. "I'm on my way to the gate. I'll meet you there."

Marlon double-parked as close to the gate as he could get, then wrapped a meaty arm around her waist and all but carried her forward. He had to shove his way through the crowd, ignoring angry shouts and demands from uniformed police that they stop. The only thing that was going to stop them was a bullet, and no policeman would risk shooting them in this crowd. She hoped.

"There he is," Marlon said, shouting to be heard above the noise of the crowd and the firefighting trucks and equipment ranged inside the estate walls. They might not be able to get inside the house, but they certainly weren't giving up on fighting it from the outside.

A tall, exotic-looking black man waved at them as he stepped over to the policeman guarding the open gate and said a few words. The officer looked up, then lowered his head and triggered his shoulder radio. Almost instantly, a hole opened up in the throng to disgorge two burly cops who hustled Emma and Marlon past the wall.

"Ms. Duquet," the black man said. "I'm Jackson Hissong, Lord Duncan's Chief of Daylight Security."

"Call me Emma," she reminded him, shaking his hand quickly. "What can I do?" She ran alongside Hissong as he spun and jogged over the lawn to the front of the house where some sort of command post had been set up.

"First, you need to back me up with the fire captain. They *cannot* go in that house."

"Look, Jackson, this isn't even a real embassy, and I'm not sure what the law says about a situation like this, even if it was."

"But you're a lawyer, right?"

"Yes, but I don't have any authority to—"

"Good enough. You're acting as Lord Duncan's agent in this, and as the only individual authorized to enter the premises."

"Then, maybe I should tell the fire department it's okay for them to enter, so—"

"No," Hissong said, stopping to regard her steadily. "You absolutely cannot do that."

"But what if Duncan and the others are in there and they're hurt?" Emma asked, anguished.

"Lord Duncan knows the risks better than you do, and I've trained with Miguel for ten years. This isn't a matter of some lame protocol or diplomatic immunity. This is a vampire's residence. I already have private fire contractors on their way, but in the meantime, if those guys—" He gestured at the firefighters all around them. "—break into that house, the vampires inside will be completely vulnerable. And what if that was the plan? Most of them are probably decent, courageous public servants doing a dangerous job. But what if just one of them isn't who he seems to be? He goes in there, finds the vampires and—" He slapped his hands together, making Emma jump in surprise. "That fast, Emma. It's all over. There's a reason for these restrictions. Lord Duncan's a smart man, and so's Miguel. You have to trust them."

"I do, but—"

"No buts, babe. You back me up, or you don't talk to the fire captain at all. There's no other option."

Emma scowled. "You're serious."

"As a heart attack," Hissong replied.

Emma looked away, staring at the house. The fire seemed to be under control, but what did she know about things like that? They were still spraying water, and men were still working all around the wreckage. Her heart stopped as she recognized what she was seeing. That was Duncan's room. Or it had been. The explosion had gone off right beneath the room she and Duncan shared, blowing out windows and ripping out big chunks of the wall. She couldn't see into the house, couldn't tell if Duncan was there—the hole wasn't that big and there was water spraying everywhere, and too much equipment in the way.

Tammy Dietrich's warning that they were in danger came back to her. But she didn't trust Dietrich. Maybe the phone call had been a ploy to get Emma back here in time to die in the explosion herself.

She looked at Jackson Hissong, his dark face glistening with dirt and sweat, hands on his hips as he studied her, waiting.

"Fine," she said. "We'll do it your way."

Hissong nodded, as if there'd never been any other possibility. He took her upper arm, guiding her forward. "Watch your step," he warned. "There's a lot of crap on the ground."

Emma realized for the first time that she was still wearing the three inch heels she'd worn to the office that morning. She hadn't had time to change before racing out of her house to get back here. She sighed and was grateful for the support of Hissong's hand on her arm.

"Captain Stavros," Hissong called, his deep voice carrying despite the roar of sound all around them, not only from the equipment and the rush of water, but from the fire itself.

A tall man in yellow turnout gear finished his conversation with two other firefighters before favoring Hissong with a scowl which he quickly transferred to Emma.

"Captain, this is Emma Duquet, Lord Duncan's attorney."

Stavros' eyes were weary as he looked her up and down, but that didn't mask the clear fact that he was not impressed. Whether it was with her specifically, or lawyers in general, Emma didn't know. Either way, it got her back up like nothing else would have. She might not agree with Hissong's decision on this, but having met Captain Stavros, she would fight for it with her last breath.

"You're the lawyer?" he said doubtfully.

"Yes, I am. Is there a problem?" she said coolly, deciding a head-on approach was the only kind that would work in this instance.

"Yeah, there's a problem. We need to get inside this structure and your man here is stopping us. You're lucky I haven't had him arrested along with all—"

"Captain Stavros, you cannot have risen to the position you have in the District without being aware of the law regarding foreign embassies, which is that the embassy itself is, for all intents and purposes, the sovereign territory of the respective nation."

"Of course, I'm aware of that," he said testily. "But I'm not required to stand by and watch the damn building burn to the ground, putting other people and properties at risk. All I'm—"

"There is far more at risk here than property. This is the *vampire* embassy. There are a large number of vampires inside that house, and I'm certain every one of them is pissed as hell right now. You want your men to deal with that?"

"Hell, no, but that's a risk we take, just like every other risk on this job. Besides," he added, lowering his voice. "I thought vampires slept during the day."

Emma gave him a small smile and lied through her teeth. "You've been watching the wrong movies, Captain. Look," she continued in a conciliatory voice, "it rained last night, everything is wet, including the surrounding properties. On top of that, Mister Hissong's men activated the automated sprinkler system and with the distance between houses, the chances of the fire spreading have got to be slim."

"So, maybe I should instruct my men to pull out and let the damn house burn," Stavros replied, clearly not feeling in a conciliatory mood.

"And that is certainly your prerogative. I understand we already have private contractors en route to continue fighting the blaze."

"Son of a—" Stavros glared at her. Anyone who worked or lived in the District, especially in an official capacity, knew the minefields associated with the various embassies and their personnel. And regardless of her jab at the fire captain earlier, she knew he had to have successfully negotiated more than one such encounter in the past in order to rise as high in the department as he had.

"Fine," he snapped. "We'll do what we can from out here, but the liability is yours, lady. And you keep those damn amateurs of yours away from my fire." He stormed off without waiting for her reply, and Emma blew out a long, relieved breath.

"Nicely done, Emma," Hissong said in her ear. "I knew you had it in you."

"Bullshit," she said succinctly. "You know nothing about me. What time is it?"

"Ten minutes until sunset. Let's get you out of the spotlight, yes?"

"Yes," Emma agreed, suddenly feeling shaky. Her confrontation with Stavros had let her forget exactly what was at stake here. But now all she could think about was Duncan and whether he was still alive, or, even worse, whether he would wake at sunset to find himself and his vampires trapped in a prison of fire.

She let Hissong take her arm again, aware of Marlon on her other side as they hurried her around to the back of the residence. It was quieter back here, with the main part of the fire seeming to be concentrated on the front of the building. But there were firefighters here, too, and Emma could see the ominous orange glow of flames dancing in the many windows. The whole house would go up before long.

Emma coughed as the fire surged from an upstairs window, blowing smoke and greasy soot right into her face. Hissong moved to shelter her from the worst of it.

"Come on," he said, "the garages are clear. We can get you away from all of this." He pulled a set of keys out of his pocket and handed them to Marlon who hurried ahead.

"Have they shared any information with you about how this got started?" she asked as they detoured around the soaking wet piles of construction material.

"The fire department? No, it's too soon for their investigation. But I don't need them, I know what happened."

Emma dug in her heels, forcing him to stop. "You do? How?"

"This entire estate, including the residence inside and out, is on video surveillance during the day. The man who started the fire is already in custody."

"The police have him?"

"Not the police, Emma. As you pointed out to Stavros, this estate is vampire territory. You may have been bluffing with our local fire captain, but as far as the vampires are concerned, this is vampire business, not human. Lord Duncan will do the questioning and no one else."

"What if . . ." She swallowed, reluctant to say the words. "What if Duncan . . . can't do it?" she finally managed, staring up at Hissong.

"Then God save us all, because Lord Raphael will be out for blood."

"Raphael? You mean Duncan's Sire?"

"The very same. Come on, Marlon's got the garage open."

Marlon stood at the open side door waiting for them. "Should I hit the lights, Jackson?" he asked.

"No," Emma said quickly. She didn't know what would happen when the sun set, but if it was bad, if the worst happened, she didn't want her grief spotlighted for everyone to see. "I don't want to call any attention to us or to what we're waiting for."

"Right," Hissong said.

They stopped a few feet inside the door, leaving it open. Emma could smell the fire, a scorched, acrid scent that stung her sinuses and made her eyes water. She knew her face must be coated with black, that her hair must be greasy and gray with ash. No wonder Stavros had doubted her credentials. She probably would have too.

With a rumble of sound, the ground shook beneath her feet. Emma froze, staring at the burning house. All around her conversation ceased. Despite the steady roar of the equipment, the absence of voices was as palpable as if the night had been perfectly still. And then the house itself shivered.

"What is that?" Emma whispered, more to herself than anyone else, but Jackson Hissong was at her ear.

"You ever see a really powerful vampire get angry, Emma?" She shook her head silently. "Well, you're about to," he added.

"It's coming down!" someone shouted. And then everyone was yelling again, rushing to pull back personnel and equipment for fear the house was about to collapse.

Emma watched it all with growing distance, feeling like a spectator at a play, as if this was all unreal. There was a mounting pressure on her brain, a presence that she couldn't quite touch, as if she only needed to open a door and there would be . . . Duncan?

* * * *

The sun hovered over the horizon, moments from dropping below the edge. Duncan raged, trapped in his mind as his power stirred, coiling with him, straining to get out, building like an explosion that would take down the house and everyone around it. The very air trembled, the ground shaking, the ancient timbers of the house creaking ominously. He fought for the control that had always come so naturally for him. But this fury was far greater than any he'd ever felt, his power aching to break free and avenge the wrong done to him and his people, to . . . Emma.

The thought of her banked the hunger of his power. It withdrew, curling deep inside, waiting. He had to remain calm. He needed information. Where was Emma? Had she been here when the fire hit? Was she lying injured, dying, while the humans fought the blaze, not knowing she was inside? He let his mind roam free, his thoughts searching outward. His vampires slept all around him, some already beginning to gain awareness, others too young to wake while the sun still hung in the sky.

He searched farther, beyond the confines of the dreary basement beneath the east wing, where he and his vampires had slept since moving into this unsuitable, old house. He found nothing but fire. Its heat surrounded them, greedy flames eating up the timbers like a ravening beast, drawing ever closer, threatening the primitive sleeping quarters Alaric had thrown together as a temporary measure. There were humans all around. Duncan could feel their presence too, far too many for just his daytime security. Their emotions—fear, excitement, curiosity—bombarded him, making it difficult to weed out any one person, to determine how bad it was. A strong mind flashed through his awareness and he grabbed onto it. This one was energized, rather than excited, and determined. A man of some authority, although it was impossible to say whether he was one of the firefighters or a policeman, or maybe even a powerful neighbor watching from the street. Whichever it was, Duncan slipped his own consciousness into the human's brain, weaving the two seamlessly until he could look up and see—

His heart nearly stopped when he saw the damage to the house, the fire still raging around what must have been the focal point of an explosion—his bedroom, the bedroom where Emma slept. His power roared back and it had only one goal.

"Emma!"

* * * *

"Duncan?" Emma whispered. She whipped her head in the direction of the house.

"What is it?" Hissong asked intently.

"I don't know. I thought I heard—"

"What?"

"Duncan's voice . . . in my head. He called my name. It doesn't make any sense, but—"

"It makes perfect sense. Where did the voice seem to come from?"

"Be quiet!" she snapped, and then more quietly, "I'm sorry. Let me concentrate." Emma felt foolish. Duncan had told her he couldn't read her thoughts, but he'd also said that the more they exchanged blood, the closer their minds would come. And Emma liked to bite. She'd taken a little of his blood every time they made love. Was it possible?

"Duncan?" she whispered in her mind, and then she shouted, *"DUNCAN!"*

"Emmaline," his voice came back to her, warm with feeling and as strong as if he were standing next to her. But then it faded, and Emma doubted for a moment that she'd heard anything at all. Until she felt a surge of emotion that *tasted* like Duncan. It surrounded her—calm and strong, just like he was. Emma closed her eyes against a wave of relief, leaning against the open door for support.

"Well?" Hissong demanded.

"He's alive. They're all alive, I think."

"Fuck me," Hissong swore. "We've got to—" He looked up, eyes narrowing as he stared in the direction of the house. Emma stepped far enough out of the doorway to see what had drawn his attention, her heart leaping at the possibility. But it was only a group of unfamiliar men storming across the backyard and heading directly for the three of them in the shelter of the garage.

"You," the first man called. "Hissong, isn't it?"

"Yes, sir," Jackson said, stepping out into the yard. "Alaric?" he said, clearly recognizing the man.

Emma blinked as the vampire contractor she'd seen around the house strode closer. They'd never been introduced, but she'd heard Duncan on the phone with him.

"Where's Duncan?" Alaric demanded.

"That's my question for you," Jackson replied. "They're alive in there somewhere, but I don't know where—"

"Basement of the east wing, but nothing's finished, and I got a good look at that blaze on the way here. The main section's fully engulfed, and the whole place is gonna burn." He swore viciously and stared into the distance, thinking. "All right. Best we can do is try to make it easier for Duncan. Come on, lads," he called and started across the backyard. "You, too, Hissong, and anyone else you can spare. We've got some digging to do."

* * * *

The sun finally surrendered, dropping below the horizon and freeing Duncan to act. He opened his eyes and immediately woke his vampires with a blast of power, pulling even the youngest of them out of sleep and into complete wakefulness. The fire was all around them, the main part of the house completely impassable, but even the east wing above their heads was burning now, the ancient timbers growing hotter by the minute. With a loud crack, a piece of the ceiling gave way and a tongue of flame dipped hungrily into the basement. Duncan swore as one of his vampires cried out.

"Everyone to me," he shouted, putting enough power into the words to make it a command. The room was abruptly hotter, as if that small break in the ceiling brought the full heat of the blaze along with it. He was drenched in sweat, his hair, his clothes, and as he looked around, he could see all of his vampires were in the same condition. They gathered around him, their emotions a battering ram of fear and tension pounding at the wall of his control. They were looking to him to save them, to come up with a plan to get them out of here in one piece.

"Miguel?"

"Yes, my lord," Miguel said, appearing at his side.

"We're taking the tunnel."

"Sire? It's not finished yet. There's nothing there but—"

"Trust me, Miguel. Let's go."

"Yes, my—" The rest of Miguel's words were buried under the crash of burning timbers as the entire floor above them gave way.

"Now!" His power thundered forth, holding the collapsing floor at bay while his vampires ran for the tunnel. He glanced after them long enough to be certain everyone was safe, his power casting the bronze glow of his eyes into the shadows to rival the flames themselves.

Once the last of his people was safely past, he released the burning timbers, using his vampire speed to escape as the first floor crashed into the basement. Following his vampires, Duncan sped for the minimal safety of Alaric's unfinished vault. It was a new construction, concealed beneath the backyard and reached via a tunnel from the residence. If completed, there would have been a reinforced door connected to the basement of the east wing, and another equally secure door to the vault itself. It would have been expansive, with enough room for every vampire to have his or her own small chamber.

But that had all been for the future. Alaric had finished the tunnel and the concrete enclosure for the vault, but it was still just a big box in the ground. And with the east wing burning and the electricity off, it was a big box with no exit and no air.

Duncan led his people toward the tunnel entrance, their way lit by the blaze itself. He dodged aside as another section of floor gave way, the fire licking toward them eagerly, the smoke choking and black. He stopped beneath the break, using a second push of power to blow the flames back as his vampires hustled forward. Miguel led them, but Louis stood with Duncan and willingly offered his power to augment that of his Sire. Duncan rested a hand on the shorter vampire's shoulder.

"In good time, Louis. This isn't over yet."

Louis nodded, his eyes on the vamps filing by, until everyone was past and he and Duncan took up the rear. Up ahead, the first of his vampires reached the reinforced hole in the wall where the tunnel entrance would have been. It already bore the heavy framework of support for the planned vault-style door. The relief of his vampires was a fresh breeze in his mind as they crossed into the relative safety of the tunnel.

It was dark inside, and cold. They were ten feet underground and Duncan could feel the damp earth in his bones as surely as if it were pressing into his pores instead of held back by two solid feet of concrete. Alaric had insisted on the extra thickness of the walls, reminding Duncan that Washington, D.C. was built on a swamp and that meant seeping water everywhere. But right now that extra thickness was one more barrier between his vampires and safety.

* * * *

Emma watched blankly as Alaric and his vampires began digging. She didn't know exactly why they were digging, except that Alaric had told her it would help Duncan and his vamps get out of the burning house. She'd frowned at his explanation, but was willing to do whatever it took to save Duncan, so she'd offered to help dig. Alaric had laughed and assured her his people could do it far faster. Casting about for something to do besides stare helplessly, she'd found a supply of bottled water in the garage and hauled it out to the yard. Everyone seemed to appreciate that, even the vampires, but there was only so much water one could drink. So, now she was back to watching and waiting.

Fire Captain Stavros came around eventually, stared at the diggers, then marched over to Emma.

"What the hell are those men doing?" he demanded.

Emma drew herself up and said confidently, "They're digging a rescue tunnel."

"A rescue—" Stavros glared at her, then as if a light had gone on over his head, his expression cleared and he said, "Vampires."

Emma nodded. "Yes." And then swore to herself privately because Stavros had figured it out before she did. Obviously, Duncan and his vampires slept somewhere in the basement, not on the second floor as she'd assumed. And it was equally obvious that there had to be some sort of underground escape hatch. She didn't find this sudden epiphany very reassuring, however, since it wasn't much of an escape hatch if it counted on someone digging from up above. It was like drilling a rescue hole to trapped miners. They could be anywhere, and how did you know whether the rescue hole was going to be in the same place where the miners were?

Not knowing what else to say, she handed Stavros a bottle of water, then froze when Alaric shouted and everyone stopped digging. Emma stared from one of them to another, as they grabbed their equipment and began hurriedly pulling back.

"What's going on?" she asked Alaric when he strode over to the garage and began urging her inside the structure. He didn't answer, just stepped in front of her, blocking her body as a shock wave of air roared across the yard and the earth exploded.

* * * *

Duncan forced himself to wait until all of his people were gathered in what would have been the vault. He could hear digging from above, probably Alaric's people. They'd been staying very nearby, and the old vampire would know Duncan's most likely escape route. Duncan was also aware of Emma, and knew she was very close. The thought of Emma, of what could have happened if she'd been asleep upstairs, finally cracked his patience.

"Stand back." He sent the warning to all of the vampires up above, but his own people heard it and knew what it meant. They straightened eagerly, as anxious as he was to escape their erstwhile prison. The digging stopped, and Duncan gathered his power into a single, concentrated blow, as if his fist were made of iron and the wall nothing but sand. He shot his arm forward, the gesture no more than a physical manifestation of the powerful force which slammed into the concrete wall, cracked it like an egg and exploded outward through nearly ten feet of solid earth.

There were cheers all around, from the people outside, both human and vampire, and from his own vampires as fresh night air flooded the tunnel. A hand reached down through the muddy hole and Duncan grabbed it. He heard Alaric's roar of greeting before he'd gone two steps and looked up to see the wiry vampire bearing down on him with a grin.

"Duncan," Alaric shouted. "About damn time, my lord!"

They embraced, slapping backs.

"Your woman's a tough little lady," Alaric growled against his ear. "Handled them human honchos like she was a four star general and them buck privates," he added, chuckling.

Duncan looked over Alaric's shoulder, his gaze finding Emma in the deep shadows beneath a drooping tree on the other side of the yard. She stood motionless, staring at him, her hands clasped against her mouth. He slapped Alaric's shoulder and stepped aside, starting toward her. She watched him come, her violet eyes dark, a suspicious sheen telling him she'd been crying. Her heartbeat raced faster with every step he took. When he drew close enough, her hands fell away from her face and she ran forward, his name on her lips as she threw herself into his arms.

"Duncan," she cried, then sucked back a sobbing breath.

"Emmaline," he whispered against her ear, burying his face in the warm silk of her hair, filling his arms with her softness, and drowning himself in the scent and touch of her.

"I was afraid—" she started, but he shushed her, covering her mouth with his lips and drinking her in, feeling her arms tighten against his neck as the kiss deepened, as their tongues met, twisting around each other hungrily. Duncan broke off the kiss reluctantly, aware of his vampires and everyone else watching them.

"I love you, Emmaline," he whispered. "I'll show you how much as soon as I find us some privacy."

"Oh," Emma breathed, her cheeks flushing and eyes growing wide, as if aware of the onlookers for the first time.

Duncan laughed gently. "It was just a kiss," he murmured, touching his mouth to hers quickly.

"Not *just* a kiss," Emma corrected him. "One hell of a kiss."

Duncan laughed loudly, tugging her against his chest for a hard hug, before taking her hand and turning to face the others. "Jackson," he said, searching the faces.

"Yes, my lord." Jackson Hissong stepped out from where he was conferring with Miguel and Louis.

"What do we know?"

Jackson came closer and said quietly, "We've a man in custody, my lord. But perhaps we should take this conversation to the other house. Some of what needs to be said—"

"Of course," Duncan said immediately. "And we could all use a shower and some nutrition, as well. What about the daytime guards?"

"With your permission, my lord, I'll have them remain on duty to secure the site until your vampires can relieve them."

Duncan exchanged a look with Miguel who said, "The traitor has been secured. Jackson does not believe the rest of his men were involved, although we'll check each of them before they leave to be sure."

Duncan nodded. "Very well. Emma and I will go ahead to the other house, and we'll convene there once everyone's had a chance to clean up. I'll want the prisoner made available to me."

"Of course, my lord," Miguel said, then turned away to begin organizing the guard rotation and departure.

Duncan dropped an arm over Emma's shoulder and began walking toward the ten foot wall which shielded the property from a path along the river. Emma sucked in a surprised breath when he opened a small control box and entered a code on the keypad concealed there. With a soft whir of noise, a hidden gate popped out of the smooth wall.

"Where are we going?" she asked, puzzled.

"A moonlight stroll along the river," Duncan teased.

"Very romantic," she murmured, leaning against his side. "But I'd rather have a hot shower."

Duncan laughed. "Will you share?"

"Only if you tell me where we're going."

"As Jackson said, to the other house."

"I didn't know there *was* another house!"

"I'm a vampire lord, Emma. There's *always* another house."

* * * *

Emma let her head fall back as the blessedly hot water streamed through her hair, washing away shampoo along with hours of sweat and soot. She straightened and finger-combed some conditioner in, then reached back and pulled the bulk of her wet hair over one shoulder, letting the water pound the stress from her back. Sighing with pleasure, she grabbed a bar of soap and rubbed it between her hands, generating a thick lather that had only a faint clean scent. No flowery soaps for Duncan, apparently, which was fine with her. She lifted her soapy hands to her face and began to wash gently, trying not to think about what the bar soap was doing to her skin. One night wouldn't kill her, and besides the oily residue of black soot left behind by the smoke and fire probably needed something stronger than her usual facial cleanser. She'd moisturize extra tomorrow to make up for it, once she could get to her own things. That thought made her pause. The things she'd left at Duncan's were gone, although, thank God, she'd had her laptop with her. Everything else was easily replaceable. Besides, Duncan had survived and that's all that mattered.

And speak of the devil . . . She caught a blurred shadow of movement before the shower door opened and the vampire himself stepped inside. Emma ran an admiring eye up and down his naked body. The mud and dirt which had made her look like a refugee only made him look more masculine, more dangerous. He bumped her carefully with his hip, one arm snaking out to circle her waist as he pushed her out of the flow of hot water.

"Water hog," she complained halfheartedly.

"Says the woman who's all shiny clean," he commented, then backed up a step, pulling her under the spray with him. Emma sputtered briefly before burying her face against his chest.

"You're getting me dirty," she muttered, but she wrapped her arms around his narrow waist, running her hands over the firm muscles of his back. He was like a work of art, every muscle perfectly defined and flowing elegantly over tendons and bones.

Duncan tipped his head back into the spray as she'd done earlier, letting the water run through his long, blond hair. She reached behind him and grabbed the shampoo. He was too tall for her to wash his hair comfortably, so she settled for squirting a fair amount of the gel on his wet hair, then standing back to admire the play of muscles in his arms and shoulders as he scrubbed the mud away.

"God, this feels good," he said, rinsing his hair clean.

"Being clean?" Emma asked.

"No." He opened his eyes and gave her a slow smile. "Being naked with you." His hands came down to grip her hips, and he backed her against the tile wall. "Having my hands on you." His hands dropped to her butt and he lifted her effortlessly, pressing forward until her legs wrapped around his narrow hips. She could feel his erection, hard and heavy against her thigh, as he rubbed against her gently, teasing her.

"Duncan," she whispered, pleading. But he wasn't ready to give in to her pleas. Not yet. One hand came up between them to cover her breast, his thumb playing over her nipple until it was full and hard. He bent his head to nip lightly at the plump flesh.

"I worried about you, Emmaline," he murmured, lapping at the same nipple he'd just bitten, and then biting harder until she cried out, her legs tightening around his hips as her sex clenched in need.

"Me, too," she gasped, grabbing a handful of his wet hair and tugging. "For you, I mean."

"Ouch." Duncan looked up and grinned, his hips never ceasing their maddening thrusting motion, letting her feel the length of his cock, so close, but not where she wanted it, not where she *needed* it.

"Duncan, so help me, if you don't—"

She cried out as, without warning, he plunged his full length deep between her legs, stretching her wide despite her readiness, slamming forward until their hips met with a slap of wet flesh. He waited then, watching her as she struggled to catch her breath, as her body softened to accommodate him.

"If I don't what?" he asked silkily.

Emma pulled his head forward, tugging him into a breathless kiss. It was warm and wet and soft, a slow caress of lips and tongue while below, her inner muscles flexed around his shaft with the same rhythm. Duncan hissed as his cock jerked in response, and Emma lifted her head slowly, licking her tongue along the curve of his mouth before whispering, "I love you, Duncan."

Duncan met her gaze, his expression completely serious as he began a slow, steady movement, the tight muscles of his ass clenching as his hips thrust forward and back between her legs, his erection a shaft of warm stone sheathed in satin as he repeatedly withdrew until only the very tip remained inside her, then slid deep into her body once more, a long, smooth glide of flesh into flesh. Emma crossed her ankles over his butt, trapping him between her thighs. Her arms were around his neck, her fingers threaded through his hair. Duncan's mouth moved over her face, kissing her eyes, her jaw and down to her neck. His tongue was cool against her overheated flesh as he licked the sweat and water from her skin, as he sucked hard over her jugular vein. Emma smiled to herself, thinking she'd have a hickey in the morning. She hadn't had one of those in—

She groaned with arousal as his fangs pierced her vein, as the first powerful orgasm rocketed through her body, clenching her womb and tightening her breasts. Every stroke of Duncan's rigid length produced a fresh jolt of incredible sensation, wave after wave of pleasure, as if her nerves were bare and his cock a brush of silk against them. Emma began thrusting in time with his movements, wanting him to join her, wanting to feel that moment when he lost control and tumbled over the edge with her.

His fangs still buried in her neck, Duncan groaned. The sound vibrated against her skin and raced through her veins, rumbling over her breasts and down between her legs to shiver along the length of his cock. He lifted his head, and his tongue lapped quickly at the small puncture wounds before he crushed his mouth over hers, sharing the taste of her blood. Emma met his kiss hungrily, biting as she fought to get closer to him, licking his lips in apology when she felt the warm flow of his blood, but relishing the rush of heat that came with it.

Duncan growled and began fucking her, pounding her against the wet tile, protecting her with his arms around her back as he slammed forward harder and harder, until Emma thought the tiles would surely crack under the strain. Snarling hungrily, he lifted her higher, changing the angle of his penetration, going even deeper than before, his thickness tormenting the sensitive flesh of her inner walls until her body was trembling with arousal and begging for release. Duncan slid the fingers of one hand along the crease of her ass, caressing the strip of skin stretched taut with his penetration, before dipping his finger into the tight pucker of her star. Emma gasped as a second orgasm screamed along her nerves, jumping like lightening from the touch of his hand to the thrust of his cock and up to her swollen breasts, which were crushed against his powerful chest. She bit down on his shoulder, trying to swallow the scream that surged up her throat, overwhelmed by the sensations storming every inch of her body. Her sex clamped down on Duncan's cock as he began to buck against her, his hot release coating her womb as her teeth broke the skin of his shoulder, and he lifted his head to howl his climax.

* * * *

Duncan leaned heavily against Emma, holding her up as much with the press of his body as the grip of his hands on her sweet ass. She'd wrung him dry. Or maybe it was the hot shower that was still drumming against his back, matching the heat of Emma against his chest. Her arms were loose over his shoulders, her ankles still locked around his hips, while her eager little tongue continued to lap the blood from his shoulder. He rested a hand gently against the back of her head, encouraging her. The more of his blood she took, the tighter the bond would be between them. His shoulder pulsed as he remembered the feel of her teeth in his flesh, and he grinned. She was a wildcat, his Emma. And she *was* his.

As unlikely as it seemed, he'd fallen in love again. He'd loved his wife dearly, though the memory was so old and distant, it was as if it had happened to someone else. But he could still recall the scent of her powder, the touch of her hand as she rubbed his shoulders after a hard day. She'd been a good woman who deserved better than he'd been able to give her. And far better than the end he'd brought her to.

But he wasn't that man anymore. No one, man or vampire, would touch his woman ever again. Emma was his, and he would fight to the death to protect her. Of course, Emma would probably bite him again if she knew his thoughts. She wasn't a shy flower to stand behind and let someone else fight her battles. No, she'd want to stand at his side and fight their enemies together. And that was better. Because the world was a terrible and treacherous place, and it comforted him to know Emma would be there to face it with him when he woke every night.

Emma gave his shoulder a final lick and lifted her head. "What are you thinking so hard about?" she murmured, kissing the bite she'd been suckling so eagerly.

"Only that I love you, Emmaline." He rubbed his chin against her wet hair. "Will you stay?"

She grew still. "Stay?" she asked, her breath warm on his torn flesh. "You mean tonight?"

"I mean forever."

Emma lifted her head to look at him, her eyes filling with tears. "Duncan?"

He met her gaze evenly. "Stay with me, Emma," he repeated. "Be mine."

She nodded wordlessly, tears running down her cheeks. "Okay," she whispered, then blew out a frustrated breath. "That wasn't very poetic of me."

"Poetry is overrated," Duncan commented. He stepped back and lowered her slowly, letting her slide down his body until her feet were firmly on the floor.

Emma sighed, resting her forehead against his chest. The two of them stood there, listening to each other breathe, until Emma said, laughing, "I think I need a shower."

"Yes, well," he tugged her under the water which was still running, although noticeably cooler than it had been. "I was *trying* to shower when you molested me."

"Me? You started it," she murmured absently, running her hands over his abdomen, which clenched automatically beneath her fingers. She looked up at him and winked.

Duncan groaned. "Let me at least finish washing up. If I'd have known you were this insatiable, I'd have—"

"What?"

"Fucked you into unconsciousness *before* I showered," he whispered against her ear.

"Duncan!" she gasped, but she didn't pull away.

It was a quick shower, but only because Emma declined his offer to wash away the remnants of their lovemaking between her legs. "We'll never get out of here, if you do that," she said, slapping away his hands. "I'll be a prune."

"A most attractive prune, however," he said gallantly. But he stepped out of the shower and began to dry off while Emma finished. He had pulled on a pair of sweats and was waiting with a big towel when she emerged a few moments later. Wrapping it around her, he scooped her off her feet and carried her into the bedroom. She lifted her arms to circle his neck, then sighed wearily and rested her head against his shoulder.

Duncan had already pulled the covers back and now laid her down on the fresh sheets. Placing one knee on the mattress next to her, he finished drying her naked body, then pulled the covers up and leaned in to kiss her tenderly. "Sleep, Emma. I'll be near."

She grabbed his hand when he went to stand, her eyes already half closed in sleep. "Where will you sleep today, Duncan?"

"With you, Emmaline. This house is better suited to my kind. I'll come back here to you."

She smiled, rubbing her cheek against his hand before releasing it and curling up under the blanket. She was out in moments, without any help from Duncan, although he'd been prepared to nudge her into sleep if necessary. He had a prisoner to interrogate. The man who'd set fire to the residence, and who'd clearly intended to kill Duncan along with a few of his vampires, and perhaps Emma, as well. It was not a task Duncan looked forward to, but it was something he would do and do quite well, because nothing was more important to him than the safety of Emma and his people. But somehow he doubted his beloved Emma would admire his skill when the human began screaming for mercy.

Chapter Twenty-Five

Duncan crossed his arms over his chest and leaned back against the wall of the small, barren basement room. He'd pulled a t-shirt on over his sweats and added a pair of black Nikes, but he hadn't bothered with anything fancier, because he'd fully expected to be burning the clothes before the end of the night. He'd also expected to be facing a quivering lump of terrified humanity, begging for its life. Instead what he had was a puzzle.

He frowned down at the human guard sitting across the table from him. The man's arms were handcuffed behind his back, but other than that he wasn't restrained. And he wasn't particularly frightened, either.

"My lord?" the man asked, his wide eyes guileless and confused. "Has something happened?"

This man had dragged a welder's propane tank from Alaric's construction site in the east wing, rigged it to blow like a small bomb right beneath Duncan's second floor office suite, then splashed paint thinner in a line from there to the main stairwell. He'd then walked calmly out of the house through the kitchen door in back and returned to his regular perimeter patrol, leaving plenty of time for his usual check-in. There was no question of guilt; they had security video both inside and out from the motion-activated digital feed Miguel had set up as soon as they moved into the house. Once the cameras were triggered, the images were sent to a control center in the house down the block from Victor's old residence. It was the house Miguel and Louis had lived in while preparing for Duncan's takeover of the territory, the same house they were now *all* living in until either the old residence was repaired or new quarters were found and secured.

And yet, despite this incontrovertible evidence, the guard seemed to remember none of it. He *still* should have been afraid, however. Even if he'd done nothing wrong, he should be terrified to find himself handcuffed and facing Duncan as his inquisitor.

"Mister Daniels, isn't it?" Duncan asked finally, although he knew the guard's name.

"Yes, my lord," the man said readily. "Clint Daniels."

"Tell me, what's the last thing you remember before you were brought here?" Daniels shook his head woefully. "Being handcuffed, my lord," he said, seeming confused. "I was standing by the main gate entrance, keeping the spectators out during the fire, and then Jackson Hissong showed up and had one of the guys put these on me." He tried to lift his hands behind him, but they were looped over the back of the chair and he grimaced. "I don't understand, my lord. What's happened?"

"May I touch you, Mister Daniels? It's not necessary, but it will make things easier."

"Of course, my lord."

Duncan's frown deepened. Clint Daniels obviously had nothing to
hide, or at least nothing he knew to try to hide. A suspicion took root in
Duncan's thoughts, making his gut clench with both anger and foreboding.
He straightened away from the wall and circled the table, aware of
Miguel stiffening to attention behind him as he drew closer to the
prisoner. Duncan placed his hand on Daniels's head, automatically
brushing the man's hair off his forehead in a comforting gesture as he
inserted himself effortlessly into the human's consciousness. Daniels's
emotions rose to Duncan's awareness first, and what he found only
confirmed what he'd noticed a few moments ago. Clint Daniels was
worried and confused, but he wasn't frightened. And he damn well
should be.

Duncan dug deeper, seeing the house fire through Daniels's eyes,
the crowds outside the gate. The crowds Duncan had avoided by taking
his midnight stroll along the river with Emma. The thought of Emma,
and the danger she'd so narrowly avoided, renewed his purpose, and
he burrowed into Daniels's thoughts without compassion. He was as
careful as possible, but he needed the truth.

Duncan closed his eyes and focused. He saw the surface memories,
the same ones Daniels had related to him, the bewilderment when
Jackson Hissong had ordered him handcuffed, but nothing more than
that. He delved deeper, forcing Daniels to remember. The human began
to tremble. He groaned, his legs thrashing, kicking against the table as
if trying to escape. Duncan saw the barrier then, the wall someone had
erected in this man's memories, someone skillful enough to do it without
leaving the human a drooling idiot. This wasn't Victor's work. He'd
seen the way Victor had scrambled Violet's memories, the hasty patch
that left her bewildered and unable to function. No, this was the work
of someone far more skillful and patient. Someone who'd thought ahead,
who'd set it up so Daniels could set his trap and resume his duties
without a hitch. If it hadn't been for Miguel's cameras—something
only Duncan and a very few others knew about—they probably would
never have known who set the blaze. That it was arson, everyone
knew by now, even the human fire investigators. But they might never
have traced the act back to this man.

Daniels began to weep, heartbreaking sobs that choked his voice
as he apologized over and over again, the expected fear finally saturating
his emotions. "I didn't know, my lord. I never would have—" His voice
broke again as the sobs took over.

"It's all right, Clint," Duncan said gently, smoothing a hand over
Daniels's bent head. "It wasn't your fault." He continued to stroke the
human's head as he worked, replacing the memories with ones of his
own. It was a shame. This man had been a loyal employee, a fine
guard. If Duncan had gotten to him first, this never would have happened.

But there hadn't been enough time; too many crises had hit all at once. Duncan had never found the time to check each and every one of the daytime guards for time bombs like this, and to add defenses to their minds against casual intrusion.

He sighed and released Daniels's mind, easing the man carefully forward until he was slumped on the table, fast asleep.

"Uncuff him," he told Miguel. "Does he have a family?"

"No," Miguel said, unlocking the cuffs and rubbing the human's arms briskly to restore circulation. "He's one of those I brought with me from the West Coast. A good man, my lord."

"Yes," Duncan agreed wearily. "A good man someone tried to use against us. Someone got to him, Miguel. A master vampire we've somehow missed."

Miguel shot him an alarmed look. "Could it be someone we've already met? Like that artist Erik, or his partner, Brendan?"

But Duncan was already shaking his head. "No. Neither of them is a master vampire. It's someone we've overlooked," he reiterated. *"Damn it all!* As if I don't have enough on my plate already." He looked away in disgust. "All right," he said matter-of-factly. "Send our friend here back to California, give him a good job. None of this was his fault."

Miguel nodded. "What will you do now, my lord?"

Duncan huffed a bitter laugh. "Wait for whoever did this to show himself. He knows that I'm aware of him now, and that I'll be looking for him. Better for him to act than to wait for me to find him. He'll make his move soon enough, and we'll be ready when he does."

Chapter Twenty-Six

Duncan stripped away his clothes, feeling sullied despite the fact there'd been no real violence necessary tonight. No blood, anyway. What he'd been forced to do to Clint Daniels's brain was a violation, but at least the human was still functional, still able to live his life as before.

He dropped the t-shirt on the floor and crossed to the big bed where Emma slept. She breathed deeply, evenly, her heart a steady pounding that drew him like a magnet. He slipped into bed next to her and pulled her into the curve of his body, half hoping she'd wake. She didn't. She simply smiled in her sleep and curled up against him, her soft lips touching his chest in a dreaming kiss.

He felt the sun lurking below the horizon. There were only minutes left until daylight stole his awareness. He tightened his arms around Emma, buried his face in her warm, silky hair and closed his eyes.

* * * *

Emma woke feeling more rested than she had in weeks. At least until she opened her eyes to a dark room in a strange house. She had a bad moment then, before it all came roaring back—the fire, the wait to see if Duncan and the other vampires were still alive, the shower . . . She smiled at the memory, running her hands over her body, feeling sexy and desired and very, very female. Duncan was asleep next to her, his breathing slow and steady—maybe a little *too* slow, now that she thought about it. If she hadn't known he was a vampire, she'd have been worried. Her thoughts froze and she rolled over quickly, grabbing her watch from the bedside table. It was late, little more than an hour until sunset, but still daylight for now, which explained the heavy drapes and darkened room. She turned to stare at Duncan. He wasn't just asleep. He was *asleep*. Well, this was a first—one of those moments in a relationship that you never forget. Of course, she was the only one who'd remember it, since Duncan, while not actually dead, was certainly dead to the world.

The ringing of a cell phone had her jumping from the bed to answer it before it woke Duncan. About the time her feet hit the carpet, she realized it didn't matter. The house could come down around Duncan and he wouldn't wake up. As a matter of fact, the house *had* nearly come down around him yesterday, and he'd slept right through most of it. As far as she knew, anyway. She'd have to ask him about that.

But the damn cell phone was still ringing. Emma flipped on the bedside lamp. The light was barely enough to keep her from running into anything while she followed the ringing sound to her phone. Except it wasn't hers. It was Duncan's. She stared at the caller ID. Cynthia. Who the hell was Cynthia?

Feeling somewhat guilty, she glanced over her shoulder at her sleeping lover, then answered the phone. "Hello?"

Silence. Then, "Who the hell is this?" a woman's voice demanded.

Emma's eyes narrowed in irritation. "I think that's my line, since you called *me.*"

"I didn't call *you,* I called Duncan. Where the hell is he?"

"Asleep. Which you'd know if you knew anything about him."

"Honey, I know more about Duncan than you do, including the fact that he's asleep. I expected to get his voicemail, but instead I got you. So, who are you and what the hell have you done with Duncan?"

"A lot. For hours and hours. Deal with it." Emma disconnected, feeling both petty and very satisfied. Of course, Duncan might not see it that way.

She jumped as the phone immediately began ringing again. Cynthia. What a surprise. Emma considered answering if only for the satisfaction of disconnecting again, but figured the bitch would just keep calling. Assuming she *was* a bitch. Hell, maybe this Cynthia person was Duncan's accountant or something. Emma was beginning to second guess her rudeness when her own cell phone started ringing from somewhere on the other side of the room.

"What is it with these phones?" she grumped and went in search of her jacket. Her phone, which had survived all of last night's trauma with nothing but a bit of mud to show for it, should still be in the jacket's pocket. She had a wild thought that it might be Cynthia calling her, too, but that was only the pricking of her guilty conscience. Not that Emma doubted a determined someone could find her cell number, but not that quickly. Not without even a name to go by. She finally located her clothes and dug out the phone, frowning at what she saw there. The call was coming from her office. Or rather what had been her office until Sharon fired her. Was it just yesterday? It seemed too much had happened for such a short period of time.

She debated not picking up. After all, she didn't owe them anything anymore. But it might be Noreen or one of the other legislative assistants. It wasn't their fault Sharon was an ass, or that Guy Coffer couldn't stand up to his wife. She sighed and punched the receive button.

"Emma Duquet," she answered cautiously.

"Emma, I'm so glad I reached you," a man's voice said, far too pleasantly. A politician's voice. It was Guy Coffer himself calling. This couldn't be anything good.

"Congressman Coffer," she managed. "What can I help you with?"

"Nothing at all, Emma. I'm actually calling to apologize for the way things were handled yesterday. I had no idea Sharon was going to let you go. Of course, I leave staff matters to her, but if I'd known . . ." His voice trailed off, because they both knew that even if he'd known, he wouldn't have done anything.

"That's very kind, sir," Emma said, taking pity on him. He wasn't a bad man. He simply lacked certain essential anatomical parts.

"Yes, well, I feel very guilty about how things fell out. I've written a letter of reference for you, and I've recommended you to several of my colleagues, as well. It might be best if you pick the letter up personally, however. I wouldn't want it to get misplaced in the regular office mail."

Which meant if Sharon saw it, she'd drop it in the shredder so fast she'd lose a finger doing it. Emma considered the situation. She really needed that letter, and she still had her ID, since she'd never bothered to drop it off when she left. She could make a quick run up to the Hill, grab the letter and be back here in no time. Coffer would never have suggested Emma come by if there was even the slightest chance Sharon would be around, so there was no risk of a confrontation on that front.

Emma glanced over her shoulder to where Duncan slept in perfect stillness, perfect vulnerability. Someone had tried to kill him yesterday, and probably her, too. He'd told her last night that this house was better suited to vampires, and she knew there'd be humans guarding the place during daylight, as there'd been at the old house. She frowned thoughtfully. Jackson Hissong would be around somewhere, and she was sure he'd make someone available to go with her up to Coffer's office and back.

But Duncan wouldn't like it. And he'd be right.

"I appreciate that, Congressman," she told Coffer. "But I'm not at home. In fact, I'm on my way back to the District right now. It'll take me a couple of hours to get there, and then into the office. I can't ask you to wait that long."

"It's no problem at all, Emma. I came in today for the peace and quiet, and I've got some work to do, so I don't mind."

"Well, thank you, sir. That's very kind. I'll get there as soon as I can."

* * * *

Emma walked down the nearly empty halls of the Capitol building. The office corridors were far away from the public areas of the building, and it was the weekend. No one but the occasional staffer could be seen hurrying down the usually crowded hallways.

Emma hadn't bothered to dress up. She didn't plan to be here long enough for it to matter. As it was, she'd had to go by her house to change. Everything she'd had at Duncan's old residence was gone, so she had nothing but the gray suit and silk blouse she'd been wearing when Sharon fired her yesterday. That and her three inch pumps, all of which were in desperate need of cleaning. But regardless of his promise, she'd been afraid Coffer wouldn't wait, so she'd stopped at her house only long enough to change into a pair of faded denims and a long, cable-knit sweater, along with some flat-soled boots. The flat soles

were just in case she had to make a run for it, like if Sharon happened
to show up unexpectedly. Emma chuckled at the idea and pulled open
the door to Guy Coffer's congressional office.

The outermost area was empty. She hadn't expected the
receptionists to be here on a Saturday, but the inner offices were quiet,
too. She frowned. That was more unusual, but it all depended on the
Congressman's schedule of meetings and what legislation was up when.
Two days ago, Emma could have rattled off that information without
thinking, but the knowledge seemed to have deserted her the minute
she no longer needed it.

She reached Coffer's office door and knocked quietly.
"Congressman Coffer?"

She'd barely lifted her knuckles from the solid wood before the
door was yanked open and the wicked witch herself stood there glaring
hatefully.

"Emma," Sharon Coffer sneered. "I'll take your ID now."

Emma rolled her eyes. She should have known. Guy Coffer didn't
take a pee without checking with Sharon first. "Really, Sharon," she
drawled. "If all you wanted was the ID, you could have called yourself.
I'd have been happy to mail it to you."

"I don't care about the stupid ID. I wanted to prove to myself once
and for all that I was right about you. You just couldn't pass up a
chance to get my husband alone."

"Oh, please." Emma groaned. "Why would I want to share Guy
with you, when I can have *him* all to myself?" She hooked a thumb
over her shoulder to where Duncan was strolling in from the outer
office.

"Sorry, Emma darlin'," he said, giving her a playful wink. "But
parking is terrible here. I should really write to my congressman about
it."

Sharon Coffer's eyes opened up like a cartoon character's and
she hissed like a cat. "This *creature* is your *boyfriend?"*

"Yes," Emma said proudly, "although there isn't anything *boyish*
about him" She reached up to stroke a hand down Duncan's leather
jacketed arm. "Isn't he beautiful?"

"He's a monster!"

Emma cocked her head at the other woman, finding it interesting
that Sharon had known Duncan was a vampire without being told.
Emma hadn't met that many vampires, but of those she had, Duncan
was the most human looking. She'd never have suspected him of being
a vampire—in fact, she hadn't when she'd first met him. And yet Sharon
Coffer didn't only suspect, she knew. Emma was beginning to get a
bad feeling about this. Violet hadn't identified Guy Coffer as one of
Victor's perverted partners. But then she hadn't known most of the
men involved by name, and Guy Coffer wasn't someone whose face

was on the nightly news. Then there was the unknown woman who'd been there the night Lacey died, the woman who'd been yelling at everyone as if she had a right to do so. Emma felt a thrill of fear. Thank God she'd waited until Duncan could come with her tonight. Speaking of which . . .

"Duncan," she said, letting her alarm show.

"There's nothing to worry about, Emmaline," he assured her, taking her hand and lifting it to his lips briefly. He'd caught the same oddity about Sharon's reaction that she had, of course. In fact, he'd probably made the connection before she did.

Duncan stepped in front of Emma, but didn't say a word to Sharon. He just stared down at the Congressman's wife, his head tilted curiously, studying her like she was some sort of peculiar bug. She stared back at him, her initially defiant stance softening as her eyes glazed over and her arms fell loosely to her sides. They remained that way for a few minutes, and then Duncan took Sharon's arm and turned her around, guiding her back into the Congressman's office. Emma followed, jerking to a stop when she saw Guy Coffer sitting there. Or maybe lying there was a better description. His head was cheek down on the desk, his eyes closed as if sleeping.

"Is he okay?" Emma whispered, not wanting to disturb Duncan's concentration.

"There's no need to whisper," Duncan said in his usual voice. "And, yes, the Congressman is fine. It was simply easier to deal with them one at a time."

"You guys could rule the world, you know," Emma commented, watching Duncan guide Sharon over to a straight-backed chair near the window.

"Who says we don't?" he asked absently.

Emma frowned, pretty sure he was joking. "So, what'd you discover? What do they know?"

"A great number of tedious things, I'm afraid. As for the delightful Missus Coffer's knowledge of and abhorrence for my vampire nature, however, *that* came directly from Max Grafton at a recent dinner party. Last night, as a matter of fact. Interesting coincidence, don't you think? That as I was dying tragically in a fire that one assumes will be blamed on some hate group or other, Max Grafton was already poisoning the well to explain my unfortunate demise."

"What about him?" Emma asked, pointing at the apparently sleeping Guy Coffer. "What does he know?"

"*He* is a pathetic excuse for a man." Duncan glanced over his shoulder at her. "Please tell me you never entertained any romantic notions about him."

"Ew," Emma said, wrinkling her nose. "A politician?"

Duncan laughed. "I suspect Sharon here would have the same

reaction to dating a vampire."

Emma huffed a dismissive breath. "Shows what she knows. Ask any woman, hell, probably any man, too, on Facebook if they'd rather have a vampire or a politician as a lover. Vampires would win hands down."

"Really?" Duncan said, looking far too interested.

"Not your concern, beautiful. You're off the menu. Speaking of which, what's with all these women calling to check on you . . ." Emma stopped talking, abruptly aware that Duncan might not have listened to Cynthia's voice mail yet.

Duncan grinned as he crossed the office back toward Emma, his walk a slow, lethal stroll of grace and power. Emma's heart kicked hard against her ribs, and she felt her mouth begin to water.

"Jealous, Emmaline?" Duncan whispered against her ear. His arm snaked around her waist, snugging her tight against his body, and she nearly groaned aloud as she felt the firm bulge of his arousal.

"Insanely, viciously, unreasonably jealous," she hissed back. "And I know how to use a gun."

He laughed again, then kissed her hard and fast, and pulled away. "Cynthia—and yes, I *did* listen to the message and she's *very* eager to meet you—is a friend. She's also mated to my Sire, Raphael, who is Lord of the Western Territories. In point of fact, you and Cynthia are not unalike. God save us all."

"Hey!"

He kissed her again, then spun her around, slapping her ass to get her moving out of the office. "Let's get out of here before the unfortunate Coffers awake from their naps. I have a killer to beard tonight, Emmaline, and we need to prepare."

Chapter Twenty-Seven

"Absolutely not!" Emma fumed, as she stormed across the bedroom and dropped a small gym bag near the desk. "You are not leaving me here, while you guys go out and have all the fun."

"This is not *fun*, Emma," Duncan said with that infuriating calm of his. "Max Grafton has already killed once that we know of. I'm sure I needn't remind you that he very nearly killed again when he arranged for my residence to burn. Not to mention—"

Emma opened her mouth to argue, but Duncan forestalled her with a look, and continued, "—that there's a vampire involved. A vampire shrewd enough to manipulate one of my own guards and escape detection while doing so."

"You don't know—"

"But I do know, Emma," he said implacably. "I know vampires. I know what they're capable of."

"But it won't be only vampires out there tonight," she argued. Louis had tracked Max Grafton to his residence in nearby Virginia through a skillful, and quite illegal, tap on the senator's personal phones. Grafton was hosting a dinner party at the Virginia house tonight. Unlike the earlier fundraiser, or the event last night where he'd spoken with Sharon Coffer, tonight was to be a very private affair for a few friends. "Even if there's a vampire involved—"

"There is," Duncan stated.

She ignored the interruption. "—there's no reason to believe he'll be there tonight. Louis hasn't heard anything that indicates this is business. It's just some friends, so there there's no reason—"

"Emma."

She regarded him warily. Emma might be all wild emotion, but Duncan didn't get angry, or rather, he didn't show it. He just got quieter and colder, his words more precise. And that one word, her name, had been cut with a very sharp knife.

"By now," Duncan explained slowly, as if she was too stupid to understand, or maybe because it was the third time he'd told her this same thing, "Sharon Coffer has called Max Grafton to gossip about seeing me in her husband's office."

"You don't know—" Emma started, but she stopped when Duncan gave her a flat look. She rolled her eyes and waited.

"I do know. I had Louis check the taps on Grafton's phone, because I *also* knew you wouldn't believe me."

Emma made a face at him, irritated that he'd been right. Again. It must be tough on him, being right all the time.

Duncan's mouth quirked up in a half smile as he continued. "Max Grafton, in turn, has contacted his vampire ally because he knows I'll be coming for him."

"So you know who the other vampire is?"

"I do not. Grafton's call was to a dead drop voice mail, and we haven't been able to track down the owner. My people have lived in the shadows for thousands of years, and we've gotten very good at protecting ourselves. Many of the old ones prefer the shadows even now. The point is, Emma, that the true confrontation tonight will be between me and that other vampire. No other battle will matter. And I don't want you anywhere near when that happens. If I lose that fight, I—"

Emma's heart was suddenly in her throat. It had never occurred to her that Duncan could lose. He was beautiful, strong, invincible. He was . . . Duncan. "Wait," she said. "What *happens* if you lose?"

"*If* I lose, and I don't intend to, but if I do, I need to know that you're safe. And that means far away from me."

Emma stared at him. She hadn't really considered what it meant that another vampire was involved, someone who was possibly just as powerful as Duncan. Someone so set on getting rid of Duncan, someone so vicious that they'd set fire to the residence, knowing that Duncan and his vampires would be burned alive. But rather than deterring her, that knowledge made her more determined than ever to be there tonight.

"I'm going," she said flatly. "You can leave me here, but unless you lock me up, I'll get there by myself anyway."

Duncan's eyes narrowed. "I could put you to sleep," he said softly. "You'd never know."

Emma met his gaze evenly. "I'd know," she assured him. "And I'd never forgive you."

The muscle in Duncan's jaw flexed visibly as he stared back at her. It was the only sign of whatever emotion he was feeling. "Fine," he said at last. "But you hang back, Emma. I go in first. And if anything happens to me, you run."

Emma nodded once in agreement, although there was no way in hell she was going to run away if Duncan needed her. She kept that thought from her mind, though, filling it instead with the lyrics of a particularly irritating song she'd heard on the radio today.

"So, when are we leaving?" she asked.

Duncan regarded her carefully, and Emma would have sworn she saw a flash of frustration in his brown eyes. So maybe the song lyrics were working to block him from hearing what she was thinking. She filed that information away for the future and gazed at him innocently. He snorted dismissively and said, "Be downstairs in ten minutes. I have to check some things with Miguel and Louis."

He started to turn, but Emma said, "Hey!" Duncan raised an eyebrow in question. "How about a kiss for luck."

Duncan grinned and wrapped one big hand around the back of her neck, pulling her in for a deep, satisfying, toe-curling kiss. He lifted his head at last, gliding his tongue along the seam of her lips.

"I love you, Emmaline Duquet."

"I love you, too, Duncan. So you be careful."

He touched his mouth to hers one more time, and then he was gone. Emma listened, but she didn't even hear his footsteps on the stairs. She shrugged and hurried over to the duffle bag, which was the only other thing she'd picked up at her house earlier. It held her gun and ammo, and she had a feeling she was going to need them tonight.

Chapter Twenty-Eight

Max Grafton's house wasn't so much a house as an estate. Emma had known he had money. Most senators did by the time they'd been around as long as Grafton had. But in his case, the money was in his family. Old money. Old Southern money. As someone who grew up in old Southern poverty, Emma knew exactly what a difference that kind of money meant. Still, she hadn't been prepared for the vastness of his estate. There was the house itself, which was huge, along with a second two-story building that she guessed was where the household staff lived, because with a house as big as his, he'd definitely need live-in help. There was a pool, and a pool house big enough to house a family. And then there were the stables. Emma didn't know much about horses, but if even half of the stalls she could see in the long horse barn contained animals, it had to be costing Grafton a small fortune to feed and maintain them.

The whole estate was too big to put a wall around, but there was a white rail fence along the road, and Grafton had walled off the main buildings and barns. A short gravel drive took them to a big iron gate with a stylized "G" worked into it. Two guards wearing black combat gear stood there, each cradling a matte black semiautomatic with obvious familiarity. Emma worried as their two matching SUVs rode up to the gate, wondering how they'd talk their way in, but she shouldn't have. After all, she'd seen Duncan zap Sharon Coffer with a look. Ari, who was driving Duncan's SUV, convinced the gate guard they were invited guests in less time than it probably would have taken to show their IDs if they really *had* been invited.

They drove past the open gate and a short distance up the drive, waiting while the second SUV cleared security. Once they were together again, the two SUVs started down the long twisting road to the house. A double row of trees, manicured to identical perfection, lined the drive, white lights twinkling in their boughs. It would have been pretty on any other night.

"Remember, gentlemen," Duncan said coolly as they approached the house. "We go in quietly. There will be—" He stopped abruptly, head cocked slightly, as if listening to something none of them could hear. "He's here," he said, then shook his head, scowling. "And he's not alone, but I still don't recognize him."

"Who?" Emma asked, since everyone else seemed to know.

"Max's vampire ally."

Ari parked in front of the house, backing in next to a line of expensive cars which presumably belonged to Grafton's guests for the evening. Fortunately, it was a small party, so the senator hadn't bothered with a parking service of any kind. A pair of guards flanked the front door, but unlike their counterparts at the gate, these two wore suits and carried no visible weapons. Emma was quite certain they were armed, however, and she touched her own gun somewhat self-consciously. She was wearing a jacket that concealed the Glock 9 mm tucked into her waistband in back, but it still seemed obvious to her.

"You can still wait in the truck," Duncan said, for her ears only.

She turned her head sharply and scowled. "I'm going in," she insisted.

His lips curled slightly. "It was worth a shot," he murmured, then kissed her softly and added, "Be careful, Emmaline."

* * * *

Duncan stroked his knuckles over the softness of Emma's cheek as Louis jumped out of the truck and pulled Duncan's door open. He stepped out onto the gravel drive, with Miguel right behind him. Emma made an exasperated noise and hurried to follow, but Duncan didn't wait. A whispered word dealt with the human guards as he climbed the steps and opened the front door. He found it curious that the guards were only human, when he knew for a fact that his vampire enemy was somewhere inside. Did the other vampire think Duncan could be fooled, that he wouldn't sense his presence? A vast underestimation, if true, and a fatal mistake. He'd take great pleasure in pointing that out when they finally met.

Miguel and Louis were a step behind him to either side, as he walked into Grafton's house. Ari was next, then Emma, with Baldwin right beside her and the six vampires from the second SUV ranging behind. Once through the door, they fanned out, except for Baldwin who had orders to stick to Emma like glue.

The front door opened into a huge room. The ceiling lofted overhead to more than two stories, with thick beams crisscrossing the open space. The floor was marble, and furniture was sparse, although there were plenty of plants clustered in a way that split the room into more manageable spaces while still leaving it wide open. It was a space made for large gatherings, and it was completely empty.

Duncan wasn't fooled into thinking the house was empty, however. A quick sweep told him there were roughly twenty humans in the house, most of them gathered somewhere straight ahead. There were also . . . he paused briefly . . . twelve vampires, and among them he clearly tasted the mind of the master who'd tampered with Clint Daniels's mind and suborned him into burning down Duncan's residence.

"Twelve vampires, one master, twenty or so humans," he said quietly. Most of the vampires Duncan had brought with him were strong enough to detect the humans as easily as he did, but not all of them would accurately count their vampire opponents. And Emma could do neither. He wanted her far away from the fight, but he also wanted her to know what they were up against.

Duncan started across the room, not wasting breath to tell his people what to do. These were all seasoned security operatives; it was why he'd chosen them. He slowed, then stopped a moment before the hard crack of boot heels announced what he already knew. Max Grafton was at last coming to greet his uninvited guests.

"Mister Milford," Grafton said with false cordiality, entering the room through a corner doorway and walking toward them. "I'd heard you were dead. You'll forgive me for being disappointed to find the rumors were mistaken." He stopped ten feet away. "And Ms. Duquet. You've been far more trouble than you're worth, my dear. At least Lacey—"

His next words were trapped in his throat along with his ability to breathe. There was no reason for Emma to listen to this man's poisonous words about Lacey. Grafton was grabbing at his neck in a predictable, if useless, gesture. He could slit his own throat open, but still no air would reach his lungs until Duncan decided it was time. The senator fell to his knees and his face first turned red, then took on a bluish tint before Duncan released him.

Grafton fell forward, nearly doing a face plant as he sucked in a rasping breath and began coughing. "You bastard," he gasped, glaring up at Duncan while tears ran down his face.

Duncan grinned, baring his fangs. "You're wasting my time, Grafton."

"You'll pay for this." Grafton's voice was thready, but filled with hatred. "You're not the only game in town."

"Yes, I know. Shall we get on with it?" Duncan said, affecting boredom as his mind searched the house, looking for a trap.

It was Grafton's look of shock that finally drew his attention. "You know?" Grafton sputtered.

Duncan spared the effort to look at the human directly. "That your pet vampire tried to burn down my house with me and mine in it? Of course—"

"I'm no one's pet, Duncan."

Duncan didn't move, only his eyes shifted to follow the voice, recognizing his enemy at last. "Phoebe?"

Phoebe Micheletti strolled into the room, granting Grafton a disdainful glance as she stepped around his still kneeling figure. She stopped in front of Duncan, hands on her hips. "You're surprised. Good."

Duncan gave a negligent shrug. "I am. Not surprised enough to save you, but you were very clever." Inwardly, he was seething, mostly in anger at himself. They'd never met in person before that first night at the grave site, but if he'd taken her blood oath then, he'd have known the taste of her mind and recognized later that she was the one who'd tampered with his guard. But she'd made damn certain he wouldn't think it necessary. Had she already been planning to suborn someone from his daylight guard? Or was it simply caution on her part?

Phoebe was glaring her hatred at him. "Tell me, Duncan," she said tightly. "Did you ever think to ask if any of *us* wanted the territory before you swept in like a vengeful angel? I've been waiting for more than a century—"

"That's not how it's done, Phoebe, and you know it. If you wanted the territory, you should have taken it. If it wasn't me, it would have been someone else."

"*I'm* the one who deserves it, the one who's put up with Victor all these years, while—"

"And what was it you did for him?" Duncan demanded. "Dispose of the bodies? Help him brutalize those women?"

"I cleaned up his messes, just like I do everyone else's, you bastard. That woman was already dead when I got there. All I did was get rid of her body so Victor's precious politicians could pretend it never happened. We were going to move it to someplace permanent, but then you showed up and everything went to hell."

"How many others were there? How many women were tortured while you sat back like a fat spider, watching and waiting? Doing nothing?"

"I wasn't 'doing nothing,'" she lashed out angrily. "I wasn't strong enough to take him on alone. I had to wait, to get stronger, smarter, become a better fighter, build my own backup." She made a beckoning gesture over her shoulder and vampires began to slip into the room behind her. "I've spent *decades* preparing, and now suddenly you appear out of nowhere, you and Raphael with your grand plans and your arrogance."

"Raphael has always been fair with you. He treated you with respect, admiration even."

"Oh, my." She fanned herself theatrically. "Aren't I simply the luckiest girl alive? Fuck Raphael," she snarled. "I don't need his patronage, his pats on the head like I'm some sort of clever pet or—"

"He never did that," Duncan snapped coldly. "You forget. I was there."

"Yes, you were there. Always by his side, currying his favor. His favorite lapdog. Victor had that much right about you. And now here you are, with Raphael's blessing, I'm sure. A territory of your own, a gift for serving him so well for so long. But there's something you don't understand—"

"No, Phoebe," Duncan said, cutting off her litany with a gentle smile. "It's you who doesn't understand."

He released his power then, letting it rush out of him like water trapped behind a suddenly open dam. It roared through the room like a hurricane, battering the vampires who stood staunchly at his back, sending Max Grafton shrieking across the slick marble floor to crash against a nearby trio of urns. Behind him, he was aware of Emma gasping in surprise, but standing strong, her determination to stay and fight not wavering for a moment.

Phoebe stared at him, her dark hair a wild nimbus around her head, her eyes widening briefly, before they narrowed to angry slits. Her hands fisted at her sides, and Duncan felt the draw of power as she called upon the vampires who'd chosen to stand with her against him. One or two of those sent him triumphant glances, but the others avoided his gaze, as if hoping to escape detection. He scanned their faces quickly, not recognizing any of them. A more careful examination and he realized why. These were Phoebe's own, vampires she'd made herself over the years while, according to her, she prepared for Victor's demise. But they were young—the oldest was not even a hundred years, most far younger than that—and none of them was a master. Their presence would still help Phoebe, as much as doubling her power, especially if she was willing to drain them dry in order to win. But in the end, it still came down to Phoebe versus Duncan. And Duncan would win that battle.

It would sadden him to kill Phoebe. He'd thought her a friend. Though they'd never met, they'd worked together many times over the years, consulting by phone and computer as she conducted her investigations all over the country. But she'd tried to kill Duncan and all his vampires, had been willing to let Emma die in order to get to him. He could never forgive that. And as a vampire lord, he could never tolerate that kind of challenge to his rule. She had to die.

Duncan reached out from within the depths of his power and touched Phoebe's thoughts—a brief touch, there and gone before she could sense the intrusion. He felt her determination, but also her fear for her husband, Ted Micheletti. They'd been mated far too long for Ted to survive her death.

"What about Ted?" Duncan asked quietly. "What about all of these others?" He gestured to the vampires who ranged behind her. "Surrender to me, Phoebe, and they needn't die with you."

"No!" Ted burst into the room from the hallway, pushing his way through Phoebe's vampires to reach her side. He was a big man, towering over his diminutive wife as he glared at Duncan. "Don't you dare, Phoebe," he growled. "Don't you let him sweet talk you into giving up. I'll stand with you 'til the end, my love. I want it no other way."

She spared him a tear-filled glance, then turned back to Duncan. Her jaw jutted forward with resolve. "On any given Sunday, Duncan," she said, borrowing from the idea that no contest has a forgone conclusion. "I might surprise you."

Duncan gave her the respect of nodding in agreement, though the outcome was indeed forgone is this case. Even with her power doubled,

Phoebe couldn't defeat him. She'd been deluding herself all these years if she'd thought she could have overthrown Victor, and Victor hadn't stood a chance with Duncan.

"As you wish," he said. "Miguel?"

"Yes, my lord."

Hearing the tension in Miguel's voice, Duncan gave his lieutenant a quick half grin. "No worries, Miguelito," he said fondly. "Watch my back?"

"Always, Sire."

"Emma!" he called without taking his eyes off Phoebe. "Remember your promise." He thought he heard a dismissive puff of breath from her, but it may have been his power rattling the foliage.

His point made, Duncan sucked his power in closer, aware of his vampires backing away to give him room and to avoid being caught in the deadly vortex of his defensive shield. The raw force of his unbound power, which had been tearing the room apart, shut off like a thrown switch. The room was silent in the aftermath as everyone froze, listening.

Duncan favored Phoebe with a cold look. "Ladies first," he said mockingly, intentionally pricking the pride he'd felt from her earlier, the pride that had driven her to think she could become a vampire lord.

Phoebe reacted predictably, curling her hands into claws in front of her and screaming at him in rage. Duncan strengthened his shield in reflex, a move honed into an automatic reaction over decades of practice, requiring no thought on his part. But if he'd had any doubts as to the outcome of this battle, they fled in the face of Phoebe's first assault. Driven by fury, carrying the full measure of her power, it was sucked into his defensive shield without a trace. There was not even a momentary dent to indicate its impact. Phoebe looked up and met his gaze, and he read the knowledge of failure in her eyes.

"Last chance," he called.

"Fuck you, Duncan," she snarled.

"As you wish." Duncan drew on his tremendous strength, forming a blade of pure power, invisible to the naked eye, but shining like a silver sword to those with eyes to see. Phoebe had such eyes. She saw the blade and howled in fury, dropping down to a crouch, making herself small as she sucked juice from her vampire children and wove their combined power into as tight a shield as she could make. One by one her vampires collapsed behind her as she sucked them dry. Even Ted crumpled to the floor, a trickle of blood leaking from his nose, as Phoebe pulled his small bit of energy back into herself in a desperate bid for survival.

Duncan was already stepping forward as Phoebe howled her defiance. He thrust the shining blade of his power through the spinning shell of his shield, slicing through Phoebe's defenses as if they weren't there, stabbing into her chest, shattering her ribs and piercing her heart.

Phoebe screamed as her heart exploded, as Ted convulsed and as her vampires died. Duncan held the blade in her heart until there was nothing left of the organ, until it was dust in her chest. He pulled the blade back then, drawing the power into himself, clenching his fist as if his fingers gripped a physical hilt. Dropping his shield, he took a step back . . . and stumbled, falling to his knees as a something with the force of a sledge hammer slammed into his back, tearing through muscle and bone, aiming for his heart.

Chapter Twenty-Nine

Emma knew she was being herded. She knew Duncan had appointed Baldwin as her protector, probably on pain of death or something equally unpleasant. She didn't mind, because there was nothing she could do about it. If you're going to fall in love with a big, bad, alpha male, you have to accept the mile-wide protective streak that goes with it. So, she didn't fight Baldwin when he took her arm and moved her to one side, even though it made her feel like one of the potted plants, especially when Phoebe—Phoebe!—showed up.

"I'm no one's pet," the traitorous bitch drawled as she strolled into the room, and Emma wished she had something to throw at her. Baldwin clearly felt the same way. He stiffened in surprise and took an aggressive step forward, closing ranks with Duncan's other vamps who were all bristling with anger, ready to defend Duncan. Emma stayed where she was, still and quiet, not wanting to draw any attention to herself for fear she'd be hustled right out of the room. She wanted to see and hear what was going on!

Her heart squeezed at the obvious grief in Duncan's voice when he tried to talk Phoebe out of what he clearly considered a suicide mission. Emma didn't know anything about vampire power, but she figured Phoebe had to die either way. She'd tried to burn them all alive, after all. Duncan wasn't trying to save Phoebe; he was trying to save the others. He didn't seem worried at all for himself, just sad and resigned to what he had to do.

And then suddenly everything changed. Emma's skin prickled with energy, every hair on her body standing up as a whirlwind appeared out of nowhere and filled the huge room. Ceramic vases filled with greenery toppled over, breaking against the marble floor. Dirt and leaves were sucked up by the wind and sent spinning against the walls and windows like hail. Phoebe was staring at Duncan as if she'd never seen him before, as if he was her worst nightmare come true. He was still talking to Phoebe, but Emma couldn't hear what they were saying above the noise. She heard Max Grafton scream, though, saw him rolling across the floor like a shrieking tumbleweed until he crashed into a cluster of big clay pots.

Wanting to hear what they were saying, Emma sidled a little closer, slipping behind and between clusters of plants until she was nearly even with where Duncan stood staring at Phoebe.

"Emma," Duncan called suddenly.

She froze, certain he knew she'd moved closer, that she was no longer safely hidden behind Baldwin's bulk.

"Remember your promise," he said, and Emma puffed out a dismissive breath. Like she was going to run away if things went south.

What was he thinking? But she no sooner had the thought, than everything changed again. Silence fell over the room like a thick blanket, and Emma crouched down, hiding.

"Ladies first," Duncan said, his voice thick with a mockery Emma had never heard from him before.

Electricity tingled along Emma's nerves, much stronger that what she'd felt only moments before. That had been like static electricity on a dry summer day; this was a live wire skimming along her nerves. She shuddered and closed her eyes in pain, clenching her jaw against the urge to groan. When she opened them again, Phoebe was still standing opposite Duncan, but there was a resigned set to her shoulders, a weariness in the way she held herself despite her defiant gaze.

Duncan barely moved, standing cool and calm as always, his legs braced slightly apart, his weight on the balls of his feet. He raised his arm to chest height, and his fingers curled into his palm as if holding something there. He blinked lazily and the pressure in the room began to grow, slowly at first, then building as if all the air was being sucked out at once. Emma began to pant as her lungs worked overtime trying to collect enough oxygen. A weight crushed her chest, and she leaned back against the wall, suddenly weak and lightheaded, but determined to stay, to witness Phoebe's execution. She blinked, bewildered, as Duncan stabbed his hand outward, and then Phoebe screamed in agony. The vampires who'd come into the room with Phoebe began to fall like flies, collapsing where they stood without a single sound. Not far from Emma, Max Grafton grunted, and she stiffened to attention. While she'd been watching the action and trying to breathe, Grafton had woken enough to pull himself behind one of the few chairs in the room. He was hunkered down like a nasty troll, looking pale and sweaty, pressing a hand against his ribs as if they were injured. Emma hoped his ribs were broken. She hoped he'd push too hard and one of them would puncture his lung and he'd die of asphyxiation while everyone was too busy to notice. Except her.

Lost in images of Max Grafton's imminent death, Emma glanced over and saw Phoebe had curled into a ball on the floor. She was still screaming, but weaker now, fading quickly until she literally began falling apart. Duncan stared at her crumbling form dispassionately as he took a single step backward. A flash of movement brought Emma's gaze back to Grafton, and she screamed as he brought up a gun and shot Duncan in the back.

Emma was on the move. All around her vampires were racing to Duncan's side. Miguel was shouting orders, placing himself between Duncan and what was left of Phoebe's vampires as he searched for the enemy. But Emma already knew who the enemy was. Grafton still had his gun up, still aimed at Duncan, his finger compressing for a second shot as Duncan collapsed to his knees. Emma brought up her own gun and fired without thinking, three shots, tightly grouped, just like at the range. One, two, three, and Grafton went down. Emma raced over and kicked his gun away, dropping to her knees next to him. She stared at the grimace on his face, at the blood on his chest and bubbling from his mouth, and she froze, not quite believing what she'd done.

She blinked, then whispered, "Duncan," and spun around clumsily.

"Emma," Miguel called. "Get over here."

She was there before he snarled the last word, tears filling her eyes as she saw Duncan lying on the floor, eyes closed, blood pooling beneath him. "Is he dead?" she asked, her voice catching on a sob.

"No," Miguel said shortly. "But he needs blood."

She looked up in confusion. "Blood?"

The dark-haired vamp gave her an impatient look. "Christ," he swore. "He's a vampire. He's wounded. He needs blood."

"Oh! Of course," she shook her head at her own stupidity. She handed someone her gun and began stripping off her jacket. "Do you have something—"

Miguel was already handing her a knife—a short, fat switchblade with a fancy handle, which he snapped out and handed to her grip first.

"Be careful," he warned. "It's sharp."

Emma stared at the blade, then shook her head, handing it back to him. "You do it," she said, holding out her wrist. "I don't think— Ow!" She gave Miguel a dirty look. "A little warning would be nice, dude," she muttered, but quickly eased Duncan's head onto her lap and held her bloody wrist to his mouth. Did she need to rub it over his lips? Or maybe stroke his throat to get him to— Yikes!

Duncan latched onto her wrist, his fangs sinking into the flesh. It hurt, but only briefly as the euphoric in his bite did its magic and Emma began to feel . . . wonderful. Duncan's hands came up to hold her wrist in place, and she leaned her upper body over his, needing to get closer to him, but also wanting to conceal the obvious signs of her growing desire. She only hoped Duncan would stop before too long, otherwise, she was going to—

"Emma."

She opened her eyes to find Duncan gazing up at her. He was no longer sucking at her wrist, but the heat in his eyes told her he was aware of her arousal and returned it in spades. He licked her wrist slowly and thoroughly, the coagulant in his saliva sealing the wound while the feel of his tongue against her skin did nothing to cool her hunger for him.

He gave her a half smile, then reached up and brushed his knuckles over her cheek.

"I thought you were dead," she whispered, holding on to him tightly.

"No," he murmured. "I have too much to live for."

"My lord," Miguel said, reaching out to place a hand on Duncan's shoulder.

"Right." Duncan put Emma gently aside and accepted the hand-up his lieutenant offered, while Baldwin lifted Emma to her feet and began wrapping her arm in one of the ever-present white handkerchiefs. They were no sooner on their feet than Miguel was hustling them out of the house to the waiting SUVs.

"Ari," Miguel called. "You drive. Baldwin will go with you. We'll clean up here, my lord," he added to Duncan, "and follow in the other truck."

Duncan paused on the front steps long enough for Emma to catch up. He took her hand as she emerged from the house, then he slid into the backseat of the SUV and pulled her in with him.

Two minutes later, they were racing through the night, heading back to the house in D.C.

"What happens now?" Emma asked, anxiously. "I mean what about all those other people, and—" She shuddered slightly. "—Grafton's body?"

They didn't need to worry about Phoebe's body or those of her vampires. They were already just so much dust on the floor. No one would even notice it amidst the wreckage from the fight between Phoebe and Duncan. Emma still didn't understand how that worked, but those questions could wait. On the other hand, Grafton's body needed to be taken care of *now*.

"Duncan?" she said, when he didn't answer.

"One moment," he replied, and Emma realized he wasn't talking to her. He was on his Bluetooth to someone, probably one of the vamps who'd stayed back at Grafton's. He turned, pulling her against him more tightly, tucking her head into the curve of his shoulder. "Rest, Emmaline. Everything is taken care of, you'll see. This is nothing we haven't dealt with before."

"So I'm not going to jail for killing a senator?" she asked drowsily, thinking it must be blood loss that was making her so tired.

Duncan chuckled. "No, you are most certainly not going to jail. What would I do without you?"

Emma yawned, then frowned, wondering if he'd done something to make her sleep.

"It's the adrenaline," Duncan said, reading her with his usual accuracy. "It's a rush, but when it crashes, it crashes hard, and so do you."

"Mmmm," she said, snuggling against his broad chest. She felt Duncan's lips as he kissed the top of her head, and then her eyes closed and she slept.

Chapter Thirty

"What are you reading?"

Emma managed to keep herself from jumping in surprise. Duncan moved so quietly sometimes, it was as if he appeared from out of nowhere. He kissed her bare shoulder in apology and she knew she hadn't managed to conceal her reaction after all.

Lying on her stomach on the bed with her laptop in front of her, she sneaked a peek through the heavy fall of her hair, watching as he settled next to her and sat cross-legged to work with his own laptop. As always, his presence created a strange pressure in her chest, like there was something inside that was too big to stay there. She recognized the feeling, even though she'd never experienced it before meeting Duncan. She was in love. Hopelessly, madly in love. But he was just so . . . wonderful. Not only his looks, though sitting there with his chest bare, blond hair hanging loose over his shoulders, and nothing but a pair of loose, gray sweatpants keeping him decent, he certainly looked scrumptious enough. But it was more than that. He was a good man in every way. And he was hers. She knew that for a fact. Duncan kept his emotions tightly in check most of the time, but not with her. He loved her. He told her so all the time, and he showed her in a million different ways.

She still had trouble believing it sometimes. She'd wake up and put her hand out, expecting to find the space next to her empty, expecting to discover it was all a dream. But he was always there, always ready. She smiled to herself.

"Emma?"

She blinked, startled out of her fantasies of stripping him naked and having her wicked way with him.

Duncan grinned knowingly at her. Not bothering to wait for her answer to his earlier question, he leaned over and scanned the screen of her laptop for himself. "Want ads?" He frowned. "You don't need a job."

"Of course I need a job. Even if I move in here—" His teeth closed gently on her shoulder in warning. "Even though I'm *living* here with you," she amended, and he kissed the same spot he'd bitten. "I still have expenses."

"You can work for me then," he said, as if that settled the matter. And as far as he was concerned, it probably did. He was so used to making all the decisions, giving orders and having everyone snap to. But Emma wasn't one of his vampires, and she wasn't a charity case, either.

"And what exactly would I do?" she asked skeptically.

Duncan shrugged. "The same thing you did for that limp dick

congressman you worked for."

Emma snickered at his description of Guy Coffer and asked, "You get a lot of constituent complaints from vampireland?"

"No. But I *am* the representative of vampireland to the American government, and most of that business takes place during the day. You could be my daytime face in the halls of Congress."

Emma turned her head sharply to regard him. "Seriously?"

"Of course. Why not?"

Emma considered it. Why not indeed? She was certainly qualified to do something like that, and wouldn't it chafe Sharon Coffer's ass to see Emma roaming the marbled halls of the Capitol again? She smiled to herself and Duncan chuckled.

"That's a very sinister smile you have there, Emmaline."

"I'll take the job."

"Excellent," Duncan said, absently skimming something on his laptop, probably one of the many daily reports he received from his various employees, everyone from that vampire builder Alaric to Jackson Hissong and Miguel. "We can discuss . . . well, hello there!"

Emma actually looked over to see if someone had walked into their room, then realized he was reacting to something on his computer screen. "What is it?" she asked, stretching up and trying to read over his arm.

"Tammy Dietrich is back," he said, leaning forward to read more closely.

Emma sat up. "How do you know?"

He indicated the report on his screen. "I've had someone watching her office. She showed up there early this morning, looking very furtive. Big hat and sun glasses, but it was definitely her. Apparently she heard about Max's untimely death and decided it was safe to come home."

Emma suppressed a flutter of fear. "What's the latest from the police on that? Max's death, I mean."

"They're calling it a home invasion gone bad, with Grafton shot and killed defending his family."

"The police are buying that?"

Duncan snorted derisively. "None of Max's heirs want the authorities digging too deeply into old Max's extracurricular activities, and especially not his finances. They've decided to let him die a hero."

"Bastard," Emma said, pretending it was only anger making her stomach clench.

Duncan wasn't fooled, of course. He gave her a searching look and said, "You did the right thing, Emma."

"I know that. He was trying to kill you. And he *did* kill Lacey."

"And yet his death bothers you."

Emma frowned. "Not that he's dead, it's just—"

"It's all right, Emmaline. Killing a man should never be easy." He studied her face as if trying to decide something. "I could take it away, you know. Make you forget."

Emma stared at him. He expected her to reject the idea outright. She could tell by the careful way he'd suggested it, by the way he was looking at her right now, waiting for her to blow up at him. But she didn't. She hated herself for it, but she seriously considered letting him take the whole thing away—the misplaced guilt, the fear that there was something wrong with her that she could kill a man in cold blood like that, even if he did deserve it.

"I might take you up on that someday," she said finally. "But not yet."

Duncan smiled in relief, his eyes going that warm brown that made him appear so human. "Whenever you're ready."

His phone rang, which was unexpected. It was Sunday evening and he'd decided that Sundays would be theirs alone. Miguel and the others had been told not to bother him unless it was something urgent. Emma frowned, but Duncan grinned, then leaned over and picked up his cell phone without even checking caller ID.

"Sire," he said, his tone a mixture of warmth and respect. "We are well," he continued, obviously answering the caller's query. "No permanent house yet, but that's coming along. And everyone there?" He laughed, his body language relaxed and easy. Emma rarely saw Duncan like that, except with her.

"So soon?" he asked now. "Well, that's true enough." He listened a while longer, then said, "She'll be coming with me." He laughed again and added, "It should be interesting."

Emma eyed him narrowly, since clearly he was now talking about *her*. And what would be so damn interesting?

"I look forward to it, Sire. Until then."

He disconnected and threw the phone back onto the table.

"What was that about?" she demanded.

"That was Raphael."

She already knew that. There was only one person Duncan called by the honorific *Sire,* because there *was* only one Sire, for Duncan anyway. "I know *that,*" she told him. "What was he calling about?" *And what was so damned funny?* she wanted to add, but didn't.

"There's a Vampire Council meeting in two weeks," Duncan said, giving her a brilliant smile. "We're going to California."

Epilogue

Lucas Donlon, Vampire Lord, ruler of a slice of North America that the vampires called the Plains Territory, scanned the conference room from behind his sunglasses. He didn't need the glasses. Their host for this meeting was Raphael, and unlike that lunatic Krystof, who'd hosted the last meeting of North America's Vampire Council, Raphael would never have anything as gauche as fluorescent lighting in his conference room. But Lucas kept the glasses on anyway. It made it easier to keep his thoughts to himself, among other things. There were too many nosey vamps among his fellow vampire lords, and since they'd all sworn off dipping into each other's minds, they were reduced to looking for visual clues. What a laugh riot that was.

And what a cheery group they were, too. Eight vampires ranged around a conference table that could easily have seated four times that many, because they didn't trust one another enough to sit any closer. Or maybe it was that they had no *desire* to get any closer. They met once a year to discuss matters of mutual interest, but they were hardly friends. Actually, they weren't friends at all. Lucas himself counted only one of those seated at this table as a friend, and that was Duncan. Some of the others were friendly antagonists, while one was an avowed enemy, and two were so new to the Council that Lucas had no opinion. Rajmund he at least knew from the vamp's long service as lieutenant to the finally dead Krystof—now *there* was a vampire who'd needed to be put down. But the newest member of their august circle, Sophia, he'd never even heard of until she popped up as Lord of the Canadian Territories. Not that he gave a damn either way. As long as she kept to her borders, he'd keep to his.

"Your vote, Lucas?" Raphael's deep voice interrupted Lucas's contemplation of his fellow lords. Lucas didn't move from his slouched position at the oval table. He shifted his gaze to Raphael and lowered his glasses enough to look over them.

"Affirmative," he said flatly, then raised the glasses to cover his eyes once again. Gods willing, the others would vote the same way and they could all get the hell out of here. Not that Malibu was a bad place to be. He just didn't like the company much.

It seemed to take forever, and he had to endure, or ignore, more than one boring speech, but eventually the others all voted to affirm Duncan as Lord of the Capital Territory. It was the only territory that required such a vote, and only because of the unique demands imposed on its lord. They'd all agreed to the condition about a century ago, even Victor who'd laughed at the time, assuming it would never become an issue. Arrogant ass that he was, he'd never understood that he *was* the issue. The rest of them had been waiting ever since then for someone to take that bastard out. Thank God it had finally happened, and thank God it was Duncan who'd done it. Lucas didn't think anyone else could have gotten approval from the full council.

"The resolution passes," Raphael said, stating the obvious. He stood almost immediately, seeming as eager as the rest of them to get the meeting over with. Probably more so, since it was his home that had been invaded by the lords and their security details.

Lucas unfolded himself from the chair, pushing it back from the table with the same motion. He waited while the others hurried out the door, a few stopping to congratulate Duncan, including Raj, who paused long enough to shake hands. Raj and Duncan had been lieutenants to their respective lords a very long time. Lucas supposed that created a certain familiarity with one another. And their territories shared a border, so it couldn't hurt that they were at least friendly. Of course, his own friendship with Duncan went back much further than that.

Raphael was the last to leave, his black eyes holding Lucas's gaze for a long moment despite the glasses until, finally, he murmured something to Duncan and disappeared between the big double doors. Duncan grinned at Lucas as he made his way around the table.

"Duncan," Lucas said warmly. "Congratulations."

Duncan shook the proffered hand. "You can take the damn glasses off now."

Lucas laughed and slipped the unnecessary glasses into the pocket of his suit jacket. "I only wear them to piss off Raphael. Somebody's gotta keep the big guy humble."

"Too late, my friend. That ship sailed long ago."

"Yeah, well, I do what I can. You leaving right away?"

"Tomorrow. We'll spend the night, but there's too much to do back in D.C. to remain any longer."

"We, is it? I'd heard you found yourself a honey back there."

"I could as easily have been referring to Miguel and Louis," Duncan said mildly.

"But you weren't. It's all in the *we*, my friend. So, is she a sweet, old-fashioned Southern girl then? Someone to rub your feet and wash your socks?"

Duncan laughed. "Hardly, though Emma is Southern—and sweet when she chooses. She's around somewhere. Drinking wine with Raphael's mate Cynthia, I believe, though I should probably track her down. One shudders to think what trouble those two could get into."

Lucas accepted Duncan's statement for what it was—a polite way of acknowledging that he knew Raphael was waiting to meet with Lucas. Duncan had been Raphael's lieutenant and confidante for almost a hundred and fifty years, and while his assumption of the Capital lordship took him away from Raphael's day-to-day operations, it changed nothing about their friendship. Just as Duncan's new lordship changed nothing about the friendship he shared with Lucas.

They walked out together, going their separate ways after shaking hands once more and promising to stay in touch. Duncan turned for the stairs, while Lucas started down the long hallway, heading for Raphael's office in the other wing. He'd left his security downstairs, not wanting any more witnesses than necessary to this meeting. He trusted his people, for the most part, but he was in no danger from anyone within Raphael's estate, so there was no reason to take a chance.

The black, carved doors opened upon his approach, and he considered putting the sunglasses back on. He discarded the idea almost immediately, however. They had business to discuss, and Raphael had never appreciated Lucas's irreverent approach to serious matters.

Raphael looked up from behind his desk as Lucas strolled into the room. The doors closed right behind him with a whoosh of air, barely clearing his ass. Lucas grinned briefly, but approached the desk and gave a sincerely respectful bow from the waist.

"Sire," he said. "Thank you for seeing me."

Raphael studied him for a suspicious moment, then gestured at the two comfortable chairs in front of the desk. "Sit down, Lucas. Where are your sunglasses?"

Lucas laughed then. "Duncan told me not to wear them."

Raphael permitted a smile to edge around his mouth. "Tell me what's happening."

"It's Klemens," Lucas said referring to the Midwestern Vampire Lord who'd been glaring at him across the table moments before. "He's pecking away at my eastern border. I held off until Duncan was confirmed, because you asked me, too, and because it was something we both wanted. But I can't put up with it any longer. My own people are starting to doubt that I have the will to hold on to my territory."

"Son of a bitch," Raphael swore. "What does he want?"

Lucas shrugged. "I suspect he wants my entire Plains territory to combine with his own. It's always ground at him that yours is bigger than his." He punctuated this statement with an irreverent wink, which Raphael ignored. "He'll settle for anything he can chip off, though," Lucas continued. "And I won't let that happen."

"No," Raphael agreed. "So, what will you do?"

"Nothing until after next week."

"Why next week?"

"The FBI's coming to see me," Lucas said, relaxing now that his real reason for the meeting was resolved.

"The FBI?" Raphael said. "What have you done now?"

"Sire!" Lucas said, placing a hand over his heart and pretending to be wounded by the accusation. Raphael gave him a look of disgust, so Lucas said, "I haven't done anything that I know of. Some FBI chick has been calling. And not only us, either. She called the local sheriff, too. Claims she's looking for a lost person and thinks he disappeared in our area. I've checked with my people and nobody's heard of him. If he's lost, it's either the humans or the Badlands that've taken him, not us."

"And once she's gone?"

"Once she's gone, Sire," Lucas said seriously. "There will be war."

To be continued

ACKNOWLEDGMENTS

First and foremost, my thanks go to Linda Kichline for the knowledge and nonstop hard work that go into every book. And to the talented Patricia Lazarus for another gorgeous cover.

My unending gratitude and big hugs to my critique partners and fellow writers, the very talented Michelle Muto and Steve J. McHugh, for their willingness to read bits and pieces and parts and finally the whole damn thing. And for their constant support and willingness to listen. Not that I complain or anything.

Thank you to the wonderful and oh-so-talented Adrian Phoenix for hanging around with me at RT when I'm sure she had better stuff to do, and for helping me celebrate the big win! To Kelley Armstrong for creating the best writing group on the Internet, and to all the members of OWG 6 for commiserating and/or celebrating as the moment requires!

Huge thanks to John Gorski, whose generosity in sharing his knowledge and experience shows up every time one of my characters picks up weapon. And to D. P. Lyle, M.D. (dplylemd.com) for once again answering my questions about dead bodies. Thanks also to Elizabeth from Rep. Henry A. Waxman's office, and yes, I know there are *some* congresspeople who actually do work to make things better.

Thank you to all of my readers who make it possible for me to tell my stories, and especially to those who write to let me know how much they love my beautiful vampires (and their mates, too.) And thanks also to all of the reviewers and book bloggers who help me get the word out about my vamps.

Thanks once more to my large and loving family for their ever-present pride and support. And finally, endless love and gratitude to my darling husband who still wonders what the heck his wife is doing pecking away at the computer into the wee hours of the night.

You can find me on Facebook, D. B. Reynolds, and on Twitter, @dbreynoldswrite.

Or stop by my blog at http://dbreynolds.wordpress.com for the latest news, contests, and Vampire Vignettes!

CPSIA information can be obtained at www.ICGtesting.com
Printed in the USA
LVOW061038271111

256625LV00004B/61/P

9 781610 260831